Henrietta, sitting beside the earl on the sofa, coughed loudly several times, hoping to wake her chaperon.

"Leave her," said the earl in an amused voice. "You are safe with me . . . I think."

He gave an impatient exclamation and pulled her into his arms. She made a muffled protest as his mouth came down on hers. It was meant to be a light teasing kiss, but no sooner did the earl taste the warmth of her mouth than he lost his senses and kissed her with all the passion he had never known he could hold for any woman.

He had thought it would be easy to make her fall in love with him. He had not realized until now how easy it would be for him to fall in love with her.

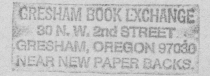

AT THE SIGN OF THE GOLDEN PINEAPPLE

Marion Chesney

FAWCETT CREST • NEW YORK

For Maria Browne
With love

Chapter One

Miss Henrietta Bascombe and Miss Ismene Hissop stood with candle-lighters at the ready, waiting for the sounds of the arrival of their first guest.

Unthinkable that they should light the candles beforehand. Henrietta and Miss Hissop were both well-versed in every penny-pinching way of impoverished gentility.

Although it was winter, the fire had not yet been lighted. Warmth, also, had to wait for the guests.

Henrietta had lately inherited a "fortune"—five thousand pounds *was* a fortune after years of trying to make ends meet—but she did not want to waste a penny of it.

Her father had been a country doctor who had earned so little that he had often acted as vet to supplement his small income. When he had died, he had left Henrietta his small house and pocket-size garden and very little money. With the sensible view that two impoverished ladies can live together more cheaply than in separate households, Henrietta had offered a home to her old friend and former schoolteacher, Miss Hissop.

Together they had worked at trying to exist on as little

as possible while keeping up appearances. They wore cotton dresses instead of silk, claiming they preferred washable materials; they bought yesterday's bread from the bakers "to feed the birds," and gave genteel card-parties where, with grim determination and flushed faces, they played for shillings and sixpences as if they were the most dedicated gamblers of St. James's, playing for thousands.

The "fortune" had come as a great surprise. The money had been left to Henrietta by the local land-owner, Sir Benjamin Prestcott, in his will. He had turned religious before his death and, conscience-stricken that he had never paid Henrietta's father for any of that poor man's excellent services, he had decided to make amends by leaving Henrietta the money with a view to providing her with a dowry.

But Henrietta had other plans for the money. So the evening's entertainment was not just a tea party. It was to be more like a council of war.

For Henrietta meant to go into trade.

In vain had Miss Hissop protested. Henrietta was determined to open a confectioner's in London's West End, and nothing Miss Hissop could say would move her from that resolve.

Henrietta would need shop assistants, and the best London confectioners always had the prettiest of girls. To that end, she had invited two ladies from the neighborhood to tea, knowing they were unhappy with their present life, and confident they would enjoy the chance to share this new adventure with her.

In them lay Miss Hissop's last hope. Both ladies were of the gentry, and she was sure their horror at Henrietta's suggestion would change that determined lady's mind.

It was not as if dear Henrietta could not get a husband easily, thought Miss Hissop. Henrietta had dark-brown glossy hair that curled naturally, a trim figure, and wide brown eyes. But Henrietta would point out that the only eligible men in the village of Partlett were antidotes. Miss Hissop could see nothing wrong with the eligibles the village had to offer.

Men were men, and it really didn't matter what they looked like. Miss Hissop often found it hard to tell them apart.

A reddish sun sparkled over the frost on the garden outside. Miss Hissop shivered, wishing the guests would arrive so that they could light the fire.

And then they were there, coming up the garden path, Mrs. Charlotte Webster and Miss Josephine Archer.

The small, dark parlor was bathed in a soft light as Miss Hissop and Henrietta lighted the candles. Then the fire gave a cheerful crackle, and the first flames shot up to disperse the bone-chilling cold of the room.

Miss Hissop removed her large woolen shawl and hurried to answer the door.

"Welcome," she said to the two ladies on the step. "Come in. Such a bore having to answer the door oneself, but our Martha has gone to visit her mother."

Miss Hissop's servant Martha was a pure fiction. Neither she nor Henrietta had ever had a servant. This was a fact well-known in the little village, but Miss Hissop had persuaded herself that everyone actually believed in the perpetually absent Martha.

Henrietta studied them with a calculating eye. Yes, they were both as pretty as she had remembered them to be, although she had not seen either since the death of her father.

Josephine was the daughter of the local squire, a

chestnut-haired beauty dressed in scarlet merino. It was hard to tell from her fashionable clothes and calm, beautiful face that she led the life of a dog with her widower father, who cursed her and beat her every time he was in his cups, which was often.

Charlotte was too thin for true beauty, and had high cheekbones, a definite setback in an age where women deliberately rounded their cheeks by stuffing them with wax pads. But she had beautiful black hair, and her eyes were sapphire. She had a natural grace and elegance.

She had married an undistinguished army captain and been thrown out by her family for doing so. The captain had died, leaving her with only an army widow's pension.

Henrietta did not know them as friends, only as former patients of her father. Josephine had been treated for cracked ribs after one of her father's more severe beatings and Charlotte for fainting fits, which turned out to have been brought on by semi-starvation.

Usually Henrietta served tiny sandwiches—yesterday's bread being carefully damped to make it appear fresh—and minuscule tea cakes.

As soon as the ladies were seated, she surprised them by serving soup laced with wine, followed by peasant-size sandwiches filled with beef.

Watching delicate color beginning to come into Charlotte's thin cheeks, Henrietta talked of this and that and held her fire until she was sure they were all thoroughly warmed.

Without opening her mouth, Miss Hissop was sending out distress signals. Her weak eyes pleaded with Henrietta to abandon the vulgar idea of trade.

Miss Hissop was much addicted to wearing cravats and jockey caps and gave all the appearance of a strong-minded woman. She was in her forties and had a harsh-featured face, weak eyes, and a thin mouth that turned down at the corners.

Only Henrietta knew that behind this formidable exterior lurked the soul of a rabbit. All Miss Hissop wanted out of life was to pay for her own funeral and not to be buried in a pauper's grave. In the way that young girls had a "bottom drawer" or wedding chest for their trousseau, Miss Hissop had a funeral closet in which she kept the little money she had saved in a tin box, a hand-embroidered shroud, black armbands for the mourners, and a long list of instructions as to the funeral arrangements.

Henrietta waited until tea had been poured and then rapped her spoon against the side of her cup for silence. Charlotte and Josephine, who had been discussing knitting patterns, broke off and looked at her in surprise.

"I have invited you here for a reason," said Henrietta.

"I am sure, my dear, Mrs. Webster and Miss Archer accepted your invitation to *tea*, you know, because ladies take *tea* and do not do . . . other things," said Miss Hissop incoherently.

Henrietta ignored her. "I have been left five thousand pounds in Sir Benjamin Prestcott's will. He was my father's patient, you know."

The ladies murmured their congratulations.

"I do not mean to use the money as a dowry," said Henrietta.

"More tea?" bleated Miss Hissop. "You will feel so much more rational after tea, Henrietta."

"I mean," said Henrietta firmly, "to go into trade."

"But there is no need for that," said Charlotte, wide-eyed.

5

"There are no men in this village I would even *look* at," said Henrietta.

"But with a dowry like that," protested Josephine, "you could go to some spa and attend balls and parties. There are plenty of eligible gentlemen at the spas. Tunbridge Wells, for example, is not so expensive as Bath."

"There you are!" exclaimed Miss Hissop, beaming all around. "*Just* what I said."

"I do not think I want to *have* to marry," said Henrietta. "I do not think I want to be married *at all*."

"In that case," said Charlotte, "five thousand pounds properly invested would keep you in relative comfort."

"But that is not the case," said Henrietta. "I want to be rich. Very rich. Now, merchants take sums of money and turn them into *more* money. We all have a talent. Everyone has some talent, but women are never allowed to exploit it. I, for example, am a first-class confectioner and baker."

There as a murmur of assent. Henrietta could conjure delicacies out of next-to-nothing. Charlotte still remembered Henrietta arriving with her father when he had attended her, bearing a small bottle of cordial and two slices of delicious home-baked cake.

"Therefore," Henrietta went on, "I wish to lease premises in the West End of London and start my own confectioner's shop. I mean to rival Gunter's."

Gunter's was the Almack's of the confectioners' trade. Situated in Berkeley Square, it attracted all the members of the ton, and Gunter's ices were legendary.

"No, I do not mean to serve ices," said Henrietta, although no one had spoken. "Not at first. I could not afford shipments of ice from Greenland like Gunter."

"I see you have asked us here for advice," said Josephine, with a sympathetic look at Miss Hissop.

"It is just *not done*. What if your venture did not succeed? What gentleman would entertain the idea of marriage to you after you had been in trade?"

"Perhaps a merchant," said Henrietta sharply. "I am tired of gentility. Look at my poor father's life. *Never* would he press for payment, because a gentleman did not do that sort of thing. Although he was from a landed family, he was nevertheless only a country doctor, whereas Mama was the *daughter* of the Honorable Edward Devere, and people told her and *told her* she had married beneath her, until she made father's life a misery, and I *swear* she died of discontent!"

"Henrietta!" exclaimed Miss Hissop. "Your poor, dear mama!"

Henrietta turned red. "I am sorry, but I only speak the truth. We are all kept in chains by the fact that we are genteel women. Let me speak plain. You, Charlotte, could do with three good meals a day. You were considered to have married beneath you, and so your family has cast you off. Josephine—well, the least said about Squire Archer the better. He would not treat a son thus . . . or a horse. No, I am determined to make my own way in life. If I am going to be a social outcast, I shall be a *rich* social outcast."

"But," said Charlotte timidly, "it appears you did not, after all, ask us here for advice. So why . . . ?"

"I am about to come to that. Now, everyone knows a good confectioner's has the prettiest of girls. You and Miss Archer are both beautiful, and so . . ."

"You are never suggesting that Mrs. Webster and myself should serve behind a *counter*?" said Josephine, two spots of color burning on her cheeks.

"Yes," said Henrietta baldly. "I am offering you both

7

jobs. I shall put up the money, and the profits will be divided among the four of us."

"The four!" squeaked Miss Hissop. "Dear Henrietta, it never crossed my mind that you would expect *me* to *work!*"

"Working in a successful business in London is surely better than living in this backwater," said Henrietta roundly.

Charlotte's long, white, almost transparent fingers fluttered helplessly. "I am sorry, Miss Bascombe," she said in a stifled voice. "It was good of you to ask me, but I must refuse."

"And I," said Josephine firmly, rising and drawing on her gloves. "I am sure that when you think calmly about the matter, you will find it would not serve. Only very common people go into business."

"I am before my time," said Henrietta sadly. "I am sorry you will not be joining me in my venture, but I shall go ahead alone if need be."

The two now highly embarrassed ladies found their shawls. With many flurried and hurried good-byes, they made their way out into the freezing cold of the late afternoon.

"Oooof!" said Henrietta, retreating to the parlor and sinking down into a battered horsehair armchair in front of the fire. "They *were* shocked."

"And quite rightly, too," said Miss Hissop. "Let us go to bed early tonight, Henrietta. I am persuaded you need more rest."

"We always go to bed early," said Henrietta gloomily. "We've never, until the windfall, been able to burn candles after the sun goes down. But, in any case, I shall need a good night's rest. It's a ten mile walk in the morning to meet the stage at Oaktree crossroads."

"Where are you going?"

Henrietta yawned. "I am going to London to lease premises for a shop."

"Oh, no," moaned Miss Hissop. "Only bad can come of this idea. I am glad, yes, *glad*, that neither Mrs. Webster nor Miss Archer encouraged you in your folly."

"They have not had time to think about it," pointed out Henrietta. "They may yet come about."

"Not them," said Miss Hissop with conviction. "Certainly not them!"

Later that evening, Josephine Archer lay in her bed, a handkerchief soaked in cologne held against one bruised cheek. Squire Archer had been drunk when she returned from Henrietta's. She had not been expecting him to be home and had therefore been taken aback by his sudden drunken appearance in the drawing room. She had let her contempt and disgust for him, usually so carefully concealed, show in her eyes. And the furious squire had struck her in the face with his fist.

Josephine eventually dried her eyes and thought about her strange conversation with Henrietta. She began to wonder if she herself would ever marry. Unlike Henrietta, Josephine had found several gentlemen in the village and local county quite pleasing.

But her father's mad drunken rages had driven away any suitable callers.

Henrietta might be lowering herself to go into trade, but she would be in *London*, not hidden away in some English village, dreading the sound of her own father's voice.

Father would chase her to London in any case, thought Josephine dismally. But just suppose Henrietta had not told anyone else other than Miss Hissop or herself or Charlotte what she planned to do. Then it would be possible to leave a note for the squire saying she had run off to Scotland with some man. Just suppose . . .

Josephine sat bolt upright in bed. Henrietta's offer, which had seemed so outrageous earlier in the day, now seemed like a golden chance of freedom. If only Henrietta had not told anyone else.

Charlotte Webster awoke during the night and lay shivering under her thin blankets. Food. Mountains of food. That's what she had been dreaming of. A confectioner's. She could see it now, the golden pineapple over the door, the piles of oranges and pineapples and dainty cakes. The smells of hot chocolate and coffee. Her stomach growled ferociously.

That is what maintaining the status of lady of the parish does for me, thought Charlotte bitterly. All I have to show for my gentle birth is a rumbling stomach and a freezing bedroom and winter days stretching out to an infinity of more rumbling stomachs and more freezing nights.

She had once been a plump headstrong girl, but hunger and more hunger had broken her spirit.

Somewhere inside her, that old rebellious Charlotte was beginning to argue, was beginning to say in a louder and louder voice, "Go to London. Go to London. Go to London, you widgeon. No one will miss you. You can *eat*. Even if the business is a failure, you will be able to eat while it lasts. Go to London!"

Henrietta, setting out the next day for the long walk to meet the stage, had two notes handed to her, one by the squire's footman, the other by a village boy.

The first was from Josephine. In it she said she would go with Henrietta and work for her provided that no one in the village, especially not her father, should find out her whereabouts. The second was from Charlotte Webster. The paper was blotted with tears, and the note said pathetically, "Thank you. I must accept your offer. I am so very hungry."

Henrietta retreated indoors to tell the startled Miss Hissop the good news and warn her to tell no one at all about the venture. Miss Hissop dumbly shook her head. She had never mentioned a word to anyone, hoping against hope that Henrietta would change her mind before she disgraced herself.

Henrietta set out again. The day was glittering with frost, but the sky was blue, and the sparkling, shining road led straight as an arrow out of the village of Partlett.

"Success is coming," said Henrietta to herself. "I can *feel* it."

Chapter Two

"What is so vastly interesting in the existence of a new confectioner's?" asked the Earl of Carrisdowne.

His friend, Mr. Guy Clifford, neatly guided his curricle between a Covent Garden cart and a hackney carriage before replying, "Nothing. If it were an ordinary confectioner's, that is. What makes Bascombe's so interesting is that Miss Bascombe is a brown-haired beauty."

"Nothing unusual in that," remarked the earl. "Confectioners are famous for their beautiful girls."

"But this one *is* Bascombe's, if you take my meaning. She started the business a month ago. And she's gently bred, and so are her two female assistants."

"It is not out of the way for shopkeepers to claim gentility," said the earl. "You know that, Guy."

"But, damme, you've only got to look at 'em, *speak* to 'em. They've even got a dragon of a lady to keep an eye on 'em."

"Are you trying to tell me that these tonnish ladies have taken to *trade*?" demanded the earl.

"Well, I suppose that's it," said Mr. Clifford awkwardly. "Ain't that just what I've been saying?"

The earl cast a cold blue eye on his friend. "I thought you were looking for a wife, not a mistress," he remarked.

Mr. Clifford flushed. "Surely running a respectable establishment like a confectioner's don't put a female beyond the pale?"

"Yes, it does, my friend," said the earl gently. "And well you know it."

Mr. Clifford set his lips in a mutinous line. Rupert, Earl of Carrisdowne, was his friend, not his guardian. But sometimes the earl went on like a guardian or a parent.

He forgot how many times the earl had pulled him out of dangerous scrapes when he was younger. The earl, like Mr. Clifford, had recently returned from the wars in the peninsula, the earl because of the death of his father, which meant he inherited the earldom, and Mr. Clifford because of a shrapnel wound. They had not seen much of each other during the past five years, having been in different regiments. Mr. Clifford was now twenty-nine. He had a comfortable income from a small Kentish estate and planned to find a wife and settle down.

The earl had readily agreed to enjoy the delights of London in Mr. Clifford's company. He was tired of war and wanted a period of relaxation before sinking himself into the cares of his estates.

He was a tall, broad-shouldered man burned brown by the Spanish sun. He had a thin, high-bridged nose and a firm mouth. His clothes were faultless, and Guy reflected enviously that the earl managed to achieve in half an hour what it took him, Guy, a good half day to accomplish.

The earl's coats lay across his shoulders without a single wrinkle, cravats fell into intricate, sculptured perfection under his fingers, and his breeches hugged his thighs like a second skin. His boots never had a mark on their glossy surface, even in the muddiest of weather.

Guy was a contrast to his tall, black-haired autocratic-looking friend. He had a fair, pleasant face and steady gray eyes. He was stocky and of only medium height.

Despite his longing for sartorial elegance, his clothes seemed to have a mind of their own. After a bare hour of leaving the hands of his valet, his waistcoat would start to ride up, and his shirt would bunch out over his breeches. The strings of his breeches would untie themselves at his knees, and the starch would mysteriously disappear from his cravat.

And yet Guy, who often resented the earl's high-handed manner and puritanical views, found that the comradeship of more easygoing friends always seemed to lead to marked cards and fast women. Despite his rather rakish past, he was a romantic at heart and was determined to fall in love when the Season started, get married, and live happily ever after.

No one could accuse the earl of being romantic. No beauty had been able to light a spark in his black, cynical eyes. At the age of thirty-three, he was still unmarried. Guy pitied the woman the earl would eventually take as a wife. He was convinced the earl would lead her a dog's life.

The earl, meanwhile, was making a mental note to have a look at this Bascombe's. It would be just like Guy to fall in love with a shop girl.

But when he made a few discreet enquiries that evening, it was to find that no one seemed to have actually gone *into* Bascombe's—only doubtfully admiring the ladies from afar.

Gunter's was the fashionable place, and no one could see any reason to go anywhere else.

"Doom and disaster," sighed Miss Henrietta Bascombe to herself as she looked out at the bleak February day. Only two months until the Season started and, unless a miracle happened, they would need to lock up the shop and go home.

Over the doorway of Bascombe's in Half Moon Street swung a golden pineapple, the sign that hung outside all good confectioners.

Inside were the most delicious cakes and confections imaginable. But the little tables stood empty, and the fashionable throng drifted past with only brief curious looks.

Henrietta, Charlotte, and Josephine were all dressed alike in striped cotton gowns and muslin aprons. Little lace caps with jaunty streamers ornamented their heads. Charlotte had put on some much-needed weight, for often they ate some of their stock at the end of the day before delivering the rest to the foundling hospital.

Henrietta did not want to leave London, particularly when things were looking so hopeful for Josephine. One of their very, very few customers, a Mr. Guy Clifford, had seemed enchanted with Josephine, and Henrietta had liked his easy, open manner.

As she stood by the window of the shop, a pale-faced young man hesitated outside. While Henrietta sent up a silent prayer, he took a few steps away, then turned back, and opened the door.

Henrietta went forward to serve him. "Just some hot

chocolate,'' he murmured, sitting down at a little table and burying his face in his hands.

Henrietta rushed to prepare a cup of chocolate and then set the steaming liquid down in front of him.

He winced as if she had presented him with a cup of poison, turned a greenish color, muttered, "I can't. The brandy, you know. Oh, my cursed head," and stumbled to his feet and lurched out of the shop.

"What on earth was the matter with *him*?" asked Josephine, round-eyed.

"He, like most of the gentlemen in Mayfair, is suffering from having drunk too long and too deeply the night before," said Henrietta crossly. "Perhaps I should have opened an apothecary's. . . ." Her voice trailed away as an idea struck her. "That's it," she breathed. "That's *it*!"

"I am glad you have realized that that is it," said Miss Hissop, who had emerged from the back shop in time to hear Henrietta's words. "Now that you have come to your senses, we can all pack up and go home."

"No, no. I mean I have hit on a plan to get the fashionables to patronize us," said Henrietta, her eyes glowing. "I still have Papa's book, where he has his recipes for various cordials, highly efficacious for the treatment of a disordered stomach and spleen. If I put them in the window with an advertisement, *that* will fetch them!"

"Nothing will fetch them," said Miss Hissop. "We are unfashionables, as I knew we should be. Dear Henrietta, let us return to our little home. I do not wish to die in London. London undertakers are *so* expensive. And in London, it costs *one shilling an hour* to hire a mute."

Miss Hissop's morbid preoccupation with her own funeral often irritated Henrietta who, like all young peo-

16

ple, thought of herself as immortal. But this new idea was burning in her brain, and she was too anxious to begin to make up the medicines and cordials to become annoyed with her spinster friend.

She worked far into the night while the other ladies went to bed in a sort of dormitory above the shop.

At last she was finished. She felt exhausted because she had had to walk to visit the herbal shops and apothecaries over in the city the previous afternoon. There was still one thing to be done, the all-important one—how to word the advertisement that was to stand in front of the bottles in the window.

It was no use hinting at the problem these prescriptions were supposed to cure. Gentlemen were too fussy in their heads in the morning to deal with subtleties. Taking a deep breath, she printed carefully,

BASCOMBE'S ELIXIRS.
FOR DISORDERS OF THE SPLEEN CAUSED
BY OVERINDULGENCE.

Was that too rude? Too blunt? Henrietta nervously chewed the end of her quill and then had to pick bits of feather out of her mouth.

"I shall leave it," she decided. "Should it prove too blunt and no one takes the bait, I shall rephrase it."

After some two hours' sleep, she awoke and roused the others. The day's baking had to commence, just as if they were expecting a flood of customers. There was always hope.

The elderly Duke of Gillingham picked his way homeward along Half Moon Street the following morning at eleven o'clock. He had been drinking and gambling at Watier's club at the corner of Bolton Street and

Piccadilly. A large breakfast, which usually put him to rights, had failed to work its magic.

His head felt hot and fevered and his stomach queasy. He felt he wanted to go home, summon his lawyers, and dictate his last will and testament. His tongue felt like a Turkish carpet that had had cigar ash spilled on it.

He was about to pass what he privately termed "that jolly little confectioner's with the pretty gels." He was often tempted to go in. But *no one* went there. It was as simple as that.

He stopped a few paces on and looked thoughtfully at the ground. Then he walked back again and raised his quizzing glass. He leaned forward, was overtaken by a sudden fit of dizziness, and banged his head against the glass. Cursing horribly, he straightened up and slowly and painfully scrutinized the advertisement.

Like a sleepwalker, he mounted the shallow steps, opened the door, and went in. He almost fled before the nauseating smells of sugar and cinnamon and chocolate.

"May I help you, sir?"

There was a dainty brunette in a striped gown and apron and a delicious frivolity of a cap curtsying before him.

"Bascombe's Elixir . . . fast," grated the duke in a rusty voice.

"Yes, sir," said Henrietta.

"Yes, *your grace*," whispered Miss Hissop, who had made it her business to discover who was who in the West End of London.

Henrietta placed the duke at a seat by the window. She poured a small bottle of the cordial into a glass and handed it to him.

He looked at her doubtfully with his red-rimmed eyes.

Then he jerked the contents down his throat and placed both hands on the table and hung on.

A warm glow spread throughout his stomach. A feeling of well-being began to permeate his whole system. He shook his head as if to clear it and looked around slowly, a little color beginning to tinge his yellowish face.

What a charming place it was, he thought with a sort of wonder. How good everything smelled! Charlotte and Josephine came in from the back shop bearing trays of cakes. What beauties, breathed the duke.

Now Henrietta had another powerful advertisement to add to the one already in the window. The Duke of Gillingham was seated at the window of the confectioner's in full view of anyone passing. He asked for chocolate and flirted amiably with Charlotte and Josephine.

One by one more gentlemen came in to take the cure and stayed to chat with Henrietta, Charlotte, and Josephine.

By the time the ladies of Mayfair set out on their calls, every fashionable man in London seemed to be crammed into Bascombe's.

The ladies could not find places, and so they were determined to get to Bascombe's the next day *before* the gentlemen arrived. A confectioner's was the only place where two ladies could meet for tea and cakes unescorted. And with all these gentlemen, it now looked a better prospect for attracting a suitable beau than Almack's.

Guy Clifford, arriving at his usual time of three in the afternoon, found he had to stand outside on the pavement and wait for a free seat.

Gloomily he watched through the window as various gentlemen ogled and stared at Josephine, and ground his

19

teeth. She should not be subjected to such vulgar company. How he longed to take her away from it all.

He flushed guiltily when he heard himself being hailed and turned and saw the willowy figure of the Earl of Carrisdowne's younger brother, Lord Charles Worsley.

"What are you hanging around here for?" asked Lord Charles curiously.

"Waiting for a place," mumbled Mr. Clifford, wondering what the earl would say if Charles told him where he had found him. "Oh, look," said Mr. Clifford suddenly, "those two Bond Street fribbles are just leaving. Come along." He seized Lord Charles's arm and all but dragged him inside.

"What's all the fuss? Why all the stampede?" asked Lord Charles. He was as black-haired and high-nosed as his brother, but where the earl's expression was autocratic and harsh, Lord Charles's was innocent and guileless.

"I don't know," said Mr. Clifford, who had been too busy watching for glimpses of Josephine to read the advertisement. "It's worse than a rout."

Charlotte curtsied before them. "What is your pleasure, gentlemen?" she asked.

"I don't know," said Lord Charles. "I was *dragged* in here, so to speak. I know, I'll have one of your wet confects."

Confectioners sold wet or dry confects. The wet ones were various fruits immersed in liquid syrup; the dry, apart from cakes and biscuits, were little figures or houses or ships made out of marzipan or fruit, beaten into a paste with sugar.

Charlotte described the various varieties of wet confects, and Lord Charles settled for apricot. Mr. Clifford asked for turtle soup. Charlotte blushed prettily. All good confectioners sold turtle soup, but since they had had no customers for it, it was an expensive business to keep making pots of turtle soup and then being forced to give it away, and so they no longer had any in stock.

"Not today, sir," she said.

"He'll have the same as me," said Lord Charles cheerfully. And as Charlotte walked away, he said to Mr. Clifford, "I'll eat yours if you don't want it. Couldn't stand to see her blush. Pretty girl. *Very* pretty girl. Do you see that beautiful shine on her black hair?"

"I say," said Mr. Clifford, hitching his chair closer to the table, "you know how authoritative Rupert can be at times."

"My brother can be a demmed bully, if that's what you mean," said Lord Charles with feeling.

"Yes, well, I told him about Bascombe's and how odd it was they were all *ladies*. He disapproved. Said they couldn't be ladies if they were working in a shop. Told him that little Miss Bascombe over there who can't be more than twenty opened up the business herself. He gave me a cold look—I was driving at the time, and I swear I felt the chill from it going right down one side— and more or less told me I was making a cake of myself. *You* know."

"So you don't want me to tell him you've been seen here," grinned Lord Charles. "Tell you what, we *both* shan't tell him we've been here, and we can enjoy the company of these pretty ladies undisturbed. Now, which one is it? Miss Bascombe, the one with the chestnut hair, or the beautiful princess in the tower who is serving us?"

"No one in particular," said Mr. Clifford airily. "Ain't much interested in ladies these days, to tell the truth."

He turned and found Josephine at his elbow and flushed brick-red.

"Oho!" grinned Lord Charles maliciously. The truth, is it?"

Instead of waiting wearily until ten in the evening in the hope of a customer, Henrietta was able to put up the heavy shutters at six. She went back into the shop and looked with dazed delight at the empty shelves. Then she groaned. It was going to be another long night of baking, and brewing elixir.

Charlotte and Josephine were sitting in chairs in the shop, looking weary but triumphant. Miss Hissop was counting out the day's takings and dreaming of a magnificent funeral with plumed horses and paid mourners.

"We should have helped you with the shutters," yawned Josephine. "In fact, the sooner we hire a man, the better. It is heavy work stoking the fires for the ovens and cleaning up."

"I am very strong," said Henrietta, "though I do feel a little weak at the moment. I must sit down and get out the order book. We are going to need large quantities of *everything*. Yes, you are right. We *do* need a boy to fetch and carry for us. Perhaps on Sunday I shall go to the nearest workhouse and see if I can find someone."

"The workhouse!" shuddered Miss Hissop, her hands full of sovereigns and silver. "Much safer to get a young man from one of the agencies."

"No," said Henrietta. "It is a chance to allow some poor boy from the workhouse a comfortable living. We are a success, ladies! Bascombe's has become fashionable.

"Nothing can stop our success now!"

* * *

A week later, the Earl of Carrisdowne stood outside Bascombe's and looked in. His younger brother and his best friend were cozily ensconced in a corner, gazing at two of the young shopgirls in a decidedly spoony manner.

He walked on, thoroughly irritated. His brother and Mr. Clifford were notoriously gullible when it came to the fair sex. Had not Guy nearly proposed marriage once to a member of the fashionable impure whom Guy had persuaded himself was really an innocent virgin?

And had not young Charles run off with an opera dancer? And would have married the trollop had he, the earl, not been home on leave to put a stop to the romance?

Nonetheless, he had almost decided to leave the matter of Bascombe's until things became more obviously serious but changed his mind because of the involvement with that wretched place of another member of the family.

His young sister, Lady Sarah Worsley, had been steadily growing as fat as a pig. She was just seventeen and had an enormous appetite for cakes. When the earl had pointed out that she was ruining her face and figure with sweetmeats, she had gone on a strict diet for a while and had emerged as a pretty girl. Now she was fat and spotty again, and he soon learned the problem was Bascombe's. Lady Sarah stated she had never tasted such delicious cakes before. The earl forbade her to visit Bascombe's, an order that Lady Sarah accepted with uncharacteristic meekness. Then it transpired that she had simply been sending round a footman each day with a long list of all the cakes she craved.

The Earl of Carrisdowne turned over the problem of

Bascombe's in his mind. What a pity the wretched place had become fashionable.

Then his face cleared.

Although he had never *tried* to be a leader of fashion, he was, nevertheless, because of the elegance of his clothes and the haughtiness of his manner, already looked up to as an arbiter of fashion.

He would make Bascombe's unfashionable.

A little word dropped here. A little word there.

It was all very simple.

Chapter Three

The Earl of Carrisdowne was to be seen gracing many balls and parties during the following week.

He always managed to turn the conversation to Bascombe's. "You like the place? How odd. I thought only peasants and mushrooms went there," he said.

Until the full force of his social disapproval hit Bascombe's, Henrietta, flushed and happy, did a roaring trade.

She had employed a boy from the workhouse. He was an ill-favored lad of fourteen called Esau. Esau had a bad squint that gave him a cunning look, belying the gentle soul within. To have been transported from a miserable life to a West End confectioner's, to be able to eat cake for the first time in his life, persuaded the deeply religious Esau that all his prayers had been answered.

Even Miss Hissop, who had not at first approved of the boy, had her heart melted by the vast amount of work he did. Esau slaved early and late. No more did Henrietta have to nurse an aching back after stoking the bakery fires or taking down and putting up the heavy shutters. Esau was thin and round-shouldered. But he was very wiry and strong and could run like the wind.

He was to be dressed in red-plush livery as soon as his new suit of clothes arrived from the tailor, and he was to have his hair powdered.

The Duchess of Gillingham had ordered a centerpiece from Bascombe's for a dinner party. It was Henrietta's first order, and she planned to make it the talk of London.

The first signs of disaster came one day the following week. By noontime, although many gentlemen had hurried in to buy Bascombe's elixir, none had stayed to drink it. Instead, they took the bottles with them, slinking in and out of the shop with a furtive air.

Henrietta did not know that Mr. Clifford and Lord Charles had gone into the country to attend a prize fight, and so she thought they had deserted her as well.

Then the final blow fell. The Duchess of Gillingham sent a servant, canceling the order for the centerpiece.

Gloomily Henrietta told Esau to put up the shutters at six in the evening. Then she called a council of war.

"What has happened?" she demanded. "Why are we become unfashionable again?"

"London society is fickle," wailed Miss Hissop. "Do let us leave this dreadful place before we lose any more money, Henrietta."

"No," said Henrietta, her soft mouth setting in a stubborn line. "Mr. Clifford seemed much taken with you, Josephine, and Lord Charles with Charlotte. Why have they suddenly sheered off?"

"I am suddenly so very tired," said Charlotte listlessly. "I was kept going by the excitement of success. I cannot *bear* to think of making and baking cakes again for people who do not come. Now, even the duchess has canceled her order. Could you have done it anyway, Henrietta? It is very difficult to make one of those elaborate centerpieces."

"Yes, I could have done it; better than Gunter's, too," said Henrietta. "Sir Benjamin Prestcott's chef used to let me watch how he created miracles out of spun sugar. I would spend my time with him in the kitchen while Papa was attending Sir Benjamin. He was a Frenchman who had escaped the Terror. He was an artist."

"Something has gone badly wrong," said Josephine, wrinkling her smooth brow. "Do you think someone had a disordered stomach after eating here and talked of it?"

"No," said Henrietta slowly. "If that had happened, they would have descended on us and complained loudly. That is what they are like," she said seriously, as though explaining the customs of some strange aboriginal tribe.

"Could go to a boozing ken and find out," said Esau suddenly.

"I beg your pardon?" said Henrietta.

She waited patiently while Esau worked out a translation in his head. Esau had talked nothing but cant all his young life. He was trying hard to learn the King's English and was having as much difficulty with it as a foreigner.

"I shall go to a pub where the flash servants hang out," he said carefully, "and ask questions."

"Splendid!" said Henrietta. "Miss Hissop, give Esau a few shillings."

"He should not be encouraged to go *drinking*," said Miss Hissop stiffly.

"I'll only drink shrub," said Esau. Shrub was fruit cordial mixed with rum.

"Only one glass, then," said Miss Hissop, counting out the money.

"Give him two shillings, Miss Hissop," said Henrietta. "If he wishes to get information, he may have to buy a servant some beer."

Esau took the money and went out into the cold, blustery evening.

He had a fund of underworld gossip and knew in which pubs to find the upper-class servants, since those hostelries were often frequented by thieves looking for information on how to break into some noble's house and steal the silver.

He was gone over an hour. Henrietta heard him returning, the boy's swift, light steps coming running along the street from Piccadilly. Esau never walked.

She went to the door and let him in.

"I found out, mum," he said triumphantly. He started on a long story. Henrietta had to take him back over it time after time to iron out all the cant phrases so that she could understand. At last she had it all.

"Only peasants go to Bascombe's," the upper servants had told Esau.

"Why?" Esau had asked, and had kept on asking until it had come out that that was what the Earl of Carrisdowne was saying, and what the earl said was law.

"Oh, dear," said Miss Hissop, when Henrietta repeated Esau's story. "You know, Lord Charles is the earl's younger brother, and he has been paying a lot of attention to Charlotte. This must be the earl's way of trying to put us out of business."

"But did you not say that Lady Sarah is his sister? She still sends a servant for cakes."

"Fat as a pig," said Esau suddenly. "Earl don't like that neither."

"It *must* be to put us out of business," frowned Henrietta. "This earl has not been here himself. He probably disapproves of Lord Charles's visits."

"Not 'arf," said Esau. "Nor Mr. Clifford's neither."

"But what has Mr. Clifford to do with the Earl of Carrisdowne?"

"Chums," said Esau. "Close as inkle weavers, they is. Carrisdowne said t'other night . . ." here Esau's voice rose to the strangled falsetto he considered upperclass, " 'Any fellow going to Bascombe's is indeed *making a cake of himself.*' "

"Is this earl so powerful?" marveled Henrietta.

"Oh, yes," said Josephine sadly. Josephine picked up a great deal of gossip from the lady customers. "All the debutantes talk of little else. He is the catch of the coming Season. Rich, handsome, titled. The ladies say he looks deliciously like the wicked earl in a circulating library romance—all dark and overbearing."

"He is a monster," said Henrietta. "He must have so much money, and we have so little. Why cannot he leave us alone?"

"Lord Persham's underfootman told me real ladies don't work in shops," said Esau. "I drew 'is cork—may the good Lord forgive me," he added piously.

"You did the right thing," said Henrietta firmly. "But it is Lord Carrisdowne who should have his nose punched. Do you know, Esau, I am beginning to understand every word you say."

"I knew I could talk flash if I put me brainbox to it," said Esau proudly.

"Then, that is that," said Charlotte, her eyes filling with tears.

Josephine began to cry as well. "I h-have never m-met anyone as n-nice and *kind* as Mr. Clifford before," she sobbed. "Now all I have left is a future of being beaten day and night by my papa. And I shall n-never s-see Mr. C-Clifford *again*."

"Fustian," said Henrietta. "What we need is someone more powerful than the Earl of Carrisdowne to bring us *back* into fashion. There is the Prince Regent."

"No one seems to follow the Prince Regent, not when it comes to fashion," said Charlotte, drying her eyes. "Mr. Brummell is still the leader. No one talks about anyone else but Brummell and Carrisdowne. But I believe he is harder to reach than the Prince Regent."

"Of *course*," breathed Henrietta. The fame of the great dandy had reached even the village of Partlett. Beau Brummell was an intimate of the Prince Regent. He had changed fashion by introducing impeccably tailored clothes, clean linen, and starch—'plenty of it.' Although the Beau himself was reported to be a miracle of understated elegance, most of his followers overdid his advice. Sometimes young men wore their neckcloths so high, and stiffened with so much starch, that the wearers could not turn their heads.

One young man was reported to have turned up at a dinner so starched that when he wanted to speak to the footman standing behind him he had to bend his head back until his face was horizontal. Another young man burned his chin by trying to iron the bows of his neckcloth after it was tied.

"I have an idea . . . I think," said Henrietta cautiously. "I must find out what Mr. Brummell looks like. Where does he live?"

"I'll find out, miss," said Esau, pulling his forelock.

Again he disappeared into the night, while Henrietta and the other ladies grimly set to work, trying to preserve as many of the day's uneaten delicacies as they could.

After only half an hour, Esau was back. "Mr. Brummell lives at 13 Chapel Street, which is just at Park Lane, off a South Audley Street, just a few streets away, miss."

"Good," said Henrietta.

"What do you plan to do?" asked Charlotte.

"I shall tell you after I have had a look at this famous Beau," said Henrietta, "but let me tell you one thing, Charlotte and Josephine. You may dry your tears, for Bascombe's is *not* going to fail!"

Henrietta had learned quickly that the ton did not keep country hours. The gentlemen who crept into Bascombe's at ten in the morning for their elixir were usually going home.

So at two o'clock the following afternoon, on a freezing day with the metallic smell of approaching snow in the air, Henrietta set out to walk to Chapel Street, a sketch pad under her arm.

The wind beat against her thin cloak and set it flapping about her ankles. When she got to Chapel Street, she was forced to keep walking up and down at a brisk pace, not only to keep warm, but to stop drawing any gentleman's attention to her.

Any woman strolling about at a leisurely pace, unescorted, was bound to be taken for a prostitute. She wished she had brought Esau with her.

How would she recognize the famous Beau, he who had evidently said that if people turned to stare at you in the street, then you were badly overdressed?

Just as she was about to give up, for flakes of snow were beginning to fall, she saw a slim young man emerge from Number 13. Two giggling debutantes, passing by with their maids in attendance, cried, "Only look! There is Mr. Brummell!"

Henrietta, now stationed on the opposite side of the street, whipped out her sketch pad and began to draw rapidly.

Almost as if he had noticed her and was gratified at the attention, the Beau posed on the steps of his house, slowly pulling on his gloves.

He was wearing a blue swallowtail coat, tailored by the famous Weston, over a fifteen-guinea waistcoat from Guthrie's. His pantaloons were buff-colored and tucked into glossy Hessian boots. Gentlemen were beginning to adopt pantaloons because "Napoleon and his upstarts" had adopted breeches. He had a high-crowned beaver hat on his head of light-brown curls. His face was humorous, the nose flattened and upturned, the result of a horse having kicked it.

While Henrietta sketched busily, he finished drawing on his gloves and strolled into South Audley Street, his toes turned outward as he walked, evidently heading for St. James's.

Henrietta closed her sketch pad with a sigh. Her plan *must* work.

After the confectioner's had closed that evening and the chores had been done, Henrietta set to work in the kitchen with the sketch pad beside her.

Charlotte and Josephine were curious as to what she was planning, but Henrietta sent them all to bed, saying she would need as much help as she could get on the morrow, for they were shortly to be fashionable again.

When they all appeared in the kitchen for breakfast at six in the morning, it was to find Henrietta asleep with her head on the table. In front of her stood a foot and half high statuette of Beau Brummell, made out of spun sugar and colored with vegetable dye. They circled around it in awed silence. It was, they were sure, Beau Brummell to the life. They knew that Henrietta had gone out to sketch him, but not that she meant to create a confection from that hurried drawing.

Even the Beau's eyes sparkled where Henrietta had placed a coarse grain of sugar near the center of each pupil to catch the light. His cravat of white sugar was as delicately sculptured as the original.

Henrietta stretched sleepily and yawned, and then grinned up at the circle of admiring faces.

"It is wonderful," said Miss Hissop. "I knew you were a good artist, Henrietta. I never realized to this moment that you were a *genius*!"

"Are you going to display it in the window?" asked Charlotte.

"No," said Henrietta. "Esau's new livery arrives today. He is to be washed and brushed and then he will take it to Mr. Brummell as a *present*."

Esau was so excited at the idea of his new livery that he even submitted to taking a wash in a tin bath in the kitchen behind a sheet pinned up as a screen.

He privately thought the whole business of bathing was shameful and indecent and had anyone other than Henrietta told him to scrub himself, he would most definitely have refused.

But Henrietta's soft voice and large brown eyes, which smiled on him in such a merry way, had done more for poor Esau than any workhouse whippings. What Miss Henrietta wanted, Miss Henrietta should have. The bathwater was scented with rose petals, and Esau began to find the novelty of washing quite pleasant.

Miss Hissop thought Henrietta had gone too far by insisting the boy wash himself all over. But Miss Hissop had to admit to herself that Henrietta had very odd notions when it came to washing and even soaped and washed her own hair, which everyone knew could lead to all sorts of agues and fevers.

Dressed in his best and looking even more sinister with his hair powdered—it seemed to accentuate his squint—Esau set out.

He came back quite crestfallen. He had hoped to have presented it to the Beau himself, but Mr. Brummell's servant had simply taken the large beribboned box and told Esau rudely to "hop it."

Although Beau Brummell's household effects boasted a dinner service of twelve oval dishes, twenty soup plates, and seventy-eight meat plates, as well as nine wine coolers, three claret jugs, a dozen hock glasses, and forty others, Mr. Brummell usually dined out at friends' houses.

But that very evening he was holding one of his rare dinner parties. Henrietta's statue was not exhibited on his dining table, but on a special stand placed in the middle of his chintz-upholstered, Brussells-carpeted drawing room upstairs where he received his guests.

Candles had been arranged to set the grains of sugar in the candy eyes sparkling to perfection. His guests exclaimed, admired, and all began to gossip about Bascombe's. "Who is saying it is a common establishment?" asked Mr. Brummell crossly. "In my opinion, it is the home of a genius. And you say Bascombe is not some ancient pastry cook but a pretty, genteel lady?''

''Carrisdowne says no one who's anyone goes there,'' was the reply from all sides.

Mr. Brummell said gently, ''When could Carrisdowne—such a stiff soldier one expects him to wear a cannonball in his stickpin—*when* could our military friend ever appreciate the finer things of life, whether a painting, a pretty ankle, or . . .'' he waved his quizzing glass at the statue'' . . . a work of genius?''

Mr. Brummell had only a nodding acquaintance with the earl. But he was vastly annoyed that society should follow anyone else's dictates.

''I have heard that he is a bully, horse-whipping sort of fellow,'' went on Mr. Brummell. ''Oh, he is a fine figure of a man and dresses almost as well as I myself. But he has such a *badly dressed mind*.''

''Such a badly dressed mind,'' muttered everyone gleefully, saving those bon mots to pass around at less exalted gatherings.

''Now Gunter's,'' went on the Beau pensively, ''has become quite dull. I actually brushed shoulders with a merchant there the other day, and had to ask my valet to throw the besmirched coat away.''

Mr. Brummell's views could not damn socially such a marriageable man as the Earl of Carrisdowne. But they could, and did, bring Bascombe's roaring back into fashion.

By the end of another week, Henrietta had the pleasure of being able to save a daily table for Mr. Clifford and Lord Charles, who had arrived back in London and to employ three kitchen maids.

The Duchess of Gillingham renewed her order for a

centerpiece. Henrietta sent her "Hannibal Crossing the Alps," taken from Turner's famous painting, which had just been exhibited at the Royal Academy. Marzipan elephants strained up sugar mountains, laden with baskets of tiny sweetmeats wrapped in gold and silver foil.

Bascombe's appeared for the first time in the social column of the *Times*.

Mr. Clifford, grown courageous, laughed in the Earl of Carrisdowne's face and accused him of behaving like a Methodist. "Imagine," said Mr. Clifford, "what a figure of fun you look trying to stop your brother and your best friend from visiting a respectable confectioner's in the middle of the afternoon. You have a badly dressed mind."

"So I keep hearing," said the earl dryly. "It seems I am become an ogre even to my best friend."

Mr. Clifford blushed. "It ain't that I'm not grateful to you for all the messes you've pulled me out of in the past, Rupert, it just seems terribly stuffy to go on like a Dutch uncle over an innocent taking of tea. When did you ever think it odd to look at pretty girls?"

"Never," grinned the earl. "What has made this Bascombe's so violently popular again?"

"Haven't you heard? Little Miss Bascombe sent a statuette of Brummell to him, made out of sugar, the most wonderful thing anyone has ever seen."

"Clever of her," said the earl thoughtfully. "Very clever."

"Why don't you have a look at the place for yourself," said Mr. Clifford eagerly. "I know what it is—you're worried about Sarah stuffing her face with cakes. You're not really worried about Charles or me. It's not as if we aren't old enough to look after ourselves. But Sarah has always had a terribly sweet tooth, and if you forbid her to either go or send the servants to Bascombe's, she'll simply go back to Gunter's. Besides, you can't stop anyone eating these days. There's such a monstrous deal of food around.''

''For those that can afford it,'' said the earl. ''And those that can could exist on a fraction of what they eat. Someone who shared dinner for two at Lord Stafford's told me they dined on soup, fish, fricassee of chicken, cutlets, venison, veal, hare, vegetables of all kinds, tart, melon, pineapple, grapes, peaches and nectarines, and with six servants to wait on the two of them.

''But I shall certainly call on Bascombe's, Guy. It is ridiculous of me to damn a place I have never set foot in.''

The earl appeared at Bascombe's just before closing time. He had decided that his fears were groundless and that the ladies there would prove to be quite ordinary shopgirls pretending to be duchesses.

He ordered turtle soup and sat at a small table and looked at Henrietta, Charlotte, and Josephine with a sinking heart. They were each of them beautiful in quite a different way. They were undoubtedly ladies by birth, although their present occupation had certainly reduced them to the ranks of the demimonde. But the earl knew how terribly susceptible his younger brother and best friend were. Beauty decked out in domestic aprons and surrounded by food. The combination was hellishly seductive.

Henrietta studied her customer curiously. He was drinking his soup as though it were poison. She decided he was by far the most attractive man she had ever seen since she had come to London. The exquisites were too

37

feminine, the masculine members of the Corinthian set too brutish in their sports and manners.

This gentleman, mused Henrietta, looked powerful and strong, and yet there was a certain sensitivity in his harsh face and drooping eyelids. He glanced up and caught her staring at him, and looked steadily back, his black, black eyes giving nothing away. Henrietta stood rigid, one hand on the counter of the shop, feeling as shaken as if he had tried to assault her.

Josephine passed close to her with a tray of confectionery. "One of the ladies who has just left," she murmured in Henrietta's ear, "said that *that* over there, eating soup, is none other than our enemy, the Earl of Carrisdowne."

"Oh," said Henrietta weakly. "He is not at all what I expected."

She had built up in her mind a picture of a middle-aged tyrant with a brutal face—despite the fact that the lady customers had said he was handsome. Anyone with a title and a fortune was vowed handsome, that much Henrietta had learned very quickly.

Since six in the evening was now the regular hour for closing, by ten to six the last of the customers had collected hats and canes, shawls and reticules, and were making their way out. Still the earl stayed.

Charlotte was the next to flutter up. "That is Carrisdowne," she whispered, and when Henrietta nodded, added, "Why does he not *go*?"

"Because I think he wishes to speak to me," said Henrietta. She was now calm. The earl was a man like any other. He had a great deal of power but fortunately not more than Mr. Brummell.

"Get Miss Hissop and Josephine, and stay in the back

shop with Esau until I call you," muttered Henrietta. "I can handle this better alone."

The earl sat listening to the hissings and mutterings as the ladies tried to stay while Henrietta shooed them all into the back shop.

Then she walked to the door and drew down the blind and, turning to the earl, said sweetly, "We are now closed, sir. I do not wish to hurry you, but as you have finished your soup . . ."

The earl's black eyes locked with Henrietta's brown ones. "I stayed quite deliberately, madam," he said. "I have something to say to you."

Henrietta unpinned her apron and folded it neatly on the counter. Then she unpinned her frivolous cap with the jaunty streamers. She would face this adversary as a lady, not as as shopgirl.

She sat down opposite the earl. "Very well, Lord Carrisdowne," said Henrietta Bascombe. "What is it you wish to say?"

Chapter Four

The earl looked thoughtfully at Henrietta's flushed face and bright eyes.

"I shall speak to you plain, Miss Bascombe. My brother, Lord Charles Worsley, and my friend, Mr. Clifford, are frequent customers here."

Henrietta nodded. "They come every day when they are in town."

"Delicious as your confections appear to be, I am persuaded that the attraction is either yourself or the two other ladies who work for you."

"Indeed?" Henrietta tilted her little chin defiantly.

"Yes, indeed. Both Mr. Clifford and my brother are gullible young men."

"I would not call Mr. Clifford exactly *young*," interrupted Henrietta.

"How old are you?"

"Nineteen," said Henrietta.

"Mr. Clifford is twenty-nine but is young for his years. Charles is twenty-three. I have rescued both in the past from unsuitable alliances—an opera dancer and a member of the fashionable impure, to be precise.''

"Since no one here belongs to either set, I do not see—''

"Madam, I wish you to repel any advances these two men might make to you or your companions, or it will be the worse for you,'' grated the earl.

"How *dare* you!'' raged Henrietta. "We are all *ladies*.''

"It seems to me,'' he said calmly, "that you *were* all ladies at one time. But not now. Ladies do not go into trade.''

"Let me tell you, my fine buck,'' said Henrietta, "that I do not consider *you* a gentleman. Making malicious remarks to stop society from coming here. What on earth do you have against four poor women trying to make a living?''

"Women such as yourself, whom the good Lord has seen fit to place among the gentry, do not work. They marry.''

"Pooh,'' said Henrietta. "I do not wish to get married. I am much better off as I am.''

"You . . . do . . . not . . . wish . . . to . . . get . . . married?'' The earl looked dumbfounded. There had been an unmistakable ring of truth in her voice.

"No.''

He looked at her shrewdly. "And your female assistants. Do they feel the same?''

Henrietta bit her lip. The truth was that despite her desire to turn Charlotte and Josephine into businesswomen, she knew that in their hearts of hearts they were ashamed of being in trade and had their lives back in Partlett not been so thoroughly nasty, they would have returned on the first available stage.

"They are as competent as myself when it comes to making their own way," she said. "Tell me, my lord, I can understand you forbidding your younger brother to go anywhere of which you disapprove. It amazes me, however, that you should be able to command Mr. Clifford."

"I do not *command* my friend to do anything. I merely suggest—"

"And tag on a warning."

"No. I merely point out the obvious. You have all gone into trade, and therefore you are none of you marriageable."

"Let me tell you, my lord, that somehow, somewhere, there must be a man who does not care—who would be *proud* of us. We have proved that gently bred ladies can earn their wages."

He rose to his feet. "Let me know when you find him, Miss Bascombe. I have never yet met a saint."

"Oh, do not rush off," said Henrietta sweetly, "without telling me what you will do should I not carry out your wish regarding your brother and friend."

"If either my brother or Mr. Clifford should be so addlepated as to propose to one of you and be accepted, then I shall . . . I shall—"

"Yes, my lord?"

"Damn you, madam, I shall be very angry indeed!"

Henrietta's enchanting trill of laughter followed him out into the street. He marched to the corner of Half Moon Street and Piccadilly and stopped. He turned and looked back.

It had been snowing lightly that day, a fresh fall. The warm lights from the confectioner's shone a welcome into the cold street. The golden pineapple above the door swung in the wind.

He felt an odd mixture of fury and exultation. She had had the better of him, but By George he was looking forward to the forthcoming battle! But what on earth could he do to them now that they enjoyed the patronage of Mr. Brummell?

Every woman had her price, the earl thought cynically. Imagine any woman declaring—and meaning it—that she had no interest in marriage.

Although he had not yet met any woman who had found enough favor in his eyes to make him want to take her as wife, he was well aware that, for their part, the ladies fell before him like ninepins. He had not been back in London a week before they were up to every plot and plan to catch his attention. But cynical acquaintances were quick to point out that his title and fortune were the attraction. And I imagined it was because I might be perhaps as handsome as they claim I am, the earl had thought gloomily.

"Miss Bascombe has now made me feel that *she*, at least, would not take me under any terms," he muttered to himself.

He walked up Piccadilly past the Green Park, still deep in thought, with a bright little picture of Henrietta, all flushed face, bright eyes, and heaving bosom, dancing before his eyes.

Suppose . . . just suppose he made Miss Bascombe fall in love with him. . . . She was the owner and the driving force behind the business. Were she in love with him, she would gladly go for walks and drives with him, and the business would falter and die. By the time she discovered he really had no interest in her at all, other than keeping her and her assistants away from his brother and friend, it would be too late.

He had never *tried* to make a woman fall in love with

him before. But it should be quite easy. Women had nothing else in their heads but fashions and flowers, beaux and romances.

Yes, definitely a challenge. And by pretending to court Henrietta, he could visit the shop often and make sure Guy and Charles were behaving themselves.

Something, also, would have to be done about Sarah. Although he was quite good at disciplining Charles, he had never been able to do anything with Sarah. His face cleared. His mother, the Dowager Countess of Carrisdowne, who had been taking the waters at Bath, had written only that day to say she was much improved.

Very well. Sarah should be sent to Bath. Instead of making her come-out at the Season in London, she could make her debut at the famous spa. It would not matter if nothing came of it. She was still very young. But Mama would see to it that she kept away from treacherous confectioners and their devilish wares.

The problem of Sarah having been dealt with, the earl turned his mind once more to Miss Bascombe. He enjoyed thinking about her. She was such a defiant little miss. It would be enjoyable to bring her down a peg. He could hardly wait to begin.

"And," ended Henrietta, looking around the kitchen, "do you know what his terrible threat was? He threatened to become very angry with me." She laughed and laughed, until she realized no one was joining in.

The kitchen maids had returned to their homes, and Henrietta was seated at the kitchen table surrounded by Charlotte, Josephine, Miss Hissop, and Esau.

"What is the matter?" she cried. "There is nothing to be afraid of. He can't do anything to Bascombe's."

"No," said Charlotte sadly. She stood up and kissed

Henrietta on the cheek. "And now you must excuse me. I am so very tired and shall feel better for an early night."

"I, too," said Josephine, trailing out after her.

"Going out for a bit, mum," said Esau, sidling out the back door.

Henrietta looked in amazement at Miss Hissop. "What is wrong with them? I *told* them the wicked earl cannot do anything to Bascombe's."

"I think he can, however, make sure that Mr. Clifford and Lord Charles do not marry either of them," said Miss Hissop quietly.

"Oh." Henrietta put her hands up to her hot cheeks. "I was feeling so triumphant at having got the best of him that I quite forgot. Bascombe's means so very much to me. But alas for Josephine and Charlotte. All they want to do is fall in love and get married. It is most odd of them."

"Henrietta," cried Miss Hissop. "I beg of you . . . you are not talking sense, you know. What is it all for? The Season and the gowns and the duennas? Almack's, the Italian opera, the routs, the fetes, the breakfasts? Why . . . so that John may marry Jill! There is *no other future for a lady*! If she does not marry, and the family is not rich, then she may be lucky enough to find a post as a companion . . . or governess.

"Have you not considered my plight? We are making a great deal of money, but we also spend a great deal creating novelties. Flour is a wicked expense. What if we lose all? And I . . . poor Miss Hissop . . . am buried in a pauper's grave? Have you no feelings? Why not be done and give my poor old body to the anatomists at St. George's Hospital? Oh, lovely black horses and weeping mutes, where are you now? Gone. Alas, all gone.''

''If only I were a man, the Carrisdownes of this world would not plague me so,'' said Henrietta. ''Please, do not distress yourself. We are all so tired. So very tired. You may stay in bed tomorrow, all day long, and rest.''

''No,'' said Miss Hissop, striking her scrawny bosom with her fist. ''I shall see it through. When Bascombe's lies at my feet in ashes and ruins, I shall say *hah* to the Fates.''

''Go and say *hah* to your pillow, my good friend,'' said Henrietta gently. Miss Hissop was behaving so oddly and so . . . well, insanely . . . that her conscience was smiting her. She should never have persuaded this timid spinster into coming to London.

Had the shrewd Earl of Carrisdowne been there, perhaps he might have told Miss Bascombe that Miss Hissop was enjoying her dramatics immensely. But he was not, and so Henrietta led her old friend upstairs to the dormitory, waited until she had undressed, and then tucked her into bed as if she were a child.

''Do not worry about a thing, dear Ismene,'' she said, kissing a worn cheek. Henrietta had never called Miss Hissop by her first name before, but the older woman now appeared to her as defenseless as a child.

Henrietta quietly blew out the candle beside Miss Hissop's bed and left the room—but not before she had heard a stifled sob from Charlotte's bed.

''Should I have left them all behind?'' anguished Henrietta to herself. ''But Josephine might have been beaten to death by now, and Charlotte might have died of cold or starvation, or both.''

Then she thought of the earl. Somehow, things would work out. She would *make* them work out. If only for the pleasure of showing the earl that he could not stop her.

Why, oh *why*, had Josephine and Charlotte had to fall in love so soon? Henrietta had planned to amass a fortune and then persuade Miss Hissop to take them all to Bath and chaperon them at the assemblies. They would be respectable again by that time and with large dowries. Henrietta did not plan to find a husband for herself. She had only dreamed of the pleasure of seeing Josephine and Charlotte comfortably settled.

She tidied up the remaining dishes in the kitchen and washed out the sticky metal trays.

Water was supplied to the shop—as it was supplied to all the houses of the West End—only twice a day, and then it had to be pumped up into a cistern on the roof. It was one of Esau's many chores.

Esau. Esau, too, would need to be taken care of. He must never return to the workhouse.

Feeling suddenly exhausted, Henrietta went out into the street and paid the night watchman sixpence so that he might shout extra loudly outside their shop at six in the morning and wake them up.

The next day they were as busy as ever, and each had little time to worry about personal matters. Mr. Clifford and Lord Charles were, however, upset to find that neither Josephine nor Charlotte had a smile for them.

Lord Charles and Mr. Clifford finally took their leave and walked along the street, arm in arm.

"Not so jolly there today," remarked Lord Charles casually. "Pretty widow, Mrs. Webster. Don't like to see her so quiet and withdrawn."

"Miss Archer didn't even look at me," said Mr. Clifford, tossing a coin to a crossing sweeper. They gloomily picked their way across Half Moon Street and into Curzon Street.

"Tell you what it is," said Lord Charles. "I think Rupert's behind this. Think he's scared 'em off."

"Think you're right," said Mr. Clifford.

"By George," said Lord Charles, "I wish I could handle him like Sarah. She ups this morning and tells him he's a horrible martinet, has no soul, no feeling, and is nothing more than a piece of cannon fodder in dandy's clothing."

"Did he whip her?" asked Mr. Clifford with interest.

"Not he. Wouldn't strike any woman, especially not his own sister," said Lord Charles. "He'd told her she was to go to Mama in Bath and drink the waters and forsake the confectioners, so she ripped up at him."

"But she went, didn't she?" asked Mr. Clifford.

"Yes."

"Well, ain't that what always happens? He always gets his way."

"But, dash it all, she's only seventeen and has been summoned by Mama as well as being bundled off by Rupert. Not the same as me."

"Isn't it?" said Mr. Clifford, giving him a sidelong look. "I think Rupert will be more circumspect if he wants to spike my guns this time. Trouble is, the man ain't ever been in love."

"And are you?" asked Lord Charles anxiously.

"Yes. Yes, I am. Very much so. Right up to the neck in love."

"Not . . . not . . . Mrs. Webster?" asked Lord Charles.

"Who? Oh, *her*. No, of course not. T'other one. Miss Archer."

"Let me shake your hand," cried Lord Charles, "and wish you luck."

"No need to be so violent. It's a hand, not a pump handle. Oh, I say, you ain't spoony about Mrs. Webster?"

"Love her madly," said Lord Charles. "Terribly, awfully, madly."

A cloud of worry once more dampened Mr. Clifford's high spirits. "I'll help you if you help me," he said. "But it's going to be deuced awkward. If only Rupert would fall in love. *Then* he would know what it's all about!"

"If only Henrietta would fall in love," muttered Josephine to Charlotte as they loaded confections onto trays in the back shop of Bascombe's. "Then she might understand our misery."

Charlotte sighed and brushed a strand of black hair from her hot forehead. "I think Henrietta loves confectionery and nothing else. What's more, I don't think she ever will."

"Well, it's nearly closing time, and it's Saturday," said Josephine. "Lovely Sunday. I shall sleep all day, and Henrietta can pay my shilling fine for not going to church."

She opened the door to the shop with her shoulder, saw the gentleman who was just entering, and swung back into the kitchen again. "It's Carrisdowne!" she said.

"What does he want?" squeaked Charlotte.

"I do not know. Let me put this tray down." Josephine opened the door and peered round it. "He is saying something to Henrietta. He is standing very close to her and whispering something."

"Threats?"

"No, she is smiling. She is shaking hands with him. He has ordered something and is taking a table. Oh, Charlotte. Perhaps everything is going to be all right after all."

Inside the shop, Henrietta busily served customers and wondered what had come over the Earl of Carrisdowne.

Her first thought when she saw his tall figure was that he had come to make trouble. But he had bent his handsome head very near to her own, so near that his breath had fanned her cheek, and had said in a low voice, "I am come to apologize for my boorish behavior. Please say you forgive me." And then he had smiled into her eyes. Henrietta, feeling weak at the knees, had taken his proffered hand and mumbled that, yes, she forgave him.

He ordered a portion of orange salad and then, after greeting various acquaintances, went and sat down.

Henrietta nervously spooned the salad into a small glass dish. She had made it from oranges, muscatel raisins, brandy, and pounded sugar. She placed it in front of him, bobbed a curtsy, and would have left, but he looked about him as if searching for a topic of conversation. "Stay a moment," he said. "Tell me, why do you not have ices?"

"Perhaps I might begin to make ices in a small way," said Henrietta. "I have not even tried, because I am always aware of the great competition from Gunter's. *They* ship their ice from Greenland. I could perhaps buy ice in London and the machinery to make ices—but the equipment costs a great deal of money, so perhaps I shall wait a little longer until my finances are more secure."

The earl looked around the busy little shop. "I should have said they were secure already."

"Not quite. People are ordering elaborate center-pieces for their tables. What if . . ." Henrietta paused. She had been about to say, "What if we should become unfashionable again?"

She said instead, "What if they cancel their orders? Even just one canceled order would mean a loss of money. I shall go carefully for the moment."

"Very wise." Again the earl smiled at her. "You do not work on Sundays?"

"Of course not," said Henrietta. She blushed at the lie, for she knew that Sunday was the day she went over the accounts, but even in this godless age, the earl might find that rather shocking.

"I go to church, of course," she added quickly.

"Then, in that case I should consider myself honored if you would allow me to escort you. Do you go to St. George's?"

Henrietta shook her head. "Grosvenor Chapel."

"And may I have your company?"

A customer behind Henrietta rapped angrily on the table with his fork for service. "I shall return in a moment, my lord," she said.

As she busily attended to the needs of the other customers, Henrietta thought quickly. The earl's presence in Bascombe's, after all he had said about it, was occasioning pleased surprise and comment from the other customers. It would do no harm to encourage the earl. And what could be more respectable than attending church with him?

When there was a lull, she returned to his table. "I am most grateful to you, my lord," she said. "I shall accept your escort. Do you mind escorting Miss Hissop as well? She never misses church service.''

''By all means, Miss Hissop, too,'' he said, rising to his feet. He paid for his salad, made Henrietta a magnificent bow, and left.

Henrietta could hardly wait for the shop to close so that she could discuss this new development with the others.

Charlotte and Josephine were delighted. Esau said nothing, but he was privately worried. It would be just like a beauty like Miss Henrietta to go and get married, he thought. And then what would become of poor Esau? The horrors of the workhouse rose before his eyes. He remembered being subjected to blows, starvation, and putrid air, the lice, itch, and filth, and always surrounded by the plaintive cries of the dying. He ran a hand down the soft plush of his livery.

Henrietta *must not* marry. He had overheard her saying she did not want to.

Miss Hissop voiced her disapproval. ''Dear child,'' she exclaimed, ''dear Henrietta. Only consider. Man in Carrisdowne's position . . . don't mean anything respectable. Ah, I see it now. The silks, the jewels, the apartment in Jermyn Street, the villa in Kensington . . . then, 'You weary me, Miss Bascombe, I shall pass you on to Sir Evil Nasty' . . . then cheaper addresses and muslin, no carriage, one maid . . . then passed down to a merchant . . . then crying for shillings at the opera. Oh, my doomed child!''

Henrietta looked at Miss Hissop in exasperation. ''I am not going to fall in love with the earl, Miss Hissop— only *use* him. Now that even *he* has been seen at Bascombe's means assured success for us.

''And Charlotte and Josephine, I know you have

formed certain *tendres* for Lord Charles and Mr. Clifford, but that is because you have not been in the way of meeting a *variety* of gentlemen."

"Many gentlemen come to the confectioner's," said Charlotte stiffly. "Lord Charles and Mr. Clifford are the only two who treat us as ladies. The others treat us simply as shopgirls, and once they find out we are not interested in a dubious relationship with them, then they confine their interest to sweetmeats and leave us alone."

"But listen!" cried Henrietta. "I have never outlined my plans for you and Josephine. If we make a great deal of money during the Season, then we shall go to Bath or some other fashionable watering spa and, with dowries apiece, we shall be able to *choose* husbands."

"I thought *you* were not interested in marriage," snapped Josephine.

"Not for myself. But for the both of you," pleaded Henrietta. "Only give it a little time. Do you know"— she rested her chin on her hands and looked round at them with sparkling eyes—"it will be interesting to see if I can make the great Earl of Carrisdowne fall in love with me."

Josephine and Charlotte exchanged glances. If only Henrietta herself would fall in love. *Then* she might not be so insensitive to their plight!

Chapter Five

For most of London society, Sunday was a boring twenty-four hours stretching between one gambling session and the next. Never had gambling fever been so great. Both men and women of society spent long hours at the tables.

Although Methodism and Evangelism flourished among the lesser breeds, the ton politely suffered God and all his angels on this one day of the week. There was a general uneasy feeling that religion had no place among the top ten thousand. It was enough that God had placed them in their exalted stations. They would much rather have gone on enjoying being exalted without the labor of sitting in a cold church, praying fervently for the service to end.

Henrietta was unfashionable enough to enjoy her weekly visits to church. She always left after the service feeling refreshed and with courage to face the week ahead once more renewed.

Josephine and Charlotte, however, had decided to stay in bed. They envied Henrietta her stamina. Despite the new addition to the staff of three daily kitchen maids, they found the long weeks of work beginning to take their toll.

Josephine had sleepily told Henrietta to help herself from her wardrobe. Josephine had the most fashionable clothes of the three girls. Determined to enchant the earl, Henrietta cheerfully selected one of Josephine's best day ensembles.

It was a promenade dress consisting of a Spanish pelisse of white-and-lilac shot sarcenet, trimmed with Chinese scalloped binding, and worn over a white muslin gown. On her head she wore a woodland hat of lemon-colored chip straw, decorated with a curled ostrich feather of lilac and white. She was drawing on a pair of lemon-colored kid gloves and peering through the shop window for a sight of the earl's coach when Miss Hissop came down to join her.

Miss Hissop had, for the moment, forgotten her distrust of Lord Carrisdowne's intentions and was happily excited at the idea of making her entrance in church on the arm of a member of the nobility. She was wearing a purple velvet walking dress, and on her head she wore a large black-velvet turban. Henrietta noted that Miss Hissop's gown was sadly "seated" at the back where the velvet had grown shiny with age, and she was about to urge her to borrow one of Josephine's shawls when the earl suddenly arrived. A quick glance out of the window showed no coach outside, and she realized with surprise that the earl had come on foot.

He offered an arm to each. He was in morning dress, the plated buttons of his coat of Bath superfine winking in the pale sunlight.

The day was very cold. The snow had melted during the night and had then frozen during the morning. As they walked along, Henrietta shivered miserably and wondered how on earth she had ever been stupid enough to think she could attract such a man as the Earl of Carrisdowne.

As they turned along Curzon Street in the direction of South Audley Street, Henrietta looked at the other ladies heading in the direction of the church. Some were attired in thinner clothing than herself, muslins fluttering in the biting wind.

"I shall never follow the dictates of fashion again—not on a cold day, at least," said Henrietta.

The tall earl smiled down at her. "There is a tinge of lilac in your cheeks that matches the color of your pelisse."

"Meaning I am blue with cold," said Henrietta crossly.

He turned and raised his hand. His footman, whom Henrietta had not noticed, had been following some distance behind. The earl stepped aside and said a few words to him, and the servant hurried off.

Miss Hissop, who had been silent up till then, decided the time had come to show the earl that dear Henrietta had a protector. "I am surprised," she said, "to hear you talking thus about fashion on the Sunday morn, Henrietta. You usually have a mind above such petty things. Henrietta," she added, fixing the earl with a basilisk stare, "is *very* devout."

The earl nodded politely.

"We *never* miss church on Sundays," went on Miss Hissop. "Never. We go in the rain, the sleet, the snow, and the scorching days of summer. *Always.*"

"Miss Hissop," said Henrietta in stifled tones, "I am sure my lord does not wish a sermon *before* he gets to church."

"But you know it is true," expostulated Miss Hissop. "I feel it is the only place—church, that is—where a young maiden is free from the perils of this loose and decadent society!"

As they reached the steps of Grosvenor Chapel, a pleasant little church built in 1730, the earl's servant came hurrying up with a huge fur cape over his arm. The earl took it from him and put it around Henrietta's shoulders. Henrietta felt she should protest, for several members of the ton were staring at them with open curiosity, but the warmth of the fur was so wonderful that she merely murmured her thanks.

Henrietta had forgotten that no one was equal in this house of the Lord. The rich had their pews near the pulpit. The servants and shopkeepers such as herself sat on plain benches at the back.

The Earl of Carrisdowne usually attended church service at St. George's, Hanover Square. It was unthinkable that he should sit with the common folk at the rear of the church. In a whisper, Henrietta urged him to share the pew of one of his friends. But the earl replied in a low voice that, for his part, he really did not care where he sat.

Henrietta was conscious of the sensation they were causing as they sat down, although the earl appeared indifferent to it. Some of the nobility were standing up on the benches and leveling their quizzing glasses over the tops of their pews to get a better look at the Earl of Carrisdowne sitting with the common people.

"Didn't know Carrisdowne was a Jacobite," said the Duke of Gillingham, creaking down, after a good look at the earl, to sit beside his wife.

"He's been away at the wars too long," sniffed the duchess. "If he wants to make that confectioner girl his mistress, then he shouldn't make a parade of the fact in church.''

Henrietta hugged the fur cape closely about her and decided to concentrate on the service. There would be no reading from the New Testament, of that she was sure. Society preferred the blood and thunder of the Old Testament, free from any nasty remarks about the rich having a hard time getting into the kingdom of heaven.

There was not much of a sermon. Even that relic of Puritanism was slowly disappearing, and the days when the sermon was the highlight of the service, to be discussed and debated afterward, had been slowly dying out.

But the feeling of content that Henrietta usually experienced in church would not come. She was very conscious of the earl as a *man*. He was very tall, very strong, and very masculine. He had removed his gloves to turn the pages of the hymnbook for her, and his hands were long-fingered and tanned, with square nails, a contrast to the hands of the other aristocrats, which were usually white-leaded on the backs to make them appear delicate, and painted pink on the palms with cochineal.

Why had he decided to be pleasant to her and seek her company? Had he some plot in mind? The more Henrietta thought about it, the more odd and out of character his apology appeared. She realized with a start that the church service was over and that she had not heard one word of it.

Miss Hissop was thoroughly embarrassed by all the attention. Like Henrietta, she had forgotten about the seating arrangements in the church. She had vaguely thought that, by his very presence, the earl would be able to conjure up a private pew.

The earl stopped outside the church to chat with various friends, all of whom were Henrietta's customers. Each time, he drew Henrietta and Miss Hissop a little forward and introduced them. But hard eyes stared insolently, and hard voices said, "Hah, yes. Been to your shop."

What if they think I do not know my place and will punish me by not coming to my shop? thought Henrietta miserably. Did the earl know this? Is *that* why he took me to church?

The earl was engaged in talking about the war in the peninsula to an elderly gentleman. He half turned to introduce Henrietta and Miss Hissop, but the old gentleman caught hold of his sleeve and asked him whether the war was not, as the Whigs declared, a monstrous waste of men and money.

The earl turned back, and Henrietta decided to escape. "Come along, Miss Hissop," she whispered.

They hurried off down the street, but the earl caught up with them as they were rounding the corner into Curzon Street. "You should have known I meant to escort you back, Miss Bascombe," he said severely, "if only to get my cloak back."

"You were engaged in conversation," said Henrietta. She drew a deep breath. "We occasioned too much comment by being seen in your company in the common seats, my lord."

"You have already occasioned much comment by running a shop," he replied, taking her arm and offering his other to Miss Hissop. "I was under the impression you did not trouble yourself over the rules of society."

Alarmed that, by this statement, the earl meant he considered Henrietta an immoral hoyden, Miss Hissop burst into incoherent speech. "Not at all . . . dear Henrietta, *very* well brought up . . . would never tie her garter in public . . . strictly chaperoned . . . I did not realize my lord meant to join us at the back of the church . . .'' and on she went until they reached the shop.

She finally ran out of breath as Henrietta opened the shop door. Swinging the cape from her shoulders, Henrietta handed it to the earl. "Thank you, my lord," she said. "It was kind of you to escort me. I fear, however, I have made us both look ridiculous."

He looked down at the dignified figure in the lilac pelisse. He saw the worry and concern in the large eyes looking so directly up into his. "It was not to make you unfashionable again," he said gently. "On the contrary, those who have not yet met you will be beating a path to your door to have a look at you."

"Nonetheless, it is all very unpleasant," said Henrietta firmly. "I do not wish to be such an object of curiosity. It makes me feel like one of those poor shabby animals in the Tower zoo."

"My apologies," he said. "I should have taken you to St. George's, where my family has a pew. Come driving with me this afternoon, Miss Bascombe. There is nothing more respectable than a drive in the park at the fashionable hour."

"No, thank you," said Henrietta firmly. "I have caused sufficient comment for today. Besides, I have work to do."

"Liar," he mocked. "And you said you never worked on a Sunday."

"I meant work at my prayers," said Henrietta crossly. She curtsied to him and went into the shop and closed the door.

The earl stood with a half smile on his face. She certainly was an enchanting creature—but one who did not seem in the slightest interested in him.

He turned and walked away, signaling to his servant to take the heavy fur cape from him.

"It's just like a battle," he thought to himself. "The trouble is I have no real plan of campaign. First, I must earn her gratitude. . . ."

By the next morning Henrietta was already regretting having turned down the earl's invitation to go driving in the park. Charlotte and Josephine had looked worried and anxious when she had told them. Secretly both had hoped that Mr. Clifford and Lord Charles would ask *them* to go driving if they saw the Earl of Carrisdowne was not too high in the instep to be seen around with Henrietta.

Just before the shop opened, two servants dressed in the Earl of Carrisdowne's livery appeared at the shop door. They had, they said, a present for Miss Bascombe.

Henrietta looked at the huge parcel in dismay. Then the earl's intentions *were* dishonorable. This should have come neither as a surprise, nor should it have caused such a sharp pain around the region of her heart, but Henrietta was upset nonetheless. Gentlemen might send bouquets of flowers or poems to a lady they admired. Only members of the demimonde received expensive presents.

"Convey my thanks to your master and tell him I am unable to accept this," she said, backing away from the huge box.

"Begging your pardon, miss," said one, "my lord told us you might say that, and said to urge you to examine the contents before you refused."

"Very well," said Henrietta, "but I shall probably send it back just the same."

With the help of the two servants, she opened the box and then looked with amazement at the contents. Never before, surely, had a gentleman sent a lady such an unromantic gift.

In the box were all the ingredients to make ices. There was a large tub, big enough to hold a bushel of ice, a freezing pot made of pewter, a bright spaddle made of copper, and even a cellaret where the ices could be stored for a short time.

To Henrietta, blinking away sudden tears, it seemed as if the earl, by his gift, had declared his approval of her being in trade. She had not realized until that moment how very much she had minded the censure of society.

"Thank my lord very much," she said. "And tell him I am delighted to accept his gift."

Henrietta sang to herself as she went about her work that day. Mr. Clifford and Lord Charles arrived at their usual time. Josephine and Charlotte were lucky. There was a lull in business, and they were able to engage in brief conversations with the gentlemen.

But soon the little shop was busy again, and Mr. Clifford and Lord Charles took their leave. Henrietta found herself glancing hopefully at the door each time the little bell above it tinkled to announce a new customer. The earl must surely come, if only to find out how she liked her gift. But by closing time there was no sign of his tall figure.

After the daily maids had cleaned up, and Josephine, Charlotte, Esau, and Miss Hissop had retired to the back shop to take tea, Henrietta sat behind the counter of the shop and looked out onto Half Moon Street.

Esau appeared briefly to ask if he might put up the

shutters, but Henrietta told him to leave them for the moment and sent him back to join the others.

Snow was beginning to fall gently. What a cold spring! It was now March. The Season began in April. One profitable Season might bring them their dowries, mused Henrietta. But although many of the aristocracy ordered set pieces that were expensive to prepare and took long hours to make, they seemed reluctant to pay their bills. There must be *some* way of getting them to pay, thought Henrietta, without offending them.

Her heart gave a lurch as she recognized the earl's footman, the one who had followed them to church on Sunday. He walked up the steps and rapped on the door. Henrietta ran to open it. He handed her a letter, touched his hat, and left.

Henrietta carried the letter back into the circle of candlelight and broke open the seal. The contents were brief and businesslike:

Dear Miss Bascombe,

I am giving an entertainment this Friday at my town house at 12 Upper Brook Street. I wish to order a centerpiece. The subject I shall leave to your imagination.

Carrisdowne

Well, thought Henrietta breathlessly, what else did I expect? It is a business letter to a businesswoman, nothing more.

For one moment, she felt very young and alone. It flashed through her mind that it would be wonderful to go to the earl's as a guest, not as a shopkeeper making deliveries, to return to a pleasant town house with her parents afterward, instead of back to her place of work, to be loved and cossetted, instead of having to be responsible for, love, and cosset her companions.

Then she shrugged away these odd thoughts. Tonight she would try to make her first ices. Then she would need to create a very special centerpiece, something to show *him* she was an artist as well as a tradeswoman.

She had not even thanked him for the machinery he had sent! Henrietta rushed to find pen and paper.

As she composed the stiff, formal phrases of thanks, her mind drifted off, wondering what the earl's entertainment would be like. What a pity she could not go herself. But Esau would deliver the centerpiece in the new handcart she had recently bought, with BASCOMBE'S in curly gold letters on the side.

Then she remembered one of the customers telling her that Gunter's confectioner often went himself and put the finishing touches to the centerpiece just before it was carried to the table. But that would get her only as far as the kitchen.

Would he have a hostess? Henrietta drifted off into a rosy dream where she was standing by the earl's side, receiving his guests. She finally gave herself a little shake, signed the letter, sanded it, and sealed it. Her only interest in the earl, she told herself firmly, was to keep him amused and attracted enough to keep Bascombe's fashionable. Still . . . if she took the centerpiece along herself, she might be able to catch a glimpse of the ladies and see what they were like and what they were wearing. How could she know what kind of lady the earl found attractive if she never saw him with any?

Chapter Six

A further formal note from the Earl of Carrisdowne requested that Miss Bascombe bring the centerpiece to his house at seven on Friday evening so that it might be displayed to advantage in the refreshment room.

Henrietta toiled through the long nights before that Friday creating her masterpiece. The subject was the famous "Battle of Salamanca," which had taken place the previous July. It was the battle that did for Wellington what none of his previous battles had achieved. The world realized he had become "almost a Marlborough"—to use the expression of General Foy, the only French commander to survive the battle with his corps intact.

As Josephine, Charlotte, Miss Hissop, and Esau watched, fascinated, the university city of Salamanca rose under Henrietta's inspired fingers. She had read long descriptions of the battle in the newspapers. There were the three forts, built out of the ruins of twenty colleges and thirteen convents, which had been garrisoned by Marmount when he retired from Salamanca at

Wellington's approach, all made out of spun sugar and colored with caramel. There, created in miniature, was the River Torres with its green mats of waterweed, its sandbanks, and ancient water mills. A tiny, beautifully sculptured figure of Wellington on his horse stood in the plaza mayor while dainty Spanish ladies held out bouquets of flowers to him.

The Spanish ladies were all dressed in the fashion of Regency England because although the accounts that Henrietta had read of the battle were very extensive, none were detailed enough to sidetrack into a dissertation on the gowns worn by the ladies of Salamanca. Still, the confectionery figures wore mantillas of spun sugar and had black eyes made of tiny pieces of currant, so that their high-waisted gowns did not make them look so terribly un-Spanish.

Esau became worried again. He was jealous of the love and concentration Henrietta was lavishing on the centerpiece. Surely love for the earl, and only love, could inspire her thus. Esau had nightmares of Henrietta leaving on the arm of the Earl of Carrisdowne and not even throwing him one backward glance.

By Friday, Henrietta was finished and knew she had achieved something so great that she could never hope to repeat it.

The snow had melted and a soft wind, harbinger of spring, was blowing through the drying London streets. Blackbirds were caroling on the sooty roofs, and the sky above the twisted chimneys was a delicate violet as Henrietta and Esau set out with Henrietta's "miracle" packed in layers of tissue paper on the handcart.

Henrietta had chosen to wear one of Josephine's warmer gowns. It was of gold velvet, high-waisted and buttoned with little velvet-covered buttons up to a small lace ruff at the neck. Over it, she wore a heavy blue-wool cloak of her own.

When they reached the earl's house on Upper Brook Street, Henrietta felt her mouth grow dry with nerves.

Obviously she and Esau should maneuver the centerpiece down the area steps, which led under the main entrance to the kitchens below. But she persuaded herself that so much artistry should at least be rewarded by seeing the earl's reaction to it.

She left Esau on the pavement with the handcart and boldly mounted the front steps and sounded a brisk tattoo on the knocker.

The butler opened the door, looked at Henrietta, hatless and wrapped in a cloak that had seen better days, and demanded frostily, "Yes?"

"I am come at Lord Carrisdowne's request," said Henrietta grandly. She presented a visiting card turned down at the corner to show that she had called in person. "Be so good as to take this card to his lordship."

Impressed by her manner, the butler bowed and took the card. Then he saw Esau squinting up at him from the pavement. "You, boy," said the butler. "Be off with you, and don't stand there gawking."

"That is my servant," said Henrietta. "Be so good as to take my card *immediately* to his lordship."

The butler's face cleared. "You're Bascombe's," he said, looking at the curly lettering on the side of the cart. "That must be the centerpiece. Wait there, and I'll send a footman to help you down to the kitchens with it."

But, having come so far, Henrietta was not going to back down. "I think," she said sweetly, "you will find his lordship expects to see me *in person*." The butler hesitated. "And," went on Henrietta, "I am sure he will be most annoyed if you keep me waiting out in the street much longer.''

''Very well,'' said the butler reluctantly. He stood back and held open the door.

Henrietta blushed as she realized she would first have to help Esau lift the handcart up the shallow steps.

''I don't know as I should be allowing you to bring that in the front door,'' muttered the butler as they trundled the cart past him. He turned and went up the stairs, leaving Henrietta and Esau standing in the hall.

Esau looked about him in awe. Apart from the cheerful crackling of logs in the hall fire, the town house was very hushed and quiet. The black and white tiles of the floor gleamed like glass. A chandelier of Waterford crystal sent prisms of colored light over the pictures and wood paneling. A clock in the corner suddenly began to boom out seven o'clock, and Esau jumped.

And then they heard the earl's voice. ''It is all right, Yarwood,'' he said. ''Miss Bascombe is a friend of mine.''

The earl came slowly down the stairs, followed by his butler. He was already dressed for the evening in a black coat, black knee breeches, and shoes with diamond buckles. A large diamond flashed among the snowy folds of his cravat, and diamond rings sparkled on his fingers. His black hair was brushed and pomaded until it shone like a raven's wing.

Esau executed a clumsy bow from the waist, and Henrietta sank into a deep curtsy.

''Good evening, Miss Bascombe,'' said the earl. ''The dining room—that is the door on your left—is to be used as a supper room this evening. If your servant will bring the centerpiece in there, we can arrange it to advantage.''

His manner was courteous and formal. Henrietta felt she had made a terrible mistake by entering by the front door. He led the way, and she turned to help Esau lift the centerpiece in its wrapping from the cart.

"My footmen will do that," he said sharply.

But Henrietta shook her head. "It is too fragile. Esau and I are used to handling these delicate confects."

He gave an infinitesimal shrug and held open the door of the dining room. There was a long table against the wall, laden with plates, glasses, and knives and forks. Other long tables, spread with white-linen cloths, were set about the rest of the room.

"The food will be here," said the earl, pointing to the table against the wall. "My guests will fill their plates and then find a place at one of the other tables. The centerpiece goes on that raised platform in the middle of the table. I hope it is large enough?"

"Yes," said Henrietta. Her heart was beating hard as she and Esau unwrapped the centerpiece and then lifted it gently onto the platform.

The earl was putting a log in the fire when Henrietta said, "Do but look, my lord. I hope you are pleased with it."

The earl turned and walked slowly back to where Henrietta was standing. He looked at the centerpiece, at the little figures, at the forts and the green river of angelica, at the Spanish ladies, and then at Wellington on his horse.

He looked at it a long time without saying a word. Henrietta felt tears start to her eyes. He did not like it! And oh, how very tired she was.

"It is a masterpiece," said the earl at last.

"You *like* it?" Henrietta blinked away her tears.

He raised her hand to his lips and kissed it.

"I was there," he said, "at Salamanca. You might have been there yourself, your work is so very good. It is amazing to think all this art is merely sugar to be eaten. How can I bear to let my guests even touch it? Miss Bascombe, please be my guest this evening. An artist such as yourself must see my friends' faces when they look on your work."

"I should like that above all things," exclaimed Henrietta. Then her face fell. "But will it not be considered very odd to entertain your confectioner?"

He smiled. "I think genius transcends social laws."

"Perhaps if I am not *of* the party but merely sit in a corner and *observe*," said Henrietta seriously, "it would not be considered very odd."

"As you will. My guests will sit down to supper at midnight. Come before then if you wish."

"Midnight will do very well."

"Good-bye, Miss Bascombe," said the earl formally, his face once more unreadable.

After Henrietta and Esau had left, the Earl of Carrisdowne stood looking thoughtfully at the centerpiece. I cannot put her out of business, he thought. Such artistry must surely come before any plans to prevent a mistake by Charles or Guy. I am sure their intentions are not serious. They appear content to carry on mild flirtations. Perhaps I should mind my own business for a change.

Like Cinderella in reverse, Henrietta sat demurely in a corner of the Earl of Carrisdowne's dining room. When the clock struck twelve, her moment of glory would come.

She had been instructed by Josephine and Charlotte to observe Lord Charles and Mr. Clifford and see which

ladies they conversed with, and if either of them favored
any one in particular.

Henrietta was wearing a pink-satin slip with a Grecian
frock of white Persian gauze, fastened up the front with
silver filigree. The bottom was trimmed with a deep
flounce of Vandyke lace. Everything she had on had
been culled from all their wardrobes at the confectioner's. The gown was Josephine's, and the pearls around
her neck belonged to Charlotte. They were Charlotte's
most prized possession and the very last valuable thing
she owned, all the rest having been sold. The silk flowers in Henrietta's glossy hair had been saved by Miss
Hissop for twenty years and, unlike most of that poor
lady's belongings, were as good as new, Miss Hissop
having had to wear caps since her twenty-third birthday
as befitted her spinster state.

The earl had ordered his servants to carry the food in
after the guests were all in the dining room. He did not
want anything to detract from the centerpiece.

The clock struck twelve.

Two liveried footmen opened the double doors.

The Earl of Carrisdowne entered with a beautiful lady
on his arm. Behind him came the rest of his guests.
They clustered around the centerpiece, exclaiming in
wonder and admiration.

But Henrietta heard none of it. There was a queer
little ache at her heart as she watched the earl's handsome head next to the calm oval face of the beautiful
woman. Who was she?

Not, thought Henrietta firmly, that I have a *tendre* for
Carrisdowne or anything stupid like that. It is just . . .
it is just that it would be wonderful to *belong* somewhere, instead of being a sort of strange social animal
on the fringes of society.

Servants began carrying in dishes of meat, fruit, sweetmeats, and jellies. Henrietta's stomach gave a miserable rumble. She had been too excited to eat anything before leaving the shop.

Mr. Clifford and Lord Charles were surrounded by a bevy of delightful-looking debutantes. "And how can I tell either Josephine or Charlotte *that*?" worried Henrietta.

Henrietta sat as still as a statue in a dark corner of the room, partly hidden by a lacquered screen. The earl appeared to have forgotten her presence.

Henrietta would have been amazed had she known that he was aware of her presence during every minute of that supper.

Time dragged on. Henrietta wished she had not come.

Then finally the earl rose to his feet and proposed a toast to the King, the Prince Regent, and to the Duke of Wellington. He signaled to a servant to fill his glass again and said, "My final toast of the evening is to the genius of Miss Bascombe, who created the centerpiece. Ladies and gentlemen, I give you . . . Miss Henrietta Bascombe."

"Miss Henrietta Bascombe," they all murmured.

Lord Charles, following his brother's gaze, cried, "Why, there she is, over in that corner!"

Henrietta blushed with embarrassment and hung her head as every curious eye in the room turned in her direction.

The beautiful lady seated next to the earl broke the silence that followed Lord Charles's announcement.

"Well, it *is* for *eating*, isn't it?" she demanded.

"Lady Clara, it is much too beautiful to touch," protested Mr. Clifford.

"Nonsense," said Lady Clara. She rose gracefully to

her feet and walked over to the centerpiece. "See!" she cried, picking up the Duke of Wellington. "I shall let you all know if our Iron Duke tastes of iron or sugar." She bit off the little figure's head.

Almost everyone laughed, got to his or her feet and started snatching at pieces of the confection.

Lady Clara *who*? thought Henrietta. Miss Hissop will know.

Henrietta, sensing that the people in the room had forgotten her existence once more, felt more at ease than she had earlier. She carefully observed Lord Charles and Mr. Clifford. They did not seem at all interested in any of the ladies present. *They* had not rushed to help destroy the centerpiece, nor had the earl. Of course, this was not really seeing society at its best, thought Henrietta charitably. A great number of them, the ladies as well as the gentlemen, were in varying stages of intoxication. And why should she, Henrietta Bascombe, take such a fierce dislike to that Lady Clara?

My centerpieces *are* for *eating*, Henrietta told herself firmly.

The earl rose to his feet once more and announced that dancing would begin in the ballroom upstairs. The guests began to leave the dining room, first in large groups, then one by one, until Henrietta was left alone, except for the servants who were clearing away the plates.

She got to her feet and walked across the room and looked down at the ruin of her centerpiece. One tiny little Spanish lady stood amid the wreck of sugar, marzipan, and caramel, her tiny bouquet held up to where the figure of the duke had been.

"I do not know how they could bear to eat even a bit of it," said a voice behind her. "It was so beautiful."

Henrietta turned around and found Mr. Clifford had come back into the room.

"Usually I do not witness their destruction, Mr. Clifford," she said. "But imagine if people could not bear to eat any of my confects. I should soon go out of business."

"How is Miss Archer . . . and Mrs. Webster?" asked Mr. Clifford.

"Very well. They are asleep by now. Poor things! They are beginning to feel the strain of all those weeks of hard work."

Mr. Clifford glanced over his shoulder nervously. "Miss Bascombe," he said, "since Bascombe's *is* your business, I feel you are responsible for Miss Archer. May I have your permission to call on her?"

"Yes," smiled Henrietta.

"And, oh, I say . . ." Again that nervous look over the shoulder. "Charles—I mean, Lord Charles—well, he begged me to ask you on his behalf. If he could call on Mrs. Webster, that is."

"Perhaps Lord Carrisdowne would not approve," said Henrietta cautiously.

"If he didn't know about it, he wouldn't have to worry about it," said Mr. Clifford.

The earl's voice, giving orders to the servants, came from the hall outside.

"*Please*, Miss Bascombe," said Mr. Clifford urgently.

How ridiculous to be so afraid of the disapproval of one's best friend, thought Henrietta. Aloud she said, "You and Lord Charles may come for dinner next Sunday—at four."

The Earl of Carrisdowne walked into the room.

Mr. Clifford pleaded with his eyes for Henrietta's silence, and Henrietta gave him a slight nod to signify assent.

The earl looked from one to the other suspiciously.

"I am just leaving," said Mr. Clifford hurriedly. "Your servant, Miss Bascombe." He bowed and left. The earl swiveled and looked after him.

"Dear me, one would think Guy was making an assignation."

"With me? No. We were just admiring the last survivor." Henrietta held up the sugar figure of the Spanish lady.

"Yes." He took it from her and turned it around in the light. "I must confess my heart sank when they started tearing into it like wolves. Perhaps I was too conscious of your clear gaze looking upon my friends, for I confess they seemed a shabby lot to me this evening."

"I know most of them by sight," said Henrietta. "They are my customers. They are all very pleasant and quite witty. I had not, however, seen Lady Clara before."

"But you know of her?"

"No. I heard her name mentioned."

"She is Lady Clara Sinclair, daughter of the Earl of Strathbane."

"Oh."

"She is this season's beauty."

"Ah."

"She is accounted a wit."

"Mm."

"As you so cynically remark, 'Mm' indeed. Lady Clara told a very funny story at supper that went on for quite half an hour. It was about Lord Trumpington, who was asked to lay a foundation stone at a new printing works in Kensington. He was given a silver trowel to perform the ceremony. He expected to keep the trowel as a present but, to his fury, the printers demanded it back. He was, says Lady Clara, very *mortar-fied.*"

Henrietta laughed dutifully.

"Don't force yourself," he drawled. "I cannot stand puns either. My face is stiff with forcing smiles onto it. Can I persuade you to come and watch the dancing?"

A shadow crossed Henrietta's face. Of course he could not ask her to dance with him.

"No, thank you, my lord," she said. "It is time I returned to my shop. The baking for tomorrow has still to be done."

He looked down at her, noticing for the first time the violet shadows of fatigue under her eyes. "I would you did not have to work so hard," he said. "Come driving with me on Sunday, Miss Bascombe."

"I cannot," said Henrietta, with a faint blush. "I am entertaining guests for dinner."

He looked at her sharply.

"*Female* guests?"

"I must go," said Henrietta, not answering his question.

"Where is your servant?"

"In bed."

"You cannot walk unescorted through the streets in the middle of the night. I shall send a footman with you. No, I shall go with you myself."

"My lord . . . your guests."

"So busy polishing their puns, they will not miss me."

Henrietta enjoyed a novel sensation of power. It was very pleasant to think she could make the earl leave his guests.

To her surprise the earl, as he had done when he escorted her to church, elected to walk. This was decidedly odd behavior in an age when one traveled by carriage even to the next street.

"Tell me about yourselves," said the earl. "Where did all of you come from?"

Henrietta hesitated. For the sake of Josephine's safety, she did not wish to mention the name of the village. She still did not trust the earl.

"We all come from the same village in the country," she said. "My father was a doctor, who died leaving me hardly any money. Miss Hissop is a retired schoolmistress. We decided to pool our small savings and share a house. A certain landowner who had been attended by my father during his lifetime and had never paid his bills left me a sum of money in his will. I decided to go into trade. The landowner's chef had trained me in the confectioner's art. Mrs. Webster is an army widow with practically no money at all. She is only twenty-two years of age. Miss Archer has a brutal father who beat her every time he was drunk. They elected to join me in my enterprise."

"And what draws Mr. Clifford and Lord Charles to your shop? Yourself?"

"I think gentlemen of the ton enjoy the sweetmeats and the comfortable atmosphere," said Henrietta.

"That is not answering my question. What was Guy talking to you about?"

"He was regretting the destruction of my centerpiece."

"And that was all?"

"Lord Carrisdowne, you must not quiz me about who said what to me. I am too tired."

"Do not encourage them," he said in a serious voice. "Marriage is out of the question."

Henrietta rounded on him. "May I suggest you run your *own* life and stop meddling in affairs that do not concern you!"

Henrietta was shaken by fury and bitterness. He had more or less told her she was not worth considering when it came to marriage. He had told her as much before but, oh *how* it hurt this time. Her eyes filled with tears, and the parish lamps became a flickering blur.

He stopped and swung her round to face him. He took out a handkerchief and gently dried her eyes. "Ah, no, Henrietta," he said softly, "you must not cry. It was your evening of triumph." He bent and kissed her cheek.

Henrietta trembled, looking at him wide-eyed.

He wanted to pull her into his arms and kiss her breathless. He wanted to do just that with an intensity of feeling that shook him. Instead he tucked her hand under his arm and started to walk again.

"How did you know my Christian name?" asked Henrietta.

"I asked someone. It is not a deathly secret, you know. The other ladies in the shop call you Henrietta frequently."

They had reached the shop.

Henrietta turned and faced him. His diamonds glinted in the faint light thrown by the parish lamp outside the door of Bascombe's. But his face was in shadow and she could not read the expression in his eyes.

"I did not like to see you sitting in that corner while I entertained much less talented people," he said. "Allow me to entertain you to dinner tomorrow night."

"I cannot go to your house alone," said Henrietta, backing away.

"Then bring your dragon, what is her name . . . Miss Hissop."

Henrietta was about to refuse. But it was so very tempting—tempting only because it would be wonderful to be waited on for a change.

"Yes, my lord," she said. "At what time?"

"Seven o'clock. I shall send the carriage for you."

He raised her hand to his lips, and his kiss seemed to burn through her glove. Then he stood back and waited until she had unlocked the shop door before walking away.

I only think I am enchanted with her because I see so little of her, thought the earl. Tomorrow evening she will be out of place and gauche, a country girl out of her depth. That should cure these odd feelings she arouses in me.

Henrietta nearly fell over Esau, who was sleeping like a dog on the floor of the shop behind the door. "I waited for you, miss," said Esau, jumping to his feet. "I got something to show you."

He led the way into the kitchen. There on the table was a sugar dragoon on a sugar horse. The horse was excellent. The figure on its back was somewhat lumpy.

"It is very good, Esau," said Henrietta. "Very good indeed."

She leaned forward, studying the figure closely while her mind worked busily. Here was surely Esau's future. If she could manage to get Josephine and Charlotte settled comfortably, then Esau could be trained to take over the business.

"You need some lessons, all the same," said Henrietta slowly. "As soon as the business settles down, I shall begin to train you to be a confectioner."

"Oh, thank you, miss. You should ha' let me come to fetch you. Don't do to walk the streets alone."

"I was not alone," said Henrietta vaguely, her mind full of plans. "Lord Carrisdowne escorted me."

"Oh," said Esau, turning away. "He did, did he?"

Chapter Seven

Henrietta's casual remark that she and Miss Hissop were invited to the Earl of Carrisdowne's for dinner that evening burst upon the confectioner's shop like a bombshell the next morning. And when Henrietta added that Lord Charles Worsley and Mr. Guy Clifford were to be their guests at dinner the coming Sunday, excitement reached fever pitch.

Respectability at last! Josephine and Charlotte dreamed of a triple wedding—Josephine to Mr. Clifford, Charlotte to Lord Charles, and Henrietta to the Earl of Carrisdowne.

Miss Hissop was incoherent with excitement. "To think that I . . . Ismene Hissop . . . should dine at a lord's table! He means *well* . . . wouldn't have invited *me* otherwise. Dear Henrietta . . . who knows what social peaks we may scale! Why, one could even be buried in Westminster Abbey!"

The only one depressed by the great news was Esau. His active conscience told him he should wish the best for his mistress, but it was shouted down by his terror at having to return to the workhouse.

Henrietta made such an effort with her appearance that evening that Esau felt she was removing herself even more from the shop, from him. Henrietta in her apron and cap was a world apart from the grand lady who now stood at the shop door with Miss Hissop, waiting for the earl's carriage. Josephine had said that she hoped Henrietta would order some gowns for herself, for now that she had hopes of being taken out by Mr. Clifford, she would need all her own gowns.

Henrietta was wearing a dress of white leno, trimmed with a narrow edging of lace. A scarf of pink Italian gauze was tied on the left shoulder with gold cord, the gold tassels hanging nearly to the feet. She had little white kid shoes with gold roses on her feet and long gloves of white kid. Her dark brown hair was braided into a little coronet on top of her head and decorated with a single pink-silk rose.

Miss Hissop had dipped into Josephine's wardrobe herself and had chosen a brown-silk gown and a handsome paisley shawl. Charlotte's pearls were about her neck, and one of her more elaborate caps, freshly laundered and starched, covered her head.

"There is the carriage," said Henrietta, feeling quite sick with excitement. She kissed Josephine and Charlotte and then followed Miss Hissop out of the shop.

Miss Hissop exclaimed over the elegance of the carriage, at the wine-colored upholstery, at the hot bricks that had been placed on the floor for their feet. The journey was all too short—along Half Moon Street, up Curzon Street, along South Audley Street, past Grosvenor Square, and round into Upper Brook Street.

Henrietta hoped they would not be the only guests. If the earl presented her to some of his friends and showed them she was a welcome guest in his house, Henrietta felt it would set the seal on her respectability. But, as they were ushered into the Green Saloon, it soon transpired they were, in fact, the only guests. It was this fact that made Henrietta silent and awkward.

The earl put her uneasiness down to the fact that she was overawed by her surroundings. It was just as he had expected.

But over dinner Henrietta became a different lady entirely. To put her at her ease, for he was feeling sorry for her, the earl politely asked her about her late father's profession.

Henrietta, at first hesitantly and then with enthusiasm, described her father's work. "He was wont to say," said Henrietta, "that a fifth-century Greek probably had a better chance of recovery under Hippocrates than the people of today. How he had battled with prejudice and superstition and antiquated ideas! He had vaccinated the whole village against the smallpox, and mostly at his own expense. He had also written letters to Parliament and to the newspapers complaining about the window tax. By bricking up his windows, a householder could save a great deal on tax, but in doing so he shut out the sun and fresh air. Then the villagers *would* dose their children with Dr. James's Powder, and it is a wonder so many survived. My father analyzed the powder and found it contained antimony." Her soft voice went on, and her eyes glowed with enthusiasm.

She should have been a man, thought the earl. Why could she not have waited until she was married before indulging her odd tastes for independence. Married ladies were allowed great license. Not that such license included going into trade, he reminded himself firmly.

He realized with a start that Henrietta was not at all

overawed by her surroundings. On the contrary, she seemed very much part of them.

Miss Hissop, seeing his startled look, decided he was shocked that Henrietta should discourse at length on medicine, a subject that should only be debated by gentlemen. She gave a little cough, and when Henrietta stopped talking and turned an inquiring gaze on her, Miss Hissop launched into speech. "Your admiration of your dear papa does you credit, Henrietta. But to hear you speak, one would think your pretty head was full of naught but serious matters. My lord could not guess how many happy hours we have spent discussing the latest romance from the circulating library, or how we avidly study the latest fashion."

"My dear Miss Hissop," said Henrietta, "we were so busy keeping body and soul together when we were in . . . in the country, that we had no time to talk about such things. All we ever talked about then was food. All we ever talk about now is the shop. Since my lord disapproves of trade, he must be grateful that I confine my conversation to medicine."

"I like hearing about the shop," protested the earl, much to his own surprise. "Have you made ices yet?"

"Yes, at last. The first few tries were unsuccessful. I hate to waste materials. My one main problem at the moment is how to get people to *pay* for their center-pieces."

"Henrietta!" exclaimed Miss Hissop.

"But it is the truth. Here is a society that does not believe in paying shopkeepers, tailors, or jewelers until the duns come to the door. How can I make them pay?"

"It is a difficult question," he agreed, reflecting that he had not yet paid Henrietta's modest bill himself either.

"Now dressmakers do not have quite the same problem since they call on the lady of the house. Provided their fashions are in demand, the lady in question becomes afraid that if she does not pay, then she will lose her favorite dressmaker," the earl continued.

"Now, you, Miss Bascombe, could request the money *in advance*. Say firmly that you wish to buy the best of materials and cannot do that without money in hand. At the moment, it is fashionable to have one of your centerpieces rather than one of Gunter's. Society will always pay to be the fashion. It is rumored that Mr. Brummell once paid his tailor."

"What a good idea!" cried Henrietta. "It will make me appear very mercenary and pushing, but I cannot let niceties get in the way of making a profit."

"Does money mean so much to you?" he asked curiously.

"All the world!" laughed Henrietta. "It means all the world to me. It can buy warmth and comfort and food, all those things of which I have been too long deprived. I would do anything for money!"

"Anything?" he mocked.

"In the way of business," said Henrietta severely.

They eventually retired to the saloon, the earl electing to join them rather than be left to his wine in solitary splendor.

Miss Hissop, overcome by too much food and wine, fell asleep in a chair by the fire. Henrietta, sitting beside the earl on a sofa, coughed loudly several times, hoping to wake up her chaperon. But Miss Hissop began to snore gently.

"Leave her," said the earl in an amused voice. "You are safe with me . . . I think."

He took both her hands in his and looked down into

her eyes. He had thought it would be easy to make her fall in love with him. He had not realized until now how easy it would be for *him* to fall in love with *her*.

She tried to pull her hands away, but he held on to them tightly. Her soft mouth trembled, and her eyelashes were fanned out over her cheeks.

He gave an impatient little exclamation and pulled her into his arms. She made a muffled protest as his mouth came down on hers. It was meant to be a light, teasing kiss, but no sooner did the earl taste the warmth of her mouth and feel her bosom pressing against his chest than he lost his senses and kissed her with all the passion he had never known he could hold for any woman.

He was brought to his senses by Henrietta's little hands beating frantically against his shoulders.

"Forgive me," he said huskily.

"No," said Henrietta crossly, moving away from him. "You would not have behaved *thus* with a lady."

"I have never been so bewitched in my life before," he said. "Oh, Henrietta, come driving with me on Sunday—alone."

"My dinner party."

"To the deuce with it. Who are these people who are so important?"

Henrietta longed to tell him, but he might grow hard and angry again—and he might try to ruin her business.

"No one of importance," she said, hanging her head.

Miss Hissop awoke with a start. Henrietta rose to her feet, saying she must leave, the hour was late, and she had work to do.

The earl longed for another moment with Henrietta so that he might try to find out the names of her dinner party guests. Why had she not invited *him*, damn it, he thought furiously, forgetting that only a short time ago he would have considered Miss Bascombe to be addled in her wits if she had issued such an invitation.

Henrietta was silent on the road home, wrestling with uncomfortable thoughts. She had wanted the earl to go on kissing her, and surely no lady entertained ideas such as that.

But her eyes were soft, and her face was glowing as she stepped into the shop. Sadly Esau watched her. Unless he thought of something, and quickly, then Henrietta would be leaving him to get married.

The earl met his friend, Guy Clifford, in Gentleman Jackson's Boxing Saloon on Saturday afternoon. "There's a prizefight in Cobham on Sunday," said the earl. "Care to come along?"

"I can't," said Mr. Clifford, turning away. "Have a most important engagement."

"Where?"

"I don't need to tell you everything," said Mr. Clifford. "You ain't my father."

The earl let the subject drop, although his mind began to race.

He stayed for a bout with the famous Jackson and then strolled homeward. His younger brother was just leaving as he arrived at Upper Brook Street. "Off to Bascombe's again?" asked the earl sweetly.

"Go there too much," said Lord Charles airily. "Get a bit tired of seeing nothing but females. Taking myself off to the club for a rubber."

"Learning sense in your old age," grinned the earl. "There's a prizefight at Cobham tomorrow. Care to accompany me?"

"No, no," said Lord Charles hurriedly. "Doing

something else. Forget what. But definitely something else.''

He hurried down the street and left the earl looking suspiciously after him. ''Now,'' thought the Earl of Carrisdowne, stroking his chin. ''I wonder. I just wonder . . .''

Henrietta's dinner party was a delightfully informal affair. It was served at the country hour of four in the afternoon. Charlotte and Josephine were looking their prettiest.

Lord Charles was amazed when Miss Hissop told him that she and Henrietta had been to Upper Brook Street for dinner. ''What a sly fox Rupert is,'' said Lord Charles. ''I was away that evening at a play and then a rout. He said nothing to me.''

''Well, seems he can't say anything about *us* socializing,'' said Mr. Clifford cheerfully.

Both gentlemen suggested they take Josephine and Charlotte out driving. Henrietta was closing the shop during the last week in Lent to get in extra supplies for the Season. Mr. Clifford proposed they should all go for a picnic if the weather should prove fine, ''and no doubt Rupert will want to go with us.''

''I should not say anything . . . just yet,'' advised Henrietta.

''But he can't ask *you* to dinner and then forbid *us* to take out Mrs. Webster and Miss Archer,'' protested Lord Charles.

''He just might,'' said Henrietta. ''Which is why I did not tell him you were both coming here today. Oh, do not look so downcast! Let us not talk about the Earl of Carrisdowne.''

The dinner proceeded merrily until at last Lord

Charles and Mr. Clifford rose to take their leave. Henrietta waved to them from the step.

From the corner of Half Moon Street, Jean, the earl's devoted Swiss valet, watched them go. Some ten minutes later he was standing before his master in the earl's study.

"Yes?" said the earl curtly. He was feeling rather grubby. It had seemed a good idea when he had sent Jean to spy on Bascombe's. Now he was so sure Henrietta's dinner guests would turn out to be a mere gaggle of females and leave him with all the guilt of having been suspicious of her.

The Swiss looked at the cornice. "Lord Charles and Mr. Clifford were the guests," he said. "Miss Bascombe herself waved good-bye to them. They appeared to be on the best of terms."

"Thank you," said the earl quietly. "You may go. I need not remind you, I trust, to be discreet?"

"I am always discreet," said Jean, adding with the license of an old and trusted servant, "as you have reason to know."

When he had left, the earl sat glaring at the wall opposite, consumed with rage. Henrietta Bascombe was not an innocent. She was devious and scheming. The very fact that she had not told him the names of her guests showed that she wished to entrap one of them for herself. When she might have had *you*, jeered a little voice in his head. "I was never, at any time, in danger of allying my great name with that of a shopgirl," he told the uncaring serried ranks of books above his desk.

He tried to force himself into a calmer frame of mind. To rail at Guy and Charles might give Henrietta the added luster of forbidden fruit. What was she playing at? I shall ask her, he thought.

And so Henrietta, who was helping the others to wash and put away the dinner dishes, was startled at the sound of loud knocking at the door.

Religious Esau had gone to evening service.

She went to the shop door, raised the blind, and looked through the glass—and reeled backward before the angry glare of the Earl of Carrisdowne, who was standing on the step outside.

She knew, instinctively, that somehow he had found out about the visit of Lord Charles and Mr. Clifford.

She signaled to him to wait and, without telling the others anything, ran upstairs to fetch her bonnet and cloak. Anything the Earl of Carrisdowne had to say to her, he could say out of the hearing of the others. Josephine and Charlotte must not have their splendid day spoiled.

The earl was just raising his hand to knock again when he saw Henrietta on the other side of the glass, unlocking the door.

She put a finger to her lips as he would have burst into angry speech there and then. "Walk with me a little, my lord," said Henrietta. "I do not wish to upset the others with an angry scene."

"And just how do you know it is going to be an angry scene, Miss Shopkeeper?"

"Because you are breathing fire and brimstone," said Henrietta calmly. "Hold your fire until we get to the Green Park."

"I do not think I want to walk about a damp park in the darkness," he said.

"You have no choice, my lord," replied Henrietta, "for I am not going to have a verbal boxing match with you in the street."

They entered the park and walked a little way under

the trees. Finally she stopped and turned to face him. "I surmise you have discovered my guests today were Lord Charles Worsley and Mr. Clifford."

"Yes."

"And why should that make you so very angry?"

"I *warned* you, madam, that I would do my utmost to protect my brother and friend from making unsuitable alliances."

"Then, perhaps you should set a better example. Inviting me to dinner encouraged both to believe they might have your approval."

"Don't play Miss Innocent with me," he said, his voice low and intense. "You refused to name your guests. *That* shows a guilty conscience."

"You did not tell either Lord Charles or Mr. Clifford that *I* had been *your* guest."

"That is different."

"I see no difference."

"You are mocking me," he raged, "because you have managed to enslave my friend and my brother."

"No!" exclaimed Henrietta, too surprised to do other than tell the truth. "Mr. Clifford favors Miss Archer and Lord Charles, Mrs. Webster. Now Charlotte, Mrs. Webster, has been married before, but that is all to the good. She has a certain wisdom and maturity beyond her years that balances Lord Charles's lack of both."

"How dare you criticize my brother!"

Henrietta spoke in a weary little voice. "It is of no use. You are determined to find us all socially unacceptable. But think, might Lord Charles not be better with a lady of gentle birth who works in a shop than some debutante who will marry him for his money and title and then will probably be unfaithful to him after marriage, like so many of the married women in society. And Miss Archer—Josephine—what is there so monstrous about *her* to merit your censure? She is not bold, nor vulgar. But all this is a mere waste of time. I will not apologize to you for inviting Mr. Clifford and Lord Charles, neither will I apologize for not telling you that they were to be my guests. You are every bit as angry and unreasonable as I expected you to be."

"I . . . am . . . never . . . unreasonable," he grated.

"Then, you might appreciate the reason in this. Since it is obvious you will never leave us in peace, I shall tell Josephine and Charlotte that they must never see either your brother or Mr. Clifford again.

"You, my reasonable lord, must also understand that I never want to see *you* again. Just leave my business alone." Her voice broke on a sob as she added, "I am so very tired, you know, and . . . and . . . there is so much work to be done. I have neither the time nor the energy to cross words with you."

She turned and began to walk slowly away from him across the grass, a dim figure under the trees.

"Wait!" he cried. "Please wait, Miss Bascombe."

One thing she had said burst upon his brain like a skyrocket. Neither Charles nor Guy were interested in *her*. She had merely been trying to do the best for her friends.

He must not lose her.

"What is it now?" demanded Henrietta in a tired little voice.

The great attraction she held for him battled with his pride. Attraction won.

"Forgive me," he said. "I have been autocratic . . . bullying . . . hasty. There has been much care and responsibility put on me since the death of my father. I spoke rashly. I shall not stand in the way of either

Charles or Guy. There! Please smile and say you will let me take you driving. Or to the theater.''

Henrietta's spirits rose from the depths to the heavens in one bound. She could not stay angry with him. Was he smiling? She wished it were not so dark so that she might see his face.

''I should like that very much,'' she said, and the bewitched earl felt he had never before heard such beautiful words in his life. ''Only wait until the shop is closed during the last week in Lent. *Then* I shall have some free time.

''In fact, Mr. Clifford and Lord Charles plan to take Mrs. Webster and Miss Archer on a picnic during that week. Perhaps we could go with them.''

''Of course.'' He wanted to pull her into his arms, but something held him back. Not knowing that that *something* was the first little step toward marriage, the Earl of Carrisdowne drew Henrietta's arm through his and, in a companionable silence, they walked slowly together, back to the shop on Half Moon Street.

Chapter Eight

Before the great day of the picnic, Lord Charles Worsley met Mr. Guy Clifford on New Bond Street. It was Lord Charles who had now become the intimate of Mr. Clifford, the earl being immersed in various business ventures on the stock exchange. Gentlemen could gamble on the stock exchange. That was not sullied by the name of "trade." The two had been drawn together by their love for the ladies of the bakery.

They did not know of the earl's increasing fondness for Henrietta, only that, somehow, he had found out about that dinner party and had surprised them by appearing amused rather than angry. He had next amazed them by saying he planned to be present at the famous picnic. After much debate and decision, a journey to the Surrey fields was settled on.

"Where are you bound, Guy?" asked Lord Charles.

"I am going into labor," said Mr. Clifford.

Lord Charles pursed his lips in a soundless whistle. "Going into labor" meant being fitted into a new pair of leather breeches. Mr. Clifford must be very much in love to elect to go through such an agonizing performance.

"I'll come with you and be in at the birth," said Lord Charles.

They turned in at the breeches maker—this personage was never called a tailor; breeches makers working in leather were considered of a higher order.

Mr. Clifford groaned in anticipation as the new leather breeches of pale leather were produced.

The breeches maker summoned four sturdy assistants, and Mr. Clifford lay on a blanket on the shop floor.

Lord Charles lent a hand and all pulled and tugged and strained to fit the skintight breeches up over Mr. Clifford's thighs and bottom.

"Wriggle a bit," said Lord Charles. "Try a bit harder. We're nearly there."

A final massive pull and the breeches were safely up around Mr. Clifford's waist. A special instrument had to be produced to button them.

Then, stiff as a board, Mr. Clifford was lifted and propped upright. He had to be supported while he kicked out with one leg and then the other to ease the stiffness of the leather.

"Very nice," commented Lord Charles. "Like the ladies' muslins, they leave little to the imagination. Now, we'll all need to take a deep breath and get 'em off again."

"No," said Mr. Clifford, "Leave 'em on, for pity's sake. I'll sleep in them if need be."

"Yes, but you do have a tendency to creak," protested Lord Charles as they strolled out of the shop—or rather Lord Charles strolled while Mr. Clifford took painful mincing steps.

"What color d'ye call that?" demanded Lord Charles,

leveling his quizzing glass at the breeches. "Mud of Paris," said Mr. Clifford. "It was a choice between that or Emperor's Eye."

"Horrible names they have for colors," sighed Lord Charles. "Slaves of fashion, that's what we are. Now take these pantaloons of mine. Don't like the color. But my tailor tells me I must have pantaloons of a reddish color. 'All on the reds, now, my lord,' he says, and so red it is. We are tyrannized by this street." He waved his quizzing glass at New Bond Street. "One week it's one thing and the next, t'other. Do you remember a couple of years back when all our boots had to have leather wrinkled on the insole and all *that* did was to retain the dirt and baffle the shoe-black. As for the ladies—twenty years ago they all had waists and hoops. Now that they've started casting off their clothes, they don't know where to stop. You're never wearing those torture chambers of breeches to the picnic?"

"Of course I am. They will have eased out by then."

Perhaps if Mr. Clifford had worn the breeches during the days before the picnic, they might have become more comfortable but, having got them off that night, he found himself very reluctant to put them on again.

But love gave him the courage to suffer and, when the great day dawned, bright and sunny, he was crammed back into them by his valet, his cook, and his knife boy.

They set out in procession from the bakery, the Earl of Carrisdowne driving Henrietta and Miss Hissop, Lord Charles in his carriage driving Charlotte and Josephine and Guy Clifford and, behind that, the earl's fourgon with his servants and enough food and drink to feed a detachment of dragoons.

Although the earl was supplying food and servants for the outing, Mr. Clifford was the one who had chosen the spot for the picnic. To his dismay, when they arrived at the chosen spot, he found it occupied by a band of evil-looking Gypsies.

The earl, who was chatting to Henrietta and Miss Hissop about a play he had seen the previous week, was content to leave it to Mr. Clifford to find somewhere else.

Mr. Clifford, thrown into a fever of anxiety and wanting only the best for Josephine, directed Lord Charles's carriage to lead the way, and then hung on to the guard-rail, shouting from time to time, "Stop! No . . . that will not do. Try farther on."

At last the earl became aware that he was very hungry and that they had been traveling for quite a long time, and called sharply to Mr. Clifford to find *somewhere,* or they would all find themselves in the Channel.

Josephine said timidly that she was feeling very hungry, too, and alarmed that he should cause his beloved the slightest distress, Mr. Clifford picked the first lane that led to the nearest field and declared it was just the thing.

Stiffly they all climbed down from the carriages and looked about them. It was a square field bordered by a high thorn hedge, nothing more. No stream, no trees, no pretty prospect.

Above, the blue of the sky had changed to a milky color, and a scudding, irritating little wind had got up, snatching at hats and bonnets.

The servants spread rugs and cushions on the grass and began to unload all the impedimenta of spirit stove, hampers, and bottles.

The wind grew stronger. The earl suggested that they

move everything to the edge of the field so that they might gain some shelter from the hedge. But Mr. Clifford, exhilarated with being in command for once, poohpoohed the idea and said they were all to sharp-set to fuss.

Conversation grew desultory as bits of grass blew into glasses of wine, and the increasing chill of the wind cut through the muslins of the ladies.

"It will not do," said Miss Hissop at last. "I am sure the damp from the ground is seeping through this rug. I shall catch the ague. Woe is me! Oh, that I must be snatched from this earth before my moment of glory!"

"What moment of glory?" demanded the earl, eyeing the steadily darkening sky uneasily. They had traveled in open carriages and he was now worried they would be soaked before they could reach London again.

"Everlasting glory," said Henrietta, throwing Miss Hissop a warning look. She knew that Miss Hissop dreamed of attending all three girls as bridesmaid.

The earl, who had now heard Miss Hissop talking about her plans for her own funeral several times, accepted Henrietta's explanation and assumed Miss Hissop was thinking of the hereafter, unaware that the spinster obviously expected her moment of glory to come in this world and not the next.

Henrietta was disappointed. She had looked forward to a sylvan setting where Charlotte and Josephine would stroll beside a little stream, talking to their beaux. She had never thought for a moment they would be attended by a retinue of servants. It made the whole business as formal as a dining room.

There were fortunately plenty of fur carriage rugs to supply cloaks for the ladies, but the wind was growing colder by the minute. With cold fingers, they nibbled at wafers of Westphalian ham and slices of chicken. No one felt like eating much in such uncomfortable circumstances.

At last the earl rose. "Walk with me a little," he said to Henrietta. "I fear we must leave soon. I cannot blame Guy for his lack of organization. We were all mad to venture out on a picnic when the leaves are not yet on the trees. The poet Milton describes the souls of the condemned as being hurried from fiery into frozen regions. Perhaps his imagination was fired by such a day as this. I consider myself a sensible man, and yet, like most Englishmen, I am frequently surprised at the vagaries of the weather. We all put ourselves at the mercy of this fickle climate. Why do we not warm our rooms like the Germans, with a closed stove and pipes to carry the heat around the walls? Because we say we like to see the fire. 'It is so dismal not to see the fire,' we say. And so, for the sake of seeing the fire, we are frozen on one side and roasted on the other. We have more women and children killed because of hearth deaths, *burned* to death, in one year than all the heretics and witches who were ever burned at the stake. We—"

"If you wish to continue your speech," interrupted Henrietta with a shiver, "pray let us go over by the hedge, where we may be sheltered from the wind."

They walked over and stood by the tall thorn hedge. The wind moaned and hissed through its branches, making a desolate sound.

"There will be hot tea soon," said the earl, looking along the line of trees to where his servants were crouched round the spirit stove, trying to shelter the flame from the wind.

"Poor things," said Henrietta, meaning the servants. "They must be very cold. At least *their* carriage is covered, and they are not in danger of freezing on the road back. Being a sort of servant oneself changes one's view of things very much.''

''I do not like to hear you talk thus.''

''But it is true,'' said Henrietta, looking anxiously up into his face. ''I now belong to the serving class. There is a poem on the kitchen wall left by the previous tenants. It goes:

Next, as we're servants, Masters at our Hands
Expect obedience to all just Commands;
Which, if we rightly think is but their Due,
Nor more than we in Reason ought to do.
Purchas'd by annual Wages, Cloths, and Meat,
Theirs is our Time, our Hands, our Heads, our Feet:
We think, design, and act at their Command,
And, as their Pleasure varies, walk or stand;
Whilst we receive the convenanted Hire,
Active Obedience justly they require . . .

''I have forgotten the rest. But, you see, I cannot help noticing that your butler is quite blue with cold and that the serving maids do not have cloaks or pelisses to keep them warm.''

''I am not a monster,'' said the earl impatiently. ''My servants are well housed and well fed. The reason they are not more warmly dressed is for the same reason *we* are not warmly dressed. They are English, too, and like all the English, they have only to see a sunny morn to be convinced the day will remain fine until sundown.

''Were my Swiss here, he would now be muffled to the eyeballs, having brought along suitable clothes for at least six changes of climate. But if it distresses you to see cold servants, then warm servants you shall have.

I do not think we should freeze in this drafty field, waiting for tea. I shall send them all home, and I suggest we repair to the nearest inn and sit in front of a roaring fire and drink tea there.''

One large flake of snow spiraled down over the hedge and landed on Henrietta's nose. He took out his handkerchief and brushed it away. "See what I mean?" he teased. "We are about to find ourselves in a sort of arctic if we do not move." He walked away to order the servants to go.

Henrietta happily saw that Josephine and Charlotte now appeared impervious to the cold as they chatted to Lord Charles and Mr. Clifford. Charlotte looked a different girl from the pale beauty of the Charlotte of the village. Her cheeks were tinged with healthy pink, and her eyes sparkled. As Henrietta crossed the field to join them, the wind struck her with a roar, and the field all but disappeared in a roaring white blizzard.

The horses had been unharnessed from the carriages and allowed to graze. The earl called to Lord Charles and Mr. Clifford to help him harness them up so that the servants might be free to pack everything away in the fourgon.

The ladies were bundled up in rugs in the carriages. Miss Hissop was gasping and wailing that the end was nigh, and Henrietta resisted a strong temptation to slap her. Yet Henrietta was so busy mourning the wreck of the day for Josephine and Charlotte, she had little time to examine her own feelings.

She persuaded herself that she was glad the earl showed no signs of wanting to kiss her again. She admitted she enjoyed his company, but that was a good thing, and a bonus in a way, since her only interest in him lay in keeping Bascombe's a fashionable establishment.

As they inched their way through the blinding, wet snow, the earl, on the other hand, was thinking a great deal about Henrietta, and had to admit to himself he was puzzled by her attitude.

Although she appeared pleased to be with him, there was a certain detachment about her. Remembering that kiss that had meant so much to him, he decided reluctantly that it had meant very little to her. She did not appear at all embarrassed or flustered in his company.

Only that morning the earl had thought it folly to take her out, feeling that was the sort of behavior expected of a gentleman who was courting a lady. He had not yet admitted to himself he would even consider marrying Henrietta.

But her very apparent indifference to him made his great democratic gesture seem as nothing. He felt she might at least have shown some awareness of his great condescension. Since he had come into the title, he had been toadied to quite dreadfully and, not having had a very high opinion of women at any time, he assumed he had only to smile at one of them for her to flutter eagerly in his direction.

Through the snow, he saw the blurred image of an inn sign and turned into the courtyard. The servants would need to join them. The weather was too bad to allow them to risk trying to get to London by themselves.

It proved to be little more than a hedge tavern, but the landlord looked clean and decent and was overjoyed at a chance of entertaining members of the quality.

The little inn was empty of other customers because of the terrible weather, and soon they were seated by the tap in front of a roaring fire, drinking hot punch and feeling like a band of explorers who had come down from the glaciers. The servants were ensconced in the kitchen.

Mr. Clifford thought it all very romantic. He sat close to Josephine on a high-backed wooden settle beside the fire. She had placed her ruin of a bonnet over the poker to dry. Her springy chestnut hair shone with threads of gold in the firelight.

Mr. Clifford looked cautiously around. The earl was telling Miss Bascombe about one of the famous peninsular battles. Lord Charles was telling Charlotte all about Gentleman Jackson's Boxing Saloon, and Charlotte was listening to him with as much interest as if he were telling her the latest court gossip. Miss Hissop had fallen asleep.

Mr. Clifford felt the time had come to declare his intentions. There was no need to ask little Miss Bascombe or Miss Hissop for permission. Their approval of him was all too evident. To compose himself and to find the right words, he stood up with his back to the fire. He would take Josephine's hand, he decided, when no one was looking, and ask her what she thought about marriage. Yes, that would be a good start.

He went to sit down beside her again. But his breeches, his new leather breeches, had dried onto him like a second skin and refused to sit down when he did. He let out a cry of agony and slid down onto the floor.

In vain did he try to get up. Lord Charles and the Earl of Carrisdowne came over and hoisted him to his feet. But the wretched breeches seemed to be getting tighter by the minute. Mr. Clifford was now very white about the face and looked on the point of fainting.

103

"It's those cursed breeches," said Lord Charles. "You'll need to get 'em off."

"Shhh!" said Mr. Clifford feebly. "Ladies present." he swayed, and the earl caught him just as he collapsed in a dead faint.

"Ladies," said the earl, "Mr. Clifford is suffering badly from constriction. You must leave the room until we attend to him."

The landlord was summoned and offered his own parlor as sanctuary for the ladies. They woke Miss Hissop, and then they all left the room.

"Now, lay him down on the floor," said the earl, "and let's get these things off him."

But the buttons could not be moved. "Cut them off," said Lord Charles. "It's the only thing to do. He's turning blue about the mouth."

"When I was a boy," said the earl, producing a penknife, "I used to see ladies get into this coil through too much tight lacing." He cut the buttons and then had to saw the leather of the breeches on either side while Lord Charles held burning feathers under Mr. Clifford's nose.

The landlord came in with a pewter bowl filled with snow, and they pressed some of it to the back of Mr. Clifford's neck. He slowly recovered and then sat up clutching his head.

"Easy," said the earl. "You had better wrap your nether limbs in a blanket, Guy. We had to send the ladies from the room."

"And I was just on the point of proposing," said Mr. Clifford dizzily.

"Drink some brandy," urged the earl, "and then let us discuss the matter of marriage while the ladies are absent." He waited while his brother hoisted Mr. Clifford back onto the settle and gave him a glass of brandy.

The color returned to Mr. Clifford's cheeks. "Oh, my breeches," he mourned.

"Never mind your demmed breeches," drawled Lord Charles. "My dear brother is about to deliver himself of a jaw-me-dead about the folly of marrying into a shop."

"I was merely going to point out the folly of leaping into marriage before you have properly courted the girl," said the earl. "It is not fair to Miss Archer. What do you know of each other? Snatched conversations in a busy shop, one dinner, and one disastrous outing."

Mr. Clifford scratched his head. "Seems to me it doesn't really matter," he said, puzzled. "Can't say I've felt like this before. Never wanted to *cherish* any of the others, if you know what I mean."

"Nonetheless, you must admit you were about to be hasty."

"Perhaps you have the right of it," said Mr. Clifford reluctantly. "I'm certainly not going to propose now, not with a blanket wrapped around me. So long as you're not going to mess things up for me, Rupert, I don't mind waiting."

"I never messed things up, as you put it, for you before," said the earl. "As I recall, you were deuced glad I came to the rescue."

"Well, it ain't that I'm not grateful," said Mr. Clifford. "But it don't follow I'm naturally about to make another mistake."

"And what about you, Charles?" demanded the earl, fixing his brother with a steely look.

"Oh, I don't mind biding my time," said Lord Charles airily. "Early days yet."

The earl looked at his younger brother suspiciously.

It was hard to tell half the time what Charles was really thinking.

"And what about you?" rejoined Lord Charles. "Never say you are squiring Miss Bascombe for the sole purpose of keeping an eye on the pair of us. Too Gothic."

"I enjoy Miss Bascombe's company, that is all," said the earl repressively. Privately he thought things were moving too fast and was glad he had dissuaded Guy from proposing. What did they know of these women?

When Henrietta was next to him, the earl found it very hard to think clearly. But when she was not, all of his old caution and all his distaste for her manner of earning her living returned in full force.

The ladies were brought back in. Modesty forbade them from mentioning the reason for Mr. Clifford's constriction. It was politely assumed his cravat had been too tight, and eyes were delicately averted from the blanket wrapped about his nether limbs.

The landlord appeared to say that the snow had changed to rain and that the roads were clearing fast. Soon they were able to arrange themselves in the carriages with rugs over their heads to make the journey back.

Because of the miserable weather, it was a silent journey home, the earl breaking the silence only once to beg Henrietta to attend a play with him the following evening.

Henrietta accepted, feeling as if spring had come at last. She felt warm and elated. Here was more proof that the earl had forgiven her for being in trade; for an outing to the playhouse was even better than a picnic. He would be seen with her before the eyes of society.

As the carriages with their sodden occupants turned

into Half Moon Street, the sun burst through the ragged clouds, gilding the cobbles and shining on the golden pineapple above the door of Bascombe's.

Josephine and Charlotte began to chatter like schoolgirls as they unwrapped themselves from the wet rugs. Lord Charles and Mr. Clifford were teasing them both and saying that if they had not both died from rheumatism by the morrow, they would take them driving at the fashionable hour. The earl jumped down and, after helping Miss Hissop, lifted Henrietta down from his carriage.

She felt the strength of his hands at her waist and noticed the evident reluctance with which he released her when he had set her on the ground. He raised her hand to his lips. "Tomorrow?" he asked.

"Yes, tomorrow," said Henrietta huskily. He kissed her hand. He said, "The play begins at seven, but most of the ton do not attend until nine."

"I have never been to the playhouse before," said Henrietta. "I should like to see the play from the beginning."

"It is Shakespeare's *A Winter's Tale*. The performance is said to be very fine. I shall call for you at six-thirty."

He bowed and jumped up into his carriage.

Mr. Clifford and Lord Charles were standing on the pavement laughing and joking with Josephine and Charlotte. Miss Hissop stood by the shop door, waiting for Henrietta to unlock it and wondering why the girl was still standing on the pavement, her hands to her lips, watching the earl drive away.

Chapter Nine

The next evening as Henrietta was preparing to go to the theater, Josephine and Charlotte sat on their beds to watch her dress for the great occasion.

Both girls had returned from the park, much elated at the success of their outing. The sun had shone, the afternoon had been fine, and it was evident from their report that both Mr. Clifford and Lord Charles had gone out of their way to present them to many leading members of the ton.

"And that must surely mean marriage," ended Charlotte. "Lord Charles's whole manner toward me is not that of a man who is seeking an idle affair."

"Yes," agreed Henrietta. "Both Lord Charles and Mr. Clifford appear to behave very prettily."

"We *all* have beaux now," said Josephine.

"Not I," said Henrietta, twisting this way and that in front of the looking glass.

"But Carrisdowne *is* your beau," protested Charlotte.

"I am merely allowing Lord Carrisdowne to squire me to the play because it keeps Bascombe's in fashion."

"Dear Henrietta," said Josephine tentatively, "I should not like to think you were encouraging Lord Carrisdowne merely to promote the happiness of myself and Josephine. Although you say it is all for the sake of the shop, I know you have our welfare at heart. *I* think Lord Carrisdowne is a dangerous-looking man. So fierce! You must not play with his affections."

"His affections!" laughed Henrietta. "He does not have any." Then she remembered that kiss and blushed.

She still did not quite trust the earl or his interest in her. She sometimes suspected him of playing a deep game, suspected him of staying close to her so that he might find a way of alienating the affections of Lord Charles and Guy from Josephine and Charlotte.

"I confess we owe you much," said Charlotte. "Never did I think I should have such a wonderful time. I do not even feel tired anymore. But *if*, as you say, you are not interested in Lord Carrisdowne, why did you get the dressmaker to work all last night and today to supply you with that very splendid ensemble in time for the theater?"

Henrietta was wearing a dress of spotted India muslin with puckered sleeves, the front richly ornamented with silver trimming and lace. Over the dress she wore a Persian robe of rich-figured amber sarcenet, made without sleeves and loose from the shoulders. A rouleau of silver muslin bound her glossy curls. The dress had armlets of gold, studied with paste rubies, and was confined under her bosom with a golden girdle.

"I felt I must look my best," explained Henrietta. "I am by way of being an advertisement for Bascombe's. Besides, Miss Hissop has new finery, and *she* is not going to the play."

Henrietta had felt obliged to order new clothes for

Miss Hissop. Unthinkable that she, Henrietta, should spend so much on just one gown when poor Miss Hissop was in such dire need of new clothes.

Miss Hissop was proudly wearing the first of several gowns Henrietta had ordered for her. It was a soft dove-gray velvet, and Miss Hissop had cried tears of gratitude after she had tried it on, saying that it was so very beautiful she had a good mind to change the instructions for her funeral and request that she be buried in it.

Although the profits from the confectioner's were to be divided equally among the four of them, all had agreed to live as frugally as possible, saving all they could for the girls' dowries and Miss Hissop's retirement. But when the others had insisted that Henrietta's theater gown should be paid for from their joint savings, she in turn had been equally insistent that all their clothes in that case should be charged to the profits before they were divided up.

Henrietta had become very fond of Josephine and Charlotte. Although both girls were older than she, Charlotte being twenty-two and Josephine twenty, Henrietta at nineteen felt older than they. If only she could keep Lord Carrisdowne amused and interested, then Mr. Clifford and Lord Charles might propose to the girls very soon.

Her hopes for them took predominance over her own desires. The earl was an enigma, but he was an intelligent man and courteous company.

Having convinced herself that all her excitement at the prospect of spending an evening in his company was dictated by her delight in being shown to society in such exalted company, Henrietta was quite unprepared for her own reactions when she saw him again.

Esau came shuffling reluctantly up the stairs to scratch at the door and announce that "him" was below.

The earl was standing in the middle of the shop in black evening dress and diamonds. Henrietta came down the stairs so softly that he was not aware of her approach. She stood looking at him for a brief moment, her heart doing a somersault. He looked so very grand, so very masculine, the cascading white muslin of his cravat setting off the hard firm lines of his tanned face. His black evening breeches were molded to his legs, showing all the strength of the muscles in his thighs. He looked cool and remote and every inch the aristocrat.

Why does he bother with me? thought Henrietta in sudden panic. Why?

The earl turned and saw her. A smile softened the harsh lines of his face. Those black eyes of his that gave so very little away studied Henrietta in silence. Then he said, "You look like a fresh rose with the dew on it, sparkling, untouched, not yet full-blown."

"A pretty compliment, my lord." Henrietta avoided his intense gaze. "Shall we go?"

The press of carriages as they approached the Theater Royal, Drury Lane, was so great, and Henrietta was so anxious not to miss the beginning of the play that they alighted from the carriage a few streets away and walked to the theater.

A covey of bloods came barreling along the street, and the earl pulled Henrietta tightly against his side and swung her away from them so that she would not be roughly knocked. That brief contact made her feel dizzy. It was weak and humiliating to have such violent physical reactions to a man who did not seem too much moved by the same contact.

They were only two playhouses in London: the Theater Royal, in Drury Lane, and the Haymarket Theater. It was a sad change from the days of Queen Elizabeth and King James I when London, then only a tenth of its present size, contained seventeen theaters. But the two remaining playhouses were enormous. Old people said the acting was better in their young days because there were more schools for actors then, and the theaters were so small that the natural voice could be heard and the natural expression of the features seen, and therefore rant and distortion were unnecessary.

As Henrietta and the earl approached the Theater Royal, they saw the soldiers stationed at the doors in case of riots, and as they drew nearer they were pestered by women trying to sell them oranges and boys selling playbills.

Once inside, Henrietta was overawed by the size, the height, the splendor, and the beauty of the theater. The pit was capable of holding a thousand people. Above it, on three sides, rose four tiers of boxes supported by thin iron pillars and above them, two galleries, the higher at such a distance that anyone taking a place there had to be content with the spectacle, for it was impossible to hear the dialogue. The theater was decorated in colors of blue and silver and the whole illuminated with chandeliers of cut glass.

The people in the galleries were very noisy as Henrietta and the earl took their places in his box. They were whistling and calling to the musicians and passing the time waiting for the play to begin by throwing orange peel at the audience in the pit.

Although both pit and galleries were already full, the earl explained that the lower side boxes, of which theirs was one, did not begin to fill up until toward the middle of the first act, because, he told her, that part of the audience considered themselves too fashionable to come on time, and in any case came to see the other fashionables and to be seen themselves rather than to listen to the play.

He did not tell her that the front boxes—those facing the stage—did not fill until halfway through the play, when they would be swarming with prostitutes and the men who came to meet them. There had been a move to prevent prostitutes from entering the theater, and men had been placed at the doors during the previous year to keep them out. But, alas for the fashions of the Regency! It was so hard to tell lady from prostitute! The whole plan was abandoned after two aristocratic ladies with highly painted faces and transparent muslin gowns had been marched off to the nearest roundhouse.

The play began. Henrietta watched the stage, and the earl watched Henrietta. He was fascinated by her rapt attention and the expressions that flitted across her face.

Noisy fights broke out during the play between the men in the front boxes vying for the custom of the prostitutes, but Henrietta did not even seem to notice. The play had lately been revived to display to advantage those two stars of the English stage, Mr. Kemble and Mrs. Siddons.

When the play was finally over—there were no intervals; they only had those on benefit nights—Henrietta heaved a sigh of pure delight. "Do you wish to stay for the afterpiece?" asked the earl. "It is *Don Juan*."

"Oh, *yes*," breathed Henrietta.

With all the candles blazing in the theater, making it as bright as a sunny day, Henrietta became aware that many glasses were being turned curiously in the direction of their box.

Then, from the leering stares, the malicious giggles

of the ladies, and the occasional loud remarks, the deeply humiliated Henrietta realized she was being regarded as Lord Carrisdowne's latest mistress. There were many jokes about the earl's "sweet tooth."

The earl looked thoughtfully at Henrietta's flushed and unhappy face, such a contrast to the childlike wonder that had transformed it during the play. He seemed to come to some decision.

He rose to his feet. "Before the afterpiece begins," he said, "I should like you to meet someone. She is only two boxes away."

"Who is it?" asked Henrietta nervously.

"My aunt, Lady Browne. She will not eat you."

Henrietta was escorted by him from the box and soon found herself in the presence of Lady Browne, a terrifying-looking old dowager with a gimlet eye.

"Well, Carrisdowne?" she demanded. "Never say you have brought a lady to meet me at last."

The earl performed the introductions.

"And how did you find the play, Miss Bascombe?" demanded Lady Browne.

"It was very fine. I-I thought it was wonderful, in fact. You see, I had never been to the playhouse before."

"Such enthusiasm does you credit. I cannot abide these young misses who consider it fashionable to find everything a bore. Tell me, Carrisdowne, how goes Emmeline?"

It transpired that Emmeline was the earl's mother. Henrietta listened while the earl discussed his mother's health. Then, "We must leave," he said. "*Don Juan* is about to begin."

Henrietta curtsied low. Lady Browne took her hand and drew her face down to her own and kissed her on the cheek. "I hope you never lose that fresh look," she said. "There are too many jaded women in London."

The introduction and that kiss were noticed by many jealous female eyes. Miss Bascombe was *not* the earl's mistress, or he would not have introduced her to his aunt.

Lady Clara Sinclair clutched her fan so tightly that she broke one of the sticks. Until a few weeks ago, she had entertained hopes of a proposal from the earl. He had escorted her to the opera and had finally invited her to that dinner party where she had taken the role of hostess—although it was a role he had not asked her to assume.

She had believed his recent absence was due to his business affairs. Now it appeared all too plain that it was because of that sly Bascombe creature.

Spoiled and willful, Lady Clara was used to getting anything she wanted. And she wanted the Earl of Carrisdowne. There must be some terribly simple way to drive that Bascombe woman out of London.

The old story of Don Juan was performed as a pantomine. It was a favorite spectacle everywhere. The London audiences were delighted when the statue came to life, and the sound of his "marble" footsteps always struck a dead silence through the theater.

At last it was all over. The earl's coachman had battled and fought to find a place for the carriage at the front of the theater.

They chatted about the play on the road home, Henrietta cheerful and animated and, for that short time, very much at ease in the earl's company.

Before he left her at the shop door, he wanted to kiss her very much indeed. But he knew in his mind that he had come to a point, to a crossroads, where he must decide what his own intentions were before making any more advances to her. He wanted her desperately. But always between him and his desire rose up the great wall of his pride.

After he had gone, Henrietta let herself into the sugar-smelling darkness of the shop. She twirled around, humming snatches of a popular ballad. Then she stretched her arms up to the ceiling. "What a *wonderful* evening," she cried.

Esau, crouching in the darkness of the shop, felt his heart sink. He could smell the stench of the workhouse in his nostrils and feel again the cut of the lash across his back. Something must be done to prevent Henrietta from marrying the earl.

"Something must be done to stop Carrisdowne from marrying that Bascombe shopgirl," said Lady Clara.

Her brother, Lord Alisdair Sinclair, lounged in a chair opposite her in the sitting room of their family's town house. His feet in their muddy boots rested on a marble console table.

"Take some of my chums and break up her shop," said Lord Alisdair. He was a dissipated young man who roamed the lower and dangerous parts of the town with his drunken friends.

"No," said Lady Clara crossly. "Carrisdowne would get to hear of it and you would be blamed, and then I should be suspected of having put you up to it. Everyone knows of my hopes of marriage to Carrisdowne."

"That's 'cos you talk too much," said her brother.

"Instead of sitting there criticizing me, you might put what's left of your brain to the problem and come up with something *sensible.*"

Lord Alisdair stretched and yawned. "Begad," he

said, "the simplest way is always the best. Smoke her out."

"Smoke her out? She is not a *cobbler*." It was considered prime sport among the bucks and bloods to blow cigar smoke into a cobbler's little closed stall where he slept during the night so that they might enjoy the jolly spectacle of seeing the cobbler come staggering out, gasping for breath.

"I mean, set fire to her shop."

"And if someone sees you?"

"No one will see *me*. Don't do my drinking in Tothill Fields for nothing. Plenty of villains down there'd jump at the chance to do it for a golden boy."

"Only a sovereign to get rid of that Bascombe?" Lady Clara smiled, a slow, catlike smile. "The only bargain to be found, little brother, in these expensive days. Very well. Burn her out! Carrisdowne hasn't yet proposed, evidently, or we'd have heard of it, and without a place to stay she will need to return, even if temporarily, to where she came from. That will leave the field open for me."

"And what if Miss Bascombe and her ladies perish in the fire?" Lord Alisdair fixed his sister with a beady eye.

"Dear Alisdair, what with pestilence, fires, riots, and hangings, London is full of dead bodies. A few more won't make any difference. Besides, the Bascombe creature is in *trade*. She is not one of us. She is no more one of us than any of those wretches we saw being hanged at Newgate t'other week. Do not tell me you are become overnice in your feelings?"

"Not I, sis. Oh, no, not I."

Chapter Ten

The next day Henrietta served the Duke of Gillingham with bergamot chips instead of apple salad and left the turtle soup to boil over on the kitchen fire.

The more she thought about the evening at the theater, the more dazed she became with happiness. The great Earl of Carrisdowne was turning out to be her *friend.* She could hardly believe her good fortune. Perhaps, one day, he might even begin to entertain warmer feelings toward her. She was sure he had only kissed her because he had considered her far enough beneath him to accept such easy familiarities. But he had introduced her to his aunt. Miss Hissop, on hearing of this, had said he must have serious intentions, but Henrietta felt that was too optimistic a hope for the moment. It was enough that he liked and respected her. Her mind shied away from examining her own feelings too closely. The marriages of Josephine and Charlotte still held predominance in her thoughts and each mark of the earl's respect seemed to bring the realization of that ambition closer.

She had not slept very much the night before and so she was exhausted by the time the chores of the day were completed along with the lengthy preparations for the next.

By ten o'clock, she was fast asleep.

By eleven o'clock, the other girls and Miss Hissop were asleep as well, while downstairs, in a makeshift bed in the back shop, Esau tossed and turned, plagued by uneasy dreams.

At two in the morning, Lord Alisdair's ruffians held a piece of brown paper smeared with syrup against the glass panes of the door. One of them tapped against the paper with a hammer until the glass broke. They gently lifted out the broken glass stuck to the paper and stuffed a pile of oily rags through the hole they had made so that the rags fell onto the floor of the shop. Then they lighted a torch and threw it in on top of the rags.

There were so many fires in London that had it not been for an amazing coincidence, Bascombe's might have been burned to the ground. Fires were usually caused by exploding coals or candles. Only the week before a gentleman had set the tail of his shift afire by climbing into bed with his back to his bed candle. The flames from his blazing shift had caught the bedcurtains, and, although the gentleman had escaped, his house had burned to the ground.

All the insurance companies had fire engines and firemen, but if you were not insured—and Henrietta was not—or if you had not paid up your premiums, then they would drive past without even stopping to watch the blaze.

There had been inventions for preventing fires, but they had come to nothing.

A Mr. David Hartley had suggested lining every room

119

with metal, and Lord Stanhope had invented a kind of mortar for the same purpose, but they were not adopted because no law was passed to compel the adoption. Houses in London were built for sale, and the builder did not want to incur the expense of making them fireproof, because, if the house went on fire, then he would not be the one to be burned.

As far back as 1724, inventor Ambrose Godfrey had produced balls filled with chemicals that would extinguish a fire. The Royal Society of Arts even built a house in Marylebone fields to try out his invention. His devices were thrown into the burning rooms where they exploded, and the fire was successfully quenched. But it was a trade in England to put out fires, and "All trades must live," as the current motto went. So the firemen and the funeral directors got together, and when Godfrey or any of his friends tried to mount a ladder to throw one of his balls into a burning building, they simply pulled the ladder from under him, until the life of every person using them became endangered. And so that was the end of fire-extinguishing devices.

As Lord Alsidair's ruffians ran off down the street, coincidence in the form of the Earl of Carrisdowne turned the corner of Piccadilly onto Half Moon Street.

He had been playing cards at Watier's on Bolton Street and had persuaded himself that it was just as quick to walk home along Piccadilly and down Half Moon Street as it was to go via Berkeley Square.

He tried to ignore the little voice inside that kept telling him he was behaving like any love-smitten youth and was really hoping for some sign of Henrietta. Perhaps she might still be awake and working in the kitchen.

He saw the two dark figures running away, and then

a tongue of flame leaped through the door of Bascombe's. Shouting for help, he ran toward the shop.

Esau awoke with a start. He always slept lightly. In the workhouse it had been a mistake to indulge in heavy sleep when even the skimpy rags might be stolen off your back. He smelled smoke. He faintly heard the earl's shout. He staggered to the door of the back shop and flung it open.

The pile of oil rags had blossomed into a sheet of flame. Esau screamed, a terrified animal scream.

Henrietta, almost as light a sleeper as Esau, leaped from bed and rushed down the stairs to the shop. Esau was standing helplessly, whimpering and wringing his hands.

"Water!" shouted Henrietta. "Fetch water, Esau."

And then a tall figure hurtled through the flames and fell onto the shop floor, rolling over and over to extinguish the greedy flames licking at his coat.

"Carrisdowne!" cried Henrietta. Galvanized into action, Esau ran to fetch water.

"Blankets," rapped out the earl, jumping to his feet. "Blankets, Miss Bascombe."

"Esau's," said Henrietta. "The back shop."

She ran into the back shop and snatched up Esau's blankets and then thrust the bundle at the earl. He threw them over the flames and then stamped on them, cursing as a tongue of flame singed the black silk of his breeches.

Esau staggered in with two pails of water. "More," ordered the earl, snatching them from him.

"The curtains," gasped Henrietta, for the pretty chintz curtains were ablaze. He threw the water over them and then ran about like a madman, stamping down

121

the flames, kicking off bits of flaming rag that stuck to his shoes.

Esau came back with more water, and it was thrown on the dying blaze. The earl went with Esau this time to the scullery pump.

When they returned, Henrietta was beating down the remaining flames with a broom, unaware of the fact that she was clad in nothing but a flimsy nightdress and a frivolous frilly nightcap.

"That's it," said the earl with satisfaction as the water he and Esau had brought doused the rest of the flames.

"Go upstairs to the cupboard on the landing and get more blankets for your bed, Esau," said Henrietta. "If the others are awake, tell them what happened."

People in the street outside were clustering around the burned and shattered door. The earl took off his coat and put it around Henrietta's shoulders.

"Go away," he snapped at the curious faces at the door.

One by one they drifted off. "I shall send my servants round with some sort of door or piece of wood to keep you secure for the night," said the earl.

"Oh, th-thank you," whispered Henrietta, now shaking with shock.

There was a sooty smut on one cheek, and her large eyes were full of tears. He drew her gently into his arms and held her against his breast.

"It's all over," he murmured against her hair. "Do not cry. I shall take care of you." He tilted her chin up. "Smile. There is nothing to be afraid of."

Henrietta gave him a watery smile. He kissed her gently on the mouth, feeling such a mixture of sweetness and passion that he forgot where he was.

The noise of female screams and exclamations coming down the stairs finally penetrated his brain, and he reluctantly freed his lips.

Miss Hissop burst into the room followed by Josephine, Charlotte, and Esau. They cried and exclaimed over the blackened mess of the room, hugged Henrietta, praised the earl for his bravery, and told Esau he was the best servant in London.

"So terrifying," gasped Miss Hissop. "We might have all been burned to a crisp, and then what would have happened to my funeral? Oh, to think all my dear funeral instructions might have been burned with me! Henrietta, my funeral instructions must from now on be lodged at the bank."

The earl took a deep breath, and when all the exclamations and cries had died away, he bowed to Miss Hissop, and said, "Miss Hissop, I shall call on Miss Bascombe in three days time. I would I could make it sooner, but I have matters to attend to. May I have your permission to see her alone? I have something very important to ask her."

"Yes," said Miss Hissop, startled into uttering only that one monosyllable.

Henrietta looked up at him as he raised her hands to his lips.

"I shall leave you now and send my servants with something to board up the door for the rest of the night."

"Bascombe's will not be opening for a few days," said Henrietta ruefully. "What a mess! But we shall come about. At least any orders for centerpieces are to be delivered next week, so I shall have time to make this shop sparkling again. Oh, and thank you for your advice. I have been unfashionable enough to start demanding money in advance."

"Till Friday, then. At six o'clock," he said, kissing first one hand and then the other.

"Friday," echoed Henrietta softly.

"Now," he said, turning to the others, "I must report this fire to the authorities. It was set deliberately. I saw two men running away from the door of the shop."

Miss Hissop let out a faint scream.

"Someone is jealous of your success. I suggest that in future Esau sleeps in the shop itself."

After he had left, they all clustered around Henrietta. The earl quite obviously meant to propose to her. Would she accept?

And Henrietta, thinking of his handsome face, the touch of his lips, and the sweetness of his smile, gave a little gulp and said, "Yes. Yes, I will. Yes, I *will* marry the Earl of Carrisdowne."

They were so busy laughing and hugging her that they did not notice Esau creep sadly away, an Esau tortured with fears for his future now that his mistress was to wed.

The earl did not tell Mr. Clifford or Lord Charles of his appointment with Henrietta, but both men heard about it when they visited the shop the next morning to find the door boarded up and a sign in the window saying that Bascombe's was temporarily closed because of fire.

Charlotte saw them at the window and let them in. The story of the fire had to be told again and again, and it was only at last that they learned how Carrisdowne had asked Miss Hissop's permission to call on Henrietta.

They set to with a will, helping the girls to clean the blackened floor and scrub the soot from the shelves, although Henrietta protested, saying that the maids who were at work in the kitchen would help with the shop later. But it was all a novelty to Mr. Clifford and Lord Charles. Each man was elated at the thought of Carrisdowne proposing to Henrietta.

They left late in the afternoon, saying that the next morning, the Thursday, they were setting out for Newmarket, and promising the girls that they would return as soon as possible.

When they had walked away from the shop, Lord Charles murmured, "As soon as he pops the question, we'll pop ours. Let him go first."

"Don't see why we should wait," said Mr. Clifford. "Let's go back now and ask 'em."

"Oh, let Rupert have all the fun of first proposal. He's not such a bad old stick."

"Hope it's going to be all right," said Mr. Clifford. "When's he seeing her? Friday? Whoever heard of a man proposing on a Friday?"

Friday was considered an unlucky day in England. Friday was the usual day for executions, the idea being that it gave the condemned time to travel to heaven on the Saturday and get through the pearly gates by the Sunday. No one ever married on a Friday, and sailors would not put to sea on that unlucky day, even if the winds were favorable.

"It will be all right," said Lord Charles soothingly. "Forgot to ask Charlotte . . . little Miss Bascombe's going to accept him, isn't she?"

"Yes, definitely. Told them all she was."

"There you are! Never believed that stuff about Fridays anyway."

Esau worked and listened to the chatter in the shop. He worked and worried. There must be some way to stop Henrietta from marrying. He was to be paid on the tenth of June. Once he had his wages, he would feel more secure. Somehow matters must be delayed until then.

He felt sure the minute Henrietta accepted the earl's proposal, she would promptly close down the business. Even Esau knew it was unthinkable that the great Earl of Carrisdowne should have a fiancée in trade.

A busy time made the hours fly past until Friday. The carpenter hung a new door, and Henrietta herself repainted the shop walls.

On Friday Bascombe's opened again, but there were very few customers, nobody thinking they could get on their feet again so very quickly.

The day passed very slowly for Henrietta. She planned to close the shop as early as half past five.

A coachman and carriage had been hired to take the girls, Miss Hissop, and Esau for a long drive in the park while the important proposal was going on.

Miss Hissop had protested strongly, saying that Henrietta must be chaperoned, but Henrietta said that, being the owner of Bascombe's, it was perfectly correct to see the earl alone.

The shop was closed at last. The rest left in the hired carriage to take the air. By six, Henrietta was sitting by the window in a pretty gown of sprigged muslin, heart beating hard, waiting for her lord to come.

The little French gilt clock up on the shelf chimed six. She waited with increasing impatience. What if he did not come? What if that great pride of his had persuaded him that to propose to a shopgirl was folly? And if he changed his mind, what then would become of Josephine and Charlotte?

Would he never come? Henrietta began to pace up

and down. The others would not be back until after seven. But the precious minutes were ticking away.

She heard footsteps in the street outside and rushed to the window.

Lady Clara Sinclair stopped outside the shop on the arm of a thin, dissipated youth. Henrietta did not know that the youth was Lord Alisdair.

"Pity it did not burn properly" came Lady Clara's voice. "You must have hired fools."

"Try again another time," drawled the young man laconically.

They moved off. They had not seen Henrietta because she had moved behind the curtain as soon as she had recognized Lady Clara.

She sat down suddenly. So that was who was behind the attempt to burn the shop.

Where was the earl? *He* would know what to do. If he had changed his mind, if he had decided he did not want her, then she would indeed feel friendless. Only the earl could advise her as to how to go about bringing aristocrats like Lady Clara into court.

How very beautiful, how very fashionable, Lady Clara had looked. How could the earl look at *her,* Henrietta Bascombe, shopkeeper, when there were so many beauties about?

And then she heard his firm step. She knew instinctively it was he. Henrietta stood up, her hands clasped to her bosom, her heart in her eyes.

Chapter Eleven

The earl would have been on time for his appointment with Henrietta if he had not met Esau, who was sitting forlornly on the steps of the Grosvenor Chapel.

Esau had asked to be set down, saying he did not feel like going for a drive. Miss Hissop, cross that their male servant should not wish to accompany them, pointed out that the doors of the church were closed.

But Esau, showing a rare streak of stubbornness, insisted, and Miss Hissop, who secretly admired Esau's religious fervor, gave in.

The earl recognized the servant by his familiar squint and red plush livery. Esau was small for his age, and he looked a sad little figure sitting on the church steps.

"Why are you not in the shop?" asked the earl, stopping in front of him.

"Mistress sent us away," said Esau. "The rest of the ladies is gone to the park for a drive."

The earl smiled with pleasure at the prospect of seeing Henrietta alone. He was about to take his leave when he noticed large tears were standing out in Esau's eyes, making the squint more pronounced.

"What ails you?" he asked gently. "It is the shock from the fire, no doubt."

Esau solemnly shook his head. The reason for his tears was because he was sure the devil had sent the earl. Esau had long debated telling the earl some lie so that the proposal would never take place. He had gone to the church for comfort and had quite resolved to behave himself and accept the inevitable. But here was the earl, and here was the opportunity. Still, he hesitated, but the noise and the filth of the dreaded workhouse rose before his eyes.

"I am in sore distress about mistress," he said, enunciating slowly and clearly.

"Miss Bascombe? What is the matter with Miss Bascombe?" The earl's voice was sharp with anxiety.

"She's a good lady," said Esau, "and I don't like to see her going on the way she does. She would do anything for money, she says, not wanting to be poor again, but it goes against my pinsipulls."

"What goes against your principles?"

"Her selling herself," said Esau in a low voice. "First to the Duke of Gillingham, then to Mr. Brummell, and now she's going to sell herself to you."

"Do you know what you are saying?"

Esau quailed before the blaze of anger on the earl's face. He, Esau, might quickly be found out in his lie and lose his employ, but he was shrewd beyond his years and knew that in their heart of hearts most gentlemen were prepared to believe the worst of the ladies. He had often returned to the servants' pub to keep up with the gossip and had heard the servants faithfully repeating their masters' cynical opinions about Lady this and Miss that.

"Yes," said Esau. I've lied now, he thought, and may God forgive me, but I'm going to make this a really big one. Aloud, he added, "I would give her my wages if I thought it would stop her. I would work for *nothing*."

A red mist of anger rose before the earl's eyes. He did not want to believe Esau, but why should this child-servant lie to him? What did he really know of Henrietta Bascombe except the little that she herself had told him, and that very little had included her statement to him that she would do anything for money. Besides, she had gone into trade.

Esau knelt at the earl's feet and clutched the hem of his coat. "Leave her alone, my lord," he sobbed. "She's good reelly."

The earl jerked his coat hem from Esau's grasp. "You no doubt think you have done me a favor," he grated. "But you are a disloyal servant."

Esau shrank away from him and put up his hand to ward off the expected blow.

My world has fallen in ruins, thought the earl bitterly, and here I stand berating a child! He gave Esau a curt good-bye and strode off back the way he had come.

Esau dried his eyes on his sleeve. At least the earl would not be going to Bascombe's to keep that appointment.

But the earl was too furious, hurt, and sick to let matters rest. Instead of going into his house, he walked on past it, turned down Park Lane, along Curzon Street, and onto Half Moon Street.

He kept remembering her saying she would do anything for money. She was no better than an abbess, no doubt renting Charlotte and Josephine out to the highest bidders. And not content with that, she had nearly trapped *three* of London's most eligible gentlemen into unsuitable marriages. He could only be glad that Guy and Charles were safely on the way to Newmarket.

He hammered on the shop door.

The light died out of Henrietta's eyes when she saw the expression on his face.

"Are we alone?" he demanded harshly.

"Y-yes," faltered Henrietta.

He stood looking down at her, at the delicate pink of her cheeks, the softness of her mouth, and the swell of her bosom under her gown.

The shop had not yet been cleared of sweetmeats, cakes, jellies, and fruit. She looked as edible and delectable as one of her confections. The shop glowed with color. There was a sweet smell of sugar and spice.

He pulled her roughly into his arms and crushed her mouth under his own. She returned his kiss eagerly, sweetly, and with newfound passion, and it was only after a few dazed moments that she realized how much he was punishing her mouth and that one expert hand had slid inside the neck of her dress to find her breasts.

Alarmed and shocked, she pushed him away with all her strength. Breathing heavily as if he had been running, he stood back, his black eyes sparkling with contempt.

"How much?"

Henrietta put a shaking hand up to her bruised mouth. "I beg your pardon, my lord," she said faintly.

"I said, how much?" he demanded. "How much did you get from Gillingham and Brummell? You no doubt set your favors high. Well, madam, I am prepared to meet your price. I ask you again. How much?"

Henrietta took a few steps back from him until her back was against the polished wood of the counter.

"I do not know what you are talking about," she whispered.

"I am offering to set you up as my mistress," he said. "You may come with me in the morning to my lawyers, and we shall arrange the terms. I cannot promise to keep that harem of yours as well, but no doubt they are experienced enough by now to look after themselves."

"No!" cried Henrietta, white to the lips. "You cannot mean it. You took me to the theater, you introduced me to your aunt. You have been drinking!"

"I shall apologize to my aunt, and, no, I have not been drinking. I have never been more sober in my life. You are a pretty baggage, Henrietta, and 'fore God, you still manage to look the picture of innocence. Come here!"

Anger rose up in Henrietta, suffocating anger. "Get out!" she cried.

"Why?" His voice was cold, mocking. "I am very rich. Rich enough to purchase anything *you* have to offer."

"Get away!" said Henrietta shrilly, as he took a step nearer. "You *disgust* me."

"Oh, hoity-toity, miss. I never like bargaining. Is this how you put up your price?"

Henrietta felt beside her on the counter. Her hand encountered the thin stem of a tazza which held a gooseberry jelly. Henrietta had been proud of that jelly. She had added a little coloring to it. It was as green as grass, as green as jealousy.

As the earl took another purposeful step toward her, she raised the tazza and flung the contents full in his face.

"Hellcat!" he shouted, wiping green jelly from his face. "I'll have you for that!"

Henrietta went completely insane with anger. As she darted about the shop, as he tried to catch her, she threw everything at him she could lay her hands on—tarts, crystallized fruit, wet confects, dry confects, cream cakes, and followed it all up by hurling a whole regiment of marzipan soldiers at his head.

"Be damned to you," he shouted, blinded by cream and pastry. He scrubbed the mess from his face and strode to the door, opened it, and marched out into the street.

A large apple pie caught him right on the back of the head.

He hailed a passing hack and climbed in.

Henrietta sat down amid the wreck of her confectionery, amid the wreck of her dreams, and cried her eyes out. She was still sitting there, sobbing, when Charlotte, Josephine, and Miss Hissop came back.

Bitterly she sobbed out her tale of the earl's iniquities. Josephine and Charlotte began to cry as well. There was no doubt in their minds that Mr. Clifford and Lord Charles had the same low ideas about *them*. Just like Mr. Clifford and Lord Charles, the earl had *appeared* to show Henrietta every respect and attention before this last terrible visit. The stigma of being in trade weighed heavily on their souls. It stopped Josephine and Charlotte from thinking clearly. The attentions of such great personages as Lord Charles and Mr. Clifford had always seemed too good to be true.

Esau crept quietly in and set about clearing up the mess. He felt a mean and evil person. He was sure now that God would punish him. In fact, he became so sure of the divine wrath about to be visited on his head that he finally threw down his cleaning cloth into the bucket and sat down on the floor and added his sobs and wails to the general lamentation.

Henrietta was the first to dry her eyes. "London is a wicked and evil place," she said. "I was overambitious in setting up business here. Thank goodness we have made enough money so that we may close up here and open somewhere else."

"Where?" sobbed Josephine.

"Bath," said Henrietta. "That's it! We'll go to Bath. I could not bear to stay here, knowing everyone considered us no better than doxies."

"Could we not just go home?" ventured Miss Hissop.

"No," said Henrietta. "Josephine would be beaten, and there is not enough money yet to set up Charlotte for life. Esau must be taught the trade, and I must have a thriving business to turn over to him. He is a good and loyal servant."

Esau rolled about the floor in an agony of guilt and remorse when he heard Henrietta's words. He had been so unused to any kindness in the past that it had never crossed his mind that she would make provision for his future at all, let alone such a magnificent offer.

Henrietta knelt down beside him. "You take our troubles too much to heart. Do not cry, Esau. I really always wanted to go to Bath. And do you know, I don't care a fig for the Earl of Carrisdowne."

Esau stopped crying and sat up. "Do you mean that?" he asked eagerly.

"Yes, Esau," said Henrietta, clenching her fists. "I hate that man as I've never hated anyone in the whole of my life. Oh, and there is another reason why we must leave." She told them about Lady Clara. "So you see," she ended, "there is no point in trying to take her to court. It would only be my word against hers—and what judge is going to prosecute Lady Clara Sinclair? Let us get away from this wicked city before it kills us!''

Mr. Clifford and Lord Charles had gone to Newmarket to see Lord Charles's horse, Calamity, run in the races. They had not wanted to leave London, but it had been learned that Lord Charles's jockey was a trifle overweight, and although he was reported to be stewing between two featherbeds to get down to the right weight, Lord Charles felt he should be there in person to make sure the man was trying hard enough.

Mr. Clifford had a bet of a thousand pounds on Calamity. It was the largest bet he had ever laid on anything. He hated leaving Josephine, but he was determined to be on the spot to assist Lord Charles in bringing about a successful race.

The horse won, Mr. Clifford was considerably richer, and both men made their way back by easy stages to London. Life appeared very sunny and secure. Not for one moment did they doubt that the earl and Henrietta would be engaged on their return. It was over a week since they had seen the girls, and so they decided to call at Half Moon Street first.

"That's deuced odd," said Mr. Clifford as they turned the corner from Piccadilly.

"What is?"

"Look! No golden pineapple. It's gone."

"Probably taken it down to get it cleaned."

They drove up to the door of the shop. The windows were shuttered and the door boarded up. A sign on the door proclaimed the shop was available to rent.

"Gone!" Lord Charles pushed back his beaver hat and scratched his head. "They *can't* have gone."

"Oh, I have it," said Mr. Clifford. "You know what a high stickler Rupert is. He'll have got Henrietta to close down immediately. He'd never stand for having his fiancée working in a shop."

Lord Charles's face cleared. "That's bound to be the reason. Let's go to Upper Brook Street immediately and offer our congratulations."

Lord Carrisdowne, they were told in sepulchral tones, was in the study. They both breezed in and stopped short on the threshold. The earl was sitting in an armchair by the fire, a glass of brandy in his hand.

"Well, well," he said, his voice slightly slurred, "the lovers have returned. I can save you a visit to Bascombe's. Or perhaps you might have more success than I if you send your banker first."

"What are you talking about, Rupert?" Lord Charles walked forward and stood over his brother.

"Miss Henrietta Bascombe," said the earl in a weary voice, "is a slut and a whore. To think she sat in this house and told me she would do anything for money, and I believed she was referring to the selling of confections. She meant herself, her favors, her body. Gillingham and Brummell have already had the pleasure. She is nothing more than an abbess, running a genteel brothel with a row of pretty cakes as a smoke screen."

"Never!" cried Lord Charles. "I will not believe you. Charlotte Webster is the sweetest angel I ever beheld."

"Then, go and ask them if you do not believe me."

"But they've gone," said Mr. Clifford. "Where have they gone? The shop is closed and shuttered and being offered for rent."

The earl half closed his eyes as a great black wave of misery engulfed him. "So," he forced himself to say with a shrug, "they have fled, and London is well quit of them."

"Where did you come by this information? Surely Miss Bascombe never demanded money from you."

"Her servant told me," said the earl.

"Her *servant*!" Mr. Clifford gave a scornful laugh. "A boy she took from the workhouse. When did you ever pay any heed to servants' gossip?"

"The boy was crying with distress. I have no reason to doubt his word."

"But what in heaven's name did Miss Bascombe say when you taxed her with it? Or did you simply walk away and never see her again?"

The earl shook his head as if to clear it. After all, what *had* she said? He remembered vividly the look of shock and betrayal on her face. But *he could not be wrong*.

"She threw the contents of the shop at me."

"At you? At one of the richest men in England? And yet you still believe her to be mercenary?"

"She was playing for higher stakes. She had expected an offer of marriage. I took her to the play and introduced her to Lady Browne in front of everyone. I asked Miss Hissop's permission to call on her."

A mulish look settled on Mr. Clifford's face. "I don't believe it. I simply don't believe it for a minute. I think they are all as sweet and innocent as they appear. You're very high in the instep, Rupert, and I'm sure you readily believed the servant because you've always thought there was something demmed unladylike about them going into trade. Begad, man! I do not mind you bringing about the ruin of your own hopes, but to ruin my future and Charles's . . ."

The earl held up his hand. "Enough! Did I not receive just such protestations before when each of you was about to form a mésalliance with a disreputable female?"

"When real love comes along," said Lord Charles simply, "there ain't any doubt about it. You *know* . . . that is if you ain't blinded with your own pride. Where have they gone?"

"I neither know nor care."

"But you *must* know," said Mr. Clifford. "When you saw Bascombe's was closed . . ."

"I did not know it was closed. I have hardly stirred from this house for a week."

Mr. Clifford and Lord Charles exchanged surprised glances over the earl's head. So he *had* been hit harder than they had thought! It seemed Lord Carrisdowne had at last been wounded in his heart as much as in his pride.

"We'll find 'em," said Mr. Clifford. "They're bound to have told *somebody* where they were headed. You can't move a whole shop without someone stopping to ask where you're bound. And it isn't any use you trying to stop me, Rupert."

"*I* shan't," said the earl, filling his glass again. "I'm weary of the whole thing. The pair of you may go to hell for all I care. Just never mention Henrietta Bascombe to me again!"

At first neither Lord Charles nor Mr. Clifford could believe that the ladies of the confectionery had disappeared without a trace. They asked and asked. But no one had even found out where they had all come from in the first place.

As the days passed into weeks, and the Earl of Carrisdowne appeared at fewer and fewer fashionable functions, Mr. Clifford and Lord Charles became moody and depressed. Lord Charles saw as little of his brother as possible, and Mr. Clifford, seeing the earl in the street one day, pointedly crossed over to avoid him.

The earl tried to forget that scene in the confectioner's. But in the middle of restless, sleepless nights, Henrietta's shocked face would rise up to haunt him. The little voice, which at first had nagged at him that he should not have listened to Esau, gradually became a shout. He could have gone and taxed Brummell or Gillingham and asked them about their relations with Henrietta, but he shrank from doing so. They would either confirm his worst fears, or, if the girl proved to be innocent, his very questions might lead both men to think her a jade.

Lady Clara had been persistent, sending letters and presents. He had burned the letters and returned the presents. Finally he had become tired of finding her "passing just by chance" when he left the house and had given her a cruel set-down.

As the longing to see Henrietta became stronger and stronger, as he became more convinced he had damned her without a hearing, he became determined to find her. But inquiries at livery stables and coaching inns drew a blank. It was as if there had never been a Bascombe's, as if Henrietta, Josephine, Charlotte, and Miss Hissop had never existed.

Lord Alisdair Sinclair returned home one evening to find his sister, Lady Clara, in tears.

"Haven't seen you cry this age," he said. "What's to do?"

"It is Carrisdowne," said Lady Clara. "He told me if he found me waiting outside his door again, he would

need to order his servants to tell me to go away. He said
. . . he said he was tired of being *annoyed* by me."

"Never say you've been hanging about his doorstep
like a trollop?"

"No, it was coincidence, nothing more," lied Lady
Clara, not meeting his eyes. "I often walk down Upper
Brook Street on my way to the park."

Lord Alisdair wondered whether to point out that his
sister always went to Hyde Park in the carriage and
walked as little as possible but decided against it. Lady
Clara's temper could be vicious.

"Well," he said, "that's the way of it. He don't want
you. May as well cast your eye elsewhere. You've ruined a whole Season. Now we're all off to Brighton,
you'll be able to put him from your mind."

"No," said Lady Clara mutinously. "He loved me
once. I am convinced he will love me again."

"Don't look like it."

"It's that Bascombe woman."

"Can't be. No one's seen hide nor hair of her. Must
have got a fright after the fire."

"Toby Miles said t'other day that Carrisdowne had
emerged from the confectioner's covered in cream, and
before he could get into a hack, a pie came sailing out
and struck him on the back of the head."

"Did it now," grinned Lord Alisdair. "I'd give a
monkey to have seen that—the great and stately Carrisdowne getting his comeuppance. It looks, then, as if
Miss Bascombe took against him, doesn't it? I mean,
you don't go around shying pastry at someone you respect."

Lady Clara tapped her foot impatiently. "Listen! It is
no secret that Carrisdowne's servants are trying to find

out where the Bascombe creature has gone to. He must be obsessed with the woman.''

"You are all about in your upper chambers, sis. Leave Carrisdowne be. You will have gallants aplenty in Brighton.''

"I want Carrisdowne," said Lady Clara shrilly, reminding her brother forcefully of the days when they had both been in the nursery and baby Clara had wanted one of his toys.

"You can't have him," he said, "and let that be an end to it.''

"Even you have deserted me," said Lady Clara, beginning to sob again.

He looked at her impatiently. There was little room in his weak and selfish heart for love or affection, but what little there was, he reserved for his sister.

"Don't cry," he sighed. "I shall find the Bascombe woman. I'll let Carrisdowne find her for me. Our servants will be given instructions to ask his servants about his movements. As soon as he shows any signs of leaving town, we shall follow him. But how we are going to ruin La Bascombe is another matter.''

"Find her," said Lady Clara, drying her eyes, "and I shall think of something.''

Chapter Twelve

Although still one of the most beautiful towns in England, Bath had seen better days. When the great Beau Nash had acted as master of ceremonies, he had made the Bath assemblies as exclusive as Almack's. He had ruled with a rod of iron. Ladies who turned up at his assemblies not dressed according to his rigid standards were turned out. At the end of his life he had become helpless and poor and had died neglected and miserable. The inhabitants of Bath then erected a statue to this man they had suffered almost to starve.

His loss was felt keenly. Only a short time before Henrietta's arrival, two ladies of quality had quarreled in the ballroom. The rest of the company took part, some on one side and some on the other. Beau Nash was gone, and they stood in no awe of his successor. They became outrageous, and a real battle royal took place, and the floor of the ballroom was strewn with caps, lappets, curls and cushions, diamond pins and pearls.

The town was full of cardsharpers and adventurers,

and it had more of death's advance guard than anywhere else in Britain as the sick and self-indulgent filled the pump room to take the waters.

Henrietta had been lucky in securing the lease of a shop in the center of the town. With it went the apartments above so that they each had a bedroom and a cozy parlor.

Although she herself was regarded as highly unfashionable, Henrietta's confectionery was not. Her cakes and confections insured her success, and so long as Miss Bascombe and her ladies remembered their place and did not try to attend any of the assemblies, then society was pleased to give her its custom.

Henrietta was disappointed. She had hoped to provide Josephine and Charlotte with some social life. But the only men who seemed interested in any of them were seedy adventurers prepared to marry into a profitable business.

Josephine and Charlotte appeared resigned to their fate, Esau was receiving a full training in the making of confectionery from Henrietta, and Miss Hissop enjoyed their unadventurous life of hard work and sedate walks.

Henrietta marveled at her friends' seemingly cheerful demeanors. She herself kept as busy as possible, but there was always a dull ache at her heart, always an irrational surge of hope when she saw a tall black-haired man at a distance. The most bitter thing she had to live with was the realization that she had fallen in love with the Earl of Carrisdowne, and though her mind daily lectured her emotions on their folly, there was nothing she could seem to do to alleviate the hurt and the longing.

The sight of the earl's sister, Lady Sarah, sitting in a corner of the shop, wolfing cakes and sweetmeats, did nothing to help. Despite her plump appearance and fat cheeks, Lady Sarah had the earl's black eyes and high-bridged nose.

Henrietta knew the earl would be furious at his sister eating so many cakes, but Henrietta could hardly turn her out of the shop.

And then one day, the Dowager Countess of Carris-downe accompanied Lady Sarah on one of her visits. From their raised voices, Henrietta learned that Lady Sarah was supposed to have been visiting her music teacher all the times she was actually in the confection-er's.

"So this is where you go," demanded the countess, black eyes snapping, "and I would not have found out except I met that music teacher of yours in the street and asked him why he did not call at our house to give you lessons. He said you had had one lesson of him, and then had given him a letter, supposed to have come from me, canceling the rest of the lessons."

The countess waved an imperious hand and sum-moned Henrietta. "I believe you are in charge of this establishment," she said.

"Yes, my lady," replied Henrietta, who knew the countess by sight, having often seen her passing the shop, attended by her footman. She looked very like her son the earl, although her hair was snow-white.

"In future, I beg you, do not supply my daughter with any confections. Is that understood?"

"Yes, my lady," said Henrietta meekly.

"I think it is ridiculous," pouted Lady Sarah. "Skinny ladies are not the fashion, as well you know, Mama."

"A certain pleasing roundness is one thing," said the countess acidly. "Letting oneself become fat and spotty is quite another."

"May I take your order, my lady?" asked Henrietta.

"No, you may not." Then her harsh features softened. A sweet smile lighted up her face, reminding Henrietta painfully of her son. "I do not mean to be angry with *you*, miss . . ."

"Miss Bascombe, if it please your ladyship."

"Ah, of course, you are *Bascombe's*. Well, Miss Bascombe, I think it monstrous enterprising for such a young and obviously gently bred lady as yourself to make her own way in life. I always did admire spirit in a woman. But this silly girl of mine must be protected from herself. Nonetheless, I am giving a dinner in two weeks time—let me see, Friday the thirteenth—and would like you to send a centerpiece to my home. Nothing military. Something pretty will do very well. Do you know where I live?"

"Yes, my lady," said Henrietta. "The Royal Crescent, number 9."

Henrietta had once walked past the house, drawn there by lovesickness, dreaming of seeing the earl arriving to call on his mother, although the gossips said he avoided Bath like the plague.

"You may send me your bill along with the centerpiece," added the countess. "I believe in settling my accounts promptly."

"Dinner is at five—I do not believe in these newfangled hours—so have it to me by four in the afternoon at the latest. Come along, Sarah."

Sarah trailed out miserably after her mother. They started arguing again as soon as they reached the street. Henrietta turned away to serve another customer and therefore did not hear the countess's threat. "You are become unmanageable, Sarah. This is what befalls me for having a child so late in life. I am too weary to cope with your nonsense. I shall write to Rupert this day and tell him of your lies and of your visits to that confectioner's.''

The Earl of Carrisdowne had just returned from Brighton. He had been summoned there by the Prince Regent to join the round of pleasure. Brighton had been one frivolity after another. Lady Clara had been there, her hungry eyes following him round the room when he had attended one of the assemblies at the Ship Inn. He began to wonder whether she might not be a trifle unbalanced, and that thought made him gloomier than ever. It appeared a female would need to have more than a touch of madness to fall in love with *him*.

He set about making preparations to move to his estates. Mr. Clifford and Lord Charles, who had also gone to Brighton, were still there. They had recovered some of their spirits, but they still shunned the earl.

How easily they seem to have forgotten, thought the earl. For his part, he was still plagued day and night by longing for Henrietta. The more he thought about her, the more bitterly ashamed he became of his easy belief in Esau's story. The Duke of Gillingham and his duchess had also been in Brighton. He had observed them closely, and it was forcefully brought home to him that the old duke had no interest in any female whatsoever—even his wife.

He sat down to deal with the post that had piled up in his absence, separating bills from invitations and invitations from personal letters.

He started by reading his personal correspondence first. There were various letters from relatives and one from his mother. He recognized her heavy seal. The one from his mother would no doubt contain more complaints about Sarah. He decided to leave it to the last.

When he finally opened it after snapping the heavy seal and reflecting his mother must have used one whole stick of wax, the word *Bascombe's* seemed to leap up out of the page. His hands shook slightly as he smoothed out the parchment and carefully read the letter.

In it, his mother, as usual, complained of Sarah's gluttony. She added that Sarah had been frequenting a confectioner's when she should have been at her music lessons. *Not that it is not an exceptionally respectable establishment,* the countess had written, *and the little lady who runs Bascombe's appears to be a superior type of person.*

Bath!

The earl slowly lowered the letter. Henrietta was in Bath.

A bare two days before the earl had discovered the whereabouts of the missing Miss Bascombe, Lord Alisdair Sinclair sat in a Brighton coffeehouse, nursing an aching head. He could not tell whether the damage had been done by last night's rack punch or last night's wine or last night's brandy.

A surly gentleman slumped down at the table beside him. Lord Alisdair raised red-rimmed eyes and looked into the unsavory blue-jowled features of the Honorable Toby Miles. ''Under the weather, hey?'' demanded Mr. Miles with a grin.

Lord Alisdair averted his eyes with a shudder. Mr. Miles's teeth had all been filed to points—the latest fashion among the bloods, who wanted to spit through their teeth like coachmen.

''Bad as that,'' said Mr. Miles. He fished in one of

his large pockets. ''Try that. Set you right in no time at all.''

Lord Alisdair took the little bottle Mr. Miles was holding out to him. His gaze sharpened as he read the legend BASCOMBE'S ELIXIR on the side.

''Where did you get this,'' he asked as casually as he could.

''M'father sent me a dozen. Very old, m'father. In Bath to drink that filthy water. Got gout.''

''And he bought this in Bath?''

''Stand to reason, don't it? Bascombe is probably some apothecary or quack. Place is crawlin' with 'em.''

''There was a Bascombe's on Half Moon Street,'' said Lord Alisdair, ''which sold an elixir.''

''Well, I wouldn't know that, would I?'' demanded Mr. Miles testily. ''Never go near the place if I can help it. No race meetings in London; no prizefights neither.''

''And your father, has he been in London this year?''

''Not left Bath this twenty year past. Are you going to drink that stuff or aren't you. 'Cos if you ain't, I'll have it back.''

''No,'' said Lord Alisdair, sliding the bottle into his own pocket. ''Take it later. Just remembered. Have an urgent appointment with my sister.''

Life had never been better for Esau. It was a warm August. Bath was bathed in sunlight. Henrietta appeared to have forgotten the earl, the business was flourishing, and he, Esau, was to have the honor of making the centerpiece for the Countess of Carrisdowne. At first he had hesitated, frightened of running into the earl. He made the excuse to Henrietta that he was frightened of Lord Carrisdowne, as only a frightful person would have treated Miss Bascombe so badly. Henrietta assured him the earl was not in Bath, and, from gossip she had overheard, was not likely to visit the place. He had said he detested the town.

Henrietta had drawn up the plans for the centerpiece, and Esau worked long days and nights over it. At last he had created Pan sitting by the toffee rushes playing his sugar pipe while shepherds and shepherdesses danced about. Sometimes his touch was still too clumsy, and Henrietta had to help him finish some of the figures, but most of it was all his own work, and he was very proud of it.

The only thing that marred his pleasure was that he had to deliver it on Friday the thirteenth. What could be more unlucky! But Henrietta said roundly that this fear of Friday was nothing more than an old superstition.

Henrietta decided to let Esau deliver the centerpiece alone. The sooner she forgot all about the Earl of Carrisdowne the better, and seeing members of his family would do nothing to help.

Esau set out to climb up the cobbled streets to the Royal Crescent, pushing the handcart with the centerpiece on it.

Like most religious people of his time, Esau was also deeply superstitious. Huge black thunderclouds were building up to the west, and the sky above was brassy. The farther he got from the shop, the more apprehensive he became. Thunder grumbled in the distance. Esau had an uneasy feeling he was being followed. From time to time, he stopped and turned about. It was always as if someone had just dived for cover before he was able to set eyes on him. The thundery air felt heavy with menace. Despite the heat, Esau shivered in his plush livery.

Then he heard the light patter of footsteps behind him.

Marion Chesney

"Young man!" called a hoarse voice.

Esau turned about and let out a squawk of fright. A Gypsy woman was standing there in her black and red clothes. Her black hair was coarse and matted under a scarf decorated with gold coins. The fringed edges of her shawl rose and fell in the hot, damp wind.

"What do you want of me?" demanded Esau, backing away.

"It's Friday the thirteenth, Esau," cackled the Gypsy.

"How do you know my name?"

"I know everything," said the Gypsy. "I know there is bad luck everywhere this day. If you do not accept my help, your pretty sweetmeats in that cart will be ruined."

Esau rallied. "Then, you don't know everything," he said. "This here is a centerpiece what I made myself."

"You are a good boy, Esau, and I would help you. Let me sprinkle a little magic sugar over it and all will be well."

Esau relaxed. If that's all she wanted to do, let her. A little sugar dusting wouldn't mar the centerpiece. And he would be shot of her."

"Oh, go ahead," he said.

She took a silver sugar shaker out of her pocket. Esau gently parted the tissue paper wrapping, and the Gypsy shook the shaker over the centerpiece.

"Can I go now?" mumbled Esau.

"Go, and remember, you will thank me for my help before this day is over."

She turned on her heel and strode away with long mannish strides. Esau picked up the handles of his cart and continued on his journey.

What a strange encounter! And yet, he felt happier as

he quickened his pace to reach the Countess of Carrisdowne's before the storm broke. Thank goodness he had left early. It was only three-thirty.

Miss Hissop glanced nervously up at the sky as she walked in the parade gardens. So kind of dear Henrietta to allow her so much free time, but it looked as if it might rain. She glanced at the watch pinned to her bosom. Five o'clock. Perhaps just a look at the river and then she would return to the shop. She always found it soothing to the nerves to watch the water tumbling over the weir.

As she stood behind a pillar on the promenade above the roaring water, she heard a man on the other side of the pillar call out, "There you are, sis. Well, the deed's been done. You might have performed the murder yourself."

"It isn't murder, Alisdair," answered a clear, high, arrogant voice. "Probably only make them sick. Where was the delivery going to?"

Miss Hissop stiffened.

"The Countess of Carrisdowne, no less."

"Zooks! Would you poison the very man I am trying to marry?"

"Relax, my sweet. Carrisdowne was reported to be in London when we left Brighton. It is well-known he never comes to Bath. You do not care madly for his family."

"No, I do not," said the female voice. "The countess said in my hearing I was too bold a minx."

"When was that?"

"Early this year."

"Oh, the vengeance of Lady Clara."

Miss Hissop trembled. This, then, must be Lady Clara

Sinclair, and the man called Alisdair must be her brother. What had they done?''

As if in answer to her unspoken question, Lady Clara asked, ''And how did you do your dark deed?''

''Well, as you know, we took turns watching the shop and found out the names of everyone in it, apart from La Bascombe. So when you told me their servant was setting out with a delivery, I rushed back to our lodgings and changed into that Gypsy-woman costume—you know, the one I wore to the Pantheon two years ago. I followed this Esau and told him to let me shake a little lucky sugar on what turned out to be a centerpiece. Of course he let me, being as superstitious as any other peasant. So not only will La Bascombe be ruined, but very probably hanged for murder as well. Nothing like a touch of arsenic to brighten up the dinner party.''

With wide frightened eyes Miss Hissop looked down at the watch on her bosom. Five-fifteen and Henrietta had said the dinner was at five!

Miss Hissop slid out from behind the pillar and started to run. There was no time to go to the shop first. She, Ismene Hissop, must save Henrietta from the gallows!

Chapter Thirteen

The Earl of Carrisdowne looked quite satanic, as one elderly guest at his mother's dinner table remarked to her companion. He had arrived just before the dinner was about to begin and had been "press-ganged" as he put it to himself, by his mother to attend.

His original plan had been to change out of his traveling clothes and immediately walk down to the center of the town and seek out Henrietta. But the rain had begun to descend in torrents almost immediately after his arrival, and he did not want to be pestered by maternal exclamations over his desire to plunge back out into the storm. Because Bath was so hilly, very few used carriages and sedan chairs with their chairmen in dark-blue coats and cocked hats were a feature of the town. All the countess's servants were on duty at the dinner party, and to send a footman down into the town to find a sedan would occasion even more surprise.

He attended the dinner party with great reluctance. Sarah, he noticed sourly, was fatter than ever. The rest of the guests, to his jaundiced eye, appeared to be in their dotage.

Great cracks of thunder following blinding flashes of lightning made the elderly guests twitter with alarm. At least, thought the earl, the dinner would not last very long. His mother did not believe in multiple courses. The meal had begun promptly at five. Surely it would soon be over and leave him free to look for Bascombe's.

"I have a surprise for you," he realized his mother was saying. She clapped her hands. The double doors to the dining room were thrown open, and two footmen carried in a centerpiece and placed it reverently in the middle of the long table. There were admiring oohs and aahs as the company creaked from their seats to gather around it for a better look.

"Isn't Bascombe's marvelous?" said the elderly lady next to the earl.

"I used to visit their shop when they were in London," he said. "Miss Henrietta Bascombe was famous there for her centerpieces."

"It seems such a shame to destroy it, but it *is* for eating," said the countess. She signaled to the butler that the centerpiece was to be removed to a side table and cut up.

Two footmen walked forward to pick up the confectionery; the elderly guests resumed their seats; Lady Sarah eyed the centerpiece greedily. Then before the centerpiece could be removed there came a sound of crashing doors and a female voice screaming.

Everyone froze.

The earl rose half out of his seat.

There came the sounds of a scuffle from the hall outside.

Then the double doors burst open, and Miss Hissop

154

stood on the threshold with a footman hanging tightly onto either arm. Her clothes were drenched and sticking to her body. Her face was a bluish color.

"Don't eat it," she wailed. "It is poisoned."

"What is poisoned?" said the countess testily. "Who is this madwoman? Take her away. Ladies, gentlemen, we will continue with our meal as if nothing had happened."

Before the earl could intercede, Miss Hissop screamed *"No!"* With the strength of the madwoman the countess believed her to be, she shook off the restraining arms of the footmen. She hurtled across the room and leaped into the air. With a cry of triumph, she landed belly-down right in the middle of the centerpiece. *Smash!* Pieces of confectionery flew about. A cloud of sugar dust rose in the air and hung like a nimbus around the candles.

Ladies fainted and screamed. Servants tried to drag Miss Hissop off the wreck of the centerpiece, but she clung on grimly, kicking out behind her at her tormentors with a serviceable pair of half boots.

"Leave her!" The Earl of Carrisdowne walked down the table and leaning down, peered into Miss Hissop's contorted face.

"Miss Hissop," he said mildly. "Are you trying to tell us that centerpiece is poisoned?"

"Yes," gasped Miss Hissop. "Lady Clara and her brother tricked Esau, our servant . . . shook poison over it . . . Alisdair is her brother, is he not?"

"No one shall eat any of it," said the earl firmly.

"Oh, thank goodness," sobbed Miss Hissop. "They would have poisoned your family and guests and seen Henrietta hang."

It all seemed so farfetched, so incredible. The guests were clamoring for explanations.

Lord Carrisdowne helped Miss Hissop from the table. She was a sorry mess, soaking clothes covered in sugar. He told the footmen to remove the centerpiece, to sweep up every bit of sugar, put it in a bag, and keep it in the kitchens.

"Will *no one* tell me what is going on?" cried the countess. "Who is this woman?"

"She is one of the ladies from Bascombe's," said the earl. "Go on with your dinner party, Mama. Let me take Miss Hissop into the study until I get to the bottom of this."

They watched in silence as the earl led the now-weeping Miss Hissop from the room. Then as the doors closed behind them, a babble of noise broke out. The elderly guests were fast recovering and beginning to enjoy the unexpected excitement.

In the study, the earl placed Miss Hissop in a chair in front of the fire and then stood looking down at her. "I shall make sure you have a change of clothes and something to help you recover from your shock. But it appears to me you have made a very serious charge. Begin at the beginning. Take a deep breath and talk slowly and clearly."

Miss Hissop did as she was bade. Although she still strongly disapproved of the earl, it was wonderful to feel that the terrible responsibility of dealing with the nightmare situation had been taken from her shoulders.

She took a deep breath and began. "I was walking by the river when . . ."

"Where is Miss Hissop?" said Henrietta. She opened the kitchen door and let in a breath of sweet rain-washed air.

"She probably took shelter during the storm," said Charlotte. "It is only just over. She will be here presently."

Henrietta leaned against the doorjamb and looked out into the weedy garden at the back of the shop. "I do hope the countess liked the centerpiece," she said.

"Bound to" came Esau's voice from behind her. "I was worried about it being Friday the thirteenth and all. But after that Gypsy woman sprinkled it with her lucky sugar, I reckoned that nothing bad would happen."

Henrietta turned slowly round.

"You did not tell me about any Gypsy woman, Esau."

"It was when I was on me road to the countess's. Oh, it was that hot pushing the barrow up them hills. She run up after me, and she even knew my name."

Henrietta felt a stab of fear. "And . . . ?" she prompted.

Esau told the story about the lucky sugar and how it must have been very lucky because the countess herself had descended to the kitchens to have a look at the centerpiece and had given him a florin.

"There is no such thing as lucky sugar," said Henrietta. "Esau, if someone who wished us ill put something into one of our confections and one of our customers were harmed because of it, then Bascombe's would go out of business."

Esau flushed. Friday, unlucky Friday, would soon be over. Nothing terrible had happened. He felt he had been very silly in believing the Gypsy woman.

"I don't think she meant no harm, mistress," said Esau.

"No," said Henrietta, "I don't suppose she did. The

only person who has ever really threatened us is Lady Clara, and it's a mercy she is not in Bath.''

Josephine was stirring something in a pot over the fire. She brushed back a damp lock of chestnut hair from her forehead and said, "But she is! I meant to tell you, but we were so very busy today, and . . . and . . . I saw a young man walking along Milsom Street, and he looked so very like Mr. Clifford that I began to feel miserable again and could think of nothing else *but* him.''

Henrietta licked her dry lips. "When did you see her?''

"This morning, walking past the shop. I am not exactly sure it *was* she, for as you know I never met her, but one of the customers exclaimed, 'Surely that is Lady Clara Sinclair.' ''

"Do you think," said Henrietta, "that Lady Clara might have dressed as a Gypsy woman and put something in the centerpiece to discredit me? Something to make the countess ill?''

"No," said Charlotte. "I am sure she tried to burn down Bascombe's because she was jealous of you. It was well-known she had hopes of marrying Carrisdowne. But . . . well, dear Henrietta, no one could possibly believe Carrisdowne has the slightest interest in you *now*.''

"I suppose not," said Henrietta.

But worry nagged at her mind. And where was Miss Hissop? Henrietta decided to walk up to the Royal Crescent and just look at the house and perhaps watch the guests leave. If they appeared normal, happy, and animated, then she would know nothing bad had happened. And she could look for Miss Hissop on the way.

Not wanting to frighten the others with her worries, she murmured something about going out to get a breath of air. She took off her apron and, still wearing her shop outfit of striped cotton gown and frilly cap, she set out through the rain-washed streets.

People were beginning to move about again. As she turned into the circus, she heard herself being hailed from a sedan. The aged face of one of her regular customers, Mrs. Cunningham, peered out. "Miss Bascombe," she called. "How is Miss Hissop?" Miss Hissop was a great favorite with the elderly ladies who visited the shop.

"I hope she is well," said Henrietta. "She has not yet returned, and I admit I am becoming anxious."

"I think the poor lady has had some sort of brain seizure," said Mrs. Cunningham. "Just when the storm broke, as Mrs. Brockett and I were sheltering under the colonnade, Miss Hissop ran past. She looked quite deranged, and she was muttering 'Arsenic . . . poison . . .' as she ran.

"Thank you," gasped Henrietta. She set off at a run, the streamers of her cap flying. The Gypsy woman! Miss Hissop must have found something out.

Panic lent her wings. She did not stop to look at the countess's house as she had planned but hammered with her fists at the front door.

The butler opened the door, and Henrietta flew past him into the hall, shouting, "The centerpiece. What happened? Have they eaten it?"

"No," said a cool voice from the shadows of the hall. "No, Henrietta. Come here. It is I. Carrisdowne."

She flew toward him, questions tumbling one after the other from her lips.

Quietly he said, "Miss Hissop saved us all from poisoning. Come into the study, and I shall tell you all. Miss Hissop is abovestairs resting. She has had a bad fright.''

They stood in the study, facing each other in front of the fire, each thinking how very different this was from the meeting of which they had both dreamed.

The earl looked very grand and formal. Henrietta, amid all her worries, wished in a very feminine way she was wearing something other than her shop clothes.

In a cool, steady voice the earl told Henrietta of Lady Clara's crime. Henrietta sat down suddenly, her legs shaking.

"It is as well I recognized her," said the earl. "For she did look deranged. Had I not been there, then I am sure my mother would have succeeded in getting the servants to throw her out.

"Although she succeeded in smashing the centerpiece, little parts of it had gone flying about the table, and someone like my greedy sister Sarah might have picked a piece up.

"The authorities have gone to arrest Lady Clara. The centerpiece has been taken to the apothecary's. I am sure traces of arsenic will be found. She is mad, quite mad. I began to suspect as much when I saw her in Brighton. And yet, earlier this year, I was happy to enjoy her company."

"She was the one who arranged for Bascombe's to be burned down," said Henrietta. "I would have told you, but I only learned that evening . . . that evening you . . .'' Her voice trailed away, and she looked miserably at the fire.

"Ah, yes, that evening," he said. His voice sounded stiff and cold. "I met your servant, Esau. It was he who told me you had already sold yourself to Brummell and Gillingham.''

''Esau? Nonsense. Esau is devoted to me. What reason would he have to tell such monstrous lies? And what reason had you, my lord, to believe such stories even if he did tell you such things? Perhaps because that monstrous pride of yours was all too ready to believe the worst of a woman who stooped to run her own shop!''

''Listen,'' he said desperately. ''I admit—''

The door opened, and the countess walked in. ''There you are!'' she cried. ''Ah, Miss Bascombe, you have no doubt come to collect Miss Hissop. Rupert, the watch, the constables, and the magistrate are all in the hall to see you. Lady Clara and her brother have somehow managed to escape out the back door of their lodgings, and no one can find them.''

''Very well, Mama,'' said the earl. ''Miss Bascombe . . .''

''I shall attend to Miss Bascombe. Please hurry, Rupert, and see to those gentlemen.''

The earl left. His mother signaled to Henrietta to follow her upstairs.

''I am sure you will find her quite recovered,'' said the countess. ''What a drama! My dinner party will be the talk of Bath.''

Which, reflected Henrietta bleakly, was one way of looking at attempted mass murder.

Miss Hissop, attired in one of the countess's best gowns and pelisses, not to mention one of the countess's smart bonnets, chattered the whole way back to the shop about her adventures. She seemed more overwhelmed by the countess's condescension than by any of the drama of her heroic rescue. ''Put in the *best* bedroom,

my dear, and attended by the countess's own lady's maid
. . . not put in the kitchens, which one would have expected them to do, considering our class of person . . .
or rather the class of person we have become by being
in trade. And Carrisdowne! So opportune that he was
there. No one else recognized me, for although some of
the ladies were our customers, I was so wet, so wild,
my own sainted mother would not have recognized me!''

"Yes, we are that class of person now,'' said Henrietta bleakly. "It was indeed condescending of Carrisdowne to entertain me in the study when I was dressed
in my shop clothes.''

"Yes, wasn't it?'' said Miss Hissop brightly. "And
the clothes the dear countess gave me. I would like to
be buried in them with a little note, you know, pinned
on my bosom giving the name of the donor. I might get
a better place in heaven that way, don't you think?''

"I can't think,'' said Henrietta crossly. "My head
aches. Oh, Miss Hissop, you are a heroine, and I have
no right to snap at you. I am an ungrateful girl.''

"Not at all. No one can call Henrietta Bascombe ungrateful. Think how this affair will help our trade? Bascombe's will be crowded tomorrow.''

"I have no doubt,'' said Henrietta wearily, thinking
that they must prepare extra cakes and sweetmeats.

"And Carrisdowne,'' said Miss Hissop, peering at
Henrietta's face in the darkness. "Had you not told me
of his insolent behavior to you, I would not have believed it. So courteous, so nice in his manners!''

"Miss Hissop, it appears for some reason Esau told
him I was a slut.''

"Esau?''

"Yes, Esau.''

"Well, blood will out. That sort of low person always betrays their origins."

"Not another word about Esau until I question that young man," said Henrietta firmly.

But when they arrived at the shop, Henrietta had to wait patiently while Miss Hissop showed off her clothes and told the astounded Josephine, Charlotte, and Esau of their adventures. Esau was white to the lips at the thought of what might have happened if Miss Hissop had not overheard Lady Clara and her brother. He went even whiter as Miss Hissop began to babble on about the Earl of Carrisdowne.

They were all standing in the shop. "Why do you not take Miss Hissop up to the parlor," said Henrietta, "and hear the rest of the story in comfort. Not you, Esau. You stay with me."

"Got pots to wash," said Esau, edging toward the kitchen door.

"Wait, Esau," commanded Henrietta sharply. The others threw her curious looks as they made their way out.

Henrietta waited in silence until she was sure they were all settled upstairs in the parlor. Then she turned to Esau. "Why?" she said. "Why did you tell Carrisdowne those filthy lies."

Esau fell to his knees, a miserable-looking figure.

"I am waiting," said Henrietta sternly.

"I was frightened," said Esau. "I thought if you married, then I would be sent back to the workhouse. I wasn't to get me wages until June. All I wanted to do was to put off the engagement until then. Oh, mistress, you don't know the fear o' the workhouse, the smell, the hunger, the cold. How was I to know you wouldn't cast me off? I never met anyone like you afore. In the workhouse, we're mean and savage like beasts cos that's what being poor does to a body. You got to care for no one but yourself. For if you don't, you die.''

He burst into tears, bending his head to the floor and covering his face with his hands.

"You did wrong, said Henrietta. "You must never tell lies again, Esau.''

Tears were spurting through Esau's fingers.

"Oh, don't cry, Esau,'' sighed Henrietta. "If only you had told me. . . . But he believed you, and I do not want any man who would believe such things of me.'' She walked over to him and drew him to his feet. "Do not cry anymore. Go to your room, and pray that tomorrow will bring a new life, new hope, and a new Esau.''

When Esau had stumbled from the room, Henrietta took off her cap and tossed it on the counter. With her hands on her hips, she surveyed the shop. "This is my domain,'' she said aloud. "I never really accepted it. But here I am, Henrietta Bascombe, spinster of Bath, and shopkeeper for life.''

She went into the kitchen, took her sheaf of recipes, and sat down at the kitchen table and began to read through them.

She had not been so ambitious in Bath as she had been in London with her confections. But tomorrow would be a bumper day. She was a shopkeeper. She must cash in on her notoriety.

Josephine and Charlotte came in, asking if they could help, but Henrietta wanted to be alone and sent them to bed.

Josephine stopped outside the door of her room. "She looks so grim,'' she whispered to Charlotte. "When I heard Carrisdowne was there, I could not help hoping . . .''

Charlotte miserably shook her head. ''There is no hope in Henrietta's face, and that means no hope for us.''

Henrietta worked on, glad to be alone, glad to have her work to keep her thoughts at bay. It was approaching midnight when she heard a gentle tap at the shop door.

Lady Clara! That was Henrietta's first terrified shock. Then she told herself that with the law looking for her, it would be unlikely that Lady Clara would call at Bascombe's. But Lady Clara *must* be mad, and who knew what a madwoman would do next?

Henrietta walked softly through the open kitchen door into the shop. She had turned the back shop into a kitchen rather than to have to work in the original kitchen, which was in an airless basement.

''Who is there?'' she called softly.

''Carrisdowne.''

Henrietta opened the door.

''What do you want, my lord?'' she demanded, barring the way. ''The others are asleep.''

''Oh, let me in,'' he said wearily. ''I have much to tell you.''

''Very well.'' Her voice was curt. ''Come into the kitchen. I can continue my work while you talk.''

He followed her into the kitchen. Lips primed into a firm line, Henrietta stooped over the fire, stirring hot sugar and fruit juice in a pot.

''Turn around,'' he commanded. ''I must see your face.''

Henrietta carefully removed the spoon from the pot

165

and laid it on the hob. She turned about, arms folded. "Yes?" she said coldly.

"What I want to say to you is . . . what I must tell you. Damn it, Henrietta, my heart has been breaking, and you must say you will be my wife, because I love you; so don't stand there glaring at me, or I will *shake* you."

"You believed all those lies Esau told you."

"Pride. Wretched pride. What did I know of you? Henrietta, let me put it another way. If you do not forgive me and marry me, I shall wring your neck!"

Henrietta stood staring at him. He strode up to her and took her by the shoulders. "Well, what is it?" he said harshly. "A wrung neck, or marriage."

"Oh, Rupert," sighed Henrietta. "Yes."

"Thank you," he said formally. "Now, take note of my restraint, Henrietta. I am not about to kiss you and maul you. I respect you."

"When will we be married?" asked Henrietta, her eyes like stars.

"Just as soon as I can arrange it. Send all this," his arm encompassed all the pastries and jellies, "to the workhouse. Bascombe's will not open tomorrow. You can take down that golden pineapple over the door and keep it as a souvenir."

"What of Josephine and Charlotte?"

"I have already written this evening to Charles and Guy. I am sure they will arrive with all possible speed."

"But Esau?"

"Surely you are not still concerned with that miserable, lying whelp!"

"Oh, Rupert, only hear why he did it." Henrietta told him Esau's morbid fear of being sent back to the workhouse. "And I still plan to let him run the business," said Henrietta stubbornly.

"My sweeting, you may do as you please. I think one day I may be able to forgive Esau."

Henrietta, suddenly shy, turned back to the fire and began to stir the pot again.

"Lady Clara has been found," he said, and that brought Henrietta about to face him again. "There was no sign of Lord Alisdair. Clara was found wandering in the fields outside Bath. It appears she has completely lost her senses."

"But Lord Alisdair is still at large!"

"Lord Alisdair did what he did out of love of his sister. He is weak and shiftless."

"Was she in love with you? Is that why she tried to ruin me?"

"I believe that to be the case. You would have been up on a charge of murder if it had not been for your intrepid Miss Hissop."

"I have not yet had the full story. I know she smashed the centerpiece. Did she do it with her fists."

"No," said the earl. "She . . . sh-she . . ." He collapsed in gales of laughter.

"Rupert! What *did* she do?"

The earl pulled himself together with an effort. "She took a flying leap and landed right in the center of your confection and hung on to the table like grim death. Bath has never seen anything like it."

Henrietta began to laugh.

"How wonderful to see you happy again," he said softly. "Come here until I kiss you."

"You respect me," said Henrietta, her eyes dancing. "You will not kiss me or maul me or . . . oh, *Rupert.*"

He pulled her into his arms and kissed her breathless.

Then he sat down at the kitchen table and took her on his knee and began to make love to her with single-minded thoroughness, taking them both off into the dizzy realms of passion while the golden pineapple outside the confectioner's creaked in the rising wind, and the syrup boiled over on the stove.

A Dad of His Own
Gail Gaymer Martin

Steeple
Hill®

Published by Steeple Hill Books™

STEEPLE HILL BOOKS

Steeple
Hill®

Recycling programs
for this product may
not exist in your area.

ISBN-13: 978-0-373-87657-0

A DAD OF HIS OWN

www.SteepleHill.com

Printed in U.S.A.

May your unfailing love rest upon us, O Lord,
even as we put our hope in you.

— *Psalms* 33:22

As always, love and thanks to my husband and best friend, Bob, who blesses me with his support, devotion and especially his sense of humor. Thanks from the bottom of my heart to my agent, Pam Hopkins of Hopkins Literary Associates, and to my editor, Patience Smith. They have both been cheerleaders from the beginning of this amazing career, providing guidance and support, with many laughs added to the mix.

Chapter One

Lexie Carlson peeked into the meeting room of Mothers of Special Kids. She hated being late, and the reason for her delay had plunged her spirit to the pits. Despite trying to slip in unnoticed, her friend Kelsey Rhodes, the meeting moderator, spotted her. She sidled the few steps to Lexie's side, a frown etched on her face. "Something wrong?"

Lexie shook her head, uncomfortable with Kelsey's attention, especially with the intriguing guest speaker standing nearby. A grin curved his full lips, and smile lines crinkled the edge of his gray eyes canopied by the thick blond lashes. His honey-colored hair glinted with copper highlights.

As much as she wanted to shift the focus, she leaned closer to Kelsey, managing as pleasant a look as she could. "No. Just a phone call." Hoping to end the questions, she slipped into a nearby chair and turned to the front.

Thank goodness Kelsey had moved away, relief spreading across her face. Relief. Lexie welcomed the expression from women like her who faced life with seriously ill children. Their support brought her here weekly and had become her mainstay.

"As I was saying," Kelsey said, sending a teasing smile her way, "I'm glad so many of you are here today since we have a special guest." She motioned toward the good-looking man a few feet away from Lexie.

Something about him captured Lexie's attention. His gray eyes glided past her with a twinkle that matched his grin. A giddy feeling swept over her, causing her to grin back. The ridiculous reaction unsettled her.

Kelsey beamed at the women. "This is Ethan Fox, who sits on the board of Dreams Come True Foundation, and he's here to tell us about a wonderful opportunity for you and your family."

He swung his hand in a brief wave. "Happy to be here."

The women applauded.

Lexie liked his voice, warm and rich as a cinnamon bun fresh from the oven. Guilty pleasure swept over her at the thought of the sugary treat. It was one of her vices.

Kelsey motioned Ethan forward. He strode to the center, slipping one hand into his pocket while the other clutched what appeared to be a stack of brochures. His shirt had thin blue stripes on a white background. Lexie liked the way he coordinated his attire with his beige and navy tie. He looked like a spit-polished executive minus the suit jacket.

Ethan's gaze locked with hers and he smiled.

A flush warmed her neck, and Lexie glanced away, but the look hadn't escaped her friend. She ambled closer to Lexie and arched a brow. Lexie drew in a breath and gave a quick shake of her head, immediately wishing she hadn't responded to Kelsey's implication.

"I hope most of you have heard about the Dreams Come True Foundation." Ethan scanned the group of women.

His comment yanked Lexie's attention. She'd never heard of his organization. She surveyed her peers to see how many had. Only a few women nodded. Most gave Ethan blank looks that probably matched hers.

He shook his head. "I'm disappointed. I had hoped most

of you knew about Dreams Come True, but this makes me especially pleased that I'm here today." He handed Kelsey a stack of brochures and refocused on the women.

Kelsey stood at the end of the first row of chairs and counted out the brochures, but Lexie didn't keep her attention on her friend for long. She studied Ethan Fox.

"Dreams Come True is a foundation that provides children who are surviving a serious illness with the means to reach a dream. By this, I mean the foundation plans, arranges and finances your child's dream. This is not a national organization, but one founded in South Oakland County by an anonymous donor. He doesn't serve on the board, and he is contacted solely through an attorney."

Kelsey appeared, slipped a brochure into her lap and settled into the empty chair beside Lexie. She avoided Kelsey's direct look. She wanted no more arched eyebrows. Instead she scanned the brochure as she listened to Ethan.

Sincerity always captured her attention, and she suspected the man had a love for what he did for kids, but the foundation sounded like a fairytale, where happy endings were the norm. Long ago Lexie had given up wishing on a star and singing down a well. Her prince had galloped right past, taking the glass slipper with him, and at this point in her life, she didn't expect another heroic knight to pass by.

Ava Darnell's hand shot up.

Lexie liked Ava, although her curiosity sometimes took precedence over wisdom. Ava's son and hers shared a similar disease. They'd both experienced the ups and downs of cancer, and being alone, Lexie empathized with Ava's struggle as a single mom.

Ethan gave her an acknowledging nod, and Ava lowered her hand. "Does the donor live in the area?"

Ethan lifted his shoulders. "I don't know for sure, but I suspect he does."

"Do you think he's a teacher or something? Someone who knows—"

"Those of us on the board have no other information. As I said, he's an anonymous donor." A frown flashed across his face. "But that doesn't diminish the wonderful opportunity that you have as parents to apply for one of these gifts."

Ava lowered her head, but her mumble could still be heard. "But why? I don't get it."

Kelsey rose from her chair and took a step closer to Ethan. "It's difficult for us to imagine such kindness from a stranger, someone who doesn't know our children, but we appreciate learning about this wonderful charity."

Lexie tried to cover her grin. Kelsey served as the meetings troubleshooter even when she wasn't the moderator. Lexie wished she had Kelsey's knack to calm a crisis and soothe people's hearts, but she approached trouble with common sense. Avoid emotion. That's how she'd survived.

Ethan's expression relaxed. He gave Kelsey a pleasant nod as she settled back in her seat. "It is a charity of a sort, but please don't think that your family's income is considered. This donor wants to give a sick child something to look forward to. To experience something that seems—or seemed—impossible. It's more than a charity. You have all been faced with family adversity, watching your children suffer from a variety of serious illnesses. The Bible tells us to be imitators of God and live a life of love, just as Christ loved us." His gaze scanned the women. "I think that's what the donor has done. He wants to bring unexpected joy into your children's lives and into yours."

Tears welled in Lexie's eyes. Though she had never been a person of faith, what he said made sense. Sick children deserved happiness. So did their parents, but most of all, the point he made struck her. Charity was more than generosity. It was giving from the heart as an act of love. That's what parents did for their sick children. They gave, never expecting any repayment except to see their children well and happy. That was payment enough.

Surprised by her reaction, she brushed tears from her eyes, and when she focused again, Ethan's expression alerted her he'd noticed. The man seemed tuned to people's needs. Though the attribute was admirable, it didn't set well with her. She liked to keep her problems private. Lexie dropped her musing. What difference did it make what he thought?

Another hand shot up. "What kind of dreams are you talking about?"

Ethan's eyes sparkled. "Glad you asked. Some kids want to meet a sports figure or a popular singer or band. Young girls often want to meet Hanson or the Jonas Brothers, for example. And vacations. Many children want to see the ocean or mountains or even go on a Caribbean cruise. Others want to visit a popular amusement park. It can be anything."

"And you can arrange that?"

Ethan grinned at the woman, a newcomer, in the front row.

Lexie's pulse zinged.

Ethan's gaze swept the audience. "We sure can. Sometimes the dream is as simple as learning to ride a horse or riding on a fire truck. Every dream, no matter how simple or elaborate, we do our best to make it come true."

Murmurs rose from the women, including Kelsey, who joked about her dream to have her bills paid. Lexie liked that dream herself.

While other women posed their questions, Lexie sank into her own thoughts. She pictured Cooper asking her if he could go to school today. That was his dream, and it hurt to tell him no once again. He was in the second grade. Time flew. It seemed only yesterday he'd been a toddler. She ached thinking of how much school Cooper had missed since his diagnosis. She'd asked herself why so often, but no answer came, and she didn't expect one. Her life had been filled with unanswered questions, but she wasn't one to pity herself, and she didn't plan to start feeling that way now.

Cooper was her joy. Her son. No illness could take that away. A wave of shame rolled through her. She'd made the worst mistake of her life falling in love with his father, and afterward she'd dealt with more than her share of sorrow before Cooper's birth. But once she looked into her son's face, she melted and knew she'd made the right choice. Even now with everything that had happened.

Lexie flipped open the brochure. Thoughts of taking Cooper on a trip to one of the major amusement parks or to the pyramids in Egypt struck her as impossible. Yes, she loved to dream, too, but dreams only led to disappointment. Oh, how she knew that. She pressed her lips together, forcing back the sudden surge of emotion that caught in her throat.

More random questions were posed while Lexie sank deeper into her thoughts. She envisioned Cooper healthy and happy, having all his dreams come true. Her longing sizzled to frustration. She'd asked herself many times if Cooper's illness had been punishment for her bad choices. What about Jesus? What about the loving God she'd heard so much about? Would God hurt a child to get even with a parent? A loving God would not. She forced her thoughts away from her eternal struggle as her pulse slowed. Time to cling to her optimism. She coped better that way.

"If there are no more questions, let's give Mr. Fox a round of applause for coming here to share this wonderful opportunity."

Kelsey's voice jerked her to the present. Surprised that she'd returned to the front of the room without her awareness, Lexie's dropped the brochure to her lap and clapped her hands with the other women, her gaze on the man with the engaging smile.

Kelsey stepped away as a few members surrounded Ethan, and drawing up her shoulders, Lexie rose and slipped the leaflet into her shoulder bag. She glanced at her watch, thinking how quickly the time had passed before she remembered she'd been late for the meeting. She'd missed the women's time to share their weekly ups and downs. Today she appreciated not having to add their emotional needs to her own.

As she reached for her bag, she felt Kelsey's hand rest against her shoulder. "Interesting idea?"

Her mind pulled itself from her muddle of thoughts. "What idea?"

"Dreams Come True."

A moment passed before she found a response. "For some, it is." She grabbed her purse and then looked up. "Cooper's not well enough yet."

Kelsey's face sank to a frown, but as her expression flickered, her hand flew to her mouth. "Oh, Lexie, I should have guessed. The phone call. Was it bad news?"

"No worse than usual. It was the doctor, but nothing drastic. Just discouraging. Cooper's last treatment didn't show any improvement. His white cells are still too low." Saying it made it too real. Her chest emptied of air, but she grasped the positive. It could have been worse. The test could have shown he'd regressed and it hadn't.

"I'm sorry the news wasn't better."

"It's part of life, right?" She curled her arm around Kelsey's back. "How's Lucy doing?"

"So far so good. Tumors are shrinking. You know how it is. It all takes time." She gave Lexie a squeeze and lowered her arm. "Speaking of time, it's shopping day for me. Groceries. Pharmacy. Service station." Her head bobbed as she listed her tasks. "So I need to run, and…" A playful grin curved her mouth.

"Sure you do."

"Maybe you could wait until Ethan's finished before leaving. I hate to rush off without seeing him out of the building."

"Good planning, Kelsey." Lexie shook her head at her friend's obvious plot.

"Thanks." Kelsey wiggled her fingers in a silly goodbye. "I saw the eye contact." The words flew over her shoulder.

Before Lexie could rebut the insinuation, she'd vanished beyond the doorway.

Lexie tossed the strap of her bag over her shoulder and rocked back on her heels, eyeing Ethan as he spoke to the last woman. They seemed so eager for information, and part of her wished she could be as enthusiastic.

Turning her back on them, she dealt with her feelings as she dug into her shoulder bag for her car keys. Brain tumors. Leukemia. Heart disorders. So many illnesses were part of life for the people who attended. Yet some had higher hopes than others. Some children were in remission. Some weren't—like Cooper. But Cooper could be worse, and she had to remember that. No progress was better than his exacerbating. Big strides were wonderful, but small steps moved them forward. She'd learned to find joy in small steps. Each time she looked into Cooper's face her heart filled with the same kind of happiness.

When she found her keys, Lexie stepped back and smacked against someone. As she spun around to apologize, her shoulder bag slipped down her arm and dropped to the floor beside a pair of men's shoes.

"Sorry about that." Ethan bent to retrieve her purse. He smiled as he rose. "What do you carry in that thing? A wrench?"

Lexie gathered her composure and managed a friendly smile. "You never know when you'll need one."

Ethan chuckled and returned her bag. "You're a woman after my own heart. Always be prepared."

If only she were. Lexie's pulse escalated. "Thanks, and it was my fault, you know." She slid her bag onto her shoulder again, realizing it was heavy.

"Michigan has the no-fault ruling."

"That's for cars." Silly talk, but she enjoyed it.

Ethan rested his hand on the back of a chair. "No men in this group, I see."

"The *M* in MOSK stands for mothers. Mothers of Special Kids." Still, he'd made a point. She studied his face, wondering why support for men interested him. "A number of us are single mothers, and the married women haven't asked." But the question did arouse her curiosity. "You're a man. Do you think—"

"Glad you noticed." A twinkle lit his eyes.

His look tripped her pulse, and she worked to regained her composure. "As I was saying, do men really want to talk about their feelings?" She eyed him. "I thought men preferred to take action. We have so little we can do to make things better. It's the emotional ups and downs that cause us problems."

His smile had faded. "True for many men, too." He motioned toward the front of the room. "So, what did you think?"

"About Dreams Come True?"

The corners of his mouth edged upward.

"The idea is wonderful, but…" Why had she added "but"? From his expression, she'd put a damper on his excitement about fulfilling the hopes of sick kids. "My son is not well enough. He's being homeschooled right now. Clawson district has been great with his schoolwork, but it's not the same. A child wants to attend school."

"They miss the friendships and being part of it all. It makes learning more fun."

"I think it does, too." His compassion touched her. "It's not that your foundation isn't a lovely idea. It is. Whoever started this certainly has a generous heart."

His eyes searched hers.

Perspiration dampened her palms, and she ran her free hand down her pant leg while her other clung to her shoulder bag strap.

A faint frown darkened his face. "But it won't work for some kids. That's what you're saying."

She closed her eyes and opened them again, releasing a ragged breath. "Yes. Some aren't well enough to enjoy trips or days at an amusement park."

"But one day maybe. Illnesses go into remission. Sometimes they nearly vanish. Isn't that true?"

"True." Curiosity spiked Lexie's thoughts. "Have you had a child with—"

"I don't have any children."

From his sad expression, she feared she'd caused him to feel ill-at-ease.

His shoulders lifted. "I'm not married, and I've only read up on children's illnesses and read about remissions that cause physicians to marvel. I realize that's nothing like living it."

Not married. Single as she was. She studied his face, wanting to know more about him. "It's thoughtful that you've taken the time to understand what our kids go through."

His expression softened. "But it's not just the children. It's families. So many without hope."

He'd hit truth on the head. She'd tried to keep hope foremost in her mind.

Lexie glanced behind her and realized they were the only

ones left in the room. When she turned back, Ethan was eyeing his watch. She took a step backward. "Kelsey, our moderator, had to leave, but I want to thank you for the presentation and for reminding me that things can get better."

"You're welcome." He studied her a moment.

Lexie's skin prickled with his look. "I'd better be on my way. I have a sitter."

He took a step toward the door. "I'm heading out. I'll walk with you." He beckoned her forward and fell into step beside her along the hallway to the exit. Neither spoke, and though she wanted to say something meaningful, she felt tongue-tied.

Outside the April sunshine warmed Lexie's spirit, as did the memory of Ethan's smile.

"My car's this way." He pointed two rows over. "I wish we had time to really talk. I'd like to know more about the group, but I know you have things to do."

She wished the same, but it was one of those strangers-in-the-night moments, like the old song. "I need to relieve the sitter."

He lingered a moment before he turned toward his car.

Something in his eyes intrigued her. A sensitivity better than compassion. Compassion mixed with sincerity. And hope. She needed uplifting. That's why she came to the MOSK meetings. She didn't share much, but when Cooper had good times, she listened to members who were dealing with difficult situations, and while her heart broke for them, she realized how lucky it was when things were going well for her and Cooper. Then she had clouds beneath her feet rather than the usual black muck of depression.

As she watched Ethan reach his car, a white SUV, Lexie faltered. She'd never introduced herself. Too late now and probably just as well. If she ever fell in love, which she wouldn't, it would be with a man like him. He sent her pulse skipping, gave her food for thought and, best of all, made her smile. Today, she'd found a real white knight.

And the knight didn't even know her name.

Pulling herself from her ridiculous ideas, Lexie trudged down the asphalt toward her car. She hit the remote's unlock button, and as she grasped the door handle, her gaze fell on her front tire. Flat.

She slapped her hood. "No. No. No." But her words didn't change a thing. She walked to the wheel and knelt down. The tire couldn't get flatter. She rose and dug out her wallet and cell phone. Road service. Now how long would she have to wait?

Ethan sat behind the steering wheel watching...who? She'd never introduced herself, and he'd never asked. She hadn't moved from where he left her, and that made him curious. Finally, she headed down the aisle and stopped at a burgundy sedan. His interest in her seemed so unlike him. When she'd indicated she was single, his interest heightened, and he realized he was in trouble. He knew many single women, but meeting this stranger today was different. He'd felt a spark.

She was lovely. He'd been drawn first to her long brown hair with those wispy waves that looked as if she'd been caught in a breeze, but later he'd been struck by her almost straight brows and wide-set eyes, ice blue in color, yet with a warmth that drew him into their depths. But it was even more than that. Something else about her had gotten under his skin.

As he watched, she stood outside her car as if she'd lost her keys, but he'd heard them jingle in her hand as they walked, so it wasn't that. He eyed her car and shook his head.

His key dangled from the ignition. He reached to turn it but stopped when the woman slapped her car hood and walked forward. He waited until she rose and dug into her handbag. He noticed she'd grasped her cell phone.

He seized his key, then opened the door and strode from the car. "Is something wrong?"

She didn't respond, and he hurried between the cars toward her. "Can I help you?"

This time, she looked up. Relief filled her face. "I have a flat."

"Flat?" He slipped past her and crouched. "It's flat all right." He rose and grinned. "Now's a good time to pull out that wrench."

She eyed her purse and shrugged. "Sorry." A grin stole to her mouth.

Ethan's chest tightened. "Better yet, a jack will do."

Her grin deepened. "I think I actually have one of those." She motioned toward the trunk. "And thanks for noticing my predicament." She brushed a strand of hair from her cheek with her cell phone. "I realized after you went to your car, I hadn't introduced myself. I'm Alexandria Carlson, but everyone calls me Lexie."

He grasped her warm hand, feeling its slender shape, while his gaze swept over her again and tangled in the strands of brown hair with streaks of gold. He apprehended his senses. "Do you have a spare?"

Her smooth brow wrinkled. "One of those spares that's not a real tire."

"A donut." He noticed how the purple color of her sweater made her eyes even more amazing.

"Yes, a donut." She gave him a quizzical gaze.

Apparently she'd noticed him gaping. "You can't go far on one of those, anyway. It's better we just take the tire in for repair."

"No. You don't have to do that." She held up her cell phone. "I'll call for road service."

Her expression sent his pulse hopping. "I can't leave you here without knowing everything's okay." One of the idiosyncracies his wife had always teased him about.

Her eyes widened. "You're a real gentleman."

"Thanks. I try, and who knows how long road service would take? Anyway remember, I wanted time to talk." His ulterior motive turned to guilt. "I'll pull your tire off, and we can have it fixed. There's a place right up the street."

"Okay. I'm not silly enough to argue. Thanks."

"You're welcome." He grinned and held out his hand. "I need to get into your trunk for the jack."

Lexie dropped the keys into his palm and stood back. Ethan rolled up his sleeves and went to work. Grateful that the lug nuts came off without a hacksaw, he pulled the tire from the axle and leaned it against the car. "I'll pull my car up and throw this in my trunk." He slid past her, brushing his arm against hers, and felt like a teen again. "Make sure your door is locked." He strode to his SUV, telling himself to stop whatever crazy thoughts were in his mind and be the gentleman she'd said he was.

When he reached her car, Ethan jumped out and opened the passenger door. She slipped in, her cell phone absent from her hand. Somehow he twisted that fact into the thought that she trusted him. Otherwise she would have had her fingers ready to call 911. He stepped back and rolled his eyes. He'd been attacked by the crazies. After he tossed her tire into his trunk, he settled back inside and shifted into gear.

"I hope I'm not making you late for work."

He forced his eyes to stay focused on the road. "I kept the morning open for the meeting, so no problem. I'm a contractor for a construction firm and spend much of my day on the road. No one misses me except my clients." He gave her a smile. "And I don't have an appointment until this afternoon."

"Then I can relax, I guess."

"You sure can." He pulled into the street. "I think our meeting was meant to be."

She faced him with a questioning look.

"You'd be waiting for road service." True, but he meant much more than that.

A grin played on her mouth. "You're right." She leaned against the headrest. "How did you get involved in Dreams Come True?"

"Short story. When the foundation was looking for people for the governing board from a variety of businesses in the community, I volunteered."

"You volunteered." A quizzical look played on her face. "Any special reason other than you're thoughtful?"

A knot tightened his throat. Did he really want to get into all of that? He glanced at her and noted her apologetic expression.

"I'm sorry. I didn't mean to pry."

As always, he tensed when he talked about Laine. "It's fine." Getting it out in the open. "This is the hard part."

Lexie touched his arm. "No. Please. You don't have to tell me. I prefer my privacy, too. I didn't mean to—"

"It's not prying. When my wife died, I realized how lonely life had become."

Her face washed with sadness. "I'm sorry, Ethan."

He kept going, wanting to tell the story, then move to something less depressing. "We had no children, although we'd wanted them, and when my wife died, I was alone. No longer a family. Nothing. It took a while to find my identity as anything more than a contractor for Pelham Homes." He slowed at the traffic light and stopped.

Lexie nodded as if she understood.

"When I learned about this organization that did great things for sick kids, I hoped it would be a way to show compassion, and on a personal level, it helped me connect with children. Sometimes I still wish we'd had a child, though I know it would have made my life even more difficult to raise one without her."

She shifted to face him, her eyes filled with tenderness. "How long has it been since your wife died?"

"Four years. I've been functioning for about two." He managed to smile, not wanting her to think he was still the mess that he had been. Watching the woman he loved suffer and die from ovarian cancer had been a nightmare, but he'd pulled himself together. Only his faith had gotten him through.

"I think it's admirable, Ethan. You volunteered and turned a negative into a positive. Everyone should do that."

The light in her eyes told him so much. "You've done the same, haven't you?"

"I try. It's not easy."

"Nothing worthwhile is."

She looked thoughtful and seemed to ponder his words. "You're right. I'll keep that thought for times when things look dark."

When things look dark. Ethan had a difficult time picturing her letting things knock her down. She exuded strength. The light turned green, and he moved ahead, then past the intersection, he pulled up to the tire shop.

Lexie had become quiet, but when he turned off the ignition, she opened the door and stepped out before he did. He met her by the trunk, and she followed him inside with her tire.

Once the mechanic had written up their order, Ethan motioned toward the chairs. "We might as well sit."

She sank into one, but before joining her, he spotted a vending machine. "Want a pop?"

"Do they have water?"

He ambled to the machine and nodded. He dropped in

the coins and pulled out a bottle of water for her and a cola for himself. Before he gave her the bottle, he unscrewed the cap.

She grinned. "Thanks. Always the gentleman."

Ethan gave her a playful shrug and settled beside her. Back in the meeting room, he'd longed to get to know her better, and now he couldn't help but grin, recalling he hadn't even learned her name until the tire incident. *Thank you, Lord, for that flat.*

Lexie's intense look warned him he'd been quiet too long.

"I was just thinking. Earlier I'd said I would like to know more about…the group." Good cover. "And here we are."

"The group?" She gave a shrug. "Everyone has a sick child, as you know, but I don't know them all. I'm good friends with Kelsey. She was the moderator. Her daughter has a brain tumor, but Lucy's doing well." She quieted a moment. "And Ava…you remember her. Her son Brandon has Hodgkins lymphoma."

"Ava?"

Lexie grinned. "She's the one with all the questions about the foundation donor. She's curious to a fault."

He chuckled at her description. "Curiosity is okay." His own had reached fever pitch.

"Tell me about your son."

Her face brightened. "Cooper." She ran her finger around the rim of the water bottle. "He's my joy. Cooper's seven. A second-grader. He'll be eight soon. He was diagnosed with leukemia a year ago."

Leukemia. The word hit him hard. Cancer. He managed to maintain his composure. "That's very hard on you."

"It's harder on him." She lowered her head. "He's a great kid. You should meet him."

A jolt of panic shot through him. He'd like to meet her

son. He'd like to get to know her, but cancer? Again? "You sound like a proud mom."

"I am. He's a brave boy. Never complains about the treatment, and he's very optimistic."

The urge to flee came over him, soon usurped by shame. A little boy without a dad. Or maybe he had a dad who spent time with him. "I'm sure his dad's proud of him, too."

Her face darkened, and Ethan realized he'd made a grave error.

"Cooper doesn't see his father." Her jaw tightened, and she looked away.

"Mrs. Carlson."

Lexie's arm jerked as Ethan looked up at the mechanic.

"I found a nail embedded in the tire. The repair will take about twenty minutes."

She glanced at him. "Ethan, is this okay with you?"

He nodded, his mind scrambling to find a new topic to discuss. His job—anything to keep him from thinking about the little boy with cancer and no dad.

"I should call the sitter. She might worry." Lexie dug into her bag and pulled out her cell. "I'll just step outside."

She rose and strode to the door while Ethan watched her through the window, disappointed at his sense of relief. Somewhere in his crazy mind, he'd been attracted to this woman with the amazing eyes and captivating manner, but his dream had been shot down by one word. Cancer. Laine's face filled Ethan's mind. They'd had such hopes and dreams. She'd looked radiant when her CA 125 test came back with good results, and she'd been so brave each time the report was bad news. He'd lived with heartbreak for over two years. He couldn't watch it happen again. Not to a little boy.

Chapter Two

❧

"Can I go to school today, Mom?" Dressed in his jungle-print pajamas, Cooper leaned his head against his mother's arm, his thick hair only a memory. His chemo treatments had taken their toll.

"Not today, Coop." Lexie swallowed her dismay and ran her hand across his bald scalp. She would be overjoyed when he would greet her once again in the morning with his usual bed-tousled hair. "Maybe in a couple more weeks. We have to talk with Dr. Herman first." She managed a bright smile even though she ached for him. "Brush your teeth and get dressed while I make you breakfast."

"Cinnamon buns?"

An honest chuckle lightened her mood. Her son had the same propensity that she did for those gooey, fattening treats. "Let's eat healthy today. How about scrambled eggs?"

He curled up his nose. "Okay."

While he meandered toward his room, Lexie pulled herself from the table where she'd enjoyed her morning coffee before sitting behind her computer, her graphic design program open. She'd always been grateful that her career as a graphic designer allowed her to work from home and still make a living.

She opened the refrigerator and tackled the eggs, and by the time Cooper reappeared, she'd prepared eggs with cheese—he liked that—and toast with jelly. The jelly offered him the sweet taste that took the place of the cinnamon buns he really wanted. The lesser of two evils. "How are you feeling today?"

"Good." He grinned.

Good had become his standard answer so she took that with a balance of reality. She would know soon enough by his behavior. Yesterday she'd noticed a small bruise on his arm. Bruises triggered a gut-wrenching fear when she saw them. Bruising had been one of the symptoms that caused her to question Cooper's health.

"If you're so good, then you need to study your arithmetic today. Work on your addition and subtraction."

His nose curled again, but he didn't object. If she could avoid his whining, it would be a good day for her also.

Cooper's fork dove into the eggs, and he nibbled on his toast, washing it down with milk. He had eyes shaped like hers, only a slightly darker shade of blue. His brown hair had the same highlights hers had in the sunlight, and she longed to see the day when he had a full head of hair again. She had given birth to him, and no one who saw them together could argue the point.

She smiled as she cleared the dishes, and when Cooper finished, he vanished to his room, where she hoped he was doing his schoolwork. She would check after another cup of coffee. Adding more to her mug, Lexie sank into the chair, her mind once again shifting to Ethan Fox. Questions had arisen since the day they'd met. What had happened? He'd seemed so friendly and more than thoughtful, but when he finished replacing her tire, he'd said goodbye and walked off without a look backward. The memory hurt.

Though foolish, she'd let him add a bit of excitement to her day. Even now when she pictured him, her pulse sizzled. The attraction happened fast, but the seeming rejection happened even faster. She didn't know how to handle rejections or her unexpected feelings. Too many years had passed since she'd experienced the skittering emotions she associated with going gaga over a man. The last time was college. The memory settled like a lump in her stomach.

When the doorbell sounded, Lexie sat a moment, questioning who it could be. Rosie Smith, the visiting teacher, was scheduled to come on Friday. Today was Monday. Company wasn't usual. She pushed back her chair and strode to the front door. When she pulled it open, she found Kelsey Rhodes standing on her porch with a sheepish grin.

"Sorry I didn't call. I was out and just thought I'd see if you were home."

Lexie pushed open the screen door and stepped back, feeling relief mixed with an emotion she didn't understand. "Anytime. I always like to see you." But Ethan's warm eyes filled her mind. "How's Lucy?"

"Good. She's in school this week again. No setbacks."

Lexie gave her a hug, disguising the envy she felt. "I'm having coffee. Join me. Come into the kitchen." She closed the door and led the way to the coffeepot.

Kelsey leaned against the counter, watching her fill the mug.

Lexie sensed Kelsey had something on her mind, and she knew it would take time to really get to the bottom of it. She set Kelsey's cup on the table and refilled her own. Kelsey pulled her hip away from the counter and slipped onto a chair. Lexie joined her without prodding the conversation. Kelsey would talk when she was ready.

Finally her friend broke the silence. "I've been thinking about Dreams Come True."

Lexie sipped her coffee while air escaped her lungs. Ethan

plowed back into her thoughts. He could easily make someone's dream come true.

"I'd love to apply."

Pulling her focus back to the topic, Lexie reflected on Kelsey's statement. "Then do it. It sounds like a tremendous opportunity." Cooper's eager gaze swept through her mind.

Kelsey shrugged. "I don't know. Things are going well, and I suppose I'm afraid if..."

Lexie searched her face. "Afraid if what? Lucy would be a wonderful candidate for the program. Think of all she's been through and how well she's doing now." Bitterness poked at her again. Cooper's journey had been slow, and he deserved a trip as much as anyone. He was a great kid. But reality was reality. Cooper hadn't progressed as well as Lucy.

"I worry it's bad luck." She pressed her lips together and wet them with her tongue. "I'm ashamed to say that, but that's what I'm feeling. We get our hopes up, and then they come crashing down. It's like we're tempting fate."

Lexie had to stop her eyes from gaping. "Fate?"

Kelsey flinched and lowered her head. "I know. And that's why I'm ashamed of myself. I should have faith and not worry about fate."

"Don't be ashamed. It's natural to get nervous about good things happening. We all tolerate the bad news, but..." But what? "But we just have to hang on to...hope."

Her shoulders relaxed. "You're right." A faint grin stole to her face. "It's easy to be pessimistic. It takes work to be positive."

"Now, that I agree with." Lexie watched Kelsey's grin grow. "Have you told Lucy about the foundation?"

"No. I didn't want her to get excited and then have something awful happen." She lowered her head again, her neck pivoting from side to side. "There I go again. I'll get a grip on myself, and I should talk with her doctor first."

"Good idea. He'll reassure you. Then you can decide one way or the other." Decide. Decisions were nebulous. She had so few options, which was another truth she tried not to think about. It made her feel she had no control. And she didn't really. "It's difficult to stay positive, but it's important that we do. Ethan said something about people without hope, and that spoke to me. I don't want to be someone feeling hopeless. Neither do you."

Kelsey's eyes widened. "Ethan?"

Lexie's heart flew to her throat, but she managed to give a no-big-deal shrug. "After you left, I tripped over him, and he stopped to talk."

Her wide-eyed look vanished, and she gave way to a quizzical grin. "Hmm? This sounds interesting."

Lexie shook her head. "No. Nothing like that. One thing led to another. He asked about Cooper." She rolled her eyes at Kelsey's expression. "And he helped me with my flat tire."

"Flat tire?" She chuckled. "How convenient."

"I didn't make it flat by myself."

"I know, but the plot thickens." Her grin grew to a smile, and she leaned closer on her elbows. "Tell me more."

Lexie gulped back her discomfort, but knew Kelsey wouldn't give up until she gave her details. She related their conversation about Ethan's deceased wife and about Cooper. Lexie opted not to tell her about Ethan's sudden coolness. She didn't understand it, and the situation was too personal to share.

"So that's it? He didn't ask for your telephone number?"

Lexie gnawed on the inside of her cheek, remembering how she'd said he should meet Cooper. If that wasn't a flirtation, what was? "No, he didn't ask."

"Really?"

Lexie winced.

Kelsey shook her head. "Why didn't he? He isn't married, is he?"

"No. I told you his wife died."

"Children?"

"No." She gave her the evil eye. "What are you? A cop?"

Kelsey tossed her head back and chuckled. "Maybe I should be. Ethan's a nice guy and good-looking. And single. He showed an interest in you, so tell me why no phone number." She scowled. "No hints of seeing you again."

"No. We'd just met. He's a gentleman."

"Are you crazy then? You should have asked him for a card in case you wanted more information."

"Me? I don't ask men for their phone numbers. And no, I'm not crazy."

"I question that. If you don't want him, then I should proceed." A grin grew on her face. "Forget that, but let's think of how we can fix this."

We? Lexie didn't need help in the romance department. And she wasn't looking anyway.

"Seriously, if nothing more, it would be nice for Cooper to have a man in his life. He never sees his father, does he?"

The question hit Lexie in the gut. "No." What could she tell Kelsey about Coop's father. Lexie barely remembered him, and what she remembered hurt too much.

"Okay, then. We've settled that. If you do see him again, think of Cooper." Kelsey drained the coffee mug and slipped from the chair. "Thanks for listening to me. What you said helped. I need to cling to hope. God's in charge, not me, and despite my silliness, I had really hoped that Ethan might find you interesting. I noticed he smiled at you a couple of times, and I checked his ring finger. Empty, and no telltale tan line, either." She stepped back. "I think I'll add the situation to my prayer list."

Lexie rose and gave her a hug. "I don't know about the prayer list, but thanks for caring about us." She drew back and shook her head. "Even if your ideas are a bit off the wall." But not too far off. The realization slithered down Lexie's spine. She'd had a flash of those dreams for a couple of hours.

"When I mentioned a nice man spending time with Cooper, I was thinking of someone like a big brother. You're a great mom, but Ethan or some other man like him would be nice for Cooper."

Lexie hadn't thought about that. Yes, Cooper could use a man's influence in his life. "Thanks for caring."

"Welcome." Kelsey gave a wave and strode through the kitchen doorway.

Lexie followed her to the foyer and watched her slip into her car. When Kelsey drove away, she closed the door and drew in a breath. Ethan. Why had he stepped in and out of her life in a couple of hours? Her pulse skipped, wondering what it would be like to enjoy a man's company again, and one that didn't walk away the day they met.

Ethan squinted into the sunlight glinting off the hood. He'd had a headache for the past five days, and once again he didn't have an aspirin on him. Stupid.

Everything seemed stupid. He couldn't get Lexie out of his mind, and he'd walked away from her like a coward. He'd let cancer take something else from him and hadn't even left the door open for an opportunity to see her again. All of his talk about hope, and he failed to cling to it himself.

His temples pounded as he slowed at the light. Aspirin. He remembered seeing a drugstore up ahead somewhere before Crooks Road. He glanced on each side of Fourteen Mile and spotted a large pharmacy. After waiting for traffic to clear, he pulled into the parking lot and slipped into a space. As he opened his door, his heart whacked against his chest. A

burgundy sedan sat in the spot beside him. Too coincidental.
Many burgundy cars were on the road.

But his pulse skipped as he headed inside, his gaze shifting
from one side to the other. He read the signs above the aisles
and near the back, he spotted the headache remedies.

He also spotted Lexie.

Ethan closed his eyes a moment. Guilt had riddled him
since he'd met her. God had given him an opportunity to be
a man of compassion and kindness, and he'd walked away.
What happened to the Good Samaritan in him?

When he opened his eyes, she moved. He turned, his gaze
sweeping the area. His chest tightened when he spotted her
again at the prescription pickup counter. From the back,
Lexie's long hair hung in gentle waves below her shoulder
blades. He hadn't realized the length. The strands shone in
the artificial lighting, and his fingers itched to touch the
softness.

Swallowing his apprehension, he snatched the aspirin
bottle from the shelf, then pulled himself to full height, drew
back his shoulders and planted what he hoped was a pleasant
expression on his face. When he strode close enough for her
to hear him, he said her name.

Lexie turned, a surprised look fading into a smile. "What
are you doing here?"

He managed a shrug while his mind whispered his answer.
God's plan. "I've had a headache all morning." He flashed the
bottle clutched in his hand. "You must live around here."

She nodded. "A few streets over."

Hoping she'd tell him the street, he waited. No luck. He
gazed at the prescription the clerk had set on the counter.
"How's Cooper?"

Her pleasant expression slipped away. "Having some problems today. He had chemo earlier in the week, and he's terri-

bly nauseated. That hasn't been happening lately so it worried me. I called his doctor and he called in a prescription."

"I hope it takes care of it."

"Me, too." She turned and picked up the small paper bag. "He'll sleep the day away with this." She slipped the package into her shoulder bag. "How's the foundation?"

Foundation. He blinked. That wasn't the direction he wanted to go. Now he'd have to work his way back to Cooper. "Doing some great things." He dug through his mind to remember what great things, but he knew they were planning some wonderful events for kids in the county. "One of the women from your organization contacted us. We're planning a trip for her daughter to visit New York. She wants to see the fashion industry. She'll spend some time at Parsons and we're arranging for her to meet a couple of fashion designers."

"That'll be so nice for her."

Lexie's grin failed to convince Ethan. He should have avoided details, but it was too late. "When Cooper's ready, we'll plan a great trip for him, too."

"Right now he'd give anything to go to school, but—" She shook her head. "Maybe this last treatment will turn things around."

Ethan wanted to give her a hug. "That would be great."

"It would be." She gave him another feeble grin. "His doctor is optimistic, but optimism doesn't mean much to a seven-year-old. Every time I tell him he can't go to school yet, my heart breaks seeing the disappointment on his face."

"Really tough."

Moisture filled her eyes. "Cooper's so smart. He loves books, especially about nature and beautiful places. He talks about going to see some of the national parks, and I bought him a book about them. He just stares at the photos all the time."

Her misty eyes glowed as she talked, and Ethan's chest

swelled with her description. "I love to see children interested in positive things."

"No guns and tanks for Cooper." This time her face brightened. "He likes puzzles, all kinds of them, and books. He can read, too. Easy things, naturally, but he tries to sound out larger words. I really wish he could be part of his class."

Ethan's voice knotted in his throat, and he swallowed to control his emotion. "So do I." School would mean he'd be ready for the foundation's involvement. Ethan couldn't think of anything better except for an amazing healing. He sent the thought to the Lord as a prayer.

"The teacher sends homework and a visiting teacher comes to the house. The school's been very helpful."

"The last time we talked..." Stupid comment. The only time they'd talked. He tried to relax. "I know you didn't mean it, but you said you'd like me to meet him. I've been thinking about that. I would love to meet Cooper. He sounds like a terrific kid."

He could see her struggling with a response.

She tilted her head, her eyes questioning. "But why?"

Why? Ethan could give a number of reasons. He liked kids. He understood the horrors of cancer, and he knew how hard it was to deal with it. And he felt compassion. But along with those reasons, he liked Lexie. He sucked in air, hoping he could say what he felt without coming across as a lunatic. "I admire you. I've experienced the heartbreak of a horrible disease affecting a loved one, but I love that Cooper has a chance to make it through this. I guess I'd like to see someone win."

"Win?" She appeared to toss the word around in her mind. "That's what we want." She rolled her eyes and grinned. "It's more than a want. I insist. I demand. And then realistically, I hope."

"And there we are, back where we began when we talked last week. Hope."

She shifted her weight from one foot to the other. "You're right." A sincere smile blossomed on her face. "Interesting how we always come back to that word."

Ethan had so much he longed to tell her and to ask. Was she a believer? Did she know that the Lord loved her, and she could count on Him to be with her through the good times and the bad? But he was smart enough to know coming on too strong would chase her away. A tender feeling wove through his chest. What this woman did to him felt amazing. "So what do you say?"

She scowled. "About hope?"

He grinned. "About my meeting Cooper."

"Oh." She gave a soft chuckle before looking away for a moment. "I should ask Cooper if he'd like to meet you."

"Right." His stomach sank. "Could I call you?"

She pressed her lips together, her eyes searching his again. "Give me your business card, and I'll call you."

I'll call you. He'd never heard the line personally, but he knew what it meant. He arched his back, dug out his wallet again and drew out a card, certain it was a waste of time.

When he handed it to her, she dropped it in her purse. "I'd better get home. Cooper needs these meds, and I have a wonderful lady who stays with him when I'm out and I promised her I wouldn't be too long." She stepped past him, then turned back. "It was nice seeing you again."

His "It was great seeing you" followed her as she strode toward the pharmacy exit.

Ethan slipped the papers into the folder and rose. The Dreams Come True meeting ran shorter than usual. No new requests had come in, and so they reviewed plans for a trip to New York City along with a Broadway play for one teen

girl and a day at a firehouse including a ride in a fire truck
for one young boy. When Ethan listened to the reports, his
mind drifted to Cooper. He'd hoped to hear something from
Lexie, but she hadn't called. At this point, he could do nothing but wait.

A hand clasped his arm, and Ethan looked over his shoulder at his friend Bill Ruben.

"How did the presentation go at the senior center last
week?"

"You mean the Mothers of Special Kids?"

Bill grinned. "Moms something."

"It went great." Yes, the meeting, but his head and heart
hadn't faired as well. He eyed his friend, then grasped the
opportunity. "Glad you asked." He drew in a lengthy breath.
Now or never. "Do you have a minute?"

Question settled in Bill's eyes. "No problem. Anything
wrong?"

"No." "Maybe" was the better response. "I just want your
opinion." Ethan gazed around the emptying meeting room
and motioned to a chair. "Let's sit."

Bill eyed him again as he pulled a chair from beneath the
table and turned it around. He straddled the seat and rested
his arms across the back without saying a word, though his
face showed his concern.

"It's a couple of things." Ethan shifted in the chair, his
nervousness evident in his jiggling knee. He forced his foot
to the floor, confused why he felt so edgy with Bill. He'd
thought about talking with someone, and Bill had a good
head on his shoulders. "The meeting was fine, and after it,
one of the women bumped into me as we were leaving. I'd
noticed her earlier. She had a nice smile, and…I don't know…
something about her caught my attention."

Bill's frown vanished, and a half grin took its place.

"Nothing like that." He waved his hand, but he felt like a

fraud. It had become something significant. Lexie and her son had begun popping into his thoughts numerous times a day, especially since he'd run into her again. "She had a flat when we went outside. I helped her. We talked, and—"

Bill snickered. "Love at first sight."

"No. It's…I don't know." Now Ethan questioned why he'd even brought the whole thing up. How could Bill understand his emotional struggle?

Bill leaned his shoulders over the chair back, his brow drawn. "So lay it on me. What happened? What's the problem?"

"The child has leukemia. Cancer."

Bill blinked. "Ahh." He rocked back in the chair and shook his head. "That kind of cancer is different, Ethan. The outcome can be more hopeful. You know that."

"I know that in my head."

Bill braced the heels of his hands against the chair back. "So what are you asking me?"

He blew out a stream of air. "I don't know for sure." He tried to untangle his thoughts. "I walked away that day." He allowed his eyes to connect with Bill's. "The day we met. I helped her change the tire and then left, but here's the thing. I ran into her again."

"At the next meeting?"

"No. At a pharmacy. It struck me that…I don't know. She'd been on my mind, and I'd wished that I hadn't reacted as I did. It seemed our meeting again was providence."

"You mean God planned it?"

"That sounds odd, but I felt it was meant to be. She talks about her son with such love, and I don't have kids. I asked to meet the boy. He doesn't have a dad, and I—"

"And you'd like to be his dad."

Ethan's pulse skipped. "Don't be ridiculous. The boy needs a man's attention. Like a big brother."

A faint grin etched Bill's mouth. "You have no interest in the mother, but you want to be the kid's big brother?" Bill's eyebrows arched to his hairline, and he snickered.

The comment smacked Ethan. "Okay. Whatever. I'd like to be a masculine influence for the boy. Fill that hole." Lexie's image flashed through his mind. "Not to say the boy's mother isn't doing a good job. She is."

Bill shifted and wrapped his fingers around the chair back. "Why not meet the boy? Do it if his mother approves."

"But is it right? Am I stepping over the boundary of Dreams Come True? No one said we should get friendly. We're here to plan events and trips for these kids, not to be friends."

"I don't know of any rule that says you can't be a friend." He leaned closer. "Or are you worried about some other problem?"

Ethan had to admit that was a concern. He'd been drawn to Lexie from the moment he looked at her. "That, too, I suppose."

"The mother?"

"No one's fascinated me the way she did." He shook his head. "And without saying a word to me. She was in the room with ten other women that first day." He flexed his palm upward. "And don't ask me if it's her good looks. Yes, she's very attractive, but it was something else. Maybe the purposeful set of her jaw, the affirming glimmer in her eyes. Whatever it was, it drew me like a magnet."

"And she just happened to bump into you."

"It was an accident. When she turned around, I—" Ethan gave him a shamefaced grin. "I had walked her way, hoping we might talk."

A thoughtful expression lit Bill's face before turning to a frown. "Did she flirt with you? Or encourage you to get involved with her?"

"No. She's not like that. She's careful. Strong-willed yet gentle. Lexie's focused on her son." Their conversations filtered through his mind. "She's different. Not the flirty type." He lowered his head. "Unless I'm stupid."

"That's a possibility." Bill chuckled.

He ignored Bill. "Lexie hasn't agreed to let me meet Cooper yet. She wanted to ask him first. Does that sound like a woman who's running after me?"

"No. She sounds like a caring mother." Bill straightened in the chair, his teasing expression gone. "Listen, you have to go with your heart. When Marian and I met, something happened. It's a feeling I can't explain, but it sort of felt right." He looked past him a moment as if thinking. "Like maybe God had meant it to be." He chuckled. "So maybe your 'providence' feeling was the Lord prodding you forward."

The Lord. The pit of his stomach tightened. "I'm not sure Lexie's a Christian so I doubt if the Lord had anything to do with it."

"God works wonders, pal. Don't doubt His ways."

"Doubt? No, I wasn't—" Had he doubted? "I was just—" But Bill was right. Had he been led to Lexie as a faith influence and nothing more? A hollow feeling drove through his chest and parked. The unsettling emotion forced Ethan's gaze upward. "You're right. The Lord guides us for His purpose, and maybe that's it." He rose and slid the chair beneath the table. "Thanks."

"Listen, Ethan. I wasn't trying to be a downer for you." He stood and moved the chair aside. "I'm no counselor. I'm not even good at making my own decisions. Marian's more decisive than I am."

Ethan rested his hand on Bill's arm. "What you said gave me something to think about. I need to use common sense as well as what my heart is prodding me to do."

Bill slapped his back. "You're a good man. You'll do the right thing."

He questioned Bill's confidence in him. Sometimes doing the right thing became caught up in dreams, not in reality. "I hope so."

Chapter Three

Ethan stepped from his SUV and eyed the house in front of him, a terra-cotta-colored brick bungalow, typical of many of the homes he'd passed in Clawson, but this one had a generous porch across the front, adding to its charm. Large tapered columns with timber detailing supported the porch roof, and above rose one gable with a double window. A large maple tree stood in the center of the small yard, its leaves giving a hint that spring had arrived.

His talk with Bill had resolved some of his issues, and he wanted to put it in God's hands. When more than a week passed without a word from Lexie, he chalked it up to the Lord wanting him to back off or maybe telling him he'd been too forward. The woman had a sick child and didn't have time for a stranger. But he'd been wrong. Her phone call had surprised him, and her message even more. Cooper was anxious to meet him.

He leaned back into the car and pulled out the paper bag with the local bookstore logo. The boy loved books, and Ethan wanted to give him a small gift when they met. A book seemed perfect. He shut the door, hit the remote's lock button and headed up the concrete walk. When he stepped onto the porch, he noticed a vaulted ceiling over the door.

Being a contractor, he couldn't help but appreciate the quality of the building.

When he reached for the bell, the door opened, revealing Lexie standing inside the entry. Her pleasant expression didn't hide a hint of uneasiness.

She pushed open the door. "Come in. Cooper's driving me crazy. He's been counting the hours."

The weight of Ethan's action struck him. Lexie's love of her son, the joy on her face when she talked about him, had piqued his interest, but he'd given no consideration to what the child might expect of him. He had little to offer a sick child, but he'd wanted to meet the boy who lived under the burden of a tragic illness and somehow remained eager to read books and loved faraway places. His confidence sank to his stomach.

He held out the gift bag. "I brought Cooper a present. I hope that's okay."

She gazed at the package. "That was thoughtful. You should give it to him yourself." She tilted her head to the right. "He's in the den doing his homework."

Ethan looked past the staircase to the living room with a fireplace centered across the room flanked by two windows and below them, window seats. The homey feeling warmed him. Through the archway, he viewed a dining room with another room beyond that was closed off by beveled glass doors. The den he guessed. "Nice house, Lexie. Large and open. You can't appreciate the size from the outside."

"It does fool you, doesn't it." She strode ahead of him, and as they passed through the dining room, he noticed the sunny kitchen with a large island and a plethora of cabinets.

She pushed the glass doors, and they slid into the wall. When he followed her inside, he was taken with Cooper. The boy's face radiated when he looked up. Though Cooper was bald, Ethan could imagine the boy with satiny brown hair like his mother's. And he had her eyes—a bit darker blue, but with the same inquisitive depth.

"Hi, Cooper." He strode toward the sofa. "I'm Ethan Fox."

Cooper's eyes shifted to the package in Ethan's hand. When he looked up, he grinned. "I have leukemia. That's why I'm bald." He demonstrated by rubbing his scalp. "But I feel good."

"I'm glad."

He glanced over his shoulder to see if Lexie had left. She waited near the doorway, watching them. Unexpected discomfort rattled his confidence again, and he questioned once more why he had asked to meet the child.

Cooper patted the cushion beside him. "Can you do math?"

Hearing the boy's eagerness, Ethan dislodged his confusion. "I'm pretty good with arithmetic. I'm a contractor, and I need math in my work. Do you know what a contractor is?"

A frown settled on the boy's face, and he shook his head.

Ethan sank into the cushion beside him and tucked the package between his leg and the sofa arm. "I help people decide what kind of new home they want me to build."

"You can build a house?" His eyes widened as his gaze swung around the room. "By yourself?"

"We have crews. Lots of men who build them, and sometimes I help people design additions to their houses." He gestured to the room. "But this house doesn't need any improvement. It's good just as it is."

"We could have a library in it."

Ethan's pulse skipped. "Yes, I suppose you could." He scanned the one long wall across from the large side window.

"This room could have been a library. See that wall? It could be filled with shelves."

Cooper leaned over as if he could get a better view of the wall. He eyed it for a moment. "Okay. Let's do it."

A laugh burst from Ethan. "I don't think your mom wants me redecorating your house."

"Can we, Mom?"

Lexie stepped through the doorway. "Not today, Cooper." She stood above them and grinned. "Did you want Mr. Fox to check your math?"

He nodded, and the library topic appeared to sail from his mind. He handed Ethan his workbook and pencil. "This is subtraction."

"It is." Ethan scanned the page. "Excellent. Not one wrong."

The boy beamed. "Mr. Fox said they're all right."

"I heard him. That's great."

"I think that deserves a present. What to you think, Cooper?" Ethan pulled the package from beside him and extended it.

"Mr. Fox brought me a present, Mom." He eyed his mother as if asking if it was all right to accept the gift.

"I know." She nodded. "You can open it."

Cooper reached for the bag, but Ethan didn't let go. "But only if you call me Ethan."

Again Cooper looked at Lexie for approval. She nodded, and Ethan slipped the package into the boy's hands. He pulled open the bag and a smile filled his face. "A book." He held the gift into the air. "Look, Mom."

She nodded, appreciation fluttering on her face.

"I like books."

Ethan's heart warmed. "I know. Your mom told me."

"You did?" He grinned at his mother who nodded back.

Ethan didn't notice when Lexie slipped from the room.

Cooper opened the book, and they sat side by side, mesmerized by the photographs and brief descriptions of insects and flowers, lovely close-ups that provided minute details. His chest tightened as he listened to the boy talk about the pictures and sound out the larger words. He read well, very well for a boy his age, and Ethan understood why Lexie extolled her son's ability. A sweet child. So special Ethan ached.

The ringing telephone jarred his ears, but it stopped after the first ring. Lexie must have taken the call, and he pulled his mind back to Cooper and pondered what he could do for him. How could he make the boy's healthy days more pleasant? What fun things could a man do with a child being treated for leukemia?

And then Lexie slipped into his mind. Nervous but open, that's how she'd greeted him. She'd opened the door of her home to a virtual stranger, trusting that he wanted the best for her son. And he did. Life wasn't always fair, but he couldn't question the Lord's purpose. Too often he wanted to. He remembered a book about why bad things happened to good people. That was the question that charged through his mind today.

"Are these drawings?"

Ethan jerked from his thoughts. "No. They're photographs. People took them with a camera."

"So close?"

He nodded. "They're called close-ups."

"I like close-ups." He leaned his head back against the cushion.

The boy's action stirred Ethan's concern. "Are you tired?"

He shook his head no, but Ethan read his expression. "Why don't you rest awhile? The book is yours so you don't have to look at the whole thing today."

"He's right, Coop." Lexie strode across the carpet, her look tender. But a dark shadow had settled in her eyes.

Ethan rose. He needed to leave now and not be a nuisance, even though he wanted to stay. The longing flustered him.

Cooper drew his legs onto the sofa. "My birthday is coming in a week. Will you come to my party?"

Ethan froze in place. When he thawed enough to think, he sought Lexie's eyes.

She gave a faint nod. "You're very welcome, but don't feel you have to. Cooper gets overenthusiastic sometimes."

Ethan didn't blame the boy. His life revolved around treatments and doctor's offices and not being able to go to school. A birthday party held promise of presents and cake and fun. "I wouldn't miss it." The words had flown from his mouth without him weighing them.

Lexie took the book from Cooper and tossed a pillow beside the arm of the sofa. "I want you to lie down, okay?"

Cooper gave a resigned nod and wiggled around until he had curled up into a ball with his head on the pillow. Lexie took a throw from the back of the sofa and spread it over him, then looked at Ethan. "I'll let Ethan know when the party is later, Coop."

"Okay." He gazed up at Ethan with heavy-lidded eyes. "Thanks for the present."

"You're very welcome."

Lexie strode toward the doorway and Ethan followed. He sensed something caused her change of mood and hoped it wasn't something he'd said or done. Outside the room, she slid the door closed and continued to the kitchen. Ethan paused, not knowing if he should say goodbye or follow her. He chose the latter.

She began mixing something in a bowl without looking behind her.

Ethan shifted one of the stools sitting next to the island and slid onto it. "Did I do something wrong?"

She lowered her spoon to the counter before she turned. Moisture clung to her lower lashes. "No. You've been very kind. I know Coop loved the book."

"Then what's..." Ethan searched her face. He should respect her privacy, but his unwilling heart prodded him onward. "You're upset. Can I do anything?"

A faint shake of her head gave him the answer.

"I suppose I should go then, and let you be alone." He slipped from the stool and placed it beneath the island bar.

"You don't have to go."

He faltered, juggling the questions vying in his mind until he gave in and asked. "The telephone call? Was it bad news?"

She closed her eyes. "I'll deal with it. So will Coop. We always do, but when we hear his test results, I often get discouraged until I get a grip on myself."

"You can't lambast yourself for that." He stepped to her side and rested his hand on her shoulder. "Seeing that wonderful kid sick tears me up, and I don't really know him. He's great. So bright and eager. I admire your strength. I don't know if I would be that strong."

"You were once."

Laine's struggle dropped into his mind. "I managed, but not like you." The warmth of her body traveled from his palm up his arm. His chest tightened with the closeness, and he forced his hand from her shoulder and stepped back. His lungs tugged for air. Ridiculous. It made no sense at all. He barely knew these people.

He wandered back to the island and leaned against it, keeping his distance before he did something he'd be sorry for. "When my wife, Laine, wasn't around to see me, I'd kick at stones and throw things that got in my way. I felt tremendous anger. God and I stood on opposite sides of the line. I was furious with Him." He lowered his head. "I hate to admit that."

Lexie shifted to the island and rested her elbows on the surface, the work top separating them. "Really? I have a difficult time imagining that. You seem to be a man with a lot of faith. Picturing you angry doesn't fit."

"It doesn't. But Christians are human like anyone. The belief doesn't keep us from falling prey to our own wants and our own time frame." He watched her drink in all that he'd said. "But I learned from it, too. I learned that the Lord promises to be by our side through the good and the bad. And He has been. I learned that God's time and mine are different. Things don't always go as I want them, but through it all, He's there. I only learned that when I quieted and listened. As Laine's disease worsened, I grasped those times and hung on."

Lexie closed her eyes, her full lips pressed together as if to keep herself from speaking. When she opened them, she drew in a breath. "I think I understand what you mean. It's when you stop fighting that help comes."

So simple and exactly what he was trying to say. Ethan rested the flat of his hands on the island bar. "Let me take my own advice. I'll be quiet and listen. What did the oncologist say?"

"Cooper's cell count doesn't look good." She ran her knuckle below her eyes, collecting the moisture that had formed while she talked. "Now he'll be dealing with heavy-duty treatments, and the oncologist said they'll try some new medication that can have adverse effects on Cooper, and next week is his birthday. He's so looking forward to it."

Ethan longed to hold Lexie in his arms and make things better. He longed to help Cooper become healthy again, but what he wanted didn't count. What the Lord wanted did. He sent up a silent prayer.

"So that's why Coop's birthday is up in the air. I don't know when we can celebrate it, but whatever we do, I'll let you know."

"I'll be happy to come. Just call me when you decide." His mind wrapped around the moment, wanting to say so much more, but cautioning himself, he took the chance. "I'll be praying for Coop's treatment and for your peace of mind."

She gazed at him without shifting an eye. "Thank you. I realize prayer means a lot to you, and it can't hurt, can it?"

"Not one bit." His hopes soared as he looked into her beautiful eyes.

"If there is a God, He'll hear you, and if there isn't, then it doesn't matter."

The impact of her remark struck him like a kick in the gut. He stopped himself from responding. Too much too soon. He had to let it go. Lexie was honest and direct. If he planned to be around her, he had to accept her the way she was. The comment wasn't an attack on him. She'd only stated her viewpoint.

But he didn't have to like it.

Lexie sat in front of her computer, her mind on everything but the CD cover design she'd been trying to work on for the past hour. Cooper's birthday was this Thursday, and with his new treatment happening that morning of all things, she hesitated inviting anyone to come. Ethan's image hovered in her mind while her pulse raced.

She'd liked him from the day they'd met, but seeing him with Cooper added to her attraction. Ethan demonstrated a heart of compassion and a spirit of generosity. The book he'd given to her son couldn't have been a better choice. Ethan had really listened to her when she'd talked about Cooper's interests, and that struck her as amazing.

She stared at the computer screen, eyeing the third layer of a cover design for a new children's DVD. Besides the opportunity to work at home, the career gave her a decent income. Nothing spectacular, but she could pay her bills and pay for their needs. She'd even saved a little when her work was in full swing. With Cooper's illness, she'd had to slow down, and though her parents had not been kind about her becoming pregnant without being married, they had come around when Coop was born.

Arizona eased the tension between them. Tucson and Clawson, Michigan, were separated by thousands of miles, and under the circumstances, Lexie accepted the distance with gratification. She and her parents clashed too much when they were together for any length of time. Yet despite their attitude, they had softened somewhat when Cooper came along. They'd even come for a visit and brought along gifts for their grandson.

Yesterday Cooper's birthday package from them had arrived. Though he seemed happy to see the gifts, his birthday had taken a backseat to the treatment he'd had at the end of last week. How much could a child take? And now he faced another. Her chest tightened as tears moistened her eyes. Lexie rolled back her chair and left the den. She strode to the staircase. Drawing in a breath, she climbed the steps and made her way through the large play area in the upstairs foyer to Cooper's bedroom.

Standing in the doorway, she eyed him, pale and silent against the pillow. Lexie tiptoed across the room and gazed at him. A new bruise darkened the arm that stuck out from beneath the blanket. Anger weighted against her loving heart. Her beautiful boy carried the burden of her mistake. No matter how much she tried to see the positive and talk herself out of those feelings, they hammered at her each time she watched him suffer. And Cooper suffered in silence.

She bent over him and placed her hand against his forehead. Warm, but not hot. Relief washed through her. Watching for infection, excessive bruising, anemia and a multitude of other signs kept her vigilant. The quicker his treatment could correct any oncoming problem the better.

Lexie picked up the soup bowl and spoon, then backed away, seeing the easy rise and fall of Cooper's chest against the blanket. He needed sleep as much as she needed to hold him in her arms. Turning, she tiptoed across the room and headed downstairs.

After rinsing the dishes and putting them into the dishwasher, she leaned against the counter. May 6 was the day Cooper was born. The moment she'd looked into his tiny face lived in her memory as a treasure. Everything else paled against the happiness she felt with her son in her arms. No matter how difficult life became she would never lose that joy.

She closed her eyes, clinging to those memories. When she opened them, Lexie strode to the refrigerator. She'd lost her appetite following Coop's chemotherapy as much as he did, but she had to keep herself healthy for him. She opened the door and pulled an apple from the fruit drawer. She bit into the firm flesh of the fruit. The sweet taste filled her mouth as she snatched a napkin and headed back to the den and her computer.

When she settled back into her chair, she eyed the telephone. Ethan. She promised to call him. No big party for Cooper this year unless his next treatment went dramatically better. Lexie lifted Ethan's business card laying next to the telephone and gazed at his number.

Since meeting him, Lexie realized someone besides Cooper now occupied her mind. Though she'd always been careful with people, especially ones she'd just met, Ethan's presence felt as comfortable as her favorite slippers. At first she questioned his motivation, but after his visit and seeing him with Cooper, she had a change of heart. Ethan exemplified what it meant to be a nice person. And that's what still caused concern. He talked about God and faith. Religion seemed a big part of his life. She hadn't read the Bible or attended church. She and Ethan were different, but she knew what good attributes were and Ethan had them.

When she questioned his motivation, she'd asked herself if his religion was why he'd been so kind to them. But reality finally settled in. No relationship could last based on a person needing to be kind. That had nothing to do with wanting or enjoying the relationship. She needed to pay taxes but that didn't bring her happiness. If Ethan needed to be kind because the Bible told him to, then he did it to please God and not himself. That motivation alone didn't seem to fit Ethan.

She shook her head, wishing she could make sense out of her thoughts. What did faith really mean? Often she longed to have something fill the hollow feeling that groaned in the pit of her stomach. Cooper gave her happiness, but she yearned for a kind of fulfillment she'd never had. A sense of completeness. Maybe that was it.

Glancing down at her hand, she focused on the business card and made her decision. She lifted the receiver and punched in Ethan's number. After three rings, she shifted to hang up and then heard the connection and his voice. "This is Lexie. I should have called you sooner, but—"

"Don't apologize. I'm really glad to hear from you. How's Cooper? I've been worried."

The answer caught in her throat. "I wish the news were better. He's having a bad time with his last treatment, and he has another one Thursday, but soon he'll be up and good again. I just need to be patient."

"I'm sorry he's having problems."

She swallowed. "His birthday is Thursday, but under the circumstances, I'm not planning a real party. He'll be weak, and he'll sleep after the treatment."

"That's too bad." He left a lengthy pause. "Could do something smaller."

Disappointment flattened his voice. He truly cared. Not having a party disappointed her, too, as it would Cooper. And she would have enjoyed getting to know Ethan better. He dropped into her thoughts too often. "We'll still celebrate in our quiet way. I'll bake him a cake."

"I like cake."

Lexie stared at the receiver, hearing him say what her heart wanted to hear. "Are you saying you'd like to come over anyway?"

"Definitely. I've already bought his gift."

"A gift? Ethan, you already gave him the book. That was a wonderful present."

"But it didn't come with a happy birthday card."

A grin cracked the tension in her face. "That's true." But her mind still grappled with negative thoughts. Yes or no? Encourage? Discourage? Despite the warnings that lodged in her head, she liked Ethan. She pried herself from the trench and went with her heart. "Come over about six. I'll make dinner."

"I hinted for cake. I didn't expect a meal."

Her grin deepened. "That's all the better. Is six good for you?"

"It's perfect."

"Then we'll see you on Thursday. Cooper may be sick, but when I tell him you'll be here, he'll be ecstatic. You and the book have been the topic of conversation since you were here."

"Really?"

His tone had changed, and she didn't like the sound. She'd made a mistake telling him how much Cooper thought of him. "You know kids. They love attention." She hoped that softened what she'd said.

"Yes, I suppose they do."

Silence settled over the line, and Lexie clung to the receiver wishing she'd kept her mouth shut about Cooper's excitement.

"I'll see you on Thursday at six then. And, Lexie, thanks for the invitation."

"You're welcome." She lowered the receiver and leaned back in the chair. Whatever she'd said had dampened the situation. Moments earlier the conversation had caused her to grin, and she hadn't done that in days.

Chapter Four

Ethan eyed the empty place at the table and cut into his pork chop. Lexie had dinner ready when he arrived, so serious conversation had been put on hold. He didn't want to ask questions that would make the meal a downer, and he feared talking about Cooper's illness would send their moods down the drain.

He wished he knew how to apologize for his behavior on the phone. Hearing Cooper's excitement caused a warning buzzer to sound in his mind. He didn't want to be that important to the boy, and the more he thought about the situation the more he feared he might hurt the boy unintentionally. One day he would possibly walk away, and what then? The idea ran cold through his veins. How long could a man linger around a woman and child without allowing his feelings to emerge? And though Lexie had been friendly, he sensed her interest in him was about her purely thinking of Cooper. Not of him.

Lexie gazed at him a moment, obviously noticing his focus on the empty place setting and his silence. "We'll check on Cooper after dinner." She extended the dinner rolls. "Have another. They'll go to waste here with Coop not eating much."

"How bad is he feeling?"

"Bad. He turned down dinner and said he'd wait for the cake." She shrugged. "Eating cake instead of dinner isn't very healthy, but—"

"Right. Give him what he'll enjoy. It's his birthday."

They silenced again, and he felt the stress surrounding them. He took another bite, uneasy with the quiet. "These chops are really tender. Mine always cut like leather."

"You probably fry them."

He nodded.

"These are baked. I have a pork rub that I use."

Their stilted conversation bothered him. In their short acquaintance, they had talked with ease, and right now he wished he could put them in that frame again. Instead, he concentrated on enjoying the tender chops and the mashed potatoes with gravy. She'd even prepared carrots, one of his favorites.

Lexie nibbled at her food, distracted by her thoughts, he suspected. She handed him the potatoes again but this time, he declined. His own appetite had waned with the tension he felt.

"I can't eat another bite." He straightened in his chair and shifted the plate to the side. "Thanks so much for the excellent meal."

"You're welcome. It would be a rather sad party without you."

He thought it was sad even with him being there. But he hoped that could change. "I'm glad to be here for Cooper." He clenched his teeth to keep himself from telling her he wanted to be there for her, too.

"I wish he'd eaten with us, but I knew he'd wear out too fast. I'd rather he enjoy his cake and the short celebration."

Ethan offered a mundane comment and sank back into his thoughts.

When Lexie rose and reached for the dishes, Ethan jumped to action, anxious to do something other than feel sad. He pitched in and carried the bowls and glasses to the kitchen sink, then turned on the water and ran the salad bowls under the tap.

But Lexie moved beside him and shooed him away. "You're company. I can take care of this later."

He stepped aside but didn't leave. "If we do it now, it's done." He rested his hand on her arm, relishing the feeling of intimacy standing together over the sink. "You have better things to do with your time." He stopped himself from referring to Cooper's needs.

She resigned and accepted his offer, and while he rinsed the dishes and stacked them for the dishwasher, she covered the uneaten food and placed it in the refrigerator. "Coop curled up his nose earlier, but I'm hoping he'll eat something later."

"You mean something besides cake." He chuckled, hoping the lighthearted comment might cheer her.

She grinned. "You never know." She glanced at her watch. "Let's check on him. He's rested a long time."

Ethan rose and followed her, happy to see the second floor of the house. Near the staircase, he paused. "Should I bring this up?" He motioned to the chair where he'd left the birthday present he'd bought.

"No. He'll come down, I'm sure." The tone of her voice didn't fit the positive statement.

Ethan felt the weight of her worry as he climbed the stairs. At the top, he followed Lexie to a spacious hallway as large as another den, except for the numerous doors leading to the other rooms. "I like this. It's different."

"They called it a playroom when I bought the house, but it's great for many things. I thought about moving my office from the den to here. But Cooper loves to sit by the window and do puzzles or read. The light is great in the morning. So it's sort of a...room."

He chuckled. "Rooms are handy." He scanned the wide triple windows where two easy chairs sat with a lamp table between, and another larger table farther over where one of Cooper's puzzles was partly completed. He could picture Lexie sitting on one of the chairs close to Cooper's bedroom, her feet on the ottoman, waiting and worrying alone. He adjusted his expression, fearing she would sense his thoughts.

But she had continued ahead. He watched her push open a door and stand inside the threshold. The room lay in shadow. He stood back, waiting for her to give him a sign to join her.

"Coop?" She stepped deeper into the room. "You don't want to miss your birthday party, do you?"

Ethan could make out Cooper's voice but not what he'd said.

Lexie reappeared in the doorway and motioned him forward.

An unexpected hesitation shivered through him as he pictured the clever boy bound to a sick bed. He forced his legs to move and planted a pleasant look on his face before he stepped inside the room. As he did, the darkness brightened with lamplight.

Lexie shifted away from the nightstand and beckoned him closer.

He eyed the boy's pale face, his dinner knotting in his stomach. "Happy birthday, Cooper."

The child's face was paler than Ethan remembered, with shadows below his eyes the way he recalled Laine's face after a difficult treatment. The memory deepened his sorrow for Cooper and Lexie.

Cooper gave a little wave and worked his way to a sitting position. "Did you already eat the cake?"

"Cake? No. We waited for you." Lexie rubbed the top of his bald head. "And I have some dinner ready if you feel like eating."

He shrugged, pushing back the blankets and swinging his feet over the edge of the mattress, wearing spaceship pajamas. "I don't want to miss my own birthday."

Ethan chuckled at the expression on his face. The boy still had a sense of humor. He backed away again and moved to the door, then slipped out, allowing Lexie privacy to help Cooper get ready. Trying to keep himself from dwelling on the child's illness, Ethan stood in the playroom, noticing two doors ajar revealing a bathroom and laundry room. The other two rooms were closed. He assumed they were bedrooms. While he admired the layout, Cooper's weary conversation reached him. He missed the eager lilt of the boy's voice that he'd heard before.

Rather than linger there, he crossed to the staircase and took the steps to the living room. Seconds later, Cooper made his way down the stairs with Lexie following. He'd changed into his jeans and a T-shirt with a cartoon character on the front, one Ethan didn't recognize.

"Time for the party," he said as he reached the bottom. But his voice didn't sound convincing.

"That's what I've been waiting for." Ethan ambled closer, not sure how to greet the child, but Cooper answered his question. He opened his arms, and Ethan grasped him in a hug, sinking into the child's embrace.

Lexie scooted past. "I want you to try and eat some dinner, Cooper. Then we'll have the cake."

Ethan released him and straightened. "Let's see what your mom has for you."

Cooper stuck by his side, and they strode through the kitchen archway together.

Lexie stood at the refrigerator door. She glanced over her shoulder, listing what she had for him to eat.

"Mashed potatoes." Cooper's voice sounded decisive.

"That's all?"

He nodded and headed for the breakfast nook.

Ethan watched Lexie prepare a plate, adding a piece of the pork chop and some carrots. He would have done the same. Better to tempt the child than give in. When the microwave beeped, she pulled out the food and carried it to the nook. "How about some coffee, Ethan?"

"Sounds great. Black works for me."

She motioned toward the bench seat. "Sit there with Cooper and I'll bring it to you."

He slid into the booth across from the boy, and a moment later, Lexie appeared with his coffee. She left and returned with a glass of milk for Cooper and coffee for herself. He'd expected her to sit beside Cooper, but she slid next to him. The warmth of her body stirred him, and he drew in the scent of citrus. Shampoo, he guessed. Her long hair that usually hung below her shoulders had been caught back with a cloth band.

Ethan sipped his coffee, listening to Lexie encourage Cooper to eat. The boy dug his fork into the potatoes and nibbled at the vegetable. The chop lay untouched. When Lexie mentioned Cooper had opened his grandparents' gifts earlier in the day, the boy's pale face brightened.

"I'll show you my presents. I got two videos and some puzzles."

His enthusiasm lifted Ethan's spirit. "Which videos?"

"*Shrek* and some cartoons."

"Like the one on your shirt?" Ethan pointed to the clever characters.

"No. These are my mom's drawings." He grasped the T-shirt on each side and stretched it forward. "See."

So that's what she did. He grinned at the design. "You're pretty good, Mom."

She gave him a playful grin. "Thanks."

Cooper rattled on, his spirit and energy improving, and Ethan tried to concentrate, but his closeness to Lexie distracted him. He loved her smile, even her grin, but today he'd seen too much grief in her eyes. He wanted to hold her close and warm away the sadness. When Laine had been sick, loneliness and sorrow settled around him like a blanket smothering all other emotion except anger. His bitterness had taken a long time to vanish. Now the bitterness had been replaced with acceptance. He'd leaned on the Bible during those difficult days and came to understand God's way, whether he liked it or not. But Lexie? She had little to lean on without being a believer. Her family seemed distant. No references to her husband. Death? Divorce? Separation? He would never ask.

"That's all." Cooper pushed the plate toward the edge of the table. "Let's have my birthday party."

Lexie looked at the plate, a faint frown pulling at her mouth, but she didn't comment. Instead, she scooted from the bench and carried the plate to the sink. The noise of the disposal sounded, then stopped. He watched her rinse the dish and slide it into the dishwasher.

Cooper followed her every move as she lifted the cover of a cake dish and pulled out a large chocolate creation. "My favorite. Double chocolate."

Lexie looked up and grinned. "What else for my favorite son?"

"I'm your only son, Mom."

Ethan chuckled until the words sank into his head. Only son. If Cooper didn't make it through this illness, Lexie would truly be alone. Just as he had been when Laine died. He tried to dislodge the feelings that crashed around him. Being alone. Not being a family. It wasn't how God meant it to be. God said in Genesis, *"It is not good for the man to be alone. I will make a companion who will help him."* A companion to complete him. That's what he'd missed. Being complete.

Lexie blocked their view of the cake, and when she turned around, she'd topped it with eight lighted candles. Cooper clapped his hands as she carried it toward him and set it on the table. They broke into the song "Happy Birthday" and he and Lexie joined in the clapping.

"Make a wish, Cooper." He would love to ask the boy about his wish. Where would he like to go? Who would he want to meet? What would fill him with happiness even for a short time?

Cooper closed his eyes, then opened them and blew out the candle.

They all extinguished, and Cooper beamed. "I can't tell my wish or it won't come true."

Ethan's pulse kicked. That was the myth, but he wished he knew what Cooper asked for.

Lexie slipped away again and brought back plates and a knife, slicing thick pieces of cake for him and Cooper before cutting a small piece for herself. "Let me refresh your coffee."

Before he could respond, she stepped away again and came back with the pot. "How about ice cream? We have vanilla and chocolate."

"Chocolate." Cooper answered first.

What else would a boy want whose favorite cake was double chocolate? Ethan chuckled. He was a chocolate fan, too. "Same for me."

Cooper lifted his hand for a high five, raising Ethan's spirit another notch.

While Lexie was dishing the ice cream, Ethan slipped back to the living room and brought the gift to the table. Cooper eyed it a moment, grinned and dug into his treats. Ethan placed the package beside him on the seat and enjoyed the dessert. The homemade cake was as moist and rich as he'd ever tasted, and he let Lexie know.

Cooper slowed down. He'd eaten much of the cake and some ice cream, but it was obvious he'd begun to tire again.

"Is it time for a present?" Ethan looked at Lexie for confirmation.

She agreed, and Ethan handed the gift to Cooper.

He tore off the paper and let out a yell. "A camera." His eyes widened. "My very own camera."

Ethan heard Lexie's intake of breath.

He glanced at her, hoping she wasn't upset. "I figured a boy who loves photography ought to take some pictures of his own."

"Wow! Mom." Cooper shoved the camera toward her. "Look. It's a *real* camera."

She gazed at Ethan, her eyes wide. "You shouldn't have. It's too expensive."

"They get less expensive every day, and he needs a camera."

"I need it, Mom. Maybe when I grow up, I could be a photographer and travel all over the world taking pictures of places."

The hope Ethan heard in the child's voice rent his heart. He managed to wrap his words around his tongue. "Sounds like a good plan, Coop." He'd never called him Coop before, but it seemed right.

The boy hugged the camera to his chest. "I love it, Ethan."

"I'm glad." *And I love you, too, Cooper.* He wanted to say

the words aloud. "The camera's digital so it will take lots of pictures, and your mom can put them on the computer so you can see them."

The boy continued to clutch the camera against his chest, his face tired but smiling. "Mom, show Ethan what you gave me for my birthday. It's a Wii with the sports games."

"I thought it would give him exercise when—"

"'Cuz I can't go to school." He pressed his lips together. "I really want to go to school, but the Wii will be fun, and I can invite kids over to play, too." His eyes widened. "Or you could play with me...and Mom."

His words washed over Ethan. He needed to set boundaries and expectations, but how could he discourage the boy and did he really want to? "Okay. We got a deal."

Cooper's enthusiasm subsided as his face twisted in pain.

Lexie leaned forward. "What's wrong?"

"I don't feel good."

Lexie rose. "In what way? Are you nauseated?"

"My stomach hurts." He covered his mouth as moisture dampened his eyes.

"Can you get upstairs?" Lexie leaned closer, her face pinched with worry.

He sat a moment without answering. "Maybe."

Lexie straightened as Ethan rose from the bench. "How about if I give you a birthday lift?"

"A what?"

His color looked terrible. Ethan didn't wait for the answer. He reached out to Cooper and scooped him into his arms. "I'll carry you up."

Cooper didn't fight him. He wrapped his arms around Ethan's neck as he hurried up the stairs. Lexie followed behind him, and when he reached the top, he paused. "Bathroom or bed?"

"Which one, Coop?"

"Bed."

Ethan carried him to his room and placed him on the mattress. He stepped aside for Lexie to take over. Instead of waiting there, he headed into the outer room and stood near the window. The moon rose above the next housetop, and Ethan's gaze drifted to the stars, longing to be able to wish on one. Better he prayed for Cooper and for Lexie.

When he heard a sound, he turned and Lexie stepped from the room and crossed over to him. "Thanks so much."

"You're welcome. I'm glad I was here."

She touched his arm. "So am I."

He wanted to cup her hand in his.

"I don't have people to lean on. I've learned to stand on my own, but sometimes it's nice to have someone to…"

He slipped his arm around her shoulder. "To be there with you."

She nodded and rested her head against his chest. "It's comforting."

His pulse skipped, hearing her words.

She eased her head away and raised her gaze to his. "This is one of the things that happens to Cooper following the treatment and the new medication." She motioned to the chairs and slipped away. "Would you like to sit here? I don't want to be too far away."

His arm felt empty without her there. "Smart." He glanced at the moon again, then stepped from the window and sank into the nearest chair. No one to lean on. Her voice lingered in his mind. "What's going on with Cooper? You said he had a new medication."

She sank into the other chair and lifted the footrest as she stretched her legs on the cushion. "Today he had his chemo treatment and then a spinal tap procedure. They'd hoped his ANC count would improve, but it hasn't."

"That means he has to be careful about infection."

"Right. He can't attend school until his balance is good. You hear how badly he wants to go, and it breaks my heart. He needs the white blood cells that are neutrophils. Those are the ones that fight infection. Since that's not happening, they've added methotrexate to his medication, and the higher the dosage the more adverse effects it can have." She motioned to the child's bedroom. "Tonight's an example. Nausea and vomiting can accompany the treatment, and if it gets too bad, I'll have to take him to emergency."

A helpless feeling flooded Ethan. "I can't even imagine."

Compassion filled her eyes. "Sure you can. You've experienced having someone you loved deal with a fatal illness." Her expression changed and curiosity took over.

Ethan saw the question coming, the question he didn't want to answer. He gave her a feeble nod. "I have."

She closed her eyes, and when she opened them, her gaze captured his. "Then you understand."

His pulse quickened. Her tender expression touched him, remembering his own pain. "But this is your child. Your flesh and blood. That goes against nature."

"It does." She lowered her gaze again and sank into her thoughts.

Ethan wished tonight could have been a true happy birthday for Cooper. And he'd wanted some quality time to get to know Lexie better, but this wasn't it. So many questions filled his head, but taking it slowly made more sense than acting as if he were doing a survey. "Each day's a struggle, but think of one bright side of the situation. You're blessed that you work at home. You can be with Cooper and not have to depend on childcare."

She studied him a moment. "You're right. I'm grateful for that."

"I assume you're in graphic art."

"Right. I'm a graphic designer. I love the work."

The new topic gave Ethan a reprieve. "What do you do? I saw that cartoon on Cooper's shirt."

She shifted against the cushion, her face relaxing. "I create CD and DVD covers. The project I'm working on now involves DVD covers for a company that makes cartoons and kids' animated movies with characters like the one on Cooper's shirt. When I first begin doing jobs like that and start brainstorming the cover art, I always ask myself what would catch Cooper's eye." She slipped her feet to the floor.

"He's your artistic mentor."

She grinned. "He inspires me. I figure if Coop likes it, then other kids will. It's worked so far."

Grateful for the stress-free conversation, Ethan leaned forward. "I'd like to see some of your work."

Her eyes brightened. "Anytime, but not tonight. My computer's downstairs."

"I didn't mean tonight. We're on alert here. I'm not budging."

Lexie studied him, her eyes lingering over his face, and the look sizzled in his chest. He managed to keep eye contact with her, not wanting to look away. The silence felt too important as if they were each surveying the other for answers they would never hear until they knew each other better.

"You're a nice man, Ethan."

Her statement came out of nowhere, and his chest constricted. He grasped his composure. "Thanks. I admire you, too. You've gone through so much, and you can still smile."

"It's that or sob. I'd rather smile." She glanced at her watch. "I'd better check on him."

Ethan sat on the edge of the chair and craned his neck toward the door. Only a second passed before Lexie came out with Cooper and headed into the bathroom. He sensed he was infringing on their privacy as he heard the boy's struggle in the bathroom. He should have left earlier, but he'd waited too long to leave now. Anyway, she might need him again.

Minutes passed, and Ethan rose, pacing the room and cringing at the retching sounds that penetrated the walls. He ached for the child. His pacing continued while he longed to do something. Anything.

The bathroom door opened, and Lexie faced him. "Ethan, I'm sorry, but I think I need to get Cooper to emergency."

"I'll take you." He crossed to her side.

"No. I'll manage. Don't put yourself out for—"

"I want to go, Lexie. Let me take you."

She gave a nod, gratefulness filling her eyes.

"We'd better go now." Ethan strode toward the bathroom and waited while she helped the boy wipe his mouth before he stepped inside. He cradled the boy in his arms and hurried down the stairs, his heart in his throat.

Her only son. His mind repeated the words with every step he took. What would Lexie do if the boy didn't win the battle?

Chapter Five

Ethan eyed the waiting room door for the hundredth time. He closed his eyes and sent up another prayer, asking the Lord to hold Cooper in the palm of His hand. His own hands ached with the grip he'd had on the arms of the uncomfortable chair. He loosened his fingers and stretched them, then focused on the door again.

The clock hands crept around the face. He'd compared his watch to the wall clock, and they were basically the same, both inching the minute hand forward each agonizing second.

He pushed his body upward and stood on wobbly legs. His right foot tingled with sleep, and he shifted his weight until the tingle faded. He stretched, gazing around the room at other anxious faces, doing what he had been doing for forty-five minutes. Waiting.

Magazines lay piled on a nearby table. He wandered over and shifted them, looking for anything that would grab his attention, something that would relieve the stress. Periodicals on health, women's magazines, news, sports. He tossed them down. His interest was Cooper. It began and ended there.

He turned from the magazines and strode back to his chair. As his legs bent to sit, Lexie's voice jerked him upward. She stood inside the door, her face weary, yet her eyes filled with hope.

Ethan rushed toward her, longing to hug her. "How is he?"

"A little better, I think. They gave him something to help him sleep."

He lay his palm on her shoulder, and she leaned closer, pressing her forehead against his cheek. His longing kicked into gear, and he slipped his arm around her back and drew her closer. She didn't resist. Tension gave way from her body.

She eased against him. "I'm tired."

He moved his hand across her back, hoping to soothe her. A longing rose to kiss her. "I know. It's difficult waiting."

She lifted her head, and her eyes caught his. "You've been waiting almost an hour. I'm sorry."

"Don't be sorry. I feel badly Cooper's so ill, but I told you before. I'm glad I'm here for both of you."

She rocked her head from side to side. "Ethan, you're too good to us."

She deserved so much better. That had been his prayer. "I can never be too good, Lexie. I wouldn't be here if I didn't care."

"I know, and that's what amazes me. You barely know us."

He managed to grin. "I'm getting there."

Her mouth curled upward. "I guess you are." She squeezed him, then relaxed and dropped her arms. "Let's sit a few minutes."

The feeling of her in his arms played in his memory. Soft and warm. Trusting. He'd missed those sensations, but to get through Laine's death, he'd forced the emotions away. Locked them up. Secured them so tightly he'd nearly forgotten the beauty of sharing a moment that close with another human being.

She slipped into a chair, and he joined her, wanting to offer comfort but not knowing how. He covered her hand with his and remained silent. They sat as the clock clicked the seconds, each delving into their thoughts, each feeling emotions they couldn't share. He could guess hers. A mother facing her son's tragic disease must long for a miracle, for anything to take away the fear and the pain of seeing her child so ill.

His feelings were different. For the first time in years, he'd unlocked the trunk he'd closed. He'd allowed his emotions to respond to a woman and not just any woman. To Lexie, a woman who'd opened his heart.

Lexie shifted, and Ethan pulled away his hand. She pushed herself from the chair and rose. "I think they'll keep him overnight at least." She checked her watch. "If you don't mind waiting a few more minutes, I'll go and check."

"Take as long as you need."

She turned and slipped through the doorway.

He placed his palm on his knee, asking himself questions that had no answers. What did he expect of their relationship? Could he make it through another grave battle with cancer and come out unscathed? Would Lexie open her heart when hers was tied to her child's needs? Should he be a friend and try to keep it that way or let his heart go where it willed? A thought poked him. Or was it where God willed? Did he have a choice? This relationship might be God's doing. It might have nothing to do with the kind of relationship his emotions were taking him through. Was this an act of compassion? Was he the catalyst for Lexie's faith? The questions reeled in his mind.

"Ethan."

He jerked his head upward, surprised to see Lexie had returned.

"You looked deep in thought."

He rose, willing his thoughts away from the journey they'd been on. "How's he doing?"

"They want to keep him tonight, so we can go."

"Are you sure?" He studied her.

"I'm a veteran at this. Don't worry about me. Hopefully he'll be released tomorrow."

"Is he sleeping?"

She nodded. "I kissed him goodbye. I'm okay to go. This is a natural setback with the new medication. Cooper will be fine tomorrow." Her eyes searched his with the look of confidence. "Really."

Ethan forced his legs to move. She might be okay to go, but he remembered the times he made it home only to be called back to the hospital again. He opened his mouth to voice his concern, but Lexie looked content so he remained silent.

When he pulled out onto the highway, he left Lexie in her solitude. His tongue had adhered to the roof of his mouth with words he couldn't speak and emotions he couldn't swallow. Lexie stared out the passenger window, and her silence felt deafening.

Instead of forcing conversation, Ethan sank into his own thoughts until she spoke his name. He glanced at her. "Are you okay?"

"Thoughtful." Her gaze drifted back to the window for a moment until she shifted and gazed at his profile. "Have you healed from your wife's death?"

The question knocked the wind out of him. He swallowed and asked himself where the question had come from. "As much as anyone can heal from a horrendous ordeal like that. She was part of my life for eight years. We were married seven of those, and it was wonderful."

"You still love her."

Though confused, his heart warmed. "For sure." He glanced her way, struck by the thoughtful look on her face. "How could I not love a person who brought me so much happiness?" He slowed for a light and stopped. "But she's gone, Lexie, and as much as she remains in memories, Laine is not here. It took me a few years to—"

"Four, you said."

She'd remembered. "Yes, four. Four long years to realize that she was gone but I wasn't. Laine would want me to be happy again. She would want me to have children. I have no doubt about that."

"Then…" She lowered her gaze. "Why are you still single?"

His heart plummeted to his stomach. "I haven't found—" Hadn't. He hadn't found the woman until maybe now. "I'm waiting for God's leading."

She tilted her head. "His leading? What does that mean?"

He searched for an analogy she would understand. "You know when you're trying to find the perfect outfit to wear to a party. Or you have so many choices and nothing seems the right one until you look in a new direction, and your gaze zooms in to one you hadn't noticed. Right then, you know that's the perfect choice—the perfect dress to wear. You put it on and feel wonderful in it." He chuckled, realizing how feeble his explanation seemed. "I don't hear a voice, but I feel it. Right here." He pressed his hand against his chest.

"And that's God's leading?" Her eyes narrowed, and she released a lengthy breath. "I'm not sure I've felt that."

"I'd guess you have a few times in your life." The light turned green, and he returned his foot to the accelerator, giving himself time to think. "How about when you got married? Or when you had Cooper?"

Her eyes widened. "Cooper." Tension eased on her face.

"Yes." Her head inched up and down in three short nods. "Yes. When I had Cooper, I knew it was right and beautiful."

"That's when I would know it was God's leading."

The troubled look returned. "I don't know if that…"

The expression twisted his heart. The look of anguish and doubt. He tried to make sense out of it. "Is it the idea of God? Or is it believing?"

She didn't respond.

Ethan watched moisture rim her eyes, and he wanted so badly to help, to do something to make the hurt go away. He wanted to ask about her husband. Was that the hurt she felt? Had he left her? Died? But the questions sank back into his mind. This moment was for listening and waiting.

"Sometimes I feel as if I'm missing something. I don't know if it's God or a life without sorrow." She shook her head. "I really don't know."

His chest tightened, hearing her say that much. She wanted to believe. He sensed that, but finding the Lord had to be personal and in His time. Ethan would be an example. That's all he could do. "You'll figure it out. Just keep your mind and heart open."

She pressed her lips together for a moment. "How could you believe and yet face your wife's death? That's what I don't get. I thought God was supposed to be loving."

Ethan's breath hitched, and his lungs emptied of air. He had no idea how to explain why God did what He did. Ethan trusted. That was it. He grappled to fill his lungs. "I trust Him. I'm finite. He's infinite. God knows things I don't, so I accept those terrible situations, knowing He has a reason that I will never know until I meet Him face-to-face." He dragged in another breath. "I know that sounds simplistic, but that's what my heart believes. It's trust and that's faith."

"And it's hope." She raised her eyebrows, a faint grin on her mouth.

"Yes. We're back to that."

"I admire you, Ethan. You've had your feet knocked out from under you, but you stand firm like a fortress."

He wanted to tell her God was the fortress. He was the lichen clinging to its sides. But he didn't say it. He'd said enough for now. "Thanks. I admire you, too. You've been staunch and so independent, but now I think you can relax. It's okay to ask for help. It's okay to say you need someone by your side. I don't know where you've gotten your strength."

"From experience."

She quieted again, and Ethan knew he had to let the silence remain. She needed to think, and he needed to pray that the Lord would slip between the cracks of her heart and settle there.

Lexie leaned her back against the picnic table and watched Ethan with Cooper. From what she could tell, Cooper's goal was to use every bit of the memory card in his new camera. He'd taken a couple close-ups of her, pictures of grass blades, wildflowers, leaves, a ladybug, the wood texture on the picnic bench and the apples she'd brought for them to eat.

"Mom."

She gazed at the smile on Cooper's face, and her heart warmed like the sun.

Cooper wiggled his finger for her to come, and she rose, delighted to see her boy look so happy and healthy. A glow brightened his cheeks rather than the sallow shade of his skin for so many weeks. When she reached him, he handed her the camera.

"Take a picture of me and Ethan."

She grasped the camera, her gaze drifting to Ethan's surprised expression. "Is it okay?"

"Sure." He crouched beside Cooper.

But Ethan's face showed an expression not quite as certain as his voice.

Lexie stood back, adjusted the lens for a close-up of their heads and torsos. Her heart lurched when she watched Cooper lean his knit cap against Ethan's cheek. Stress glided across Ethan's face before he covered it with a smile. She snapped the photograph and returned the camera to Cooper.

But Ethan's look troubled her, and she longed to ask him what he was thinking. Yet when questions came, she avoided prodding his thoughts. She might hear things she didn't want to hear. Though she'd been edgy at times with their relationship, she told herself she did it for Cooper. Truth be told, Lexie had to admit she enjoyed his company. He'd been a gentleman all the way, never stepping outside the bounds of friendship or making suggestive comments.

What confused her was the disappointment she felt when he maintained the boundary. Dealing with Cooper's illness had preoccupied her life, so the new emotional sensations threw her off balance.

"Mom."

She jerked her mind back to Cooper. "What?"

"Can't you see me?"

She realized he'd been beckoning to her again.

Cooper continued to motion her to come closer. "I want to take a picture of you and Ethan."

Her heart pounded. "You've taken enough photographs. You'll run out of memory in one day."

"No, I won't." He spun around to face Ethan. "You told me that we can put them on the computer, right?"

Ethan glanced her way with a subtle shrug. "Right. You save the pictures on the computer."

Cooper widened his eyes. "Okay, Mom?"

A stream of breath escaped her as she looked at Ethan.

A gentle grin swept across his face. "It's hard to fight logic."

She moved to Ethan's side, and they faced Cooper who stood back, adjusting the lens. He'd caught on so fast it amazed her.

"Closer." Cooper motioned for them to shift.

She let her arm touch Ethan's and felt his palm glide across her back as his embrace wrapped around her shoulders.

Cooper grinned. "Okay. Smile."

She smiled and her pulse quickened at Ethan's closeness. If she could understand her reaction, she would feel better. Instead of fighting her feelings, she moved away from the source and settled back on the picnic bench. Life wasn't soft and cushy. Getting used to pleasures could only lead to disappointment.

Cooper and Ethan strode her way, her son beaming as he talked with Ethan. What if...? Her stomach knotted. No. Don't go there. Questions were useless when the answers hid behind Ethan's kindness. He knew the truth. She could only presume.

"I'm finished." Cooper set the camera on the picnic table. "Can I have something to eat?"

The abrupt photo-taking end roused her curiosity, and she eyed Ethan.

Ethan gave her a wink. That was all. He must have said something to Cooper, or she assumed he'd be taking photographs until the sun set.

Lexie opened the picnic container and pulled out two apples and a banana. Cooper grasped one apple and Ethan, the other. She retrieved the banana and stripped off the peel as the sugary scent surrounded her.

Ethan settled beside her on the bench while Cooper sat behind her. Lexie swiveled on the seat and tossed her legs over the wooden plank to face him. "You look so much better, Coop."

"I feel good."

She'd heard that so often, but this time she believed him. "I know you do."

"Maybe Dr. Herman will let me go to school." Hopefulness glinted in his eyes.

The look weakened her. "Maybe he will."

Ethan gave him a high five. "That would be great, Coop. I'd be as happy as you are."

"Really?" Cooper's face glowed.

"Really."

Ethan's comment should have pleased her, but as always, she second-guessed the meaning. If Cooper were in school, Ethan wouldn't have reason to spend time with him. The thought hurt. Not only for herself but for her son. She couldn't count on this man to stay around. Ethan wanted to fulfill Cooper's dreams, and she needed to keep his purpose in her mind and stop letting other foolish thoughts get in the way of reality.

She rose and strode to a nearby trash bin. She lifted the lid and tossed the banana peel into the container. If only she could toss away her nagging thoughts. Being grateful that Ethan cared about Cooper had to become her primary focus. He visited for a practical reason. Yes. That was his motivation. She swallowed and turned to face the picnic table. "Are you ready to go?"

Cooper hopped off the bench and darted toward her. "We're going for ice cream. Ethan knows the best place. Ray's. That's what he said."

Ice cream, Ethan said. Her child beamed up at her. How could she say no?

Lexie grinned at the sound of Cooper and Lucy quibbling over a puzzle in the second-floor playroom. Kelsey's voice floated down the stairs as she tried to teach them how to compromise. Good luck, Kelsey, Lexie thought. She poured two glasses of iced tea and two glasses of milk. Then she added a few cookies. Maybe a treat would help them forget who did what to whom.

After putting the drinks on a small tray, she carried the treats upstairs and set the drinks in front of the three. She settled beside Kelsey in a comfy chair away from the puzzle table. While she had too much on her mind today to be a good hostess, the playtime was needed for Cooper. Soon he would be back in school, and he needed the opportunity to socialize with others his age.

"Cooper's doing so well. I'm happy for you both." Kelsey lifted the glass and sipped the tea.

"It's amazing. These last treatments have turned things around, although I thought they'd be the end of him." Her chest emptied of air. "I'm not kidding."

"I know you're not."

"He's been having so much fun with the camera he got for his birthday. We went to the park and took some pictures. They're pretty good." She rose. "Come with me a minute. I'll show you. They're on the computer."

Kelsey rose and followed her to the stairs. "You gave him a digital camera?"

Lexie's pulse kicked. "It was a birthday gift." She stopped before mentioning Ethan again. Kelsey made too much out of everything.

Inside the den, she hit the space bar, and the computer awakened. "I really think he has talent." She turned to Kelsey. "You know how he loves all those books with pictures of national parks and nature. One of his newest has a lot of close-ups, and he was so curious." She slipped into the chair and worked through links to the photographs, then set up a slide show. Before clicking, she rose from the chair. "Sit. You can see them better."

Lexie stepped back and motioned Kelsey to take the seat, then clicked on the tab. The slide show began, the park, wood grain, tree bark, flowers so close a bee was caught gathering pollen.

Kelsey gazed at the monitor. "These are really good."

Standing behind her, Lexie nodded, for once feeling like any proud mother. Not proud because Cooper hadn't complained during his chemo treatments or how good he was when he was denied attending school, but a normal pride of her son with a talent she hadn't known about.

The photos moved past, and Lexie chuckled at the number of shots Cooper had taken. Then her eyes widened, and Lexie couldn't do a thing. The photograph moved from the close-up of Cooper with Ethan to one of her and Ethan nestled together, his arm evident around her back.

Kelsey stared at the photo for a moment before she pivoted and grinned. "Hmm? The big brother relationship has definitely grown into something more."

Why had she forgotten the photo? Lexie wanted to explain, but words and thoughts muddled into her mind like a rock pile. She shifted one way and was tripped up by a boulder, then moved another and slipped on the stones. The fall hurt. "I'm not hiding anything. I don't know what our relationship is." She closed her eyes and pictured them together. "It's started as a friendship, and that's what it is now. He's done nothing that leads me to believe it's any more than that."

Kelsey's teasing grin sobered. "And you're disappointed."

"Sometimes." She studied the carpet wishing she had clearer thoughts. "Then I think it's good. Cooper's my priority. I don't have time to split my attention with anyone else, and I don't know of any man or woman who wants that kind of relationship."

"Someone with a good heart would. Someone who loves you both."

Her lungs constricted. "Maybe, but he's not there. Not love."

"Not yet, but don't toss it away, Lexie. Keep your heart open." She rose and embraced her. "Life is lonely sometimes, and when Cooper's well and involved with school and his life, you could be sitting on the sidelines asking yourself what happened."

"The thought of Cooper being well is all I need right now."

Kelsey released a stream of air. "I know. I've been there so often." She stepped back and drew up her shoulders. "I don't want you to close yourself from possibilities. Just be open."

"I'll try. I have dreams, too. I don't have a heart of stone."

A chuckle hit Lexie's ears. "You have a heart of gold. I wouldn't be a friend if I didn't respect you."

Respect. The conversation released another lingering thought. "This is a different subject, but I do have a question."

Kelsey studied her a minute. "Okay."

"You're a Christian."

"Sure am, and I know you question my faith, but that doesn't—"

"I'm not challenging you. I know you care about me despite that." She tried to untangle her thoughts. "When I was talking with Ethan, I asked him how he could believe and still accept that God allowed his wife to die, and he said he didn't question God because God was infinite and knew what was going to happen, that God had a reason for doing things."

"Most Christians believe God has a plan for their lives."

"Right." The idea hit her like one of the stumbling blocks she ran into. "So here's the question. If God has a plan, then what's the point? Just sit in a chair and everything will fall into place. Everyone is a puppet."

Kelsey's head rocked back and forth, and she rested her hand on Lexie's shoulder. "You missed one major point."

"What do you mean?"

"Have you ever made a plan that fell through?"

"But God, if He's so great, would make the perfect plan."

"He would and He does, but the plan falls through because we have free choice. It's one of the things the Lord gave us. We can decide to follow God's lead or we can do our own thing. We can be quiet and listen to God's quiet voice, so quiet it's only the wind in our ears, or we can listen to our own big mouth. We have free will. God doesn't want puppets. He wants children who love Him so much they want to listen and follow."

"Free will." Choices. She'd bungled many of her choices. Too many of them.

Kelsey nodded. "You want Cooper to mind you, not because he has to, but because he loves you so much that he wants to please you and do what's right."

That made sense. Lexie gave a quick nod.

"God loves us so much that He allows us to follow Him by loving Him back. And just like we do with our children, we forgive and offer them a second chance. Our Lord is a God of second and third chances. His arms are always open. He created us, and we are His."

Love that deep from a God she'd never known. But He knew her. Something moved inside her. Warmth filled her chest and tightened her heart. Lexie struggled with the sensation, unfamiliar and frightening. Except for her total love for Cooper, she had felt empty for so long. "Thanks. I need to think about this."

"Faith is a seed, my friend. It plants in our thoughts, vines its way to our hearts and grows in our souls. It doesn't happen overnight."

"But things can happen during the day." Lexie grinned and pointed to the second floor. "We'd better get up there and check on the kids, although they are quiet."

Kelsey chuckled. "That could be good or bad. Lucy may have gagged Cooper and tied him to the chair. She's pretty determined."

"Sort of like her mother." She slipped her arm around Kelsey's shoulder as they headed for the staircase.

Chapter Six

Ethan unlatched his seat belt and shifted sideways for a better view of the elementary school's entrance. His watch read two-thirty and within the next few minutes, children would spill from the school like puppies freed from the confines of their cages.

When the wide door swung open and two older boys bolted onto the sidewalk, Ethan stepped outside and rounded his car, his gaze focused on the doorway. He leaned his back against the passenger door as he watched for Cooper.

Weight had lifted from his chest two weeks ago when Lexie greeted him with the good news that Cooper's latest tests showed a favorable remission, allowing him to return to school with only a few stipulations. Wanting to attend classes so badly, Cooper didn't complain. Just being in school meant everything to him.

Ethan had his own hopes for Cooper. Dreams Come True. He hadn't mentioned his thoughts to Lexie yet, but if Cooper could return to his classes, fulfilling one of his dreams couldn't be far behind.

Warmed by the idea, Ethan closed his eyes aware that his excitement might not meet Lexie's. Her concern remained obvious. Cooper's remission could end with little notice, and he'd be back in heavy-duty treatment again. Ethan couldn't bear the thought.

He opened his eyes in time to see Cooper stride through the doors and stop, his gaze searching the line of cars for his mother's burgundy sedan. Ethan raised his arm and gave a wave, and when Cooper spotted him, a smile burst on his face as he darted toward him, calling his name.

"Hi, Coop." Ethan opened his arms to greet him. "Your mom had some things to do so I offered to pick you up. I hope that's okay."

"Okay?" Cooper's forehead wrinkled. "I like you to pick me up. It's fun."

Fun? Reality charged through Ethan's chest. The boy didn't have a dad to pick him up, and here he was playing dad to the boy. He couldn't comment. He grasped the door handle and pulled the passenger door open.

Cooper grinned at him and slipped onto the seat, dragging his backpack to the floor.

Ethan closed the door and stood a moment, calming his thoughts. He never wanted to mislead the child or make promises he couldn't keep. But Cooper's smile fluttered through his chest and encapsulated his heart, making his action seem right and good. He served as a role model. Wasn't that what his aim had been?

When he settled beside Cooper, his concern had eased and then vanished when the boy began talking about school and what he'd done all day. "I can't play at recess, though."

"But that's okay, isn't it? At least you're—"

"At least I'm in school." His shoulders lifted. "That's the good part."

"It sure is. School can be good even without recess."

He nodded as he dragged up his backpack.

Ethan concentrated on the traffic, wishing he'd thought of something fun to do with the boy. To him, picking Cooper up at school had excited him. Trying to ignore his internal motivation failed. But Cooper wasn't his son. He belonged to Lexie, and keeping that in mind had to be his priority. He couldn't step over the bounds of being a big brother, a role model or whatever he called it.

"Look."

Cooper's voice flew past him as the boy thrust a piece of notebook paper toward him.

He glanced down and spotted a big red mark at the top. "An A. Wow, Coop. That's great. What class is that for?"

"Spelling. I got an A in spelling. I wish it had been my math paper. I only got a B-plus today."

"B-plus is good, and maybe I..." His response died as Cooper's statement filled his mind. *I wish.* What did he wish? What young boy dreams did he have? It wasn't too early to gather ideas.

"And maybe what?"

Ethan's mind churned. "Maybe I can help you with your math and next time you'll get an A."

"Good idea." He grinned and slipped the A paper back into his backpack. "You can help me tonight."

Tonight? "We'll have to check with your mom. She's the boss."

Cooper giggled. "She's the boss all right."

A chuckle slipped from Ethan's throat, too. "How about a treat? We'll stop at the Dairy O. I noticed it's opened for the season." Cooper's expression answered his question.

"Can we take a cone to Mom?"

"We can call and see if she's home yet." He gazed at the child's wide eyes. "Otherwise it would melt before she could eat it."

Cooper giggled. "Then I'd have to eat it."

Ethan laughed as he turned the key in the ignition and maneuvered his exit from the school parking lot. But the boy's bright eyes and smile aroused Ethan's guilt. He wanted to talk with Cooper when they were alone. Grill him was more like it. Learning Cooper's longings, his dreams and wishes, would help Ethan begin to look into what Dreams Come True could offer the boy…and his mom. Lexie's desire to see her child healthy burned in his gut. He'd dealt with the same wishes during Laine's illness, and he prayed the result would be positive.

Cooper rested his head against the seat cushion, and Ethan recognized the tired expression on his face. School took a lot out of a child who faced chemotherapy and the fight to win the battle against cancer. Ethan was about to suggest they head home instead, but he recalled the boy's enthusiasm for a trip to Dairy O. He let his comment fade. Ice cream wouldn't take that long.

He found a parking spot, and Cooper seemed to revive as he jumped from the SUV and darted toward the outside window. Ethan gazed at the twenty-plus flavors of soft ice cream while Cooper read the choices aloud. When their turn came, Cooper ordered chocolate with sprinkles, and Ethan anticipated the rich flavor of his choice as he watched the swirl of German chocolate filling his cone.

"Want to sit outside or in the car?"

With no answer, Cooper headed for an outside table and plopped down.

Ethan grasped a few napkins from the holder on the window ledge before following him. When he straddled the chair, Cooper already had an ice cream mustache. He chuckled and handed him a napkin.

Cooper slid it across his mouth and dived back into the cone.

The boy's innocence humbled him. The child's life revolved around hospitals, chemotherapy, puzzles and longing for school. Where was the joy a child should experience?

Dreams Come True could provide at least one special week in Cooper's life. He watched the boy lick the drips from the cone. "How was school today other than recess?"

His blue eyes twinkled. "Good."

Good. Always the answer. "What's really good is you don't have to wish to go to school anymore. You're in school, just where you wanted to be."

He nodded.

Questions tumbled into Ethan's mind, but he struggled with whether to ask them. Time was available, and they were alone. He'd set up the situation, and wise or not, he wanted to know. "Now that you don't have to wish about going to school, what else would you want, Coop? What kinds of things make you happy?" There, he'd asked.

Cooper's forehead furrowed before he took another lick of his vanishing ice cream. He shrugged. "I want to stay in school and not have to do homeschool again. That would make me happy."

Ethan's gut wrenched at the simple answer. His big plans for the child sat like a massive blob in his mind. "That would make a lot of people very happy."

"My mom for sure."

"For sure, and I would be happy, too." Ethan wished he could grant that dream, but the Lord was in charge of those vast desires, and they happened in His time, not Cooper's or in Ethan's own longing. "No other wishes? Dreams?" Why did he keep probing. He needed to let the child be content enjoying school and getting better.

Cooper pushed the end of the cone into his mouth and pulled off his cap. "This." He dropped the cap on the table and ran his hand over his fuzz-sprouting head. "Hair. That's what I want."

Ethan's shoulders weighted, but he managed to grin. "I've grown sort of fond of that bald head of yours." He reached over the table and brushed his palm against the new down.

"But I look like a peach. Not like you. I want real hair." He grinned. "And not a wig. Those are for girls."

Trying to drag air through his compressed lungs, Ethan faltered. Pushing the boy for his own need to do something verged on cruelty. He managed a grin. "Men don't wear wigs, huh?"

"Nope. We just wear caps and a smile. That's what Mom says."

Caps and a smile. Lexie's determination bolstered her son's joyful spirit. He'd never heard the child grumble or whine about his rotten life. He'd tackled it like a champ. That's what he was, and Ethan realized he could learn an important lesson from the boy.

Grin and bear it. And that's what he did. He smiled at Cooper and this time with his eyes as well as his mouth.

"Are you ready?" Lexie stood at the bottom of the staircase and called up to Cooper.

"A minute, Mom."

She strode back into the kitchen and checked the wall clock before slipping the bag of potato chips into the picnic hamper. Eyeing the contents, Lexie reviewed what she'd prepared: cookies, chips, fruit, bread, paper plates, plastic silverware and condiments. The ice chest held their drinks, meat and cheese for sandwiches, and potato salad. She brushed her hands on her pant legs and headed back to the staircase. Ethan would be there any minute, and for some reason, Cooper had slowed to a crawl. That always worried her.

When she stepped into the living room, Cooper bounded down the staircase, his cap in his hand. "I don't want to wear a hat. It's too hot."

Lexie eyed his quarter-inch stubble of hair and grinned. Seeing hair made her heart sing. "You don't have to wear the cap anymore. I thought you wanted to."

His head swung back and forth. "Nope. Tired of a hat." He patted his head. "This is my itchy hair, and I'm happy to feel it."

She moved to his side and wrapped one arm around him while her other hand tousled his bristles. "They make me happy, too, Coop." Happier than he'd ever know.

"Hello."

Ethan's voice reached Lexie before he appeared peeking through the front screen door. He stood there as if waiting to be invited inside.

Lexie beckoned him forward, and he bounded in, his eyes on Cooper's hatless head. "Lookin' good." He ruffled Cooper's new hair and gave him a hug.

Cooper responded with a clinging embrace that made Lexie uneasy. He'd become too attached to Ethan, but how could she ask the man his intentions without sounding like a woman begging for a proposal?

Her heart wrestled with the idea, along with another concern. Was Ethan her soul mate? A specific set of circumstances brought them together—Dreams Come True—and once Cooper's wish had been fulfilled, what excuse would Ethan have to hang around? She admonished herself for the thought. Ethan obviously cared about her son. He'd been there for those horrible moments in the hospital and had been attentive since they'd met. But questions still rang in her head. Why? Was it compassion? Christian responsibility? Pity? The word made her cringe. Her heart stirred. Or was it the beginning of love? The possibilities bugged her.

"Cooper, quit hanging on Ethan." Irritation rattled in her voice, but it was too late.

Cooper's questioning eyes captured hers as his arms slipped from Ethan. He eased back, a hangdog look growing on his face.

Ethan arched his brow. "Hugs never bother me, Lexie."

Guilt burned on her face. "I'm sorry, Coop." She couldn't explain her worries to him. "Do you have everything?"

"How about a ball?" Ethan rested his hand on Cooper's shoulder.

"Can we play ball?" His gaze sought hers again.

"You can play catch, but no running bases."

Ethan winked at her. "I doubt if I can run bases anymore."

Cooper giggled and hurried up the stairs again to search for a ball while she stood there facing Ethan as if he were the firing squad.

"Can I help you with anything?"

Knowing where he stood would help. "Everything's packed. You can load it in the car if you'd like."

His eyes crinkled in a smile. "When it's food, I'm happy to oblige." He headed toward the kitchen. "I brought a couple of lawn chairs. I thought they would be more comfortable than the picnic benches."

"Good idea." She followed him, trying to get her head wrapped around her attitude. Part of her realized she wanted to protect Cooper, but part of her wondered if she were protecting herself. Having a man in her life was a new experience. Cooper's father had been there and gone so quickly, and he really hadn't been part of her life. At least not the life that touched the world. As she looked back, she recognized their sort of clandestine relationship. An older man and a twenty-two-year-old college girl. And she'd even hid it from her parents, knowing they wouldn't approve.

Ethan slipped the basket on top of the ice cooler and hoisted them upward.

"I can carry the basket." She tried to grasp it, but he shifted away.

"Why bother? I have everything. You have Cooper."

She chuckled, enjoying his lightheartedness. "He is more than a handful sometimes."

Ethan gave her a wink and swung past her as he strode to the front door.

She ran ahead to catch the screen and held it while he took the steps to the sidewalk. When he'd reached his car, Lexie turned back inside, lifted by Ethan's presence. Sometimes her wavering spirit irritated her. One moment she doubted Ethan's motivation and the next moment, she felt grateful.

Before she had to call again, Cooper arrived with a ball and Frisbee. His bristled head still looked strange after being bald for so long, but the evidence of health caused her to rejoice. She'd longed for this day. She hoped the good news was permanent. Learning to trust a cancer diagnosis had become a battle. Hope had become her mainstay. Then there was Ethan who leaned on prayer.

Cooper bound through the door and toward the car. She wanted to caution him not to run, but seeing his enthusiasm made her stop. She would let him enjoy his health while he had it. She longed for the day when that constant niggling concern would be gone from her life.

She grabbed lightweight jackets for her and Cooper from the coat closet and tossed her purse over her shoulder before stepping outside and checking to make sure the door locked.

Cooper beckoned her to hurry, and she plastered a smile on her face as she bustled to Ethan's SUV, ready to head for their Memorial Day picnic at the park.

* * *

Ethan wrapped a piece of bread around another slice of ham and took a bite. Though he'd avoided questioning Lexie about her edgy mood again, it hadn't left his mind. He reviewed what he'd said and done and saw no call for her edginess. Cooper hugged him. That was it. What was the big deal?

Jealousy. Could that be it? She'd been responsible for her son without interference. Coop's father had been out of the picture for years, Ethan calculated. Maybe she feared he'd become too important to Cooper. He tilted his head up, gazing at the bright blue sky and only saw the boy's eyes. Today the sky matched the color to a tee.

When he shifted his gaze, Lexie was watching him, her face showing her feelings.

"Beautiful day."

She nodded, but her expression didn't change.

So much for trying to get over that hurdle. "Good food. I think I'll stop, though." He dropped the crust of the bread onto his paper plate. "If I finish one more bite, I won't be able to toss a ball, let alone catch one."

"Or a Frisbee." Cooper had ignored the rest of his sandwich for a cookie. "Can we play now?"

"That's up to your mom." He'd learned one thing today, to take baby steps when it came to his relationship with Cooper. He'd never seen that side of Lexie before.

"It's fine, but if you start to get tired promise me you'll stop."

A smile broke across Cooper's face. "Promise." He grabbed the ball from the table and darted across the lawn away from the picnic area.

Ethan followed him. "Slow down, Coop." He caught up with him and arched a brow. "Make your mom happy, okay? Don't overdo it."

"Okay." His voice held less enthusiasm, but he nodded and glanced toward Lexie, then gave her a wave.

Ethan looked over his shoulder and saw her wave back. She unfolded one of the chairs and sat beside the picnic table, her hands folded in her lap, but her feet straddled as if ready to dart to them if she were needed. Her apprehension made him ache. He pushed her look from his mind—or tried to—and focused on Cooper.

"Ready, Ethan."

He nodded and prepared for Coop's throw.

The ball sailed his way and he caught it, then sent it back, looping it upward. It dropped into Cooper's hands. He grinned at the boy's triumphant expression.

Ethan shifted his gaze, hearing Lexie's applause. She had a good heart and did what every mother did. She worried about her child. But she had her reasons, and he could feel every bit of her concern.

He caught the next ball, but Cooper missed his throw, and Ethan decided he'd buy the boy a mitt. The ball flew back and forth until he noticed Lexie's anxious expression. "Coop, let's take a break."

His unhappy grunt drifted across the air, but he didn't argue, though his shoulders drooped as he headed back to the picnic table.

Lexie's expression brightened. "How about some fruit or cookies?"

The food bait worked. Cooper settled onto the bench and tugged out a handful of cookies from the picnic basket.

Ethan grasped a banana and pulled down the peel. The sweet scent drifted to meet him, and he sank his teeth into the soft fruit. He settled onto the bench, his back against the table. Lexie had turned her chair around, facing him and he sent her a smile. She smiled back as if her earlier tension had vanished and his own stress eased. He lifted his face to the sunny sky and drew in a lengthy breath. He wished he and Lexie could be up-front with their worries. They both seemed to harbor internal thoughts that ruined their opportunity to be open. Ethan lowered his gaze and as he did, his pulse skipped, seeing a friend approaching him. He rose and strode toward him.

"Surprised to see you here." Ross extended his hand, then glanced toward Lexie.

Ethan grasped it with a firm shake and a grin. "You never know where I'll pop up on a holiday."

Ross looked at Cooper and one eyebrow raised for a second before he recovered.

Ethan beckoned Lexie toward him. "Lexie, this is Ross Salburg. He's another volunteer for the Dreams Come True foundation." He turned to Ross. "This is my friend, Lexie Carlson."

They shook hands as Cooper sidled over, his curiosity obvious.

"And this is Lexie's son, Cooper. We're out for some sunshine and a little Frisbee."

Ross's expression wavered from confused to amused. "Nice to meet you both." He shook Cooper's extended hand. "It's a beautiful day for a picnic."

"Would you care to join us?" Lexie motioned to the extra lawn chair. "We have leftovers, too, if you're hungry."

Ross grinned. "I have some family here and my daughter's waiting." He motioned toward a group of people setting up at another picnic table.

"How is she?" Once again Laine's death shrouded Ethan's memory. Ross had not only lost a wife, but his only child suffered from the same disease.

"Peyton's been okay lately."

Ethan's heart gave a tug. "Have you planned a Dreams

Come True event yet? She's not exempt just because you're on the board."

"I know." He rubbed his face. "I can't get too optimistic. Things turn around quickly, and I still haven't had the courage to tell her a heart transplant might be necessary."

Ethan caught his breath. "Let's pray that's not the case."

Ross glanced away. "I can only wish."

Hiding his grimace, Ethan sensed a doubt in Ross's voice. He thought his friend believed in prayer, but maybe he'd been wrong.

"Listen, I need to get back to the family." Ross took a couple steps backward. "Nice to meet you, Lexie." He shifted his gaze. "And you, too, Cooper."

Ethan watched him sprint toward his family, wishing he'd had something to say to heighten Ross's optimism. As so often happened when it came to serious illness, he failed to find the words. He didn't have them for Lexie, either.

She stepped closer and touched his arm. "What did he mean about a heart transplant?"

"His daughter has cardiomyopathy. She's about ten, I think. It's the same disease that took his wife."

Lexie released a groan. "I'm so sorry. I know that's a serious illness. Worse than—" She hesitated to finish her sentence.

Ethan realized Cooper had eased between them and was listening. "She's been doing very well for a while now. The physicians have been hopeful." He swallowed. "But you know how it is. Sometimes setbacks happen. It's part of the disease."

She nodded. "I know about setbacks." Her arm drifted around Cooper's shoulders. "Getting bored?"

Coop grinned. "No, but I thought about my wish."

"Your wish?" A frown marred the softness of her face.

"What do you mean?" She shifted her focus from him to Ethan.

"Ethan asked me if I could have a wish come true what would it be." He rubbed his head. "I told him hair, but that's coming back already."

Her frown deepened. "You asked Cooper about his dreams? His wishes?"

"We had an ice cream and—"

The same defensive expression flooded her face as it had early that day.

"I only asked him what he would wish for now that his previous wish had been answered. He's in school. That's what he wanted so badly."

"I said I wished for hair, Mom, but now I think I have another wish. I want to run and play without being careful. Being careful's not very fun."

Lexie didn't respond but her glare grew deeper.

"That's a good wish. Your mom wants that, too."

She broke eye contact for a moment. "That's a good wish, Coop." When her gaze caught Ethan's again, fire burned in her eyes. "I think that's enough wishing for now. Let's just be happy you're in school and doing so much better."

Cooper glanced from Lexie to him. He knew the boy was confused. So was he. He'd meant no harm. But this didn't set well with him, either, and he needed to get to the bottom of Lexie's sudden defensiveness.

Chapter Seven

Cooper tossed his backpack on the sedan floor and slipped into the seat. He eyed his mother a moment, then settled back against the cushion.

Lexie studied him. "What's wrong?"

He shrugged and looked out the passenger window. "Why didn't Ethan pick me up today?"

Ethan. So that was it. "Two reasons. I was home and wanted to pick you up, and I haven't seen Ethan."

Cooper didn't respond, his gaze still clinging to the passenger window.

"Why do you want Ethan to pick you up?"

"He's fun."

Right. Ethan's fun. And she wasn't. She turned the key in the ignition, checked for cars and pedestrians, then pulled away. Nothing would resolve the issue so she kept her mouth shut.

"Ethan takes me to Dairy O for ice cream."

Aha. Ice cream won over a mother's love. The comment banged around in her head until she faced the truth. Cooper's attraction for Ethan made her jealous. Cooper adored him. Ethan's presence stood right up there with ice cream. She kept her gaze ahead and turned onto the highway. Her mouth formed comments that she forced herself to swallow. Cooper was eight. She was thirty-three. She had to be the adult, not another child. "Would you like to stop at Dairy O? We can do that once in a while."

His head inched toward her. "Can we?"

"Sure."

He twisted his body and straightened in the seat. At least the offer of ice cream had melted his downtrodden look. She'd tried to hide her irritation with Ethan, but apparently she hadn't done a very good job. Ethan hadn't said much on the way home from the picnic, and he hadn't called afterward. She hadn't called him, either, but she should apologize. Sometimes Lexie didn't understand herself. With Cooper being in such good health and spirits, she should be buoyant with happiness. Instead she looked for problems. Ethan was often the center of them.

Fear. Confusion. She'd asked herself what life would be like again without Ethan and the answer stunned her. He'd become as important to her as to Cooper. That was the problem. She had no confidence in how Ethan felt about her. Sometimes she sensed his feelings had grown to include her in his attention to Cooper. Another day she feared it was pity or only his desire to bring one of Cooper's dreams into reality. Then he'd be gone from their lives.

Maybe that's what she should do. Encourage Cooper to tell Ethan his dream, let him fulfill it, and then say goodbye. Get it over with. The anticipation stung as much as what might really happen. And then maybe she'd blown it all out of proportion. Still, removing Dreams Come True from the equation made sense. Would Ethan stay or go?

She pulled into the Dairy O parking lot and stepped outside. Cooper beat her to the window. He ordered a chocolate cone with sprinkles, and she chose black cherry. As she headed back to the car, Cooper veered toward the outside tables. She curved her path and joined him.

Sitting in silence, Lexie studied Cooper, wanting to ask questions but not wanting to stir up problems again. "Is the chocolate good?"

He nodded and swiped the edge of the cone with his tongue. Ice cream smeared on his chin. Lexie rose and headed back to the window to grab some napkins. She handed Cooper a couple, and he wiped his mouth before eyeing her cone. "Ethan had German chocolate."

"He did?"

Cooper nodded. "We both like chocolate."

Her defenses flared until she slid her rebuttal comment—*I like chocolate, too*—out of her mind. She ignored his comment, knowing it was safer. But the questions returned as they sat there, and she drew in a lengthy breath, wanting to hold them back but sensing she would lose the fight. "When did Ethan ask you about your dreams?"

"Dreams?" His forehead wrinkled. "You mean what I wished for?"

She nodded.

He shrugged before his eyes widened. "When we were here. He said now that I had my big wish what other wishes did I have."

This time, she couldn't hold back a frown. "What big wish?"

"Mom." He dragged her name out as if she were stupid. "School. I got to go to school."

She laughed, watching his expression and his reaction. "Silly me."

He laughed, too. "That was my most important wish. Now I just want to stay better and grow hair."

His wishes were too practical. Little boys should want so many things that he'd never allowed himself to long for.

Ethan's idea made sense and maybe she should encourage Cooper to think outside his small box of expectations.

Ethan stepped into the Dreams Come True meeting room and spotted Ross. When they'd met in the park, Ethan had been uneasy, because he hadn't told anyone about his relationship with Lexie other than Bill Ruben. And then he didn't know what he felt for sure. He still wondered how orthodox it was to spend that much time with a child and his mother whom he'd met through the foundation. He knew his concern had little to do with ethics and more to do with his own confusion.

Losing a loved one to a horrible disease warped many people and introduced unreasonable fears. Miscarriages caused women to fear pregnancy again. Having a child die bred deep anxieties. People clung to fears rather than worked at reasoning them away. One miscarriage and one loss didn't mean others would follow.

Ethan looked up to see Ross standing a few feet away, peering at him as if he'd lost consciousness. He pushed a grin to his lips and headed for him. "Did you have a good time on Memorial Day? The weather was great."

"It was nice." Ross's comment slipped out followed by the question that he'd probably had in his mind the day they'd met at Clawson Park. "I didn't know you were dating."

Ethan's jaw dropped. Was he dating? Is that what Lexie thought? He called it spending time. Visiting Cooper. He'd called it everything but dating. "We're friends. Good friends."

A grin stole across Ross's face. "Okay, if that's what you want to call it."

Ethan opened his mouth to rebut but closed it again.

Ross rested his hand on Ethan's shoulder. "Where did you meet her? She's gorgeous."

Yes, she was. Yet her looks had only captured him for a moment. Instead he'd become enthralled with so many other things about her. "She's a member of Mothers of Special Kids. I did a Dreams Come True presentation for them, and we started talking. It just went from there."

Ross's eyebrows raised. "Mothers of Special Kids?"

Ethan studied Ross's curious expression.

"You know I'm a strong person."

Where did that come from? Ethan gave a nod. "Always."

"I've been strong with Peyton's illness, but I feel…"

"Alone." Ethan knew that feeling so well.

Ross nodded. "Alone and I've thought it would be nice to have some support. Is there a group for me? Fathers of Special Kids? If so, I'd like to hear about it."

He'd asked the same question the day he'd met Lexie, and her answer had stuck with him. "I don't think so. I asked Lexie, but she said something about men didn't like to talk about their feelings. They wanted action. You know, men want to do something."

"But there's not much we can do."

The intense look in his eyes pierced Ethan's heart. "I know. I understand."

"So…"

Ethan felt at a loss. "I could ask Lexie if they thought about adding men to their group." But he'd already heard Lexie's reaction. It wasn't hopeful.

"Great. Would you?" A look of hope sprang in his eyes.

"Sure, but I'm guessing they'll say—"

"Hey, you could ask, right? I might be the first to open the door for other guys."

But what about feelings? Could he talk about those deep things? Things that showed his helplessness? He looked at Ross's face and kept the thoughts to himself. His own concerns faded away. "I'll check on it the next time I see her. How's that?"

Gratefulness filled Ross's eyes, and hopelessness filled Ethan's chest. But he'd promised, and he would ask. If not a door, maybe he could open a window.

Knowing Cooper was in school gave Lexie a great feeling as she entered the senior center and strode down the hall-way to the MOSK meeting. Even though the meetings were important, twinges of guilt rattled through her when she had to leave Cooper with a sitter.

When she stepped through the doorway, Kelsey stood at the front table, her eyes on her clipboard. Being well orga-nized, Kelsey always had an agenda. Kelsey looked up and noticed her. She set her clipboard on the table before heading her way. "How's it going?"

Specific or general? "Fine." The word slipped out with-out thought. Her "fine" was like Cooper's "good." Watching Kelsey's expression, Lexie knew she'd given herself away.

"Fine." Kelsey's eyes narrowed. "It's not Cooper, is it?"

"No. He's great so far. In school every day and loving it."

Relief flashed across Kelsey's face. "I'm so glad." She turned and eyed the room filling with women. "Want to talk later?"

Lexie's shoulder lifted in a shrug. Though she needed to talk to someone, she preferred to handle it. Lately she'd stopped doing that. Ethan's face filled her mind. "Fine."

A flicker of a grin swept across Kelsey's face.

The magic word. Fine. Lexie grinned back.

The meeting began as it always did as each woman intro-duced herself, gave a brief review of how her child was doing, and then the floor was open for discussion. She half listened today, her mind wavering in one direction then another.

Kelsey had wisdom and hopefully their talking would help Lexie's indecision.

When she tuned into the discussion, Lexie listened to the others, happy to hear that many of the children were doing well. One mother announced that her daughter would be going to Hollywood to be on the set of one of her favorite television programs. Lexie realized she didn't know which TV program was Cooper's favorite.

To her relief, the meeting ended, and the women left, some pairing up to go to lunch. Ava stopped to invite Lexie to join them, but she declined with a smile. When the room emptied, Kelsey relaxed her shoulders. "Finally." She brushed a strand of hair from her cheek and ambled to Lexie's side. "If it's not Cooper, then it must be Ethan."

"Why do you say that?"

"Your job is secure. You look healthy. Cooper's doing well. So what's left?"

Lexie chuckled. "Okay, it's Ethan."

Kelsey settled beside her. "He's not seeing you anymore?"

"No. He is, but..." She hated admitting what she feared. "I think I'm jealous of his relationship to Cooper."

Kelsey's eyes widened in a look of surprise.

"I should be grateful, right? I don't know what's wrong with me, but I resent their closeness sometimes, and—"

"It's natural." Kelsey patted on her arm. "Cooper's been your focus for a long time. You've had no one else in your life. Your family doesn't live in the area. Cooper's father is out of the picture. It's been just you in Cooper's life. Don't you think it's a normal response if you see someone else stepping into your shoes?"

Pressure grew in her chest. "I suppose, but envy makes me feel shallow. I should be grateful."

"I think part of you is, but look at yourself, Lexie. You

ask nothing from anyone. You want to do it yourself. Some of us have tried to support you, but you don't seem to want it so we back off. The only person I know you to depend on beside yourself is your sitter, Mrs. Beckmeyer."

She pictured the kindly neighbor's face. "You're right. I've never learned to expect help from anyone."

"But you don't have to expect it. You can accept it. There's a difference." A frown crept to her face. "Does Ethan take over? Does he try to tell you what to do with Cooper or—"

"No. No. He's been nothing but kind. He always tells Cooper to get permission from me for everything. He's been great."

"Then accept it, Lexie. He sounds like a gem to me."

She lowered her head as Ethan's concerned expression filled her mind. "He is a gem."

Searching her face, Lexie captured her gaze. "Is that all that's bothering you?"

A lengthy breath escaped her. "No. I suppose it's not. Obviously I met Ethan when he did the presentation for Dreams Come True." She filled Kelsey in on Ethan's probing Cooper about his dreams and wants. "When Coop said he'd thought of a wish, I felt left out. Ethan hadn't asked me about heading in that direction, and I'm not sure Cooper's ready. I don't want anything to go wrong and disappoint him again. He so longed for school, and I lived in fear that he'd get back into school and then have to drop out again. I just—"

"You can't live in fear. You don't want to keep Cooper from every experience in case his remission fails."

"I don't want to hold him back, but—"

"Wouldn't Cooper enjoy something special, and so what if it can't happen as you want? If he does have a setback, he still knows that an opportunity can happen again. It gives him something to look forward to, especially with summer coming. It's a long summer for him to sit at home and wait to get sick again, Lexie."

Tears sneaked onto Lexie's lashes.

Kelsey leaned forward and grasped Lexie's hand. "I'm sorry. I didn't mean to come on so strong. I only wanted you to—"

"It's okay. It's fine. I needed to hear that." Lexie brushed her fingers beneath her eyes to wipe away the telltale tears. "I'm frustrated with myself for being so negative about this. I pride myself on being positive."

"You're one of the most positive people I know, but sometimes we all fall apart a little. Don't be mad at yourself. Just make it better. Be open with Ethan. I'm sure he'll understand."

Be open. She'd been thinking about that herself. "I'll call him. I think I owe him an apology." She leaned closer and gave Kelsey a hug. "Thanks." She definitely had the skills of a peacemaker, and Lexie needed to learn forgiveness and accept reconciliation in more ways than one.

Ethan tucked his cell phone into his pocket, happy to have received the call he'd been waiting for. Lexie apologized and said she wanted to talk to him. She gave no hint as to what had changed her mind, but at this point he didn't care. Filled with relief, he finished the job he was winding up, said his goodbyes to the clients and strode to his car.

In minutes, he pulled into her driveway, but then it struck him. Besides the apology, Lexie sounded decisive and commanding, as if she had a sense of purpose that needed to be addressed. This wasn't necessarily good news. The awareness took the edge from his excitement. He grasped the door handle and paused, bowing his head and not only talking to God but to himself about acceptance. If Lexie wanted him could make come true. He deserves to have fun in his life. I want to change. You've shown real concern, and you've allowed me to lean on you." She captured his gaze. "You see, that's another thing I never do. I depend on me. Just me." A shudder rippled through her chest. "That scares me."

"But why?" He rose and settled beside her on the sofa. "We talked about this before. No person is meant to bear the burden alone. Burdens are meant to be shared."

"With Jesus."

Her response startled him. "Yes, the Lord, too, but I'm talking about people sharing burdens. I grieve with friends who are dealing with problems. You met Ross. He lost a wife and now his daughter suffers from the same disease. I empathize with his plight. I care what happens to Peyton."

She gave a faint nod. "I guess I do, too. When Lucy was so bad, it broke my heart. All the women at MOSK help carry each other's trials, but I probably avoided saying too much. I don't want people's pity."

"Do you pity Kelsey? Do you pity the other women in MOSK?"

"Pity?" She blinked as the color drained from her face. "No. I understand what they're going through."

"And that's how they feel about your troubles. Why do you assume people pity you? I don't pity you, Lexie. And I definitely don't pity Cooper. He's an amazing boy. I love him and I care." From the look on her face, he'd said too much. He'd let the word love slip into the discussion, and it had taken its toll on their openness.

Her eyes narrowed. "Do you really love him?"

The question kicked him in the gut. *Lord, what should I do?* he silently prayed.

Love does not delight in evil but rejoices with the truth.

Ethan felt the Bible verse wrap around him. "I do. Laine and I never had kids. I wish we had. I know Cooper's not my child, but I found myself cheering him on and being proud of his courage. He's bright and positive. It just happened. I do love your son." He longed to know her reaction, and when it came, it was better than he'd expected.

"Thank you for caring so much."

Tears brimmed her eyes, and he lifted his finger and brushed them away. The warmth of her cheek stirred his heartbeat, and he slipped his other hand behind her back and pressed her closer.

"I'm not accustomed to all of this, Ethan, so be patient with me. You've become a special person in my life, and I know I've been leery. I really couldn't understand why anyone could care so much about us."

"Get used to it, Lexie."

She lifted her chin and smiled. His gaze drifted to her full lips, the slight curve like pink petals opening to the sun. His heart beat in his throat, and the longing rose until he couldn't stop himself. He lowered his mouth to hers, tasting her sweetness. He felt her shudder, and he drew back, fearing he'd undone all the good that had happened. He was wrong. Her eyes were still closed, and as she inched them open, a hint of amazement glinted there.

He lifted his hand and brushed her cheek, allowing his fingers to glide across her lips, their eyes linked in anticipation. He leaned forward, his hand at the back of her head, her thick hair cushioning his fingers as he lowered his mouth to hers again.

Lexie's palm pressed his cheek, drawing along his afternoon stubble, and as she drew back, she released a shaky breath. "I haven't been kissed in many years."

"Neither have I." A grin tugged at his mouth, and he let it happen.

Her body relaxed, and she pressed her hand against his.

out the front window, watching for Cooper. His gaze drifted to the sofa where he'd kissed Lexie, and the warmth of their kiss flickered down his spine. He could have said so much more. He'd admitted loving Cooper. But what about Lexie? He needed to understand if his feelings were real and lasting. Could he handle their tension when her protectiveness pushed him away? Could he handle her resentment again when it happened? And it would.

Chapter Eight

Lexie heard Cooper's voice screeching Ethan's name as he charged into the house. She hurried to the front door to wave thank-you to Kelsey before facing Cooper. Cuddled in Ethan's arms, Cooper rattled on about all the things he'd done with Lucy. Lexie had always been the one to listen and hold him. Envy sputtered through her before she took control. Why couldn't she let go and be thrilled that someone else loved her son, too?

She wandered to the archway and looked into the living room. "So you had fun?"

"Mom, Lucy has some new puzzles, and she has a game that we played with sticks. We had to pick them up without touching another one."

Pick Up sticks. Lexie grinned at Cooper's exuberance. Such an old game and she'd never thought of it. "We'll have to buy it."

"And me and you and Ethan could play."

Ethan tousled his hair. "Sounds like fun."

"I'd better get dinner." She reached the archway before stopping. "Wash your hands, Coop."

"Ethan, too." Cooper grabbed his hand and tugged him up from the chair.

They hurried past her to the bathroom off the kitchen, and she set the table and checked on the rolls, now golden and ready for serving. She pulled them out. Voices drifted to her with Cooper's never-ending conversation when Ethan was near. Her heart squeezed as a new sensation warmed her chest. Cooper loved Ethan. He loved Cooper. She loved Coop. And she loved… Her heart constricted again as heat rose on her face.

"We're clean."

Ethan's voice caught her in the midst of her admission. She faced him, her cheeks warm from her thoughts.

"You've been hanging over that oven too long."

She sent him a feeble smile. "Can you put some of those rolls in that basket?" She motioned to it at the end of the counter as she settled the roast onto a platter and placed the carrots and potatoes around the edge of the beef. "And you can grab the salad from the fridge." Distraction. It had worked.

Ethan slipped past her and carried both items to the table. She followed with the roast, checked the salad dressings she'd set on the table earlier, and then waved Cooper to the table. They slid onto chairs, although she noticed Ethan had tried to reach her before she sank onto the seat. She pulled her napkin from beneath the knife and placed it on her lap.

"Mom."

Lexie eyed Cooper, his hands folded in front of him.

"How come Mrs. Rhodes and Lucy thank Jesus for their food and we don't?"

Her voice left her, and the heat that had been on her cheeks turned to ice. She had no answer to his question that wouldn't upset him.

"Some people feel close to Jesus so they say thank-you for all the blessings He gives them."

Ethan's response whipped out before she could find a word.

"Don't we feel close to Jesus?" A frown had settled on Cooper's face as he studied her.

This time Ethan refrained from responding, and she grasped for wisdom. "When I was a little girl my parents didn't talk to Jesus."

"Were they mad at Him?"

She pressed her lips together not sure if she should laugh or cry. "They didn't know Him, Cooper."

"But I know Him." His eyes filled with sincerity.

"How do you know Jesus?"

"When Lucy and I read books, sometimes they're about Jesus. His father created the world and all of the people and animals." He pointed upward. "And the sun and stars and planets."

Lexie didn't know what to say. She glanced at Ethan, but his eyes were focused on Cooper.

"Then when He felt sorry for the people who were doing bad things, He sent his son to come to the world and die on a cross so that all the people could go to heaven and be saved from the devil." He leaned closer to Lexie. "The devil's bad, Mom, and Jesus did us a big favor."

Her lips pulled into a smile. "I guess He did, Coop."

"Then don't you think we should say thank-you to Jesus?"

"You're probably right."

He gave an emphatic nod. "And God, too."

"Would you like me to say the prayer?" Ethan's voice saved her from having to speak.

"Yes, please." She eyed Cooper. "Ethan will say our prayer."

He bowed his head as Ethan extended his hands across the table, and Cooper grabbed his and hers. She watched, then slipped her palm into Ethan's. The warmth of his hands spread up her arm, and the vision of his lips on hers skittered into her mind, taking her breath away. She bowed her head as Ethan and Cooper had done, and listened to Ethan's clear voice while he thanked the Lord for all things, especially the wonderful dinner she'd prepared. She joined their amens as she grappled with what had happened. Her mind spun from the kiss to Cooper's revelation to Ethan's thoughtful response.

When she lifted her head, they were looking at her. "Ethan, could you help Cooper with the salad while I carve the meat?" She managed to keep her hand calm as she sliced into the tender beef, then invited them to take the vegetables while she passed around the dressing. They dug into the food, and she slipped a fork of salad into her mouth, listening to Ethan and Cooper banter back and forth. Sometime during the meal, Ethan turned the conversation in a new direction.

"Now that you're feeling good and your hair is growing back—" Ethan gave Cooper a playful poke "—and school is letting out soon, what would you like to do or see? Where would you like to go if you could pick anything or any place you wanted?"

She chuckled at how he'd covered all bases. The hair, school and health were covered. She studied Cooper's face as he thought. "I'd like some of those sticks to play that game."

Ethan rolled his eyes at her. "Something bigger. Much bigger."

His eyes widened. "Like go to a place far away?"

"Yes, I think that's what Ethan means." She gave him an I'm-trying-to-help-you look.

He grinned.

"Okay." He pressed his lips together and closed his eyes as

if making a wish. Then a grin filled his face, and he bound from the table and darted into the den.

Ethan's eyes widened. "That's energy."

"When he's excited, it is. When it's about homework, not so much."

He chuckled and opened his mouth as if to say something more but closed it again as Cooper hurried back to the table with a book under his arm. When he shifted it in front of Ethan, Lexie recognized the cover. The national parks photographs.

"Some place in here." He poked the book with his index finger. "It's where I'd like to go." He opened the pages and flipped through.

Ethan stared at the book, his curiosity obvious.

Cooper paused, then turned a few more pages before he opened a two-page spread and paused. "Here. I want to see this."

Lexie saw the great expanse of red, orange and coral rocks deepened by a sunset. "The Grand Canyon."

Cooper's head rocked forward and back. "It's the biggest hole I've ever seen in a picture, and I'd like to go and see it for myself." His gaze latched on to Ethan's. "I could take my camera and make my own picture book."

"You could, Coop, and from what I've seen of your photographs, you have a real talent."

He redirected his gaze to her. "Can I go there, Mom?" He glanced back at Ethan. "For my summer vacation?" His expression deepened to longing. "When the teacher asks us to write about what we did in the summer, I could write about it and show my pictures."

Ethan reached across the table and patted his arm. "I know a group that helps kids pick out something they've always dreamed about and then they try to arrange their trip. Would you like me to ask them?"

Cooper leaped off the chair with such speed, it catapulted to the floor. He dove toward Ethan and wrapped thin arms around the man's neck. "Please. Please. Would you ask them? That would be the best vacation I ever had."

Lexie's chest tightened. It would be the only vacation he ever had. His illness and her pinching dollars didn't allow much more than a trip to the beach or once a visit to his grandparents. That vacation proved to be a poor choice. Now they'd changed for the better. She was grateful for that.

"And you come, too, Ethan." He glanced toward Lexie but not long enough for her to respond. "Would they let you come, too?"

Ethan's face blanched, his gaze seeking hers. "I'm not sure about that, buddy."

"Please. It wouldn't be as fun without you." He captured her gaze. "Right, Mom? It wouldn't be as fun without Ethan."

Her heart seemed to rise to her throat, and she swallowed. "I suppose it wouldn't, Coop." She drew in a lengthy breath.

"Then we can pray to Jesus, right?" He looked at Ethan first, then turned to Lexie.

Kisses, trips with Ethan and prayers to Jesus. Lexie's head spun with Cooper's chatter.

"Mrs. Rhodes always tells Lucy that Jesus hears our prayers. Is that right, Ethan?"

"He hears prayers and knows everything."

Her lungs emptied. She hoped Jesus knew she was drowning.

Ethan stood beside his car, enjoying the breeze. The air-conditioning hadn't seemed to work efficiently inside the building during the Dreams Come True meeting, although he wondered if it had been his apprehension causing him to feel so warm. He'd never introduced a trip to the group that seemed to have so much at stake. The members had received his presentation well. Empathy tugged at their faces, especially the women, when they heard about the single mom dealing with her brave son. He didn't have any answers today, but Cooper's trip had been introduced. Now the cost and arrangements would be discussed and voted on. He was certain it would be approved.

What he hadn't mentioned was his involvement, although Ross knew and so did Bill Reuben. Neither said anything, and he was grateful. Right now he'd been dealing with Cooper's request that he go along. Was it appropriate, and again, what new problem might it cause? And then Cooper had invited him, not Lexie.

Part of him longed to go. He wanted to see Cooper view the Grand Canyon for the first time. The thought of the pictures the boy would take thrilled him. Distant shots of the burnished colors of the canyon walls. Closeups of cacti, flowers and rocks. The excitement flared along his veins, yet could he ever walk away from them if he went? Could he walk away from them now?

He lowered his head and closed his eyes, sending up a prayer for God to provide him with wisdom.

"Good presentation."

Jerking at the voice, Ethan spun around to face Ross. "Thanks. The boy deserves a wonderful trip."

"It sounds like it." He extended his hand. "And thanks again for asking Lexie about adding men to the MOSK group."

Ethan squirmed. "The women vote on it, so there's no guarantee."

He shrugged his shoulder. "I know, but you tried." He drew himself to full height. "Once it's approved, will you go on the trip with Cooper and his mom?"

A kick in the gut wouldn't have knocked the wind out of Ethan any quicker. "Cooper asked me to go along."

"Sounds like a nice time."

Ethan studied his face. "But I don't think that's protocol."

"It's not typical, but if Peyton was granted a trip, I would go. Naturally I'd pay my own way."

"So would I, and I'd have my own room, naturally."

"If I were in your shoes, I'd go, I think." He gazed into his eyes. "I really think I would if they asked me to go."

"Thanks for the advice." He shook Ross's shoulder as he said goodbye and stepped away. He watched Ross for a moment, then slipped into the car and peered at his watch. School would be out soon. Ethan dug for his cell phone and punched in Lexie's number. When she answered, he told her about his presentation and offered to pick up Cooper from school.

"I'm glad it looks hopeful. How can I thank you?"

Their kisses came to mind. Kisses and Cooper's bright smile were enough for now. "You just did."

When he hung up, he headed for school and was welcomed with Cooper's enthusiastic greeting. This time he bypassed the Dairy O and drove directly to Lexie's. Cooper didn't ask and he was glad. He'd decided that for Cooper's own good, sometimes he had to say no. God's answer was sometimes no to people's prayers, and he'd wanted to tell that to Cooper the day he talked about Jesus at dinner. One day the boy needed to learn that, like a parent, permission or wants weren't always granted. God gave His gifts in His time. That difficult lesson impacted Ethan's life more than he liked to recall.

Cooper darted up the porch steps and into the house, while Ethan stood amazed at the change in the boy. When they'd first met, his illness had kept him from doing so many things.

Ethan strode inside as Cooper dropped his backpack by the staircase.

"Only four more days of school, Mom."

"I know." She noticed Ethan and grinned.

"We have exams on Thursday and only a half day on Friday."

Ethan chuckled. "Am I hearing this from a young man who couldn't wait to go to school?"

He beamed a smile. "But I need a break."

Even Lexie burst into laughter. "We all need a break sometimes, Coop." She gave him a pat on the back. "Go up and change your clothes."

He curled his nose and turned to face Ethan.

"I'll be here, buddy."

The smile returned. He grabbed his backpack and charged up the stairs.

Ethan watched him until he turned the corner and then strode toward Lexie. He longed to slip his arm around her waist, but he never knew when Cooper would appear, and he didn't want to confuse the boy. He gave her more details on his presentation, and when he stopped he noticed something in her expression. "What's on your mind?"

She lowered her eyes. "I've been thinking."

"About what? The trip?"

"Yes, but...about you."

"My coming with you?"

She hesitated, then gave a faint nod. "I'm not sure it's a good idea."

"I'm not sure, either."

Her eyes widened. "I thought you'd—"

"I'd love to be there when Cooper sees the Grand Canyon. I could help him take photographs, but I've asked myself if it's appropriate."

"Right. It looks like…" Her jaw tightened as tension etched her face. "It looks like we're…a family."

He nodded. "You know I would have my own room if I went along."

She nodded.

So what if they looked like a family? Or a couple? They were what they were. Friends. More than friends, he hoped. Yet what was best riddled him, too.

"You're afraid people will think we're a couple? Is that it?"

She lowered her eyes as a mottled flush rose to her cheeks. "Yes, but it also…might be tempting."

Tempting? Tempting to have him go or— Her meaning struck him. Their kisses, the growing feelings, the… He placed his hand on Lexie's shoulder and tilted her chin to look into her eyes. "I don't act on temptation, Lexie, until I first talk with God. You can trust me."

A shudder fluttered through her shoulder. "I do trust you, Ethan. With all my heart. I don't always trust myself."

His heart dropped to his stomach. He searched her eyes. Her meaning dissolved into confusion. Trust herself? Why?

"I haven't been with a man in many years, and until I met you, I'd forgotten what it felt like to be cared about and desired. You haven't said a thing, but sometimes I see looks in your eyes, and I know what's in my heart. I want to be true to both of us."

Her honesty bolted into his chest. "So do it. I respect you, Lexie. I'm human, and I have yearnings, too, but I can control those. I have for years."

She looked away. "I guess I have, too."

"So don't worry about that. I would never—"

"You're a gentle man, Ethan. I'm ashamed of myself for even thinking such a thing."

Heat burned in his chest. She'd spoken what he'd tried to deny. He drew her into an embrace. "Let's just remember that we are in control."

"In control of what?"

Cooper's voice jarred them apart. They spun to face him, guilt searing through Ethan's frame.

Cooper's wide-eyed gaze shifted from his mother to Ethan and back again until a curious grin spread across his face.

Ethan dragged words into his brain. "In control of life. Your mom is in control of her life and I'm in control of mine." He suspected that didn't mean a thing to an eight-year-old, but he'd found something to say.

"Me, too. And my control says, let's play a game."

Relief exploded to a laugh as Ethan tousled Cooper's hair. "What kind of game?"

"Pick Up sticks. Mom bought it for me."

"Who wants some milk and cookies while we play?" Lexie's response washed over him in a balm of acceptance.

Ethan raised his hand. So did Cooper. Lexie turned and headed into the kitchen.

"Cooper, you and Lucy finish whatever you're doing. Her mom just pulled into the driveway." Lexie turned from the stairway to the front door and watched Kelsey ascend the porch stairs. She grinned and pushed open the screen door. "You're early."

Kelsey brushed a strand of hair from her forehead. "I finished ahead of time. It's too hot to work." She stepped inside and drew in a lengthy breath. "It's cooler in here."

"Brick keeps it cooler inside." She motioned her to sit. "I told Lucy you were here." She leaned up the staircase. "Did you hear me up there?"

A double groan bounced down the stairs. "Mom, we're almost done with this game."

She looked over her shoulder at Kelsey.

"Ten minutes." Kelsey held up her fingers.

Lexie shouted the message up the stairs and then turned. "Would you like something to drink?" Then ambled toward one of the wingback chairs.

"I'm fine, thanks." She leaned against the cushion. "Any news on Dreams Come True?"

"We'll know Tuesday. I think that's what Ethan said." She sank into the cushion, wishing she felt more excited.

"I'm ashamed I haven't approached them for Lucy. She's doing so well." Kelsey leaned forward. "Cooper's doing great, and he will enjoy something special this year, but you don't look happy about it."

Lexie squirmed. "I'm nervous."

"About what?"

"What if Cooper and I get there and something goes wrong?"

Kelsey's eyes widened. "Where's that positive spirit? Nothing will go wrong." A frown settled on her face. "I thought Cooper asked Ethan to go with you. He'll be there."

She lowered her head. "I haven't agreed to that."

"I thought—"

"I'm having a difficult time with that situation." She glanced toward the stairs and lowered her voice. "Ethan guarantees me he will be nothing but a gentleman, but—"

"You mean you're worried about—"

"It's me, not him."

Kelsey whisked to her side and balanced on the chair arm. "You've fallen in love with him."

She lowered her face in her hands. "I don't know if it's love or the need to be loved. It's been a long time since I've had these feelings."

Kelsey patted Lexie's back. "Lexie, you've never said anything about Cooper's dad, but I think something went terribly wrong there. All men aren't like him. Whatever he did, Ethan's different. You know that. He's stuck by your side. He cares about you and Cooper. It's obvious to me."

A shudder ran through Lexie as she lifted her head, ashamed she'd allowed her emotions to overtake her. "You're right. I'm very confused. I want to be open to a relationship but I'm frightened. Things can turn quickly. Without a warning."

"I know all about that."

The impact of the comment struck Lexie. She'd given no thought to Kelsey's situation. She'd had to say goodbye to her husband and her friend when their affair came to light. A double betrayal would lash anyone's confidence and security. Another case of trust.

She pressed her palm against Kelsey's arm. "We both had difficult times."

Thuds sounded on the stairs, and Kelsey rose from the chair arm while Lexie worked to put a smile on her face. "Who won?"

Lucy waved. "But it was close."

Cooper shrugged. "I won last time."

Kelsey slipped her arm around Lucy's shoulders. "So how was the end of school today?"

"Fun. We didn't have regular tests. They were like games." Lucy darted to her backpack and dug inside.

Cooper leaned his shoulder against Lexie. "We had a spelling bee first and then treats."

His weight pressed against her hip, and she placed her palm on his forehead. "Are you feeling okay? Tired?"

"No." He straightened. "I'm good."

Good. Right. Worry shuffled along her spine.

Before she could comment, he darted to the window. "Ethan's here." Cooper pulled open the door, pushed past the screen door and bounded to the porch.

comfortable knowing I had someone to lean on." Her jaw tightened. "You're always telling me I should learn to do that."

His tension softened. "You should. I'm glad you're listening to me."

"Can you arrange it...if the foundation agrees to the trip."

"I'll see what I can do." He lowered his hand. "How's that?"

She nodded, but his response disappointed her. She'd hoped he would be excited, too, but she'd put up barriers. What did she expect?

Chapter Nine

Tuesday evening when Ethan pulled into the driveway, Cooper was sitting on the porch steps. He jumped up and charged toward the car, jerking the door open before Ethan could turn off the motor.

"You're certainly full of vinegar." He tousled the boy's hair.

Cooper tilted his head upward, a frown growing on his face. "Vinegar?" He shook his head. "I don't drink vinegar."

Ethan chuckled. "That's an old saying my mom used to say to me. It means you're full of energy."

He wagged his head. "I like energy. I was sick so long, and I didn't have any, but now—"

"Cooper, let Ethan get out of the car, at least."

Lexie's voice stopped him. The boy stepped back, and Ethan grinned, giving a wave to Lexie. He headed her way, gazing at her flowing hair glinting with red highlights from the sun. Her knit top matched the highlights like red raspberries. The sweater hung halfway down her knees, covering the black pants that shaped her legs.

Once again she looked gorgeous, even more amazing than the last time he'd seen her when they'd talked about emotions and longings. He'd tried to waylay her fears. She avoided anything about the past, and he sensed her husband, Cooper's father, had hurt her deeply. Sometimes an urge overcame him to ask, but the barrier would rise and undo their progress. And then, he chose not to talk about Laine, either, unless Lexie asked.

He found his smile as he stepped inside, longing to kiss her before he told her what he heard. He stopped himself, but the urge didn't waver. "I have good news."

She searched his face. "It's a yes?"

He nodded. "A rousing yes. I thought it would be. They are thrilled. You give me the dates that work with your schedule, and they'll make the arrangements."

"All of them?"

"Everything. The arrangements and expenses." He chuckled. "But then you knew that." He gazed down at Cooper whose attention darted from his mother to Ethan. "Do you want to do the honors?" He gave a slight nod toward Cooper.

"No, you should."

"Are you sure?"

She drew Cooper to her side her arm around him. "Positive." She looked over her shoulder. "But let's sit."

Cooper plopped into the first chair he found, his gaze shifting from one to the other. "Tell me what? I know you have a secret. I'm not a dumb little kid anymore."

Ethan couldn't contain his laughter. "You're far from a dumb little kid. It's your Dream Come True."

His jaw dropped. "You mean the Grand Canyon?"

"I mean the Grand Canyon."

This time Cooper's eyes widened. "Really? I can go to the Grand Canyon?"

"Really, Coop." Lexie leaned forward, grinning. "We just have to tell the people when."

Cooper leaped from the chair and grasped Ethan around the waist. "Now. Let's go now."

Ethan crouched and hugged him. "Your mom will give me dates that will work for her, and the foundation will make the plans. You have to be patient."

"I don't like being patient."

"You've been patient all your life, and that's why I'm so happy about this trip for you."

"And you'll come, too, right?" The look on his face melted Ethan's heart. He'd tossed the pros and cons back and forth many times since Lexie had agreed he join them on the trip. But until now he had no idea which way he would go. He glanced at Lexie, seeing her face as expectant as Cooper's. The words moved from his heart to his lips. "I think I can arrange it."

Cooper leaped backward and jumped into the air, clapping his hands. "Good. Good. Good."

Ethan rocked on his heels with the boy's thrust from his arms. He caught his balance and raised from his haunches. "I'm glad you're happy."

Lexie stood, gratitude reflecting in her eyes. "Let's have a treat to celebrate. Who wants ice cream?"

Cooper's hand shot up first and Ethan followed.

Lexie gave a nod and scooted through the archway to the kitchen, but before Ethan could follow, Cooper tugged on his hand. "Tell me what we'll do there. We'll have so much fun."

"There's lots of things to do there, but the best is seeing the canyon." Ethan settled onto the sofa with Cooper pressed beside him, clinging to every word he uttered. He told him about some of the tours and sights. "And you can become a junior ranger."

"Really?"

"Absolutely. You'll get maps and binoculars and have questions to answer so you can get your badge."

"A badge?"

"Yep." His chest tightened with the boy's excitement.

"And I can take pictures." He held an imaginary camera to his eye and pretended to take photographs.

The clink of dishes sounded from the kitchen, and Ethan glanced toward the door expecting Lexie to appear. "You'll take great photos, Coop."

He dropped his hands and spun to face him. "I can't wait to see the Grand Canyon." He plunked beside Ethan and rested his head against his shoulder. "But you know what I love more?"

"I don't know what could be better than the Grand Canyon, so I have no idea."

"I love you, Ethan. That's better than anything."

A dish clanged on the floor beyond the archway.

Ethan's pulse charged, digging into his chest. Lexie had heard him, and that might just rev up her sensitivity to Cooper's preoccupation with him. And now how to respond to Cooper? He loved the boy, but if he told Cooper, the boy would have expectations, and Ethan had no control over what might happen. The prospect of a committed relationship with Lexie depended on her as much as him. He could offer no guarantees to Cooper—a child with so much love to give.

He studied the boy's face and couldn't find the heart to ignore him. "I love you, too, Coop." He bent down and kissed the top of his head.

Cooper tightened the embrace and quieted a moment while Ethan struggled to regain his composure. He'd just agreed to go on the trip with them, but his greatest motivation for joining them was to grow closer to Lexie. Though she'd accepted his kiss and returned it, sometimes she backed away like a trapped animal. He needed to know why.

And the cancer. Would it stay away? Would Cooper have a full life? Ethan wasn't sure if he could deal with more loss in his life.

Footsteps alerted him to Lexie's approach. He straightened his back and pulled his arm from around Cooper. "I think it's ice cream time."

He popped up and met Lexie near the doorway.

Ethan studied her face. She didn't look him in the eye when she handed him the ice cream. He sensed she'd heard Cooper's admission.

She settled into a chair across from him, dipping her spoon into the ice cream and swirling it more than eating. She seemed as cold as the dessert.

He decided to give her an opening. "Break a dish?"

"No, but almost." She finally looked at him. "Clumsy."

Ethan let it slide and made small talk about the double chocolate with sprinkles. He sensed the fallen dish meant more than that, but Lexie kept things in. He let the situation pass. One of these days, he'd learn what she thought about Cooper's declaration of love.

Ethan gazed at the ice cream and sent up a prayer.

Lexie stood back from the rental booth in the car terminal, monitoring Cooper's unbound enthusiasm and trying to keep him from becoming a helium balloon and flying around the Phoenix airport. His feelings about Ethan had caused her to balk, but after she'd had time to think, she became rational. Children loved everything. "I love this book, Mom." "I love the Pick Up sticks. They're so fun." "I love chocolate ice cream." And he would love the Grand Canyon. She couldn't blame Ethan for Cooper's outburst of affection.

Cooper spun around again, knocking over his luggage. She'd never seen him so excited. On the plane, he made every excuse he could think of to climb over her from the window seat and head two rows back to Ethan. She'd been grateful they were seated on the side of the plane with only two seats per row.

Ethan had more patience with Cooper than she did sometimes. She had no doubt Coop plied the poor man with a million questions and asked him once again about the itinerary of their trip to the Grand Canyon. By now Ethan could recite the activities from memory.

"Cooper, stop jumping around." She straightened his luggage and set it beside her.

"When are we going to the Grand Canyon?" He looked at her with anxious eyes while he adjusted his backpack.

"As soon as Ethan finishes renting the car."

"Can I sit in the front seat?"

"No. It's a long ride. The backseat will be more comfortable for you."

His face kinked into a scowl. "But I want to talk to Ethan."

Drawing in a lengthy breath, Lexie grappled for patience and pondered how she could stop Cooper from putting Ethan in other uncomfortable situations. *I love you, Ethan. That's better than anything.* The unwanted feeling crawled over her. What about her love for Cooper? She hoped that meant something to him. Envy cut through her like ice.

Get a grip. Every boy wanted to be loved by a father figure. What she needed to do is explain that he couldn't go up to men and express his love. And when it came down to it, she'd invited Ethan on the trip, too. She knew what could happen. These days would offer her and Cooper bright memories rather than the dark days they so often spent together.

"Is it as hot at the Grand Canyon as it is here?"

"I hope not." Moisture still beaded on her forehead from the shuttle ride to the car rental terminal.

Cooper spun around, whacking his backpack into her.

"Be careful." She grasped his arm. "Have patience."

"Mom." He dragged out her title to three syllables.

Lexie couldn't help but grin. She beckoned him closer, nearly tripping over his suitcase she'd parked at her feet. "I know you're excited, but it's a long drive and we have to be grateful that Ethan is with us. I'm sure he's almost finished renting the car, and then we'll be on our way."

She slipped her hand from his head to feel his forehead. Would she ever stop hovering over him? Probably not until he'd been well for years. But would that day ever come?

When she looked up, Ethan was beckoning to them.

"Coop, let's go. Ethan's ready."

"Finally." He grasped the handle of his bag and toted it behind him.

Lexie followed. Her chest tightened as she gazed at Ethan. His face glowed with the same excitement Cooper displayed. He wore jeans and a burgundy polo shirt. As they neared, he gave her a smile. No matter how she fought the emotion, her pulse skittered up her arm.

Ethan headed toward the exit as Cooper ran ahead, and she hurried to catch up. When she hit the outside, the heat swallowed her again. As she inhaled, she felt as if she'd bent over a hot oven.

Ethan reached past Cooper and handed her a map. She eyed the picture on the folded paper, viewing a panorama of rugged mountains. She'd never seen the Grand Canyon, either, and today she admitted her anticipation had piqued, too.

"It's too hot." Cooper ran the back of his hand across his forehead. "Give me air-conditioning."

Lexie internally echoed his plea.

"This way." Ethan pointed down a row of cars, and they followed to a white sedan where a man checked his paper-work and then opened the car trunk.

After Ethan loaded the luggage, she reminded Cooper he would sit in the backseat. He tossed his backpack on the seat and climbed inside the car, his disgruntled expression obvious. In moments, he was hanging over the front seat as far as he could.

"Seat belt." Ethan gave his hand a pat. "I want to keep you safe."

He eyed the belt, a sulk returning to his face, and sat back.

Ethan waited until they all hooked up before he turned on the ignition. "Ready?"

"Ready."

Lexie chuckled at Cooper's overanxious boom.

Ethan backed from the spot and wended the car through the airport maze to the highway. Lexie leaned back and flipped open the map, eyeing the distance between Phoenix and the Grand Canyon. She'd wished they could have flown into Flagstaff, but flights were limited. The Phoenix airport met their needs.

Conversation quieted once they turned onto Interstate 10. Cooper had accepted his fate in the backseat and pulled out a video game. Lexie looked over the seat. Monopoly. That should keep him occupied for a while.

She shifted in the seat, gazing at Ethan's profile. His blond hair appeared silver-streaked with the sunlight glowing through it. His jaw looked relaxed, and from the side, she noticed his firm lips set in thought. Today his major concern, she guessed, was to arrive at the Grand Canyon safely.

She leaned back again, their conversation limited to the scenery and answering Cooper's questions—mainly how much longer before they arrived at the Grand Canyon.

When Interstate 10 split to 17, Ethan followed the new route going north. Once they'd left the Phoenix urban area, the landscape became open desert dotted with towering saguaro cacti. Heat pierced the windows, and Ethan cranked up the air conditioner. She hoped the temperature at the Grand Canyon would be kinder.

After an hour had passed, Ethan veered up a ramp leading to a place called Rock Springs. "I heard about a café here and thought we'd stop for lunch."

Cooper strained against the seat belt. "Good. I'm starving."

Ethan pulled off the highway, and in moments he rolled into a parking lot of a plain beige brick building ahead of them with a sign that read Rock Springs Café.

Lexie eyed the unlikely building. "This is it?"

He chuckled. "I expected something fancier. A friend told me they're known for their pies."

Cooper had already unhooked his seat belt and leaned on the front seat. "Yum. I like pie and ice cream."

"After you eat lunch." Lexie gave his hand a pat.

They climbed from the car and headed inside. Lexie's expectation had vanished with the sight of the drab building, yet cars lined the parking lot so she held a shred of hope. Once they stepped inside, she understood. The building held mementos of history with its knotty pine walls decorated with historic photographs and wonderful antiques. A tangy meat scent hung in the air, and she noticed diners chomping down on thick buns filled with barbeque.

After they settled at a sturdy-looking pine table, a waitress came with menus, and they perused the fare. "This is lunch, Coop."

"I know, but it feels like dinner."

Ethan chucked him under the chin. "We lost a couple of hours on the plane so it feels later than the clock says."

"See, Mom?"

Lexie grinned.

Cooper closed the menu. "Can I have a cheeseburger and fries? And I want chocolate cream pie."

Ethan folded his menu. "Sounds like a good plan to me."

The waitress arrived with water glasses tinkling with ice cubes, and they placed their order. As she left, Lexie grasped her glass and took a long swallow.

When Cooper headed for the restroom, she leaned back and studied Ethan. He was everything a woman could ask for, but too many things in her life held her back. Telling someone about her mistakes, her foolishness, rent her in two, especially a man who believed in God and followed His precepts. Her gaze shifted to his firm chin where stubble had begun to grow. She even liked that part of him. She shifted her focus to his blue eyes, always with a glint.

As she did, his gazed captured hers. "Feeling okay?"

She nodded. "I'm glad you're with us." And she was despite her earlier reservations. "This long drive with Cooper would have been tedious if I were alone trying to follow a map."

"It is long, but soon we'll be closer to the mountains. The view is magnificent." He clasped her hand. To her surprise, his fingers felt cool. "I know at first you were leery about having me come with you, but I hope I can prove that I have only good intentions."

"It's my problem, Ethan. Please ignore my foolishness." A knot rose to her throat. "I've been in some bad situations in my life that I don't want to talk about, and sometimes they overshadow the life I live now."

"The past brings up situations for everyone that we wish we could erase. But we can't. We know the Lord has blotted them out. So we go on."

The Lord. If only she could do that. She placed her free hand on top of his. "I've tried to figure out what motivates you, especially having lost a loved one to cancer. I would think that would have frightened you away from us, but here you are."

He covered her hand with his free one, his eyes searching hers.

"It's your faith, I guess. You believe in doing good deeds and showing compassion—"

"That's important, but it's more than that, Lexie. I told you the other day I have strong feelings for Cooper, and I—I think so much of you, and I told you that I admire you." He lowered his head and inched it upward, a grin on his face. "And you are a gorgeous woman. That's hard for anyone to resist."

Heat burst on her cheeks. "I'm not gorgeous. Not at all, and I don't understand why you admire me."

His grin faded. "You don't see yourself as others do." He fiddled with a napkin. "But as you said, my faith is important. We've been asked to be kind, generous, thoughtful and compassionate."

"See. I told you."

Instead of smiling, he lowered his eyes. "And I have to be honest with you."

His look caused her stomach to tighten.

"Cooper's illness did set me back. I tried to stay away for that reason. The thought of getting involved with cancer again…"

She slipped one hand from beneath his and touched his cheek. The fresh whiskers prickled her palm. "I understand. I really do. What I still don't get is your unyielding faith. Losing a wife, yet you believe. I know you talked about faith and trust, but—" How could she explain? "You must have asked God to cure Laine, but He didn't."

He started to respond, but Cooper bounded to the table and interrupted. "Mom, they have a store with all kinds of neat things. Can we go there before we leave?"

"You're going to see all kinds of shops at the Grand Canyon." She shifted her gaze to Ethan.

He leaned closer. "We can finish this talk later."

They had little choice. She didn't want to discuss her belief or lack of it in front of Cooper, but the conflict burned inside her. If she could understand that, then maybe she could make some sense out of God and faith.

When she focused, the waitress had arrived with their lunch, its aroma taunting her empty stomach. She took her first bite of barbecued pork, eager to dig into the meal and grateful for the good food. It eased her longing to finish their conversation.

Ethan tucked the park pass in his window and continued down Highway 64. Cooper and Lexie had both quieted earlier, and when he glanced at them, he realized they'd fallen asleep. The four-hour drive had taken its toll on top of their early departure from Detroit. A nap appealed to him, too, but not behind the wheel. He chuckled aloud, and Lexie stirred.

"I'm sorry. I guess I fell asleep."

"Forgiven." He gave her a quick grin. "I was thinking about doing that myself."

She gave him a playful smack. "Where are we?"

"Very close. Grand Canyon Village is just ahead."

She craned her neck. "Really? I suppose I should wake Cooper." She twisted toward the backseat, as much as her seat belt would allow, and gave his leg a shake.

Cooper groaned. "My stomach aches."

She chuckled. "No wonder. Look what you ate for lunch?" She twisted back. "Kids. What do they expect?"

Ethan took the road to Mather Point, thinking he deserved a bad stomach, too. He'd eaten too much and then added a piece of the great pie, but he'd enjoyed it. "We'll make a stop here for the first view." He rolled into a parking spot and turned off the motor. "Take a look."

Lexie's eyes widened. "Unbelievable. Pictures can't capture this." She shifted to face the backseat. "Cooper, we're at the Grand Canyon."

As if a hoist had jerked Cooper from his reclined position, he flew upright, unlatched his seat belt, and rested his arms on the seat backs, his mouth ajar. "Wow! It's huge."

Ethan stepped from the sedan, the view stretching before him—striated rocks of gray, terra-cotta and dusky rose dotted with evergreens.

Cooper leaped from the car and flew toward the railing, his stomachache apparently forgotten.

"Hold up, Coop. Wait for your mom."

He skidded to a halt, his stance ready for action.

Lexie opened the passenger door as Ethan arrived at her side. When she cleared the door, he shut it and hit the lock button. He grasped her hand, and she curled her fingers around his palm. Relief washed over him. If she had heard Cooper's confession about loving him she hadn't let it sway her from their friendship. Her smile grew and the only thing left hanging had been their discussion about God. He'd thought a lot about that as he drove from Rock Spring Café.

At the railing, she released his hand. The canyon plunged below, each rock reflecting a variety of colors descending to the canyon floor where the Colorado River flowed.

"Can we go down there?" Cooper's hopeful eyes gazed up at him.

Ethan's chest caught. "Probably not, Coop. The walk is treacherous and takes a whole day, then we would have to sleep down there and come up the next day. It's too hard for all of us, and the mule rides can be dangerous. But I have a surprise that's almost as good."

His eyes widened. "What kind of surprise?"

Lexie chuckled. "Coop, if he tells you, it won't be a surprise."

Cooper offered a disappointed grin. "When do I get it?"

"Patience, Coop." Ethan tousled his hair.

"Not you, too." His shoulders drooped as he lowered his head, then seemed to have second thoughts and pointed. "Can we walk out there?"

Ethan eyed the narrow point jutting over the Canyon. He wasn't sure he wanted to walk out there even with the railing, but he couldn't disappoint Cooper again. He eyed Lexie, and she gave a faint nod. Cooper hurried ahead but stopped before the rock projection and waited.

"Let's go." Ethan reached for Lexie's hand again.

She gave it a squeeze.

He squeezed back. The most important thing during their time together was growth for their relationship. He hoped Lexie and he would get to know each other better. He wanted to know about Cooper's dad. So many things, and Lexie hadn't learned much about him, either. He set that as his goal as he headed for the precipice.

At the point, Ethan eyed the point extending beyond a drop off more than a mile. Stepping onto the projection took faith in the same way his relationship with Lexie and Cooper took faith. His life could tumble out of control if she rejected him, but as he trusted the Lord to hold the rock in place, he trusted God to hold their relationship firm.

Though Lexie looked anxious, they all stepped to the rail, awed by the spectacular view.

Cooper spun around, giving him a plaintive look. "I left my camera in the car."

Though wanting to tell him to wait until later, the boy had lived with waiting much of his life. Ethan held up a finger and darted back to the car to locate the camera, his mind buzzing with ways to spend more time alone with Lexie.

Cooper's smile was worth the retrieval. He grasped it and went to work, viewing the scene and snapping photos.

Lexie leaned closer. "You spoil him, Ethan. He's beginning to think the world revolves around him."

"Doesn't it?"

Her scowl melted into a grin. "I guess you're right."

Her smile did wonders to his spirit. With his hand in hers, he enjoyed the scenery and the closeness he felt. Lexie and Cooper felt like the family he'd always wanted—father, mother, son sharing a special moment viewing one of God's amazing creations.

Ethan eyed his watch and veered his attention to Cooper. "Ready, Coop? We want to get settled in the hotel so we can have dinner and check out the village. After that we can see the Canyon as the sun sets." His gaze shifted to Lexie her hair streaked with gold highlights in the midafternoon sun, her eyes paler than the sky.

She looked at him and smiled.

He gazed at the view and then Lexie. Both spectacular, yet both daunting.

Chapter Ten

Impressed by the rustic charm and elegance of the El Tovar lobby, Lexie approached her suite door with anticipation. Ethan unlocked the door with Cooper at his heels and then turned to beckon her in. "This is your room."

Cooper tilted his head, a frown growing on his face. "It's our room."

Ethan looked uncomfortable. "It's yours and your mom's."

"But where are you staying?" A whine seeped into his voice.

"I'm down the hall. Not too far away." He pointed down the corridor.

Cooper spun around to face her. "But Mom…?"

She stepped deeper into the room and rolled her carry-on to one of the beds. "Cooper, Ethan needs his own room. He's right down the hall." Ethan strode into the room, guilt rising. Her earlier warning to Ethan appeared to be coming true. Cooper believed all of his wishes should come true. This one definitely wouldn't.

"Take a look here, Coop. Look at this view." He opened the balcony door and waited for Cooper to join him.

Cooper stopped his moping and headed through the doorway. He jolted to a halt. "Whoa. Mom, come and look."

Lexie stepped through the doorway and halted. "How did we get a room like this?"

Ethan slipped beside her. "The foundation works their charm. This is a corner suite. The lodge has four of them."

"Only four, and we're in one."

Ethan grinned.

"It's gorgeous." She crossed the massive balcony.

He joined her, as he admired the ornate enclosure before gasping at the view.

She touched his arm. "I feel as if I'm hanging over the Grand Canyon. It's awesome."

He eased his arm around her back, and she glanced over her shoulder, but Cooper had vanished inside, probably searching for his camera. Having Ethan close and feeling his embrace wrapped her in longing. He leaned closer.

"I'd better get to my room and unpack."

His breath brushed her cheek, his lips so near. While her heart pounded, she tried to fight the amazing feelings.

Ethan must have sensed it. He lowered his arm and glanced at his watch. "I'll be back in a half hour for dinner."

"That's fine." He stepped away, and an unpleasant loneliness surrounded her.

"I thought you might like to eat here in the lodge restaurant tonight. We're all tired, and I know tomorrow will be busy." His eyes captured hers.

She couldn't look away, drawn in the whirlpool of his eyes.

Ethan lowered his lips, a kiss so gentle and sweet she longed for more.

A sound came from the room, and Ethan stepped back and moved toward the door as Cooper veered onto the balcony with his camera. "Where are you going?"

"To my room. I need to unpack and get ready for dinner."

He looked at her. "Can I go with Ethan?"

"No, you need to get ready, too."

"Mom! Please?"

Her discomfort with nearly being caught churned into irritation. "Cooper, I'm getting—"

"I'll show him my room and send him right back. How's that?"

She gave up fighting both of them. "Fine." She focused on Cooper. "Just hurry back."

The camera forgotten, Cooper bounded through the doorway with Ethan. Lexie heard the outside door close and sank into the balcony's wicker chair. The sun warmed her arms as she flung back her head and closed her eyes. Ethan's kiss rolled through her again. She feared it, but she loved it. He'd become a magnet, drawing her to him without her giving herself permission to fall in love. He'd promised good intentions, and she didn't doubt that. His faith proved strong, and from what she knew about God's will, Ethan tried to follow the Word.

Still his romantic overture made her uneasy with Cooper around and more so since she heard Cooper's expression of love. Somehow she needed to stop Cooper from doing anything else that put her or Ethan in an embarrassing situation. In her heart, despite the lovely kiss, the realization of anything permanent coming from her relationship with Ethan seemed as impossible as ever spending a week in a room like this.

In moments she heard a knock on the door. She rose and crossed the charming suite. When she opened the door, Cooper bounded in. He grabbed her hand and pulled her into the hallway. "Ethan's room is right down there, but it's not big like this room. We have lots of space. Why can't he stay here?"

Lexie had enough. "Cooper, we need to talk." She wrapped

her arm around his back and guided him back to the balcony where the sun might brighten her attitude. He was only a child and didn't understand. She pulled him onto her lap and wrapped her arms around him. "Cooper, Ethan and I aren't married so we can't share the suite. Only married people sleep in the same room. I know you think Ethan's great. But you can't make things happen that are impossible wishes." She touched his chin and guided his eyes to hers. "Do you understand?"

He shifted his gaze away. "No."

"What don't you understand?"

"I can't make things happen, but I can pray. Jesus hears prayers."

Maybe He hears them, but He doesn't always say yes. She was sure of that. Her shoulders sank. Prayer was another thing she had to deal with. She drew Cooper closer, her mind searching for a time she could talk with Ethan alone about the situation. But Cooper's awe of Ethan made private conversation impossible.

"Get your camera." She gave his arm a pat. "You don't want to miss the pictures."

He jumped up and headed inside while she gazed across the magnificent Grand Canyon, the chasm as deep as the abyss she plunged herself into so often.

Ethan gazed out the window at the burnished hues of the Grand Canyon glowing in the setting sun. The faces of the rocks pitted with shadows and light glowed like bright pumpkins filled with candles. The sky, an abstract painting, slashes of colors from purple to red to gold covered the amazing canvas. He drew in a breath and gazed at Lexie, her eyes drowsy but searching the scene like the artist she was, perhaps to hold the vision in her memory palette.

Cooper, elbow propped on table, rested his head on his fist, and though he'd insisted he wanted dessert, Ethan wondered if he had the strength to hold a fork. "Still hungry, buddy?"

Cooper lifted his eyes, glazed and heavy-lidded. "Tomorrow I'll have chocolate ice cream."

"Good decision." Ethan beckoned the waiter. "Then I think it's time to go. We're all tired from the long day."

He paid the check, knowing this moment with Lexie and Cooper would stay with him forever. Though he longed to slip his hand in Lexie's, he didn't. But before they left the suite earlier, she'd made it clear that when Cooper was nearby they were platonic friends. His chest constricted when he thought of ever ending their relationship.

The lodge restaurant had been a good choice. When he reached his room, he paused. "What time would you like to get started in the morning?"

Lexie slowed and faced him. "Would you like to come down for tea...or coffee? I have a coffeemaker in the room."

"Thanks. I'd like that." His spirit lifted as he moved into step with her down the hall. "Tea's fine."

Inside her suite, Ethan wandered out to the balcony and set a small table beside the wicker chairs. He sank into one, gazing into the darkening sky. The fleeting sunset darkened to a golden glow over the distant rocks and a full moon rose in the distance.

He heard Lexie inside preparing Cooper for bed while he still complained about his stomachache. Moments later, he came out to say good-night and ambled to Ethan's side. He leaned down and hugged his neck. "I can't wait until tomorrow."

"Me, too, buddy. I hope you feel better."

He gave a little wave and wandered back inside. Lexie stayed in the room, and he assumed she was preparing the tea. Minutes later, she appeared with two cups, spotted the table he'd moved, and set them there. "This has been a wonderful day. Tiring but really great. Anyone who hasn't seen the Grand Canyon is missing one of the most beautiful natural wonders in this country."

"I agree." He lifted the cup and took a sip of the drink. The evening had cooled, and Ethan was glad he'd worn a jacket. "When I look at this expanse, I see God and all His handiwork."

She remained silent, her gaze sweeping the vista.

He presumed he'd made a mistake bringing it up. Yet since he'd already introduced the subject of faith, this seemed the time to talk. He steeled himself. "Earlier today you asked me again how I could lose a wife and yet still believe."

"I did." She reached for her tea and wrapped her hands around the warm cup. "What really troubles me is believing in a God who says He will give you all you ask in prayer, but He doesn't. He didn't cure Laine even with your prayers. That's what I mean."

Ethan pondered the question again though he'd thought about it during the day. Again he searched for the right words. Lexie's inquisitiveness encouraged him. She'd asked questions more than once, and he believed she was on the brink of opening her mind and heart to the Lord. But he felt the pressure. Providing the right response rested on him, and he didn't feel capable.

His chest constricted. Nothing rested on him. Truth and faith rested on the Holy Spirit working through him. He closed his eyes, his prayer rising with the speed of light.

"I don't understand everything about God, Lexie. So much depends on acceptance and faith. We've talked about that often. For example, you know the sun rises in the morning."

She sat in silence, her expression thoughtful. "Naturally

I know the sun rises in the morning. Is that what you want me to say?"

"It's something you accept. You don't doubt it will rise."

"The sun's always there so how can I doubt it?"

"That's the way my faith works. I don't doubt that God reigns over this earth. That He created it."

"But I can see the sun. I can't see God."

His lungs emptied. "You can see God, too, if you look at this canyon. If you see the amazing things that happen in this world. You feel a breeze, but you don't see it. Yet it's real. When you see disabled people rise, no longer ill, and walk away. That's not only in the Bible. It happens every day. The doctors hold no hope, and the disease vanishes. I've seen healing occur with people I know."

A scowl wrinkled her forehead. "But even if you believe how can you love a God who says no to your prayers?"

His lungs felt empty. *Father, give me words.* His mind surged. "The Lord responds to our prayers with a knowledge that we don't have, Lexie. I have to trust that He knows what is best. I'm not a preacher, but I accept that God sees the big picture. He knows our needs, and our needs are not always our wants. He comes to us with responses we may not like, but ones that are the best for us. Ones that will protect us or help us grow or save us from a deeper sorrow." He motioned toward the bedroom. "You do this with Cooper. You told me the other day I had to learn to say no, because what seems best at the time isn't always the best in the long run."

She lowered her head, and Ethan waited, giving her time to digest what he'd said. When she looked up, his pulse quickened.

Her gaze met his. "I understand, Ethan. I do say no to Cooper, because I think it's best for him."

"And God knows all things. He really knows what is in our best interest even though it seems terrible at the time."

He dug into his hip pocket and pulled out his wallet. "When Laine was ill, I struggled with this myself so I talked to our pastor. He gave me a verse that I wrote down, and I still carry it with me. I read it when I'm down or ready to give up."

Her eyes flickered with interest.

"Do you mind if I read it to you?"

She gave a faint nod, but her eyes said a resounding yes.

He opened his wallet and pulled out a dog-eared card. "It's from Romans 5. 'We also rejoice in our sufferings, because we know that suffering produces perseverance; perseverance, character; and character, hope. And hope does not disappoint us, because God has poured out His love into our hearts by the Holy Spirit, whom He has given us.'" He returned the card to his wallet and slipped it back into his pocket. "Do you understand why I still carry it?"

"Then you think when we have problems we learn something from it even though the problem is horrendous."

"Yes, I do."

"I suppose I agree with you there. All the problems in my life have helped me become stronger and more determined to survive." She tilted her head toward the sky. "I wasn't raised in a faith, but sometimes it makes sense, especially when I look at the beauty of this earth, as you said. I have a difficult time, too, thinking all the things that happened—the faithful of the seasons, the stars and planets forever in orbit—and I have a difficult time believing all of these things were an accident of nature."

He relaxed as his hope grew.

"Still the Bible's description is confusing. Six days to create this earth and everything in it?" She shook her head. "I don't know."

"Humans look at all of this with finite eyes and minds. God is infinite. We can't understand it all. His power and might is beyond our understanding. I suppose that's why we call it faith."

Her eyes searched his. "Faith and hope go hand in hand. I do hope, Ethan. Often."

Her admission fluttered to his heart. A door had been opened tonight. If not a door, a window. It's what he'd prayed for. He rose and offered her his hands.

In the light seeping from the window, question flickered on her face, but he acted as his heart demanded. When she rose, he led her to the railing and stood a moment, lost in the darkness yet drawn to the glow of the full moon shedding light on the deep canyon. He glided his arm around her back and drew her closer. She tilted her head upward, the moonlight playing on the lines of her lovely face. His lips met hers, warm and soft. Longing rose to make things right, to understand each other, to admit their feelings, but he couldn't do it alone.

Lexie trembled in his arms, and he forced himself to end the kiss. She'd mentioned fear of her emotions. The two of them were finally on a good course. He wanted nothing to happen that would mess things up now.

He rested his cheek on her sweet-scented hair and gazed at the bright moon. Everything seemed perfect, yet something inside him gnawed at his memory. Lexie had begun the trip upset with him. She couldn't hide it. Before the trip was over, he longed to understand. The more she opened up the more chance they would have to commit to what could be a beautiful relationship.

Ethan never thought he would hear himself say that.

Chapter Eleven

Lexie's feet hurt from walking for miles while Cooper filled out the *Junior Ranger Activity Booklet* that they'd picked up at the Canyon View Visitor Center. They'd searched for birds, animals, plants and trees until her eyes hurt. On top of that, she hadn't slept well, thinking of their discussion about God. And then there were Ethan's kisses.

"Come on, Mom."

Cooper beckoned to her yards ahead while Ethan stuck to his side, probably preferring his eager search for information than her silent distraction. Falling in love with a man who only wanted her for the love of her child wasn't what she'd dreamed. Truly she'd never dreamed of marrying, not after her last experience. She'd assumed some men walked away when difficult situations arose, and how would she know whom she could trust? Though she'd been wounded by his betrayal, her relationship with Cooper's father had been a bump in the road compared to the rugged journey she'd taken with Cooper and his leukemia.

Cooper. He'd coped with adversity most of his life, and he'd grown older than his years. God came to mind again. Cooper believed without any effort. He wanted to pray at meals and at night before bed. She'd heard someone say that Jesus loved children because the kingdom of heaven belonged to them. She'd always figured children's faith happened because they were more gullible, but since meeting Ethan, her feelings had changed. Now she sensed truth in God and His Son Jesus.

She'd never tried not to believe. Faith had never happened. She'd struggled much of her life to make her way, but she did, and she'd been thankful for that. Had God planned that all along? Had he given her Cooper to make her stronger and more determined? It certainly had worked. Or had God meant a child to lead her to the Lord? She'd heard Christians say that, too. Her lungs drained of air.

Ahead, Cooper and Ethan paused. She slowed to catch her breath and looked ahead to see why they'd stopped. An animal skittered through the shrubs. She'd gotten a kick out of Cooper's binoculars, which were part of the Junior Ranger equipment. He'd spent much of the day seeing things at close range, and he hadn't forgotten his camera.

She guessed the critter Cooper had spotted was another Kaibab squirrel, but she reached them in time to see a chipmunk. Nothing had been as exciting as spotting a mule deer at one of the canyon lookouts when they had taken the shuttle there that morning.

Cooper's energy thrilled her, but this morning he seemed tired and his vigor had slowed a bit. She guessed he hadn't slept well because of his tummy problems and his excitement at being at the Grand Canyon. As always, she would keep a watchful eye on him. Scanning the brush, she spotted the nervous chipmunk. "Is that a new animal for your ranger book?"

He grinned from his notes and nodded.

She eyed Ethan. "Is he about finished with the requirements to earn his ranger badge?"

He gave a nod. "We just need to check it to make sure everything's been answered."

"Good, because my feet are rebelling." She stared down the path and spotted a bench.

"How can feet rebel, Mom?"

"They're screaming silently."

Ethan chuckled, and the sound fluttered in her head.

"Give your mom a break, buddy." Ethan gave the nape of Cooper's neck a squeeze. "Let's find a bench. If you have everything, we can drop off the booklet at the visitor center and get your certificate."

"And my badge." Cooper shifted his eyes from one to the other.

"And your badge." Lexie sank onto the bench, then leaned forward. "Where did you get that bad bruise?"

Cooper looked at his arms, then at her. "What bruise?"

"The one on your leg?"

Cooper shrugged.

Ethan crouched down and studied his leg. "You have another one here, too."

Lexie's chest tightened. Bruises always frightened her, even though little boys were prone to cuts and bruises. "Be more careful, okay?"

He nodded, then turned his attention to the booklet pages.

The bench proved a respite for Lexie's feet and her thoughts for a moment as she waited. Minutes passed, and she looked at her watch. "How much longer?"

Ethan grinned. "Only a few more pages. It sounds as if more than your feet are rebelling."

She grinned. "I think I'll find a restroom while you finish."

Ethan nodded and refocused on the booklet while she walked away. Seeing Ethan and Cooper together stirred concern inside her. Coop deserved a dad, and a good one like Ethan. He'd stolen her son's heart, and some of hers no matter how hard she tried to avoid it. Ethan said all the right things, yet she continued to worry.

The familiar words tossed back and forth in her head. Faith. Trust. God. Shame. Forgiveness. Could a mighty God like Ethan's forgive people's bungled mistakes? Her parents had turned their back on her for so long until Cooper became ill. She assumed they'd felt sorry for her. But pity wasn't love.

She saw a restroom and was in and out in a minute. Though her feet were still protesting, she hurried along the path with the hope that the booklet was ready and they could go back to the hotel to rest. As she neared the bench, Cooper seemed deep in conversation with Ethan, and her interest spiked. Though guilt matched her curiosity, she eased a short distance behind them and eavesdropped.

"I love this trip. It's been so fun."

"I'm glad, Coop."

"If I had one more dream come true, you know what it would be?"

Lexie couldn't see Cooper's face, but she could almost guess he wore a silly grin. From behind, she watched Ethan tilt his head and look up as if he were thinking.

Ethan's head lowered. "I'm not sure, Coop. This trip is pretty special."

"My wish is really special." He cuddled closer and put his head on Ethan's shoulder, his arms around Ethan's body. "I wish you were my dad."

Ethan's head jerked while Lexie froze in place. She wanted to escape. To get away and not hear Cooper's plaintive admission. She'd talked to him the night before, but this was the ultimate damage. Even if she wanted to get involved with Ethan, she couldn't now. She'd questioned his motivation since they'd met, and now their relationship sank even deeper into hopelessness.

Ethan's arm enveloped Cooper. "You know, Coop, a dad is something Dreams Come True can't give you. Things like that take far more than wishes."

"Prayers. I could say prayers."

Ice seeped into her soul. Cooper had never bugged her about having a father, and he'd asked few questions about his. Once in a while, he'd hinted that he would like to have someone to show him how to do things like play ball and bait a hook, but nothing like this.

Cooper raised his head. "Couldn't I? I could pray for a dad just like you." Cooper's tone begged for validation.

Ethan appeared as startled as she felt. She backed away, embarrassed she'd listened to their private conversation. Desperation replaced her curiosity. Her son wanted to pray for a father, and not just any father. He wanted Ethan.

"You can pray for anything, but it doesn't mean God will give you exactly what you want, Cooper. You need to know that."

"But I could try. Lucy's mom says Jesus hears our prayers. So maybe He'll want to say yes."

Ethan rested his chin on Cooper's head. "Maybe He will."

They sat in silence, and Lexie adjusted her equilibrium, her legs unsteady. She struggled for air, but she had to return. She had to appear normal. She made her legs move.

"Mom." Cooper's eyes opened wide. "You're back fast."

Ethan slipped his arms from Cooper and rose. "We're ready."

Cooper hurried to her as he waved the booklet. "My book is all filled in. We checked every page. Now I can get my Junior Ranger Badge."

Ethan rose, his face mottled as Lexie's concern rose. Ethan had told her that he loved Cooper. But the look on his face confirmed he hadn't planned on commitment. Nothing like that had been even hinted at. She'd made a mistake allowing Ethan to join them, even though she loved his company. She feared being hurt to the core. Worse, that Cooper could be devastated. The child adored him.

The situation messed with her mind. Four more days together. How would she deal with this?

Tension reigned at dinner. All Ethan could think about was Cooper's newest wish. Removing it from his thoughts was like ignoring a lion watching him eat his meal, and it didn't help that Cooper looked so cute, sitting at the table wearing the Coyote Award badge pinned to his polo shirt. Lexie seemed quiet. Though she talked about the rest of the trip, the conversation seemed forced. It hadn't been easy for him, either. Once again Lexie's mood swings befuddled him.

When they headed back to the lodge, Cooper hadn't whined about wanting to do something more that evening although they'd enjoyed a full day. Ethan needed time to think, time to deal with Cooper's request. The idea had entered his mind long ago, but it hadn't moved beyond his thoughts. A few kisses, wonderful kisses, hung in his memory. Commitment meant more than kisses. It meant dealing with every aspect of life. The good and the bad. He'd dealt with enough bad for a lifetime, but his heart overpowered logic. Logic played no part in love.

At the doorway of his room, he paused, longing to tell Lexie what happened, but knowing it would upset her. Instead of dumping it on her there, he'd wait a few more days until they arrived home. It would be better for everyone all the way around. He said good-night and stepped inside.

He tossed his sport coat on the bed and slipped off his shoes, then wished he'd picked up something to drink.

His mind spun, and instead of listening to the same thoughts over and over, he turned on the TV. Working through the menu, he flipped from one program to the next. Nothing caught his attention. It was early yet. Only nine. He sat on the edge of the bed and picked up a shoe.

When the telephone rang, he jumped. Lexie. It had to be. He picked up the receiver.

"Would you like to come down? I'm making tea."

Tea? Could he spend time with her without telling her? He closed his eyes. "I'll be down in a few minutes."

Tension still sounded in her voice. Ethan shook his head. Why did he and Lexie try to second-guess each other all the time? He needed to ask point-blank and insist for honesty. They were both tiptoeing around internal scars that would never heal if they didn't get the wound open to the fresh air.

When Lexie opened the door, her expression lacked the usual warmth. Stress etched her face, and he suspected the bruises on Cooper had heightened her concern about his leukemia. He'd learned that was a sign.

Seeing Cooper asleep, he didn't speak, but she whispered she would bring out the tea. He gave the sleeping boy another look and then tiptoed to the balcony.

When Lexie stepped out, he turned from the railing.

She set the cups on the table and joined him. "Another lovely sunset."

"It is." The sky captured his attention for a moment until concern pulled him away. "I'm surprised Cooper's already asleep. I thought he'd be wound up from all the excitement."

"He was tired. The day wore me out, too."

He spotted the worry in her eyes and hoped he could lift her spirit. He braced his hands against the railing. "Tomorrow will be our big surprise for Cooper. I'm excited." He pushed his body away from the railing and wandered to the chairs.

"The helicopter ride." She followed him and settled beside him.

Ethan nodded. "He'll fly down into the canyon and see things close up. Plus the ride experience itself will be special." He lifted the tea and enveloped the mug in his palms.

"You've done a very nice thing for us—two strangers who popped into your life."

Two strangers. He felt her withdraw again. "Lexie, I know something's bothering you. I sensed it even before we left home. You close me out sometimes. Things go smooth for us for a while, and then a wall drops between us. That shouldn't happen to friends." *Friends* seemed an empty word in light of the deep feeling he had. "I wish you'd tell me what I've done or what's wrong."

Her jaw tensed, and she looked away.

His question had been a mistake. Way too blunt. He should have eased into it, but that was the problem. Two people couldn't spend a lifetime easing into conversations. A meaningful relationship needed to be open and honest.

He gazed at her while his pulse escalated. They were both tired, and another day when they were fresh might have been better, but he couldn't sleep now until he understood what caused the distance that kept stretching between them. "You know Cooper is a star in my eyes, but you're very important to me, too. I—"

"There's nothing wrong with your trying to make Cooper happy, Ethan, but I think your actions aren't really yours." She looked away. "You're being pulled like a puppet trying to please an eight-year-old, and—"

"A puppet? Have I stepped into your shoes again?" His mind spun with confusion. "I've tried to let you make the decisions. If I haven't done that, I'm sorry."

"It's not that. You've been thoughtful. You always check

with me before you respond to his crazy demands. You respect me as his mother."

"Then what do you mean, Lexie?" He rose and moved around to meet her eyes.

In the dim light, her gaze pierced his. "You know what I mean. Think about it." She drew back and folded her arms across her chest. "And if you don't, then you aren't as intelligent as I thought you were."

Her comment startled him. He drew back, reeling. "I think we need a good night's sleep. Maybe tomorrow—"

She shook her head. "Please don't play games with me."

"Games?" He searched her eyes for a trace of meaning until it struck him. He sucked in air. "Did you overhear Cooper today when you came back from the restroom?" His heart whacked against his breastbone.

She looked away. "I heard him, Ethan, and I also heard his declaration of love before we left home. I wasn't only mortified. I was distressed."

"Mortified? Why? Distressed about what?" He set his cup on the table, grasped the chair arms and leaned closer to her. "Please, talk to me."

She pulled her head back, and he straightened. He hadn't meant to be confrontational.

"I think I told you once before I don't want people's pity." Her gaze captured his. "And I don't want friendships based on pity. If you're sticking around because you feel sorry for poor Cooper without a dad and poor Lexie without—"

"Lexie, stop." He held up his hand while frustration tightened his muscles. His legs weakened, and he backed up and sank into the chair again. "Have I ever acted as if I pity you or Cooper? Have I ever done anything to make you think I feel sorry for you?"

"No, but—"

"Yes, I feel empathy because I've been through this. I

relate to the horror of cancer. I can't believe you think this is all based on pity." His fingers knotted into a fist, and he smacked it against his leg.

"Ethan, I'm not making myself clear. You've shown us kindness and—"

"This isn't all about helping you, Lexie. Don't you realize I've gained so much from knowing you and Cooper? Our relationship has given me something to think about other than my work. It's helped me look forward to getting up in the morning. I realize we met because of Dreams Come True. It's a benevolent organization for people who've struggled with adversity. But even that isn't based on pity. It's based on love and the desire to make a difference in someone's life."

"Your values are the same as the organization's, Ethan. You want to make a difference in our lives, too, so you are kind and generous."

His fist struck his leg again. "Are you blind?"

She drew back and fell silent.

"I have feelings for you. Can't you see that? When Cooper said he wanted a father like me, I was touched. Do you know why?"

She shook her head.

"Because I want a son like him."

"A child with cancer?"

Her hurtful words spewed at him, and he went numb.

"Ethan, I'm—"

"I'll ignore what you said. You're upset and so am I. Maybe I should go back to my—"

She grasped his arm. "No, please." Tears welled in her eyes and rolled down her cheeks.

Startled by her emotions, Ethan rose and knelt at her feet. "Tell me what you fear, Lexie. Help me understand why you can't trust me."

* * *

Help me understand why you can't trust me. Blood drained from Lexie's body. She felt cold even though Ethan's warm hands pressed against hers. The reasons roiled through her mind, digging deep pits of grief and shame. She'd hung on to this too long. Ethan talked about learning to lean on people. To lean on God. She'd never been able to lean on anyone.

But lean she must.

Ethan's jaw had tensed, his eyes probing hers. He deserved to know the truth, and if Cooper's dream would ever come true with Ethan or any other man, time had come to open her despised baggage.

Ethan touched her cheek. "Are you all right?"

"No." Tears welled behind her eyes. "But I hope to be soon."

A flicker of hope showed in his eyes. He leaned back looking tense, concerned. He stretched his fingers as if to relax his hands from the fist he'd formed minutes ago.

She drew in a breath, stabilizing herself for the nightmare journey she knew she must take. "You've asked me questions about Cooper's father, and I've avoided them."

He blinked and nodded.

Now that she was to begin, Lexie's confidence in Ethan faltered. His faith held him grounded to God's Word, but when the truth struck, would he crumble?

"I met Cooper's father when I was in college when he became an assistant for one of my professors. Hart—" She choked on his name. "Hartley Kurtz." Speaking his name spread poison through her body. "Hart had recently completed his master's degree and had been accepted into a doctoral program. Hart took a liking to me. I was flattered. He invited me for coffee after class one day. Asked me again a couple days later. It started innocently."

Ethan squirmed in the chair, his eyes searching hers.

Her hands trembled. She'd begun the story, and she needed to finish. "I knew Hart was older. He didn't wear a wedding ring, and I assumed he was single. One day he mentioned he had been married but was divorced. He never talked about his wife, and I blocked it out of my mind."

Ethan leaned closer and touched her hand. "What are you telling me, Lexie?"

She realized he knew. "I got involved and realized I was pregnant. When I told him, he turned cold. 'I'll pay for an abortion' is what he said. An abortion? I wasn't a Christian, but I had values, and I valued the little being inside me. Yes, I was frightened and confused, but I couldn't do what he asked. He walked away. I saw him on campus, but he never spoke to me other than to try and give me money for an abortion. I know he tried to pay me off just to keep my mouth shut."

Ethan flinched. "Lexie, I—"

"I didn't take it."

Relief broke on his face, yet his eyes had glazed as if he'd heard all he could bear.

"My parents turned their backs on me for being so stupid. They'd helped me with some of my college expenses, and I never heard the end of it.

"I'd had a small apartment near campus, and I got a job. I didn't tell them I was pregnant. I hid it for a long time. I managed. I was determined to survive. I finished college part-time, and I didn't lean on anyone. I haven't until now."

The darkness shielded Ethan's face, but tension radiated from his posture.

"That's a lot for you to digest, I know, and I'm sorry I've disappointed you."

"Lexie, you've surprised me, yes, but I'm not disappointed. I don't know how I feel, but it's not disappointment."

His words didn't comfort her.

He rose and grasped her hand, helping her rise. Ethan

drew her into his arms and held her. "Things are clearer now. You've been treated badly, and I know it's been difficult for you. But I'm not Hartley, Lexie. You need to remember that. I want to digest all of this, and now I know we can start fresh. Doors open." He pressed his cheek against her hair. "Will you sleep okay?"

She nodded, knowing she wouldn't, but tomorrow the helicopter ride offered Cooper the biggest surprise of the trip. She'd be strong for him. "Good night, and thanks for listening." She stepped from his embrace. "Other than my parents, you're the first person I've told the full story."

"Thank you for trusting me enough to tell me. I know this was a big step for you."

"A huge step."

He nodded and squeezed her hand. "Please try to sleep, and know I'm relieved you told me. I really am." He strode across the balcony to the doorway. "Breakfast at seven-thirty?"

"That's fine."

He turned into her room, and she heard the door close.

Lexie sank into the chair and covered her face. She'd said it all, all the bitter memories deep and dark that she'd tried to forget for the past nine years. "I want them gone. I want to feel clean and whole." She rose and strode to the balcony railing. The moon had disappeared behind a cloud, and the dark Canyon far below had lost its beauty until the sunrise. She tilted her head toward the sky where the moon's glow rimmed an invisible cloud. "God, if You're there, and I think You are, take the shame and sadness away."

Moisture grew along her lower lashes, and tears crept down her cheeks. "Ethan, you talked with me about a loving God who looked into people's hearts, and you told me about forgiveness. You said God can forgive, but can you?"

Chapter Twelve

The helicopter lifted and Cooper pressed against the window, his camera in his hand and anticipation on his face. Yet Ethan worried. Cooper had woken still tired and said his bones hurt. Bruises, aching joints, lack of energy—it all added up to a return of his illness. Still he prayed the symptoms were only a result of his active fun-filled vacation.

Yesterday Cooper had seemed fine. Yet when Ethan thought about it in more depth, he recalled Cooper had been more cuddly and less energetic than he'd been at home. He'd gone to bed early both nights they'd been there. Ethan drew his gaze from the amazing scenery and studied Lexie. She looked stressed, but he suspected their conversation may have caused her a restless night. He'd had no time to discuss their talk, since Cooper had been with them every minute.

The earphones he wore related the history of the canyon and provided information about the rugged landscape that stretched before them. Minutes ticked away as they crossed over Zuni Point, an amazing spectacle and then over The Confluence where the Little Colorado joined the Colorado River. As they flew past Imperial Point, the highest formation in the Grand Canyon, Ethan rubbed his temples. He wished his head would stop aching. He'd barely slept, his mind so tied to Lexie's admission. Though the information unsettled him at first, during the night he had begun to admire her bravery and her decision to have her child alone. He couldn't imagine the anguish she felt and the feeling of abandonment not only by Cooper's father but her parents, as well.

He wanted to think her parents had hoped to teach her values and intended for her to come home, atone for her mistake and receive their support, but not Lexie. Getting strength from anyone but herself seemed a major issue. Yet he recalled what she'd said last night. *I was determined to survive and not lean on anyone. I haven't until now.* Now? She meant him. A tingle ran down his spine. She did care about him. She'd relinquished her independence to his support.

He adjusted his earphones, and leaned closer, sliding the audio from her ear. "Are you okay?"

She lowered her lids and nodded. "Tired and worried."

"About me or Cooper?"

"Cooper, mainly." She motioned toward him. "He felt warm this morning. I don't have a thermometer with me, but I think he has a slight fever."

Fever. He shifted toward Cooper, patted his head, then let his hand slip to his forehead. He felt warm, but the sun burned through the windowpane of the copter and he prayed the problem came from that.

Cooper's gaze adhered to the view, and Ethan turned toward Lexie and slipped his hand over hers, hoping he could offer comfort and reassure her that her past had no bearing on her future.

The pilot's voice reached his ear, and he focused to listen. "We are heading down into the Dragon Corridor, the deepest and widest part of the Canyon. Look for the Dragon's Head formation as we go down. Here we go."

The helicopter descended and followed the river. Amazing formations came into view as the recording provided details of the Tower of Ra, an imposing butte. Within minutes, Ethan realized they were heading for the canyon floor. Cooper turned his head toward them, questions in his glazed eyes. Ethan's chest constricted. Cooper hadn't been himself, and he suspected Lexie was right.

After they'd landed, Ethan helped him from the helicopter. "Aren't you feeling well?"

Cooper evaded his eyes. "I'm good." He turned around gazing upward at the outcropping. "Is this the bottom of the canyon?"

"It is, and guess what."

Lexie stood beside them, her expression strained. "I wonder if we should go back up."

Cooper faced her. "Up? Mom, we just landed."

Ethan understood, but Cooper's eagerness stripped his common sense. He ambled closer to Lexie, keeping his voice low. "This is a great opportunity for him, something he'll remember always, and we're here. Why not stay?"

She eyed her watch. "How much longer?"

He checked the time. "We'll be back up in another hour and a half. Then we can decide what to do."

She nodded as the pilot stepped beside them. And turned to Cooper. "What do you say, young man?"

He wiggled his head back and forth. "I've never seen anything so great."

"Now that you're down here—" he pointed to a four-wheeled Ranger waiting nearby "—there's your transportation. The driver's waiting for you. You'll be on bumpy trails so hang on, and when you're back, we'll have lunch."

When the pilot walked back to the helicopter, Ethan beckoned them to follow. Once in the Jeep, they headed for the Kaibab National Forest with dense stands of firs, pines and aspen trees. The beauty stirred him, but his mind clung to Cooper who bounced beside him, and though he laughed and oohed at the ride and the sights, his weakness became evident.

Amid the amazing landscape, all he could think about was Cooper. Ethan leaned closer to Lexie. "I'll make arrangements to go home as soon as we're back."

Relief flooded her face. "Thank you." She tilted her head toward Cooper. "He'll be disappointed, but it's for the best."

Ethan slipped his arm around the boy and held him tight as he sent up a prayer.

Lexie crumpled into a chair at the MOSK meeting. Meetings had been at the bottom of her list between coping with overwhelming stress since her, Cooper and Ethan's trip to the Grand Canyon. Two weeks ago, she'd embraced hope. Cooper had been well for many weeks. Her relationship with Ethan, though shaky at times, held promise, and life had wrapped around her like a warm blanket on a cold night.

Not now. She and Ethan hadn't talked about her confession the last night at the Grand Canyon with so much going on, and she wasn't sure how it would impact their relationship for the future. Every minute since their quick return tangled in taking care of Cooper and catching up on their work. Tears sprung to her eyes as she pictured the discouragement on his Cooper's face. His confidence had been shattered when the cancer returned with a vengeance. Terror had taken control of her.

Kelsey finished speaking with the new woman and scooted to her side. "Not good?"

She could only shake her head for fear a sob would burst from her throat. Her strength and determination pooled at her feet, soon to be washed away by another storm brewing in the sky. That's how leukemia encroached on her life.

"I'm so sorry." Kelsey sank to the chair beside her and

wrapped her arm around Lexie's shoulder. "I've been worried. You told me on the phone Cooper had a relapse, but when you missed the last meeting, I suspected the news wasn't good."

"Nothing's been decided for sure, but—" She waved the words away. "Later, okay?"

Kelsey nodded and gave her a squeeze. "I need to get the meeting started anyway." She rose and took a step before turning around. "Did I tell you I presented the idea of allowing men to join our group?"

"No. I didn't realize you were doing it so soon." Emotions wavered through her, questioning her stance. She needed to think about that. "What did everyone say?"

"Mixed responses. We listed the pros and cons, and I asked everyone to think about it. We'll discuss it today and then vote in another week."

Lexie nodded. That sounded fair to her.

Kelsey opened the meeting, and Lexie tried to concentrate. She'd probably made a mistake coming to MOSK today. Her emotions were nosediving into the pits, and she couldn't control her tears. She'd never been like this, but since spending time with Ethan, she'd unlatched the bonds that held her in check. Being strong and independent was part of her identity until now when she'd almost formed a partnership. She could lean on Ethan and let him be strong for her. A mistake. No question.

When Kelsey initiated the idea of allowing men to attend the MOSK meetings, her mind bogged with thoughts, mixed reaction that made no sense. Yes. No. If voting was to be today, she needed to abstain.

A soft buzz sounded from her bag. She slipped her hand in and pulled out her cell phone. Ethan. She rose and tiptoed from the room to the hallway as she answered. "Hi."

Words skittered away, and her greeting had been all she could squeeze from her throat.

"How's Cooper?"

"Not good."

"Did you talk with Dr. Herman?"

She drew in a breath, trying to keep her voice steady, and told him the latest news.

"Bone morrow transplant?" Ethan's voice darkened. "I know you've avoided it, but it can be a cure. Don't forget that."

"Yes, but it's terrible." The tremor in her voice gave her away.

"Are you home?"

"I'm at the MOSK meeting."

"Let me pick you up, Lexie. Now."

Her chest emptied of air. "Okay. I can't concentrate here anyway. I have my car so I'll drive home first. Come to the house." Tension turned to relief. "I'll be waiting."

"I can't believe I missed all the signs. That's my job. I pride myself on being watchful."

Ethan gave her shoulder a squeeze and drew her closer on the porch glider. "You were on vacation with so many distractions. Cooper was pushing himself to see everything. It's natural that you didn't pick up all the clues."

"It came on fast this time, and that's what scares me. I should have paid attention to his stomachache, and he slept so much. He's usually too antsy and excited to sleep. I should have been more aware."

Ethan slipped his free hand into hers. "You had many things on your mind besides the trip. I know we've been dealing with our relationship. I wish that hadn't distracted you, but I'm glad you opened up."

Her eyes widened with question. "You are?"

"I admit you shocked me. You'd never hinted about not being married, and—"

"I never allowed myself to think about it. I've been ashamed for so long. Ashamed of being so gullible and stupid. Ashamed for doing something I morally didn't accept. Ashamed of the poor relationship with my parents." Her voice trembled as tears rolled down her cheeks.

He drew her head against his. "Shame isn't constructive. Guilt isn't, either. Changing your life is what counts. You've done that. You're a hard worker with a good career. A wonderful mother. A precious friend to me. Shame and guilt need to be dead and buried."

"God does that. He wipes the slate and erases our sins."

Ethan's heart rose to his throat. "Yes, and He has already done that for you. You've atoned a thousand times. More than you needed to."

Her dam of tears opened, and she burrowed her face in his shoulder.

He held her close, feeling her body quake with emotion and wanting to make it better, but he suspected only the Lord could do that.

When she lifted her head, she looked into his eyes. "Sorry. Your shirt is wet."

"Tears are healing. I'm glad you chose my shoulder." He held her tighter. "So what's next?"

Lexie closed her eyes and shook her head. "I've done everything to avoid a bone marrow transplant for Cooper. It's long and painful, and then we need a donor."

"Do you match?"

That was the million-dollar question. She shrugged. "I would have to be tested."

His chest constricted. "If not, then what?"

"Wait for months, years, until a donor matches? And

that's not the best transplant. Family gives more hope of success."

"I'll be tested, Lexie. I'm not family, but it's another chance. The longer he waits the—" He slammed his mouth closed. What? The longer they waited the higher the chance Cooper might die. He tried to speak, but his throat constricted as he fought tears growing behind his eyes.

Lexie leaned her head against his chest. "If God has welcomed me as a believer, all I can do is pray and fight with everything I have to make things go right." She lifted her head. "I'm not giving up without a fight. I won't succumb to pressure. I want to weigh all alternatives. Tomorrow I face a consultation with the oncologist."

"Do you want me to go with you?"

Her eyes searched his with a flicker of approval, but the flicker died. "I need to do this alone." Her gaze softened. "But thanks."

"You'll call me as soon as you can?"

Her mouth curved upward for the first time since they'd returned home. "You know I will."

He ran his finger along the line of her lips while his pulse played havoc with his mind. "I know our talk seems unimportant during this crisis. It's the least of your worries, but—"

"It's not the least of my worries, Ethan." Her gaze penetrated his. "A major breakthrough happened that day. An important one for me. I'd dragged that trauma in a sack of regret for years, and I couldn't let go, because I had no one to help me. You did that. You allowed me to spew my sin into the air. I've never felt such relief."

"I can't tell you how happy that makes me." Though he'd tried to ignore his feelings and his concern of reliving the past again with Cooper's cancer, his denial ballooned then fizzled.

"Lexie, I know this is a rotten time to discuss anything but Cooper, yet I have to get this off my chest."

Her gaze captured his, a look of distress growing on her face. "What is it?"

"Nothing. Nothing's wrong." As he rose, the glider swung back, and he caught his balance. He reached for her hand, prepared this time as she stood beside him, questions darting in her eyes. "I've told you that I care about you and Cooper. I've admitted I love your son, but all along, I've wondered how you've felt. You tend to fade away sometimes, and I have no idea what you're thinking or feeling." He slipped his arm around her slender waist. "My feelings for you have grown, and I want to know where we stand."

She looked into the distance without responding while emotions rolled across her face like a scrolling message sign moving too fast to read.

He remained silent.

Finally she gazed at him. "I've been fearful of relationships since Hart. Trusting another man hurts."

His stomach twisted. "Lexie, you've known me for a while now. You know you can—"

She pressed her finger against his lips. "I knew Hart much longer than I've known you, Ethan. But you're different."

Different? His emotions unraveled. Waiting.

"No matter how many times I thought about distrusting you, I found myself believing what you said and did. I looked for ulterior motives. I chalked your behavior to your faith. I told you that, but my heart insisted I was wrong."

He drew her closer. "Really?"

She nodded. "You've been my light in the dark tunnel these past months. I let go of my own inability to accept help. I've learned that sharing a problem is greater than being the sole owner. I know you love Cooper. It shows. You didn't have to tell me."

"And you?"

She lowered her eyes. "I believe you care for me, too."

"In a special way." He'd said it. Not love. Not yet, but a deep caring that would be love very soon.

"Yes, in a special way." Her body relaxed in his arms.

"Can we call today a turning point, Lexie? Can we see where this relationship can go?"

She tilted her head upward, her heavy-lidded eyes gazing into his. He lowered his mouth to hers. This was all the answer he needed.

Chapter Thirteen

Lexie looked up when she heard someone enter Cooper's hospital room. Ethan swung through the door, struggling with a feeble attempt to appear upbeat. "How's it going?"

"Cooper, look who's here."

He gazed at Ethan as a smile blossomed on his face, and he wiggled his fingers for a wave.

"Look what I brought along." Ethan lifted his laptop and set it on the edge of the bed, then bent over to hug him. "I thought you'd like to see the photographs you took at the Grand Canyon."

"My pictures? Good." Cooper used his elbows to scoot upright in bed.

Lexie stepped to his side and fluffed the pillow before cranking the head of his bed to a sitting position. "Is that comfortable?"

Cooper nodded, his eyes following the laptop.

She gave Ethan a thank-you nod. She'd totally forgotten about the photos, and they were a wonderful way to distract Cooper. He'd been through so much—rounds of chemotherapy that had drained him. Lexie wondered how much more he could take it. She didn't know how much longer she could endure this, but she'd begun to read the Bible Ethan had given her when they returned from the Grand Canyon, and she'd learned that God does not give more than He thinks a person can handle. She understood that God was all-knowing, but she questioned how well He knew her. Her resolution had lost its spark. Disappointment had overwhelmed her when Cooper's leukemia returned once again. This time she'd been more than hopeful.

She stood behind Ethan, looking over his shoulder, while Cooper studied the photographs. His pale face brightened with excitement when he saw some of the excellent shots he'd taken. "You're almost a professional, Coop."

"I am." He grinned at her, but it faded too quickly.

"Are you okay?"

He gave a faint nod, and she didn't push. Being positive provided the best chance of surviving any horrendous disease. She'd learned that over the years.

Ethan had set up a slide show, and the lovely pictures appeared, then disappeared in an amazing display. The close-ups of flowers and plants, the brilliant colors of the canyon, the vivid hues of a sunset, their smiles, the mule deer and the chipmunk swirled to the screen and zoomed off again.

"You have a real talent, Coop." Ethan folded the laptop when they were done and set it on a chair. He sat on the edge of the bed. "I'm really proud of you."

Cooper nodded, his eyelids heavy with dark circles beneath.

"When you're better, we can decide on which of these photos you want to make enlargements and you can keep them in a scrapbook." He ran his hand over Cooper's hair. "You know what that's called?"

"An album?"

Ethan chuckled. "It's an album all right, but it's also called a portfolio. Every artist has one. It shows off their best work."

Cooper nodded.

Ethan rose from the mattress, removed his laptop from the chair and sat beside Lexie. "Any news?"

Her pulse jumped. She nodded.

"Good news?"

She shook her head. "Not a match."

His heart slipped. He clutched her hand in his and held it tight. "I'm sorry." His head wagged as he spoke. "I'm really, really sorry."

"So am I." A breath rattled through her lungs. "Maybe this is one of God's ways to say no."

Ethan shook his head. "Perseverance." His focus turned to Cooper. "He's sleeping."

"He does that a lot." It broke her heart.

"I've been thinking about the procedure." He glanced again at Cooper. "Can I talk here?"

She frowned and shook her head. "We can take a walk to the cafeteria. If he wakes, he'll know I'm still here. When I leave for the night, I always say goodbye." She grabbed her bag and stood.

Ethan followed her into the hallway and slipped his arm around her shoulders. She led the way, distracted by her heavy thoughts.

Ethan ran his hands along her arm, and comfort eased through her body. The past weeks had been stressful, but Ethan had been there for her, and so had a sense that God had wrapped His arms around her, too. But her feelings didn't help Ethan. His face showed the strain of Cooper's illness, and she'd been so tied up at the hospital she hadn't given him time to talk. Time to talk. Tomorrow MOSK would vote on allowing men to join the group. The name Mothers of Special Kids wouldn't fit anymore if the women said yes. She doubted they would. Even she'd struggled with the concept.

Yet now that she'd listened to Ethan as he coped with

Cooper's leukemia, she'd begun to question her own thinking. Maybe some men needed to talk, needed to express their feelings, needed an outlet for their emotions.

In the cafeteria, Ethan offered her food, and though she was tempted by a cinnamon bun, she decided to forgo it. Coffee would satisfy her. Ethan guided her to a table near a window where the summer sun glinted on the water shooting from a lawn sprinkler. She'd missed time outside. She spent her days and some nights here, often trying to catch up on work on her laptop.

She turned from the window and faced Ethan, sitting across from her, his face serious. "What's your idea about the procedure?"

He sipped from the cup and set it down, his hand reaching for hers. She grasped his strong fingers sending warmth through her.

"I've been thinking about what you might do if your bone marrow didn't match."

That wasn't what she expected. "Cooper's already been added to the donor list."

"But that can be a long wait. And you told me, a parent or sibling has a better chance to match."

"Yes, but I'm the only parent Cooper has." She froze, spotting the look in Ethan's eyes. "No."

He drew back, his eyes widening. "No? But if you can find Hartley, his bone marrow might—"

Her heart sank seeing the disappointment in his eyes. "Ethan, the day that Hart walked away that was it. I never asked for a thing from him, and he never offered. I took care of myself. I managed. I'm not going to crawl on my hands and knees now. He doesn't care about Cooper."

"But he doesn't know Cooper. He'd be proud of his son."

She shook her head. "We'll wait and see what they come up with on the donor list."

"I'll take the test. Maybe the Lord will—"

"I don't want you to be tested for nothing."

"I'd be honored to give my marrow for Cooper." Tears rimmed his eyes. "Lexie, I can't bear the thought of—"

"I know." He'd give her son his life if need be. She had no doubt. She gazed into the coffee cup, longing for tea leaves that she could read her fortune with, but that was hokey. Right now she'd begun to grasp for anything. She lifted the cup and took a sip. "Let's drop it for now, Ethan. Pray the hospital finds a matching donor soon. I'll pray, too."

His eyes said it all. They were filled with love and concern, nothing she'd experienced since she was a child.

Ethan left his morning appointment, discouraged. His fault, not the client's. He'd had a difficult time concentrating on their construction blueprints while his mind stayed connected to Cooper's dire situation. He'd made a commitment, not to Lexie yet, but to himself. Having the joy of Lexie as a wife and Cooper as a son towered over any earthly loyalty he could envision.

He settled in the SUV and set the prints on the passenger seat. He'd lost the battle trying to work today. Maybe he could handle paperwork in the office. He didn't need to sound competent or articulate. Slipping on sunglasses to block the rays, he pulled away from the client's house and headed for work.

Why Lexie refused to consider locating Hartley Kurtz struck him as unthinking. Yes, she had prided herself in not asking for anything from the man who abandoned her when she was in need, but most important it could mean life and death to her son. She wasn't using common sense. Maybe tomorrow after thinking it over, she would change her mind.

To him, it was the best solution to the awful problem. He'd do anything to return Cooper to good health. Maybe remission forever. It happened with bone morrow transplants.

He pulled into the Pelham Homes parking lot and made his way to his office. Grateful no one stopped to talk or ask a question, he settled behind his desk, his face in his hands. His mind reeled with every question possible, and his heart joined in with a whirl of emotions. When he thought back, Ethan wondered if he'd handled Laine's cancer better than Cooper's. Probably time had eased the memory, but today Cooper's illness was fresh and he ached.

Ethan rubbed his eyes and raised his head. Even though Lexie wouldn't agree to his idea, he could be prepared in case she changed her mind. He flipped open his laptop and hit the power button. When it came to life, he pulled up a search engine and typed in Hartley Kurtz, Michigan. A list of links ran down the page. Hartley Kurtz wasn't a common name so he held his breath and hit the first link.

He'd found the man, but nothing current. Reference to his connection with Wayne State University and Marygrove College provided little information. One link after another gave details about his research and study papers, university events that he was involved in, but nothing personal. Nothing to give Ethan a hint where the man lived or how to contact him.

He lowered his head and prayed, asking God to provide a donor. His next petition rose.

Lord, if no donor is found, open Lexie's eyes to the need to find Cooper's father and help us locate him.

The prayer mingled with his thoughts, but he figured the Lord knew his heart and could sort out his words.

When his cell phone rang, Ethan's fingers bumped the

laptop keys and an advertisement for toothpaste blasted onto the screen. He lowered the volume and slipped the phone from his pocket. Lexie. "Is everything okay?"

"I'm not at the hospital, but he was sleeping when I called today so I decided to stop by the MOSK meeting. I'm leaving for the hospital now."

"Keep me posted. I can't think about anything but Cooper." He clicked off the ad and lowered the laptop. Looking at the list of links he'd been studying tempted him to admit what he was researching.

"You know I will. Why I called was to tell you that MOSK voted today on allowing men to join the group."

"Really?"

"It didn't pass."

"It didn't?" Her news didn't startle him. Lexie had made it clear she didn't like the idea.

"I was surprised. So you might want to tell your friend. What's his name? Ross?"

"Ross Salburg. I'm at the office so I'll let him know." The question niggled him. "Was it unanimous?"

Silence filled the line for a moment. "No. I changed my mind. I voted yes. But tell Ross I'll give him a list of other groups that might work. Ones that are for families."

His chest constricted. "Thanks for trying. I'll head down and tell Ross now. I know he'll be disappointed, but thanks for the list. That will give him some hope." He rolled back and rose. "Will you be home later tonight?"

"If everything goes well. Visiting hours end at eight."

"I'll drop by if that's okay, and how about if I bring you some dinner?"

"No dinner for me. I'll catch a bite at the hospital, but you know what I would like?"

He waited.

"You know the bakery that has the wonderful cinnamon buns? Would you bring one home for me? I'll make coffee."

"I'd love to." He said goodbye, a smile growing on his face. Lexie and her cinnamon buns. She'd given him the only lighthearted moment he'd had all day.

Ethan sat at the kitchen island, a steaming cup of coffee and a cinnamon bun in front of him. His heart weighted with sadness. "No donor match yet. That's not good news."

"Finding a donor takes time. We have to have patience." She broke off a piece of bun and licked her fingers. "This is pretty good."

"You look exhausted." Her eyes looked glazed with a dark tinge beneath her lashes.

"I am." She slipped the sugary bun onto a plate and shook her head. "I hate to leave Cooper there alone. I try to spend time with him especially during chemotherapy, but I'm getting behind on my project for work." She shook her head and captured his gaze. "I've thought about asking my mother and dad if they'd be tested." She lowered her eyes. "That's desperate."

"If there's a good chance they will match, you should. They can have the results sent here, can't they?"

She nodded. "But I think they'll refuse. They'll come up with a million reasons it's impossible. And I can't take any more rejection, Ethan." Tears formed in her eyes.

Ethan wiped his fingers on a napkin before rising and hurrying to her side. He stood beside her, pressing her head against his shoulder. Frustration rattled him, but he remained silent on the issue until she calmed. He kissed the top of her head and massaged her neck until it relaxed.

She tilted her head upward and kissed his lips, a quick but tender moment that made his pulse race.

"I'm fine." She straightened her back. "Once in a while it all gets too heavy to carry."

He grasped her hand. "Would you listen to me, please?"

"If it's about Hart—"

"Yes, it's about Hart." He swallowed. "I did some research." He flexed his palm to silence her. "Just in case. I got the brilliant idea, after an hour of getting nowhere, to check the white pages."

She stiffened. "Did you find him?"

His throat constricted. "I think so. I found a Hartley Kurtz living in Bloomfield Hills."

She nodded. "It could be him, but Ethan, I—"

"We're talking about Cooper's life. You can wait, but the longer you wait the weaker he'll get. I know the transplant will drain him, and if he's already in bad condition..." The rest of the sentence died in his throat. He couldn't think, let alone say, the alternative.

Lexie lowered her face in her hands, shaking her head. "It's been on my mind since you mentioned it. I couldn't sleep last night."

He ran his hand across her back. "I'm sorry, but the idea gave me hope."

"I'm being selfish." She raised her eyes to his. "For the sake of pride, I'm not doing what's best for my son." A desperate look covered her beautiful face.

Ethan's heart squeezed against his breastbone as if it had no room. "Will you give it some serious thought? I'll make the call. If it's him, then...I'll tell him or give the phone to you. Whichever you want."

"Give me a minute." She lowered her head.

He shifted away and returned to the stool. He broke off a piece of the sweet roll, needing something to do with his hands. He washed it down with coffee.

Lexie finally lifted her head. She pressed her lips together and studied him, her eyes searching his. "You think it's the best thing to do?"

"He's Cooper's father. It's the best chance you have of finding a donor soon."

Her expression sank to defeat. She nodded. "You talk. If he insists, I'll speak with him."

Ethan's pulse accelerated. How would he tell a man that his son had leukemia and needed his bone marrow? He drew in a breath and headed for the den as he pulled out his cell phone. He stood a moment to get his bearings before pulling the paper from his pocket and punching in the number he'd jotted there.

When a man answered, Ethan stomach bungee-jumped from a Grand Canyon ridge. He caught his breath. "May I speak to Hartley Kurtz, please?"

"Just a minute."

He couldn't believe what he was doing. He sent up a prayer.

Ethan heard the receiver click onto a surface as the voice yelled Hart's name. He waited, hands trembling. He never wanted to experience something like this again.

"Hello."

He wet his lips. "My name is Ethan Fox, and I'm a friend of Lexie Carlson. I'm sure the name rings a bell. Or maybe you know her as Alexandria." He held his breath.

"Sorry. Never heard either name. What's this about?"

Games. "Think back to your college days. I'm sure—"

"Look, I never knew or heard of a Lexie or an Alexan— whatever her name is."

Ethan's back stiffened. He didn't like games. "You knew her from Wayne State University."

"I went to Lawrence Institute of Technology."

"You never went to Wayne State University?"

He huffed. "That was my dad."

"Your dad?" Ethan's chest hammered. "Listen, I'm sorry about that." He cleared his throat. "Could I speak to him?"

"No."

He drew back. "No?"

"My father died three years ago. Unless you've got a special connection with the afterworld, I can't help you."

The pounding slowed. Dead end. Ethan drew up his shoulders. He couldn't give up now. "Will you give me a few minutes to explain why I called?"

"Go ahead, but make it short."

Ethan closed his eyes, pulling together Lexie's story in a neat bundle, and began. He heard Hart's intake of breath, but Ethan didn't let it slow him down.

"A kid? You mean...I have a half brother?"

The shock in Hart's voice tore through Ethan. "I'm sorry to break the news, but yes. He turned eight a few months ago."

"Eight. My parents were divorced then." Hart's voice seemed a whisper. "A half brother."

Ethan bit his lip and waited.

"Look, this is a shock though I don't know why. My dad chased after young women. We learned that when we got older. I suspect that caused my parents' divorce. But I don't plan to patch up my father's mistakes, and I doubt if we would match anyway."

He'd said *we*. "You have a sibling?"

"Yes, Jess. He's the one who answered the phone."

Two of them. Two chances. Ethan's pulse raced. How could he say no to possibly saving his half brother's life? A long shot, but maybe. "Would you please think this over? Could I talk with your brother?"

"It won't make any difference."

Ethan sent up another prayer. "Could I please talk with your brother?"

"Listen, whoever you are, we put up with our dad's antics for years. Neither one of us want to clean up his messes. You've wasted enough of my time."

"Please, may I give you my phone number?"

"No point, man. I won't change my mind." He hung up.

Ethan's body drained of energy. He lowered the receiver, gathered strength and left the den to face Lexie.

Chapter Fourteen

Lexie sat beside Cooper, her eyes on a magazine but her mind on her son. Ethan's news churned in her chest. Hart dead. He'd walked out on two sons when he divorced. She had no idea. He'd avoided conversation about himself, and what he told her had probably been a blend of lies with a smidgen of truth. How could she have been so naive? So gullible? So stupid?

She rocked her head, unable to fathom what she'd been thinking back then. A college girl flattered by a handsome man heading for his doctorate, and he had been drawn to her. Why hadn't she realized the man had probably swayed many young women into an empty romance? She'd pictured herself married to him, living in a lovely home where she would give dinner parties and talk about fashion and art.

She exhaled, her chest rattling with regret. Cooper had two half brothers. Uncaring and unemotional. Like father, like son. Now she knew what that meant.

Though she'd fought Ethan's idea to call, she'd shocked herself by being disappointed when his effort failed. Hart wouldn't have helped anyway, but not even his sons. Though unlikely matches, she'd still felt her hope crumble. Her parents were the only other options, or an anonymous donor, but as yet that hadn't happened.

Lexie noticed Cooper stir. She leaned closer and brushed her fingers along his cheek. His eyes opened. "Did you get a good rest?"

He blinked. "That's all I do, Mom." He rolled onto his side, looking thin and worn.

She stroked his arm. "It hasn't been a very good summer."

His eyes brightened. "The Grand Canyon was the best." He lifted his head and gazed around the room, then let it fall back. "Is Ethan coming?"

"In a while."

He nodded and closed his eyes.

Lexie rested her back against the chair and peered up at the TV. She should turn it on for him. Not much this time of day but news, soaps and game shows, but it would be something. She checked him again, but his eyes remained closed.

Her mind drifted to Ethan. The adventure of the past weeks with him astounded her. Once she'd told her story, she'd experienced amazing relief. She hadn't known what to expect from Ethan, but he'd give her the best gift anyone could expect—his own kind of forgiveness—acceptance without explaining her sins away. He'd dismissed them as if he'd wiped crumbs from a table. She'd become free.

Their relationship had heightened and grown since then. Without time to enjoy it, they'd accepted it. She knew he would call, and he knew she expected him. No questions. No confusion. Nothing but confidence in each other. She luxuriated in the feeling. They'd made no commitment, but they didn't have to. The unspoken concern now revolved around Cooper. If only he could be part of their joy.

When she looked again, Cooper's eyes were open, and he was watching her. "Want to sit up a little?"

He nodded. She shifted his pillows and cranked the mattress upward so he could sit. "Would you like to watch TV?"

"What's on?"

She shrugged. "Let's look."

As she grasped the remote, she caught movement at the door, and Ethan stepped into the room.

A smile grew on his face when he saw Cooper. "How are you today?" He strode to his side and gave him a hug.

Not only had their relationship changed, but so had Ethan with Cooper. He'd hesitated before with his demonstrative affection, but since they'd returned from the Grand Canyon, he'd become like a dad, and despite Cooper's illness, he reveled in Ethan's attention.

Lexie snapped on the TV and found a channel about animals. When Cooper was absorbed in the program, Ethan raised his eyebrows and gave her a cryptic look.

He leaned closer. "I have some news."

She noticed Ethan's head flick toward Cooper, and she caught on. "Good news?"

"I don't know."

That confused her.

He gave a subtle shrug. "Later?"

She eyed Cooper. The program had engrossed him, and she motioned toward the doorway. "Cooper, we're going to go down the hall a minute, okay?"

"Can I have a snack?"

"I'll ask while I'm gone." She leaned over and kissed his forehead.

Ethan had already slipped through the doorway, and she followed him. He'd waited for her a few feet down the hall.

"What's the news? What happened?"

He grasped her hand. "You won't believe this, but Hart's son Jess called me today."

Her legs became a feather pillow. "I thought the other brother wouldn't take your number."

"He didn't, but Jess found it from the telephone's caller ID." His gaze captured hers. "He wants to meet Cooper."

"Meet Cooper?" She grasped Ethan's arm to keep her balance. "But Cooper doesn't know he has a half brother. What will he think?"

Ethan shook his head. "I don't know, but he's such a great kid, mature for his age, I can only believe he'll accept it."

"When does he want to meet?"

"As soon as you're willing."

The repercussions charged through her mind. Would Cooper understand? Would meeting Cooper make a difference in Jess's decision? She leaned her head on Ethan's strong shoulder while he moved his hand along her back. "Tomorrow night? At the house, not here."

"Okay."

"Can you be there? I want to meet him first."

"I want to be there, Lexie, and I understand. You need to be cautious."

"You call him, then, and I need to find the courage to talk with Cooper."

Ethan heard a noise outside as he paced across the living room. He slipped to the window as his pulse rose. "He's here."

Lexie stood in the archway. "Would you let him in?"

Her voice had an edge, and stress showed on her face. Ethan waited for the bell before opening the door.

Jess gave him a nod, his tension evident.

"Thanks for coming." Ethan pushed open the door. He studied the good-looking young man, the shape of his face and the curve of his nose so similar to Cooper's, it gave

Ethan a jolt. He extended his hand. "I'm Ethan Fox, Lexie's friend."

The young man grinned. "I recognize your voice."

Ethan motioned toward Lexie. "This is Lexie, Cooper's mom."

Jess stepped forward and reached for her hand. Lexie grasped it. "I'm sorry to hear about your son." He brushed hair from his forehead. "I still can't believe I have a half brother."

Lexie motioned for him to sit, and he waited for her to take a seat before he slipped into the easy chair. "Tell me about Cooper."

Ethan slipped into the kitchen to see what drinks Lexie had available while she began the story. They needed privacy, and he wanted to make sure he didn't infringe on it. She had coffee made, and he found a few soft drinks in the fridge. He settled on a stool, with hope the pinnacle of his thoughts. The voices bounced back and forth from Lexie to Jess. He heard Hart's name mentioned, and he winced, assuming she had also shared the story of her relationship with Jess's father. That story had to be difficult for her to tell.

The clock ticked, and finally when he heard a chuckle, Ethan returned. "Would you like a drink, Jess? Coffee? Soda?"

"Coffee would be great. Black."

Ethan headed back to the kitchen and poured three cups, relieved to see that some of the strain had vanished from Lexie's face. Their meeting had to be difficult. When he returned, he delivered the drinks, then settled on the sofa.

Jess turned to him. "I'm glad you called, and I apologize for my brother. He's much more like my dad than I am." He glanced at Lexie. "I don't run away from problems like they seem to do." He chuckled. "Actually I didn't see this as a problem. I saw it as an adventure. It's exciting, in a way, to be about ready to turn twenty-one, and then learn I have an eight-year-old brother." He raised his cup and took a sip.

Ethan's spirit rose. "You're different, I'll admit." He gazed at Lexie. "We were both disappointed after talking to Hart."

Jess gave a faint snort. "My brother can do that sometimes...even to me." He drew in a lengthy breath. "I'd like to meet Cooper. Is that possible?" He turned to Lexie. "Would you let me? I know it might be hard for an eight-year-old child to learn he has a brother. It was shocking to me." He took another sip of coffee.

Lexie lowered her eyes. "I tried to get it out this morning, Jess, but I didn't have the courage. I promise I will tomorrow."

"Then I can visit him? Is he well enough?" A frown sank to his face. "I can't even imagine what you've been through." He shook his head. "And alone."

"I have Ethan now."

Her look made Ethan's heart sing. "Cooper's a strong, amazing boy. He's curious and takes great photographs."

"Ethan helped us arrange a trip to the Grand Canyon through the Dreams Come True Foundation."

"That's a place to take pictures." Jess's facial expression reminded Ethan of Cooper.

Lexie shook her head. "He had a wonderful time. Naturally we cut the trip short when he got sick, and now I wonder if the trip was too much for him."

Ethan rose and sat on the arm of her chair. "You know better than that. He'd been doing great." He turned to Jess. "He was able to attend school for a month or so before summer vacation. That was what he wanted."

Jess shifted his gaze from Lexie to Ethan. "I hope I can meet him."

Ethan gave Lexie's shoulder a pat and rose from the chair

arm. "Personally, I think he'll be thrilled to know he has an older brother."

Jess's grin returned as he stood. "Then you'll call me when you decide?"

Lexie nodded. "I promise I'll talk with him tomorrow."

Jess extended his hand. "Thanks for the coffee and for meeting me."

Lexie moved to his side. "It's been very nice meeting you. Your dad had charm, and so do you, but you have one thing he didn't have. A kind spirit." Instead of shaking his hand, she gave him a hug.

"Thanks. Both of you. I can't wait to meet Cooper."

Ethan opened the door and Lexie joined him as they watched Jess return to his car. When he'd pulled away, Ethan closed the door and drew Lexie into his arms. "I had no idea you blamed yourself for Cooper's relapse."

"I know better, but maybe I was so busy with the trip plans that I didn't see the signs."

He nestled her closer. "You answered your own question. You're a great mother, and you see every twinge. I didn't notice, either. Not one thing until after we were there." He touched her cheek. "Do you realize Jess could answer our prayers?" He searched her eyes.

"I have been praying. It feels strange but good at the same time."

"You amaze me, Lexie."

She lowered her eyes. "I still don't get it. I amaze you?"

"I get it." He tilted her chin as his lips met hers. Peace flooded him. Lexie and Cooper brought joy to his life. Jess had added hope. God? He had provided it all.

Her lips moved beneath his, and Ethan breathed in a new life.

* * *

Cooper shifted the pillows behind his back. "Is he here yet?"

He'd asked the question multiple times, and Lexie gave him the same answer. "He'll call us from the lobby when he's on his way up." She sat beside him on the mattress, aching as she studied his thin face and the ravages of the powerful chemotherapy. She leaned forward and kissed his head. As she did, her cell phone jingled.

She rose and pulled it from the top of her handbag. She nodded to Cooper. "It's him." She pressed the button. "Come up, Jess." She smiled at her son, seeing the excitement in his eyes.

"What does he look like?"

"You'll see in a minute, but he looks a little like you will when you grow up."

His tired eyes widened. "Mom, you're kidding."

"No. Really. I can see a resemblance. The parts that belonged to your dad."

Movement at the door caught her attention. She nodded, and Jess stepped inside, set a bag on the empty chair and stood at the foot of the bed. "Cooper, I'm Jess. I'm very happy to meet you."

Cooper studied him for a moment. "You're my brother."

"Only half, but that's enough." His face lit to a smile as he leaned down and wrapped Cooper in his arms.

Jess's greeting melted Lexie's heart. She returned to the chair while Jess settled on the other side of the bed and listened to Cooper relive the Grand Canyon trip. They talked about school, and Jess told him about college. Nothing was said about Hart Junior.

Lexie wished Ethan had come to see their meeting, but she knew he would hear about it later when Cooper latched on to him. Hope soared as she listened and watched. If Hart had done one thing right in his marriage, he'd given birth to at least one son who had both charm and goodness.

Jess grinned. "I heard you like books."

"I love books." Cooper's focus didn't shift from Jess's face. "Stories and pictures."

Jess nodded and stepped back to the chair to pick up the package. "I brought you a present."

Cooper eyed the bag. "A book?"

Jess nodded and settled on the mattress again. "If you don't feel like reading it now, you can when you're better."

"That's what I want." He lifted a plaintive gaze. "To get better. We need bone marrow for me so I can be healthy again. That's what the doctor said."

Jess glanced at Lexie. "Maybe that will happen very soon."

Lexie's heart bounced to her throat.

"Only maybe, though. It depends what the test says."

Lexie rose and rounded the bed.

Cooper nodded. "It has to match."

When she reached Jess, she wrapped her arms around his shoulders. "You're willing?"

"I am, and I'm working on Hart. That's a project, but who knows? Give me a couple more days."

Warm tears escaped her eyes, and before Cooper saw them, she brushed the back of her hand along her cheeks. "I can't thank you enough, Jess. Whether it's a match or not, I am grateful that you're willing to try. It means a great deal to us."

"I'll talk to them at the desk and find out what I need to do."

Lexie's chest constricted. "Do you understand what this entails?"

"I read up on it on the internet. An overnight stay in the hospital and sometimes a little pain that Tylenol can fix." He patted Cooper's legs. "It's easy compared to what Cooper will face."

His voice faltered, and he looked away, probably to hide his emotions.

"And if the tests don't match, I'm really happy to have met you anyway." She had so much to tell him, how meeting him had eased the feeling of desertion from his father's behavior, but with Cooper listening, she had to monitor what she said. "You've given me a better feeling about things."

Jess understood. She saw it in his face.

"I can't undo my father's inappropriate actions, but I hope it lets you know that I care."

Her tears returned, and she could only nod. She headed back to the chair while Jess and Cooper looked at the book.

Lexie wished Ethan had arrived to witness this.

Chapter Fifteen

Lexie lowered her head and let the tears flow. When she felt drained, she drew in a ragged breath and wandered to the window. Ethan said he would arrive about five to drive her to the hospital to visit Cooper, and she could barely contain herself, waiting.

When she heard a car pull up, she headed to the door, and when his hand touched the knob, she flung it open. He hurried inside and held her to his chest. "What is it? What happened?"

She shook her head, unable to speak.

"Jess's bone marrow test? Is it a go or not?"

She managed to look into his eyes and utter one word. "Not."

"Oh, Lexie, I hoped and prayed." He cuddled her against him, soothing her sorrow and releasing his own.

She struggled to get herself under control not only for her sake but for Ethan. His love for Cooper glowed like the full moon they'd witnessed at the Grand Canyon. He lit her darkest night. "Let's sit." She motioned him forward, and he walked beside her to the sofa and drew her beside him. "I need to get myself in shape. Jess said he'd drop by. I know he feels terrible, and it's not his fault. The whole thing was a long shot."

"But we both had hopes, Lexie, and it's not over. The hospital is still looking, and God provides."

She shook her head. "Maybe not for me."

He drew back. "I don't like hearing you say that. With God, all things are possible. Repeat that over and over when you doubt." He took her hand in his. "We all doubt sometimes even when we know better. God knows your heart, Lexie, and He'll never walk away."

"I'm new at this." She lowered her head again. "I'm desperate. I didn't want Cooper to have this transplant, and now I'm wondering if maybe that's why things aren't falling into place."

"It hasn't been that long." He squeezed her hand again. "I know it seems forever, but hang on and—"

The doorbell sounded, and Lexie rose. "It's probably Jess."

When she opened the door, he stood a second and then hugged her. "I'm so sorry."

She maneuvered her face as pleasant a look as she could manage for Jess's sake. He looked forlorn. "I'm grateful you tried. I told you that already." She shifted back. "Come in." She motioned him into the room.

Ethan rose and took a step forward.

"No, I can't stay, but I wanted to ask this in person. I've been talking to Hart, and he's not saying much, but I think he'd like to meet Cooper. Would you mind?"

Emotions fluttered through her. One more chance? No. She dismissed the thought. "That would be fine. Would you let me know when?"

Jess pressed his lips together. "Here's the catch. He would prefer not to meet you right now."

The idea jolted her, and she couldn't avoid her frown. "But—"

"Despite his frustration with Dad, they were probably closer than I was, and I think seeing you makes our father's thoughtless lifestyle more real."

It made sense to her. "Would you like to go up now? I'll wait and you can call when you're leaving."

He pondered her offer before pulling out his cell phone. "You know, that might be a good idea."

"If you'd like some privacy, head into the kitchen. It's right through that archway." He nodded and swept through the doorway.

"Hart…"

His voice faded, and Lexie stood beside Ethan, her mind barraged with hope, despair and possibilities. "What do you think?"

Ethan shrugged. "You made the only decision."

Lexie slipped into the easy chair while Ethan returned to the sofa.

"When I told Cooper about his two half brothers, he wanted to meet them both. I made excuses, but this can make things right." She let the comment sink in. "I hope it will."

Ethan leaned forward, his fingers woven into a knot in front of him. "If Hart agrees to visit Cooper, he'll do the right thing. I'm sure he will."

She hoped Ethan was correct. Sinking into silence, she eyed her watch and then the doorway until she heard Jess's footsteps.

"He said yes. I'm meeting him there." He crossed his fingers. "I'll call you later."

Lexie started to rise, but Jess stopped her. "I'll let myself out. Hart has a sensitive side, although he keeps it hidden. We can hope."

She agreed and waved as he slipped outside.

Ethan gazed at her. Neither had to say anything.

* * *

Ethan paced in the hospital room, dressed in a gown and mask. He'd sterilized his hands as everyone did when they entered the room. The weeks before a transplant were critical. Cooper's rigorous preparation since he entered the bone marrow transplant unit provided chemotherapy much stronger than before, and it tore him apart to see how weak and nauseous Cooper had been since then.

While pacing, Ethan listened to Lexie talk with Cooper, explaining again what he had in store. Since the day they'd heard Hart's bone marrow matched, the transplant would not leave his mind. His prayers answered, he now prayed for God's blessing on the procedure.

"I know, Mom. I'll be even sicker than I am, but you know what? I've been sick most of my life. Now I'll have a chance to get better."

"And once you're home, your grandma and granddad are coming to visit you."

"Good, and I'll feel better then."

Ethan sidled to Lexie's side. "You sure will, Coop."

Lexie slipped her hand into his. He fought back his tears while moisture blurred his vision. He walked toward the doorway and brushed his tears away. Noise from the hallway caused his pulse to rise. Soon the gurney would arrive to take Cooper to the surgery, and they would wait, an eternal wait, until the procedure had ended.

He trudged to the window and looked out at the sunny September day. School started the week before, and though they tried to avoid the topic, Cooper knew, but his hope remained solid. He'd looked at them with determination in his eyes. "Next year I won't miss one day of school, will I?"

Lexie affirmed his declaration, and Ethan nodded, knowing if anyone could go to school and not miss a day it would be a healthy eight-year-old named Cooper.

As he turned back toward the bed, footsteps sounded in the hall, and his pulse skipped, but when he looked up, he smiled. "Jess."

He stood back from the doorway. Ethan stepped into the hall and offered his hand.

Jess shook it. "I'm heading up to the surgical waiting room, but I thought I'd stop so Cooper knows I'm here."

Their relationship amazed him. In the short time Jess had been in Cooper's life, the two had become brothers. Cooper never asked for details. He'd accepted his mother's simple explanation, and it had been a blessing. Neither Ethan nor Lexie had met Hart. He'd offered his bone marrow, but that seemed to be it. He'd met Coop once, then walked away. Hart puzzled Ethan, but time could make a difference. Time and prayer.

"I wish you could come in and tell him yourself, but—"

Jess lifted his palm. "Don't explain. I understand. They offered me a mask and everything, but I didn't want to take a chance. Just tell him I'm here."

"I'm happy to."

Ethan watched him leave before returning to the room. "That was Jess, Cooper. He wanted you to know he's here waiting."

"Tell him I'll see him later."

As Cooper finished his sentence, a nurse entered with a needle. "Time for a shot to make you drowsy. Okay, Cooper?" She leaned over the bed and eyed his arms.

He rolled his head toward her. "What's drowsy?"

"It'll make you sleepy so you'll be comfortable when you go in for your transplant."

Lexie watched from the other side of the bed.

Ethan joined her and slipped his arm around Lexie's waist. "Would you mind if I talk to Cooper a second alone after the shot?"

A faint frown flashed across Lexie's face. "Okay, but—"

"Just for moment. I want to tell him something to distract him a little. I'll call it our secret, and he'll love that."

Her lips curved upward as the frown vanished. "He loves secrets." Before the nurse finished, she slipped from the room still wearing the gown and mask.

The nurse dropped the needle into the bio-hazard container and looked at him. "He'll relax now, and they'll be here soon to take him." She smiled at Cooper and swept out the door.

Ethan ambled toward Cooper and sat on the edge of the bed. "Your mom'll be back in a minute."

Cooper nodded, his eyes already heavy.

"I want to tell you something, just between you and me."

He tilted his head.

"I want to marry your mom, but I want to make sure you're okay with that."

He tugged his eyes open. "And you'd be my dad?"

Ethan nodded. "That's one of the best parts. But I don't know what your mom will say, so we have to say prayers that she'll like the idea."

"I like the idea." Cooper managed to grin. "I think she will, too."

"Good. That's what I want." As he leaned over to hug him, Cooper kissed his cheek. Ethan's heart exploded with delight.

"I see the gurney coming down the hall."

Lexie's voice startled him, and he straightened and rose. "It's your turn."

She finished washing her hands, and he moved out of her way to give her room.

"Getting sleepy?" She propped her hand against the mattress and leaned above him.

Cooper nodded. "Mom, if Ethan asked you to marry him, what would you say?"

Lexie turned toward Ethan, her eyes wide. "Where did that question come from?"

Ethan could only smile and shake his head.

She grinned. "This was the secret?"

He chuckled.

She clasped Cooper's hand and kissed it. "I would say yes."

"I say yes, too." Cooper slid his hand over hers and gave it a single pat before he closed his eyes.

At the door, Ethan and Lexie slipped out of their protective wear and waited in the hall while the escorts lifted him to the stretcher. He tucked his hand in hers and grinned. "The secret didn't work quite the way it was supposed to go. I wanted the occasion to be a bit more romantic." Her tender look washed over him.

"It was." She squeezed his hand. "It was better than romantic. It was beautiful."

They followed the stretcher to the elevator and rode to the surgical floor waiting room. He had so much more to say, but right now his focus stayed with Cooper and his long journey to healing.

When they entered the waiting room, Ethan faltered. Lexie noticed, too, because her body stiffened against his arm. Another young man sat with Jess, deep in conversation. But before the decision was made to leave or continue, Jess looked up and beckoned to them. As they approached, Jess and the stranger rose.

"Lexie and Ethan, I want you to meet my brother, Hart."

The shock of seeing the owner of the decisive voice he'd heard on the phone rattled his bones. Ethan extended his hand. "Thanks for coming."

He only nodded as he faced Lexie. "I hadn't wanted to meet you, but after I thought about it, I saw the situation wasn't your fault. Dad had moved out long before meeting you. At the time, it felt like too much reality."

No apology, but an explanation.

"Hart, I can't thank you enough for doing what must have been difficult for you, and I would have been startled, too, by Ethan's phone call." She grasped his hand. "You notice I didn't have the courage, because of my own reality."

He nodded as if he understood. "I'm not staying, but I did want you to know that I'm hoping the best for Cooper. He's a good-looking boy, and my gut says he'll come out of this well."

"So does mine. An uncanny warmth began growing inside me since I heard the bone marrow matched. I believe it was God's way of speaking in His soft, tender voice. We just need to listen and experience it. Cooper will be fine once he's through the healing. It takes time. Months. But he will be fine."

Her confession sent Ethan's spirit soaring. She'd said she believed, and he'd seen her pray, but today he saw her faith come alive.

Though neither Hart nor Jess expressed their faith, their acceptance appeared real.

Jess grasped Ethan's shoulder. "I'll walk Hart out."

Lexie said goodbye again, and the two strode through the doorway.

"Whew." Lexie lifted her eyebrows. "I wasn't expecting that." She shook her head. "He looks so much like Hart."

"He's handsome."

She touched his face. "Not as handsome as you."

Not so, but he loved what she said. Ethan motioned to the chairs the brothers had vacated, and they sank into them. The clock hands sat at ten-sixteen, and they would creep along. They always did when he was waiting.

"I wonder why Hart changed his mind?"

Lexie filled her lungs. "I've thought about that. The Bible says children are not to bear the burden of their father's sins, but I think Hart realized that he was bearing a heavier burden by acting like his father and ignoring a child's need. His half brother."

"That makes sense, and you're right. When we hang on to resentment, it eats us alive, and the person that caused our feelings wins. By letting it go, we win."

His mind drifted to Laine's illness, and how for so long, he'd blamed himself for not having enough faith and not meeting her needs. When he looked back, he'd done everything he could. Yes, he had to work. Bills had to be paid, and he'd wished they could have shared those hours he was away, but that didn't mean he'd been to blame or that he hadn't done all he could for her. He'd loved her then, and always would. But she had died, not him, and he'd almost allowed life to pass him by.

He slipped Lexie's hand into his. "We have lots to talk about."

She gazed at him, a faint grin evident. "You mean Cooper's question about my marrying you?"

He chuckled. "Right. He did the proposing, not me, but it's what I told him." He ran his finger up her arm and down again. "I don't want to live without you, Lexie. The past is gone and we have today and tomorrow, a future to share. Marrying you and Cooper is my dream come true."

"It's mine, too. You're a part of our lives, and you added the piece that had been missing for so long." A tiny scowl fluttered to her face and left as quickly. "You and the Lord. I'd lived with a huge hole in my heart and my life. Now it's filled to the brim."

"And mine's running over." Ethan squeezed her hand.

Chapter Sixteen

Lexie hooked the final string of Christmas lights to the others and stood back. Her heart glowed as brightly as the tree. "What do you think?"

Ethan turned and gave a nod. "Looks good. I like the angel tree topper." He laid the paint brush on the lid. "Do you always put a tree up here?"

"No, but I'm sure Cooper will spend a lot of time in this room. He loves to do his puzzles and read. It'll take a while before he'll feel like doing much, but I'm so grateful, Ethan. His coming home is the best Christmas gift I could have." She eyed her finger and winced. "Not counting this beautiful engagement ring."

"That wasn't a Christmas gift." He winked and strode to her side, drawing her into his arms. His lips lowered to hers and every ounce of happiness she'd ever longed for washed over her—a son who had undergone a bone marrow transplant and had come through with great promise of being cancer-free and a man who loved her dearly and loved Cooper as his son. And not just any man, either. Ethan could run rings around every superhero known.

She rested her hand on Ethan's cheek, feeling stubble and loving it. So close. So strong. So gentle. Her list of adjectives could go on and on. Her lips moved beneath his, her heart surging with love and promise.

Easing back, Ethan captured her gaze. "You are so beautiful, Lexie, inside and out."

She rolled her eyes. "And don't forget. I'm amazing."

"That goes without saying." He gave her a squeeze. "So what do you think of my finished handiwork?"

Though unwilling to leave his embrace, she shifted to face the new bookshelves. "I always thought you were a contractor, one of those guys who was a rotten carpenter so he was promoted, but you can actually build something this gorgeous."

He gave her a teasing poke. "I had to be an excellent carpenter to get my job." He polished his fingernails on his shirt. "How's that for conceit?"

She waved his comment away. Ethan didn't have a conceited bone in his body. "Cooper is going to love these shelves."

"I hope so." He grinned. "The day I met him—maybe you remember—he asked me to turn the den into a library."

"I remember." She eyed the perfect wall of shelving. "But this spot is perfect. This is where he spends his time, and before he gets home, we can put some of his books on the lower shelves so he can reach them."

"And as he grows, he can just move them up."

As he grows. The warmth of Ethan's optimism rushed along her limbs. "That sounds so good...and you know what?"

He pressed his lips together and shrugged.

"I believe it with all my heart. I know the Lord loves Cooper enough to give him years of quality life. I'm confident."

Ethan drew her closer and his eyes met hers. "Now, that's the best gift I could have for Christmas."

She grinned at his loving words. Ethan had turned out to

be a walking romantic. Lexie leaned back in his arms and slipped hers around his neck. "This Christmas will be perfect. I'll meet your parents, and mine will be coming in January when Cooper's feeling better."

"And Coop will be released for Christmas."

Her heart sang. "And he'll be home." Her lips sought his again.

January, a month later

Lexie leaned against the dining-room archway, studying the small group seated around the fireplace in her living room. A pork roast baked in the oven along with potatoes and carrots, and the aroma wafted into the room. Soon the rolls would be browned, and the salad carried from the refrigerator.

The Christmas tree stood by the front window, the white lights glowing as brightly as her heart. The doctors had released Cooper a few days before Christmas, though his weakness kept him bound to a chair or his bed most of the time. Today he sat beside her mother, dressed in a suit. His pale face and the dark circles beneath his eyes attested to the battle he'd fought and won. Though months would march past before they were certain, the oncologist had given them encouragement that Cooper could be cancer-free.

Cooper's face when he'd seen the bookshelves still glowed in her mind. She'd wished she had grabbed his camera for the occasion. He hadn't shown that much enthusiasm since the day at the airport waiting to leave for the Grand Canyon. Those days, though cut short, lived in her memory.

Her gaze swept the room, and tears rimmed her eyes, praising God for the gift and for the people around her today. Her mother's attention to Cooper touched her. She'd always seemed distant, but not today. Her father had tried to be a grandfather, but he'd struggled under her mother's heavy glare. They'd mellowed, and after all these years, Lexie was able to forgive them. And to make their visit perfect. Ethan's parents had flown in from the warm temperatures of Florida to be with them for the Christmas season. Though New Year's Day had passed, they stayed to be with them today. She loved them from the moment they'd stepped off the plane.

"Are you all hungry?" She drew in an exaggerated breath as hands waved in the air. "Mom prepared a wonderful meal for our celebration, but we're waiting for two key members."

Ross, seated beside Kelsey, gave a chuckle. "What a day for Ethan to be late."

Kelsey gave him a poke that didn't pass unnoticed. Lexie had never seen Kelsey flirt, but she was today. When she'd first met Ross, she realized he'd been the man Mothers of Special Kids had voted not to accept as a member. Lexie couldn't help but laugh out loud when Ross introduced himself.

"Hi, I'm the Ross you all voted not to admit to your support group."

Kelsey had drawn back. "Really?"

"I wouldn't kid you about that, would I?" He grinned.

A pink glow colored her cheeks. "Maybe I didn't try hard enough. Now that I've met you, I can give a personal recommendation."

Blatant flirting. Lexie couldn't believe it. Kelsey never dated. Never showed interest in any man. But then, neither had she.

Lexie ducked into the dining room to hide her chuckle, and when she slipped back into the room, the thud of a car door sent her pulse flying.

Cooper's voice split the air. "It's Ethan." He'd chosen a chair closest to the window to be lookout, she suspected.

The door opened, and Ethan stepped inside brushing snow from his coat. He hung it in the closet and then crossed the room, his gaze adhered to hers.

Lexie's heart rode a plummeting elevator. Ethan, her pillar of strength. Handsome and wonderful. He'd proven his love over and over during the past three months of Cooper's recuperation. He'd stood by her side with tears in his eyes or a smile on his lips as big as his heart.

She watched him head for her, dressed in a dark blue suit, white shirt and burgundy tie, and his pocket sprouted a handkerchief of the same color. A fresh haircut and shave advertised their special day. His tender looked warmed her. "One more person, and we're ready."

He slipped his arm around her, adding a fleeting kiss. "Excited?"

"Ecstatic."

"So am I." He turned his gaze toward Cooper. "How's my buddy today?" He strode to Cooper's side and wrapped him in his arms. "I can't get my fill seeing you home."

"It's good for me, too."

Ethan grinned as he straightened. He tousled Cooper's hair and greeted the others, but before he returned to Lexie's side, the doorbell rang. He hurried to the door and pulled it open. "Welcome, Pastor Tom."

He patted Ethan's shoulder. "I wouldn't miss this for the world."

"You better not have. What's a wedding without a pastor?" He closed the door and hung his coat in the closet. When he looked up, Lexie was missing. "Where's the bride?" He searched the room and realized her mother had vanished, too.

His mother chuckled. "What do you think? She's getting ready for her wedding. You can't see the bride in her finery before the ceremony, you know."

Kelsey stood. "I'll go check." She looked over her shoulder as she headed up the stairs. "And I get a sneak peek."

Pastor Tom made his way around the chairs to greet everyone, and then paused and took stock of the room. "Where would you like me to perform the ceremony?"

Ethan pointed to the fireplace. "Lexie thought it would be nice there." Candles lined the mantel, and a fire glowed in the grate, sending warmth through the large room.

Pastor Tom stood in front of the fireplace, waiting while Ethan's feet longed to pace. He forced himself to stand still.

"She's ready." Kelsey appeared, followed by Lexie's mother. They took their seats, and Ethan waited, his heart so filled he felt it might explode. When she glided down the staircase, he caught his breath. Lexie had always been a gorgeous woman, but today she outshone the sun. The V-neck of her ivory-colored gown glittered with pearl beads while the skirt fell in soft folds below her knees. Her hair hung in billowing waves beyond her shoulders. Ethan couldn't take his eyes from her as he walked to meet her.

He clasped her arm and stood before Pastor Tom, waiting for the moment when they would become man and wife. A smile lit Cooper's pale face, and his eyes followed every move they made.

Kelsey and Ross joined them, matron of honor and best man, witnessing their marriage and their promises. Both friends had been overjoyed for them.

Pastor Tom opened the book he held. "Today we are here to celebrate your decision to be husband and wife, a decision you both made as you put away your pasts and chose to face the future together. I know you have already shared many joys and sorrows, and I am confident that you both have enough courage and love for a relationship that will last forever."

Ethan pressed his hand against Lexie's arm. They had

gone through more than many couples experienced in their lifetime, and though he realized other problems would follow, he was confident they would lean on each other and the Lord for strength and endurance. Today his joy obliterated their tears. Today was meant for smiles.

Their vows were spoken with promises to share what was to come and to be faithful. The promise would never waver. Ethan opened his hand, and Ross dropped the diamond wedding band into his palm. Ethan slipped it on Lexie's finger, a sign of his love and faithfulness. She followed with a simple gold band. They clasped hands and bowed their heads as the pastor prayed for them and those present.

Following the amen, Pastor Tom rested his hand on theirs. "By their promises to God and to all of you present, Alexandria and Ethan have bound themselves to one another as husband and wife." He paused and they waited until he shook his head and grinned. "What's keeping you? You may kiss your bride."

Ethan chuckled before he lowered his lips to Lexie's while every ounce of his body reeled with a happiness he never thought possible.

Applause spread around the room as they turned to face their families. Ethan raised his hand. "We're so happy you're all here to share this amazing moment with us, and Cooper, you are a special gift to me. I'm so proud to call you my son."

Cooper grinned at Ethan. "Finally, I have a dad of my own."

The room filled with new applause until they heard Cooper's voice. "Now, can we eat?"

Their applause turned to laughter as they rose and headed toward the dining room.

* * * * *

Dear Reader,

I hope you enjoyed reading the first novel in the Dreams Come True series. When I decided to tackle this topic, I knew it would be a challenge, but I sensed I could do it. Creating a romance wrapped around children with serious illnesses seemed difficult, but I once wrote a novel with the hero comatose in the hospital through most of the book, and I knew if I could do that, I could do just about anything. (Chuckling here.) In the next novel of the series, you will spend more time with Kelsey and her daughter, Lucy. I look forward to sharing their story with you.

As Christians, we know when difficult times strike us, God does not walk away. He is by our side giving us strength and courage to make it through and be strong. We can understand our suffering better by studying Romans 5: 3-5. Ethan read the verses to Lexie on the suite balcony at the Grand Canyon. Lexie came to know the Lord by asking questions, but the Lord knew her forever.

Gail Gaymer Martin

QUESTIONS FOR DISCUSSION

1. Although Lexie was not a Christian at the beginning of the novel, what attributes did she have that you could admire?

2. One of Lexie's difficult situations was to learn to forgive herself for her past mistakes. Have you ever struggled with the need to forgive yourself for a past action? Were you successful?

3. Ethan had been left with scars following the death of his wife. Besides loneliness and grief, what other issues caused him to struggle with the present?

4. Ethan's attitude about being Christian was that evangelizing to a nonbeliever could do more damage than good. Do you understand what he meant? How do you feel about this attitude?

5. Lexie had a difficult time understanding that Christians believe God has a plan for their lives. How do you explain that to nonbelievers when they scoff at this part of faith? Did you find Kelsey's explanation of free will meaningful?

6. Although Kelsey is a secondary character in this book, she will be the heroine in the next book. Did you find Kelsey an interesting secondary character in this novel? What did you like about her?

7. One theme of this novel is hope. Being Christians,

our hope is tied to our faith. In what ways do you demonstrate hope in your life?

8. Again the theme of hope also teaches us about suffering. Romans 5: 3-5 says, "We also rejoice in our sufferings, because we know that suffering produces perseverance; perseverance, character; and character, hope. And hope does not disappoint us, because God has poured out His love into our hearts by the Holy Spirit, whom He has given us." Explain how this theme works in the novel as well as in your life.

9. Have you known a child who has struggled with a serious illness such as leukemia? Do you think you could be as strong as Lexie was? Explain in what ways you could show strength and in what ways you might reveal your weakness.

10. Have you had experience with a seven- or eight-year-old? Did you find Cooper to be a typical child even though he had a serious illness? Did some of his comments cause you to chuckle?

11. Have you been to the Grand Canyon? Ethan said when he looked at places like the Grand Canyon he became awed by God's handiwork. This same setting introduced Lexie's seed of belief. What things in nature awaken your faith?

12. Do you think the women at the Mothers of Special Kids should have opened the door to men in their group? Why or why not? See what happens in the next book.

TITLES AVAILABLE NEXT MONTH

Available March 29, 2011

LICNM0311

REQUEST YOUR FREE BOOKS!

2 FREE INSPIRATIONAL NOVELS
PLUS 2
FREE
MYSTERY GIFTS

When David Foster comes across an unconscious woman on his friends' doorstep, she evokes his natural born instinct to take care of her.

Read on for a sneak peek of A BABY BY EASTER by Lois Richer, available April, only from Love Inspired.

"You could marry Davy, Susannah. He would look after you. He looks after me." Darla's bright voice dropped. "He had a girlfriend. They were going to get married, but she didn't want me. She wanted Davy to send me away."

David almost groaned. How had his sister found out? He'd been so careful—

"I'm sure your brother is very nice, Darla. And I'm glad he's taking care of you. But I don't want to marry him. I don't want to marry anyone," Susannah said. "I only came to Connie's to see if I could stay here for a while."

"But Davy needs someone to love him. Somebody else but me." Darla's face crumpled, the way it always did before she lost her temper. David was about to step forward when Susannah reached out and hugged his sister.

"Thank you for offering, Darla. You're very generous. I think your brother is lucky to have you love him." Susannah brushed the bangs from Darla's sad face. "If I end up staying with Connie, I promise I'll see you lots. We could go to that playground you talked about."

Susannah's foster sister Connie breezed into the room. "I'm so glad to see you, Suze. But you're ill." She leaned back to study the circles of red now dotting Susannah's cheeks. "You're very pale. I think you need to see a doctor."

"I'm pregnant." The words burst out of Susannah in a rush. Then she lifted her head and looked David straight in the eye, as if awaiting his condemnation.

SHLIEXP0411R

But it wasn't condemnation David felt. It was hurt. He'd prayed so long, so hard, for a family, a wife, a child. And he'd lost all chance of that—not once, but twice.

How could God deny him the longing of his heart, yet give this ill woman a child she was in no way prepared to care for?

Although David has given up on his dream of having a family, will he offer to help Susannah in her time of need? Find out in A BABY BY EASTER, available April, only from Love Inspired.